FC02

W9-BMV-878

Downriver

Downriver

A BARNABY SKYE NOVEL

RICHARD S. WHEELER

western
whe

A TOM DOHERTY ASSOCIATES BOOK / NEW YORK

DOWNRIVER: A BARNABY SKYE NOVEL

Copyright © 2001 by Richard S. Wheeler

This book is printed on acid-free paper.

A Forge Book
Published by Tom Doherty Associates, LLC
175 Fifth Avenue
New York, NY 10010

www.tor.com

Forge® is a registered trademark of Tom Doherty Associates, LLC.

Library of Congress Cataloging-in-Publication Data

Wheeler, Richard S.
    Downriver : a Barnaby Skye novel / Richard S. Wheeler.—1st ed.
      p. cm.
    "A Tom Doherty Associates book."
    ISBN 0-312-87845-1
    1. Skye, Barnaby (Fictitious character)—Fiction.   2. Paddle steamers—Fiction.   3. Missouri River—Fiction.   4. Indian women—Fiction.
5. Trappers—Fiction.   I. Title.

PS3573.H4345 D69 2001
813'.54—dc21

2001040481

First Edition: December 2001

Printed in the United States of America

0 9 8 7 6 5 4 3 2 1

For my fine grandson, Remi Trottier

one

Gloom hung over the rendezvous on the Popo Agie
River. Evil rumors wormed through the gathering, furrowing brows. They were saying this
would be the last gathering of the mountain men. The American Fur Company wouldn't buy a beaver plew at all, or if it
did, it would pay so little that the mountaineers would starve.
A man couldn't keep body and soul together in the mountains anymore. There were whispers that the company's tent
store would have fewer items and these would be more costly
than ever.

It had reached Barnaby Skye's ears that the trapping
brigades would be pared down and free trappers released from
contracts; that long-term company men would be let go and
that it didn't matter how good a job a man had done. He heard
that the engagés would find themselves as useless as a lame
horse. He had heard that prime beaver pelts wouldn't bring
fifty cents, and an entire year's hard work wouldn't keep a man
in gunpowder. Those bleak rumors had built up an awful thirst
in Barnaby Skye. A jug usually solved his problems, at least until the fat moon turned skinny.

Just so long as they brought spirits, everything would be
all right. Whiskey fueled each rendezvous. Without it, the
trappers might as well go back to loading cotton or black-
smithing or plowing prairie soil or tallying waybills in a warehouse. But not one man among them believed that the year's
supplies, now being packed in from Fort Union, would not in-
clude the pure grain alcohol that would be mixed with Popo

Agie River water, a plug of tobacco or two, and some Cayenne pepper, that set the old coons to baying.

One thing wasn't a rumor: fashion had shifted. In 1833, John Jacob Astor himself had discovered that silk top hats were the vogue; that hats made from beaver felt had vanished from the shops of Europe. In 1834 he had sold out his American Fur Company, and now the Upper Missouri Outfit was really Pratte, Chouteau and Company, though no one called it that. It was said that Astor, the great fur magnate, had known exactly what he was up to, and had gotten out of the fur business in the nick of time, richer than Midas and safer than Gibraltar.

That was the dark talk those June days beside the Popo Agie, where it met the Wind River, among dour trappers waiting for the fun to begin and the trade whiskey to flow. The rest of the bad tidings wasn't rumor at all. No one had done well this year. Beaver were just about trapped out, except maybe on the streams controlled by the dangerous Blackfeet, and the competition of small outfits and free trappers had made life in the wilderness tougher than ever. No one had many plews to trade, and those few wouldn't bring much more than a few grains of DuPont powder and a bar of lead. There were men in camp who had put in a hard year's work and wouldn't get fifty dollars for it.

And so, that June of 1838, Barnaby Skye waited for what life would bring, but without much hope. Maybe this would be the last rendezvous. He would have to find some other way to survive, and so would all the rest of the mountain men gathered together for the customary trade festival and summer fun that year. What would he do? What would he become? Who would he be in the hazy future? Was this the end of his sojourn in the wilds? Would he return to the sea, from whence he came?

At least the American Fur Company had sent an outfit upriver, and it was due at any time now. The trappers could buy the traps and gunpowder and flannels and blankets they needed, and keep on going for another year if they had a few packs of skins to peddle. Maybe there was hope in that. Maybe things would get better.

The trappers knew that much, because an express rider from Fort Union, located at the confluence of the Yellowstone and Missouri, had told them the *Otter* was thrashing its way upstream with an outfit, a cargo of trade goods. But no one knew what bleak news would accompany the outfit, and not a man in that camp believed that the news would be very good. The St. Louis owners of the company had made it clear a year earlier they were losing money on the beaver business. Silk was in; beaver felt was out.

Skye had been a brigade leader, a salaried man, one of only five in camp, so he had weathered the bad times a bit better than some of the trappers. They had numbed their legs for long hours in freezing water while baiting traps with castoreum and collecting beaver, found small comfort in winter's darkness, fought their way into obscure corners of the Rockies, only to find that other, equally determined trappers had cleaned out the streams. And now the beaver had all but vanished.

Lucien Fontenelle, the veteran fur man in charge of field operations for the American Fur Company, was more optimistic.

"Beaver may be trapped out, but the company's not just in the beaver business," he confided to Skye as they lounged under a cottonwood, staring at snow-burdened peaks. "It can sell any pelt or hide we can ship."

"For less plunder," Skye said.

Fontenelle nodded. "Hard doings now," he said. "But we'll keep on going. That's what Pierre Chouteau himself told me; they'd keep on going. There's fur here and markets there. Maybe it'll be ermine or mink, deer and elk hides, weasel or otter, maybe even buffalo hides, but there's a market in the States."

Skye was not a gloomy man, nor a pessimist, but all the bad talk was eroding his joy. For a dozen years he had been in the mountains, and was considered a veteran and even an old man by the trapping fraternity, though he wasn't far into his thirties, and just beginning life.

They considered him an odd duck, perhaps because of his British ways and his peculiar looks. He had been a pressed seaman, dragooned into the Royal Navy when he was a boy in London. He hadn't escaped the iron claw of His Majesty's Navy until he jumped ship at Fort Vancouver, on the Columbia River, seven years later, and made his way into the interior, with little more than his wits and a knife and belaying pin to keep him alive.

Maybe that's why he was a more serious and somber man than most of the mountain fraternity; why he was more diligent and careful and willing to learn anything of value; why he treasured his liberty so much that he would die rather than surrender it. He had spent seven years in bondage, subservient to the whim of assorted boatswains, midshipmen, masters, captains, and lords of the admiralty, and freedom meant more to him than it did to anyone in the mountains.

Maybe he seemed odd to the fraternity because he insisted on being called *Mister*, or maybe it was because of his burly barrel-shaped body, or the seaman's roll in his gait. Maybe it was because of his giant misshapen nose, which had suffered much pulping and pounding in innumerable brawls, a hogback that now dominated his face so that his small blue eyes and thin lips shrank to nothing in comparison. Or maybe it was his battered black top hat, pierced by arrow and shot, which he wore with determined dignity in all seasons, perched on a full mane of ragged brown hair that reached his shoulders.

Or maybe they found him odd simply because he wasn't an American, and didn't speak the trapper lingo, and addressed others with politeness and civility, which were things he was born to and couldn't help. He was a man without a country; not able to return to England, yet not a westering man out of the States, so he lived in some sort of limbo, his only nation the trapping fraternity of the mountains—and his wife Victoria's people, the Crows.

But he didn't mind. What counted was their respect as well as his own respect for himself, and what else they thought of him didn't matter. He had mastered the wilderness arts in a hurry. And never stopped learning how to subsist himself in a world where there was nary a shop on any corner to sell him beef or pork or bread or greens, and nary a tailor to sew him a suit of clothes, nary a smith to fashion a weapon, and nary a doctor to tend to his ills and aches and broken bones. He had mastered the Arkansas toothpick, the Green River knife, the Hawken percussion rifle, the war axe and throwing hatchet, the savage's bow and arrow, war club and lance because there were no constables in the wilds to protect him. He knew how to build a smokeless fire, how to read the behavior of crows and magpies, how to sense an ambush around a bend. He had graduated summa cum laude from the Rocky Mountain College, where one either won a baccalaureate or died in some obscure gulch, his fate unknown.

So he, along with two hundred others, lingered in the verdant meadows where the Popo joined the Wind, awaiting whatever the lords of their fate in distant St. Louis had to offer. It was a sweet land, at least in summer, with cool evenings, and vast panoramas in which grassy benchlands surrendered to dark-timbered slopes, which in turn stretched upward in bright blue distances to snow-capped peaks that fairly cried "Freedom!"

The blue haze of campfires lay in the air, and the pungent aroma of wood smoke. In addition to the trappers, the dusky tribesmen had gathered once again to trade their pelts for all those treasures brought from afar by the white men: powder and lead, blankets, hooks, traps, mirrors, beads, and especially, the trade whiskey the wily traders concocted and sold by the cup or jug for furs.

Skye could see the tawny buffalo-hide lodges of the Crows

arrayed in a circle, and those of the Shoshones and Nez Perce, and some plenty of other tribes as well, dotting the verdant meadows. Here, on neutral trading ground, even hereditary enemies enjoyed a momentary peace, though they were all fair game for one another once they departed from the legendary trapper's fair.

Skye waited restlessly, his eyes on the low divide that would someday soon reveal a string of heavily burdened pack horses and mules, and some gaudily bedizened mountaineers driving them into the rendezvous.

He did not know what he would do if the news was bad, which is what he fully expected. There weren't enough beaver pelts in camp to pay for the enormous expense of shipping all those goods from St. Louis, much less earn anyone a profit. He had two skills: he was an able seaman, and could always ship out on any merchant vessel, and he was also an able mountaineer. He suspected he might just need to learn another trade, and he wasn't sure what it might be.

His wife Victoria was visiting with all her friends and relatives, some of whom she saw only at these annual fairs. At rendezvous time, he often went for hours, even a day, without seeing her. But whenever they were together on the trail, leading a brigade, she and he scrubbed and cooked and hunted together, lived and loved together with a unity of purpose and spirit that transcended their radically different upbringings. They were friends and lovers, hunters and warriors, and boon companions upon life's sweet walk. Except when he was enjoying his annual binge. The thought made him thirsty.

He was still young. He'd suffered hardship in the mountains, but his body was strong, and hardship had annealed the steel in him and wrought a man of rare courage and intelligence and something else: honor.

Ten days passed, then eleven, and finally on the twelfth, Joe Meek, who had been scouting up the trail for news, returned with news: The American Fur Company pack train would arrive

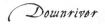

the next day. From the crest of the ridge where he had observed the distant train, he could see it was a small one, poor doings compared to the outfits the company brought in during the heyday of the beaver trade. But an outfit, anyway, and maybe there would be a few casks of spirits on the backs of those mules to gladden the hearts and bodies of the trappers.

So the next day, that June, Skye might learn his fate.

two

Barnaby Skye harbored an awesome thirst after a hard year in the mountains. He knew exactly what he would do the moment the American Fur Company store was in business: he would dicker for one quart of trade whiskey and begin sipping, and not quit until the elixir had burned a fine hole in his belly.

Ah, the joy of it. In some small patch of Eden, every ache in his battered body would vanish, every worry, every fear, and every ancient irritation; and he would know only blossoming bliss and blooming brotherhood, daisies and roses and bagpipers, visitations from angels, advice from saints, hallucinations and corporeal joys. The trade whiskey was ghastly, a devil's concoction that corduroyed the throat and shrank the gullet and assaulted the brain and shriveled the intellect, but what did it matter? After a few sips, he never noticed. A year in the mountains was a lifetime; a year without a sip was an eternity.

Keenly, his dry throat anticipating the debauch, he watched the American Fur pack train trot in, bells jangling and hooves clopping, punctuated by an occasional gunshot and many a neigh, whether from a four-footed horse or two-footed animal being uncertain and immaterial. Old Andy Drips was leading it; the gray-haired, weather-stained, plaid-wrapped veteran of the mountains had been with American Fur for years, and was second only to Fontenelle.

Along with the rest, Skye crowded about the pack train, observing its diminished size, but he was heartened by two mules carrying pairs of sturdy casks. These particular oaken kegs glowed and shimmered, as if lit by divine light, or a blessing from Saint Jerome. At least Skye thought so. The spoilsport United States government had been doing its indecent utmost to interdict shipment of ardent and rectified spirits into Indian Territory, but somehow the company always managed to supply its trappers with the nectar of life.

As famished as these gentle nobles of the wilderness were for whiskey, they were even more famished for news, news of any sort, even the topics of recent Boston sermons, and as Drips genially braced the rough knights who clustered around him, he dispensed a few St. Louis newspapers. Every word in them would be read and studied and squinted over. Every scrap of information about the States would be digested and regurgitated.

Skye had seen many a rendezvous, and remarked at once the subdued nature of this one. In times past, the arrival of a company outfit had occasioned a frenzy of shooting, whooping, mock combat, gaudy Indian parades, reckless horsemanship, and inane hollering, all intended to whet thirst. This was different. Drips was smiling, shaking hands, slapping backs, posing like a Saint Bernard with a brandy cask, but it wasn't the same. Hardly any trapper had fired his piece in welcome, because DuPont powder was scarce and costly. Even the Crows and Shoshones were watching quietly rather than curvetting their horses or dressing in feathery ceremonial regalia for the big whoop-up. The excitement swiftly subsided into watchfulness as Drips's engagés began to unload the packs and set up shop.

"Skye, you old varmint, good to see you," Drips said, embracing the Englishman.

"It's Mister Skye, mate."

Drips laughed. "Forgot. Mister Skye it is. Did you have a good hunt?"

"Beaver's scarce, Andy."

"What did you boys get?"

"Not two packs."

Drips sighed. "Same for the rest?"

"Worse, I think."

"That's what we guessed, judging from the returns at Fort Union." He eyed Skye sharply. "I want to talk to you later. Privately. Don't touch that jug until I do."

"That's a tall order."

"You let me get the store set up, and collect some news from the other brigade leaders, and then we'll palaver."

Skye reluctantly agreed. A year-long big thirst would have to continue an extra hour.

"You seen Alexandre Bonfils?"

"He's around."

Bonfils was another of the company's brigade leaders, related in half a dozen ways to most of the company's St. Louis owners. Bright, young, canny, wise in wilderness ways, and ambitious. Skye had never much cared for him, but had nothing against him, though other men did. The young man sported a tricorne and wore a medal on his chest, to let the world know he was a man of parts.

"Good. You wait for me, and we'll pow-wow."

"In one hour I'll be waiting in line with a cup, Andy."

The master of the revels laughed.

Drips, a busy man with heavy responsibilities, turned swiftly to the tasks at hand the moment he finished greeting his mountain companions, the AFC men and free trappers.

Skye waited irritably. His Crow wife, Victoria, stood with her Crow friends, studying this latest caravan from the white men's world. His mangy yellow dog, No Name, sulked at the fringe of the crowd, suspicious of any disturbance and almost invisible to most mortals. No Name was even more independent than Skye, but the dog and the man had come to an understanding about life, and formed a mutual protection society.

He eyed Victoria fondly. She was wiry and glowing, with raven hair and an unblinking direct gaze that sometimes unnerved others. She liked a good bout with the trade whiskey as much as he, and now he saw her grinning in anticipation. Only the dog, among the Skyes, scorned the annual bacchanal, and had taken to nipping and snarling at Skye whenever Skye had put away too much nectar, for which offense Skye bellowed at the dog and threw rocks at him.

The ranks of mountaineers were pretty depleted this time, but he saw Jim Bridger waiting patiently. Like everyone else, old Gabe, as he was called, worked for American Fur now. Chouteau's outfit was the only sizable company left in the Rockies. And his friend Christopher Carson was on hand, out of the southern plains, to enjoy the party. Carson usually worked with the Bent Brothers, down on the Arkansas, but this time he had drifted north.

Then, suddenly, Drips was at his side again.

"They'll be trading in a few minutes." He nodded toward the Popo Agie. "You good for a little walk?"

Skye nodded unhappily, feeling deprived. The pair distanced themselves from the hubbub. No Name spotted them and followed, stalking them as if they were game, not the source of his meat and protection.

"You winter all right?" Drips asked.

"Had some scrapes with Bug's Boys," he said, alluding to the Blackfeet.

"Anyone go under?"

"No, we got out of there. But mostly we wandered up

streams looking for beaver and finding nothing. Even the beaver dams have been pulled apart."

"That's what they expected in St. Louis. Maybe it's a blessing."

"Things pretty bad?" Skye asked.

"Yes and no. The beaver trade's over. They've been wondering what to do. Pierre Chouteau thinks he might send an outfit one more year; there's still some demand for beaver felt and trim on clothing. But mostly, he's cutting back." Drips eyed his old friend sharply. "They're letting almost all the brigade leaders go, Mister Skye. Including you. They'll send a small outfit next year, but only to trade with free trappers. No more company brigades. You'll all be on your own if you want to stay out here. Myself, I'd think about doing something else."

"That's hard news. I don't know what I'll do."

"Well, that's why I'm pulling you over here for a little pow-wow. The company's not getting out of the fur and hide business, but we're shifting operations. We can sell every ermine and otter skin we can find, and there's a market for deer and elk hides, and buffalo too."

"Forget beaver, then?"

Drips smiled.

They had reached the riverbank. The icy snowmelt gurgled past them, crystal, sweet, and delicious. A fine cool breeze eddied through the verdant spring grasses, like a mysterious finger writing the future.

"The company has plans for you—if you're interested." He waited for an affirmation. Skye nodded.

"Tulloch is leaving Fort Cass. They're looking for a replacement, a new trader for the post. You're an obvious choice, with a Crow wife. That gives you some power within the tribe, and helps the company lock down the Crow trade."

That interested Skye. Cass was a small log post, a satellite of Fort Union, located on the Yellowstone River at the confluence of the Big Horn. It did a modest trade with the Crows, Victoria's people. But the Crows weren't ardent beaver trappers and the post never did a large business.

"I might be," he said.

"There's a few hitches. One is that you're not the only man they're considering. Bonfils is another contender. And he has relatives from one end of the company to the other. There's another factor, too, which Pierre Chouteau himself urged upon me, old friend. They don't know you in St. Louis. You're a shadowy Englishman to them, known only through reports from those of us who keep an eye on the mountain trade. You'd have to go to St. Louis, meet Chouteau and his colleagues, tell them how you'll improve trade, and let them decide."

"St. Louis? That's a piece."

"No, not so long. You'd go back on the *Otter*. It's leaving just as fast as we can get these furs to Fort Union. The spring flood's already peaking and there's not a moment to waste."

"When do you leave here?"

"Tomorrow at dawn."

"Tomorrow! You just got here."

"We'll pack whatever furs we can for the riverboat. Fontenelle will haul the rest to Fort Union after the rendezvous."

"Tomorrow!" Skye didn't like that at all. He would miss the rendezvous. Miss the precious time with old friends. Miss the gargantuan drinking bout that would begin as soon as the traders could mix a kettle of whiskey.

"Bonfils will be on that boat," Drips said. "If he goes and you don't, you and the company will come to a parting of the ways. He's bright, fluent in two or three Indian tongues, knows the business inside out, has a Hidatsa woman, and their tongue is almost the same as the Crows'. He's junior to you by ten years, but he's well connected—maybe too well connected, to put it politely."

"Not even time for a drink," Skye muttered. "A miserable bloody little drink."

Drips grinned.

"Do I even stand a chance against him?"

"Certainly. Old Pierre Chouteau wants the best man, absolutely the best, and knows more about you than you might think."

"How long in St. Louis?"

"One or two days. You'll need to get a trader's license from General Clark if you're selected. Whoever they choose will start west at once. Reach Fort Cass before snow flies and relieve Tulloch. We'll be sending the *Otter* back up the river as far as it can get in low water. Whoever gets that position at Cass will be on it, and then head west from Bellevue with a small pack train, out the Platte River."

"Tomorrow!" Skye said. "I'd better talk to Victoria."

"Tomorrow at dawn. We're going to be weighing and baling furs this evening, writing chits the trappers can spend at the store, and we'll pull out at first light, moving as fast as we can. Be ready, packed and saddled and fed."

The whole business dizzied Skye.

"I'll let you know," he muttered, unable to absorb so much so fast.

Drips looked at him sharply. "One thing more. You may not want to be a trader. A man like you."

"What do you mean?"

"Just what I said. Think it over. And do it fast."

"Would you explain yourself?"

"No, and forget that I even warned you. The company will require certain things of you. That's all I can say. Some men there are who should not be traders for Pratte, Chouteau."

Skye searched the face of the man, uneasily, but found only a mask.

Andy Drips slapped him on the back. "For my money, you're the man they should turn into a trader."

That left a lot unsaid.

three

Many Quill Woman heard that her man, Mister Skye, was looking for her, but she was in no hurry to respond. He probably wanted someone to roast some meat. He could easily cook his own, but men liked to make women do it, and it didn't matter whether they were men of the People, or white men. Usually, she didn't mind, for that was what had been ordained from the beginning of the world, but at rendezvous things were different. Skye could cook his own damned meat. She was occupied.

She usually spent rendezvous apart from him. All year she toiled at his side, making camp, dressing hides, sharing his hard life and dangers, along with the brigade of trappers. But by the time rendezvous rolled around, she was weary of white men, and yearned for time among her many friends who always came to the great trapper's fair.

So she did not hurry. She had visited old friends in several Absaroka lodges this day, as well as fat grandmothers in a Shoshone lodge and some chunky Nez Perce women, and even visited with some treacherous and thieving Bannocks, who usually were at arrow's point with the Crows. That had been an act of great charity and munificence on her part; normally, an Absaroka woman never conversed with such trash. But an iron law of peace prevailed at the white men's fairs, and so it was that hostile tribes camped side by side, and even visited with one another, so she had deigned to talk briefly with a squat, ugly Bannock woman who was missing half her teeth.

She would talk to anyone at rendezvous. All except the Blackfeet. If Blackfeet had ridden to the banks of the Popo

Agie at this time, much red blood would be lying on the green grasses.

Skye called her Victoria, after the princess, now queen, of his people across the sea. She did not know what that was all about, but being named for a great woman was surely an honor, and she loved her man for it. The more names one had, the more honor. They had an uneasy relationship, divided by all the things they didn't grasp about each other, and the lives they came from. And yet, she counted herself the happiest and most fortunate of women, the envy of all her sisters among the Kicked-in-the-Belly band of the Crows.

Who else had such a man? Had not Barnaby Skye the biggest, most mountainous nose in the world? Was he not a mighty warrior, a prodigious eater, a man big across the chest and belly, though not very tall? Was he not a leader of his people? Did he not survive perils that would sink lesser men? Was he not more tender and kind and caring than any Crow man she knew? Did he not consult her and imbibe her wisdom?

Yes, she was fortunate, and she would eventually go to him and cook some meat . . . but not for a while, dammit. He deserved to wait. Rendezvous brought out the worst in him. Anyway, the traders were mixing up a great batch of whiskey, and everyone she knew was waiting eagerly to trade pelts for cups of the fiery brew that made a man or woman happy and mad, and took away the pains and sorrows of the world. Soon she, too, would bay at the moon, howl like a wolf, and laugh all night and rub her hand through Skye's whiskers.

For an hour she resisted, even though the gossips told her that her man was wandering through the lodges, bellowing her name, seeking her company. She had laughed. Let him bark at her like a lonely coyote; this was her summer time with all her friends, her People, and women from other Peoples. This was the time to see all the new babies and sorrow that she had none and probably wouldn't ever have any because this gift had just not come to them.

She loved Skye. He was in his mid-thirties, and in the prime of his life. His body had borne many wounds, and he had suffered from all the miseries that life brought; cold, starvation, sore bones and muscles, poor food, and great thirst. Yet, she had never seen him healthier or stronger or more in command of himself, of his men, or of life. A dozen winters now he had been in this country, and he bore the marks of this hard life upon every limb, and yet no warrior was stronger.

"Your man is calling again," said Arrow, her brother, testily. "Why do you defy him? You are a bad wife."

She laughed. They were watching her to see if she would ignore her man, but she wouldn't give them anything to gossip about. She rose quietly, crawled through the lodge door, and beheld him three lodges away.

He looked troubled.

"Come. We have to talk privately, away from everyone," he said.

She followed, faintly annoyed but concerned.

"When will the traders open their store?" she asked.

"It's open now."

His tone of voice was brusque.

He led her to a fallen log, once a noble cottonwood but now the home of crawling things.

"This may be the last rendezvous; maybe one more next year. I'm out of work, Victoria."

"Work? What is this? You don't have to work. We will live with the People and be happy."

"But there's something new . . ."

She gathered her spirits together. Skye was acting very strange. Maybe he just needed his jug. He was always strange until he had a few drinks at rendezvous. He was known to be crazy in the days and hours before rendezvous.

"Maybe I can be the trader at Fort Cass," he said.

"The trader? What happened to, what is his name, Tulloch?"

"He's heading for the States. The position's open. I'd be a trader, trading with your people, trying to keep all your Otter clan happy. I'm going to apply."

"I would be close to my people!"

"Yes, always close. Not roaming all over the Rocky Mountains all year."

"Aiee! This is good."

"I may not get the position, though. And even if it is given to me, I might not want it."

She waited patiently for him to explain. He did try hard to explain all these things white men do, and how they think, but often it didn't make sense. They had no gods and did not listen to the spirits. She would never understand the pale-eyes, and their ways. But that was all right. He was absolutely boneheaded when it came to understanding her people.

"There's another candidate for the job, maybe more than that. We both know him. Alexandre Bonfils."

"A boy," she said.

"He's done well, Victoria. His trappers brought back more fur this year than mine, and they got it up in the Blackfeet country without getting into trouble. I can't say as much."

"He was lucky. Good medicine. He make the beaver come to the traps, and he don't get caught. But maybe his medicine won't be so good next time."

"He's bold and young and intelligent; he may get that position. Having a Hidatsa woman who can talk your tongue helps, too."

"He has many women, not just her. And he sells her to any trapper for a pelt or two. I would not want to be the woman of Bonfils."

He smiled. She did love that smile, which wrinkled flesh around those buried blue eyes.

"Is it time to buy some whiskey?" she asked, hopefully.

He lifted that battered beaver hat, scratched his long locks, and set it back again. "No, we're not having any whiskey this year."

That jolted her. She thought he was crazy. He would have some credit at the store. They could have lots of whiskey at the rendezvous.

"You got some big reason, Skye?"

"We're taking off at dawn for St. Louis. At least I am. They want to see me. The big chiefs, the owners, they've never met me, and they don't want to put a man they don't know in a position like that. Big doings. They want me to hear how they operate."

"St. Louis?"

"On the fireboat, the paddle wheeler at Fort Union. They need to take the returns downstream before the river drops. Andy Drips will collect and bale all the furs he can tonight, and start at dawn for Fort Union. With me. With us, if you want. If you'd rather stay with your people, you could—"

"St. Louis? The many-houses place?"

"Many houses, many stores, the big river."

"And white women!"

He laughed. The biggest mystery in her life was white women. For many years she had seen these white trappers, all of them without white women, and it puzzled her. She hadn't the faintest idea where they were hidden, what they wore, or what they did. The white men said their women were back in the many-buildings places like St. Louis, and were too frail to come into the mountains like the men. They would not survive for long in lodges, or in bad weather.

All of that astonished her. She thought that white women must be greatly inferior to any other kind, and had secretly nursed a great contempt for them. No wonder white men left them behind! They were a frail and miserable and pale sex, always dying and shivering and getting themselves buried.

"When are you coming back?" she asked.

"Fast. The riverboat goes downstream much faster than

upstream. We can be in St. Louis in a couple of weeks after we leave—ah, maybe fifteen or sixteen sleeps. We would spend only a day or two in St. Louis. Then we'd outfit and ride back. If we go light, maybe three moons. Back here before it gets cold."

She squinted at him suspiciously. "Is this where the white women are?"

He laughed. "I imagine. I've never been to the States."

"Will I see what they wear?"

"You'll see everything they wear. They all dress differently."

"Will I have to ride on the fireboat? It is a beast."

"Yes."

"I could walk along the bank while you ride the boat."

"No, it goes much too fast."

"I don't want to put my foot onto a boat with fire in its belly and steam coming out. Bad medicine."

"That's up to you, Victoria. It's safe enough, but once in a while one does hit a snag and sinks. I have to go. I don't want to. I was looking forward to rendezvous. Looking forward to . . . a jug or two—"

"Sonofabitch!" she yelled. "I can't even see my friends!"

"You could winter with the Kicked-in-the-Belly people. Your mother and father would enjoy that."

"And leave you all alone? Skye, dammit, I want to see these white men's buildings worse than anything. I want to see your pale sickly women! I want to see where all these beaver furs go; where they all disappear to. I want to see where all this metal comes from, guns and powder. How do they make that? I want to see how they make blankets. Where does the wool come from? You tell me these things, but I have to see them.

"But most of all, Skye, I want to see the women. Goddamn, if I don't go along, maybe you'll throw me out of the lodge and marry one of your own kind."

Skye began to laugh. She loved his laugh. It began deep in his belly, a great rumble that shook his barrel frame, and then slowly rose up his throat and burst upon the world like a grizzly dance or a wolf howl.

"We'll take a few jugs and drink them on the fireboat," he said at last.

four

Skye woke up in a foul temper. It was going to rain; he could smell it. It had rained all June. They would be traveling in an icy drizzle.

But that wasn't the source of his ill humor. He had waited all year for rendezvous, waiting for fine times, big doings, roaring, ripping, *hoorawing* fun, belly-tickling yarns, and now he was cutting out before it started.

Victoria wasn't faring any better. She dressed sullenly, as irritable as he, her eyes accusing, her glare daring him to say one word, just one word, so it would all blow up and she would stay at rendezvous. They had the good sense not to say anything to each other.

He pulled his thick-soled moccasins up, tugged his fringed buckskins over his blue shirt, and stepped into a gray and hateful dawn. The rendezvous slept sweetly. Even the revelers had surrendered to Morpheus. He saw Gabe Bridger snoring peacefully beside a dead campfire. The rain would wake him up soon. Even Bridger, one of the partners of the defunct rival fur company, was now working for Pierre Chouteau and his St. Louis capitalists. Where else could a mountaineer go? To Mexico? No one was making a living farther south, trying to drown a few beaver for Bent, St. Vrain and Company. The good times were over, and the mountain life was going under.

Smoke from a couple of fires hung lazily over the camp, layering the air. This was the time of day of surprise attack; of hordes of vermillion-painted savages sweeping into a vulnerable and sleeping village. But that would not happen here at the great trade festival. Mountain men had fangs and two-legged predators knew it. The mountaineers and Indians guarded the horse herds well, night and day. And years ago, a few Blackfoot and Gros Ventre raiders had bumped into the rendezvous and started a war, and they weren't likely to try it again.

He headed for the river, splashed brutally cold water over his stubbled face and battered hands, dried himself with a handful of grass, and headed for the breakfast fire, walking painfully, as if on pebbles, because the chill had stiffened his limbs. Over at the store, Andy Drips's clerks were furiously baling plews, while others loaded packs onto mules.

"We'll be out of here in an hour," Drips said. "Have some breakfast. Real coffee."

"Don't touch it."

"You limeys. I suppose you want tea."

"Just some meat."

Drips pointed to a slab of buffalo loin that had been rotated on an iron spit over cottonwood flames until it was scorched outside and succulent within. Skye pulled out his Green River knife and began sawing, feeling the hot pink juices leak over his scaly hands. Buffalo was a satisfying meat, tender at the hump and loin, tough and chewy elsewhere. This was stringy meat, old bull, but tasty. It would give his teeth something to do and put some strength into his belly.

"You do a good trade last night?" Skye asked, around the meat.

"No. Not three packs of beaver from the free trappers. Few

more from the Injuns, and some weasel tails, ermine, mink, and otter."

"What happens to all these trade goods if they don't sell?"

"It'll all get packed back to Fort Union."

Skye looked at the hardware, blankets and cloth, a pathetic fraction of what usually arrived in the annual packtrain. "Don't think there'll be much to take back, mate."

"Fontenelle will bring whatever doesn't sell, and whatever furs he can still buy. We've got most of the pelts loaded. This ain't much of a rendezvous. You can feel it. Maybe it's the last. Who knows? Makes a man feel bad about things."

Skye nodded, feeling an autumnal chill, like the falling of aspen leaves, even though it was June.

He spotted the young Frenchman, Alexandre Bonfils, approaching, and studied his rival. Together they would go to St. Louis, but only one would win the trading position at Fort Cass. Bonfils peered at Skye with quick dark eyes, and then at the wavering fire. If getting up at this hour was hard on Skye, it was plainly worse for the disheveled younger brigade leader, whose lax discipline often got him into trouble.

Bonfils's life in the mountains had been a series of narrow escapes from weather, cold, starvation, Indians, and sickness. And yet the man's daring and genius, his uncanny ability to bring in the beaver was even more formidable than Skye's. Bonfils did not hesitate to take his men into Blackfoot country, moving swiftly from stream to brooding stream in virgin beaver waters, and escaping before Bug's Boys got wind of his presence.

The man affected a certain patrician elegance that shouted his superiority to the world. One of his oddities was the ever-present Royal Order of Chevaliers medal pinned to his breast. This device, a bronze medallion chased with gold, featuring the bas relief bust of Louis XVI hanging from watershot blue silk, announced the magnificence of the Bonfils name to all the mountain men, as well as stray savages. His other idiosyncracy was to have his family coat of arms sewn in gold lamé thread to his parfleches. By and large, the mountaineers enjoyed the gaudy display; beaver men could accommodate almost any attire, and the more bizarre, the better. Skye didn't mind any of it; did he not insist on wearing his own battered beaver top hat like a bishop's miter?

Bonfils poured steaming coffee into a tin cup, nodded at Skye, and grinned.

"So, my *ami*, we will go seek our fortune together on the *bateau-à-vapeur*."

Skye nodded. He knew if he opened his mouth he would regret what might come out. Bonfils had been drinking all night, yet here he was, showing no effects of the binge, while Skye, sober even after a parched year, was aching, irritable and as friendly as a lame grizzly coming out of hibernation.

"Is madame coming?" Bonfils asked.

"Yes."

"Ah, is it wise? I am lending Amalie to a friend. She would be an encumbrance in St. Louis, you know."

A mountain marriage, Skye thought. A temporary liaison between a trapper and a red woman, swiftly abandoned whenever the need arose. A man like Bonfils would have a dozen belles in St. Louis dancing in attendance, and would not let himself be embarrassed by the possessive arm of a squaw.

Bonfils's Hidatsa woman was pretty, bright-eyed young, vivacious, and a commodity the brigade leader sometimes lent to others for a favor. The young man's approach to life was to treat everything as a marketable commodity: loyalty, men, beaver, nature, women, and power. But that didn't disturb Skye. Bonfils's approach to native women was much the same as that of most trappers. Skye's enduring and committed marriage was the real oddity.

"I'm sure, monsieur, that Pierre Chouteau will want to

discuss the trading business out of earshot of your squaw. There are certain aspects of the business that are not for savage ears," Bonfils said. "Profit is everything!"

Skye nodded dourly, and sawed at the haunch of buffalo, sensing that Bonfils still wanted to palaver. For reasons Skye couldn't fathom, he had never much cared for the young Creole. The man was well educated, interesting, witty, brave, adept at survival in wilderness, a great raconteur, well liked and respected among the mountain fraternity. Skye couldn't fathom what was irritating him.

Within the hour Victoria had sullenly loaded their small seven-pole buffalo-hide lodge onto a travois, harnessed the packhorses, stuffed the panniers with their few things, fed No Name, their mutt, a buffalo rib, and was ready to go. Skye used to try to help, but she had always shooed him off, saying it was woman's work.

Drips's men were almost ready, too, and some of them were masticating meat before heading down the trail. Fontenelle, who would be in charge of the store, watched quietly.

Skye suddenly had a wrenching premonition that he would never see a rendezvous again. It tore at him so violently that he walked away from the hum of activity, down to the bank of the Popo Agie River, which ran through sedges there, and peered into the flowing waters that dully reflected in silvery images the distant mountains, their tops sawed off by a heavy overcast. Around him the rendezvous slept sweetly. Few men rose early during the summer festivals, and rare was the mountaineer who greeted the sun at any time.

An ache filled him. These mountain rendezvous were the only home he had had for many years. No matter where the site might be—Green River, Cache Valley—the great reunions were his hearth and parlor and kitchen. He was a man without a country.

He watched smoke curl sleepily from a few lodges, saw the mist obscuring the dark brush arbors where his friends whiled away joyous days, knew that if he walked through that quiet camp, he would see scores of men he cherished, like Joe Meek, or Black Harris, or Gabe Bridger, or Kit Carson, lying in shaggy buffalo robes, or between dirty blankets, or in lodges like his own, or under canvas, all of them with their Hawken or mountain gun within easy reach, trappers and warriors, storytellers, drunks, fiercely loyal colleagues, rough and violent and young and bold.

"Mister Skye," Drips called. "You think about what I said last night? About being a trader? You ready for all that?"

"No, I didn't think much about it. I don't want to think about it."

"You and old Pierre may have some different ideas about how to do things. He isn't going to let you trade your way. Only his way. The company way. You got that clear?"

Skye nodded. "We'll see," he said, cautiously. The camp tore at him; the future tore at him.

They wanted to look him over in St. Louis. It dawned on him that he wanted to look them over, too. What sort of men was he working for? Who were they, these distant lords whose command stretched even to here, in utter wilderness? Were they good men and true? Were they honorable? Did they possess that special quality of the English—moderation? Were they ruthless?

Suddenly this trip took on a new dimension. He had always been curious about the Americans, and now he would find out about them. For years he had thought about becoming an American citizen; the republic stood for things he admired. And yet, the Americans he had met were a mixed lot, some of them scoundrels and others fierce and implacable and merciless. But there were fine men among them too, men like Bridger, Carson, Fitzpatrick, and Jedediah Smith. He liked most of them. What had started a few hours earlier as a quest for a job, now loomed larger. He would see about these Yanks, and whether they were worthy of his esteem. And whether he would some day join them, swearing his fealty to them and their laws and Constitution. This trip could result in more than a job; much more. Or much less.

"Well, Mister Chouteau," he said aloud. "You'll look me over, and I'll look you over. I hope you're the man I want you to be, and your nation is the United States of America I dream it should be."

Few trappers and Indians had awakened to see them off, and these few stood silently. Scarcely one man of the mountains cared to think about what was happening: a company pack train leaving the day after it arrived and unloaded a handful of goods, after paying a lousy fifty cents a plew for what few beaver were available.

Skye didn't want to think about it either. He stepped into the high-cantled Indian saddle Victoria had gotten for him, and reined his buckskin into the procession. The caravan required no word from Drips; it simply started moving. Not even the crack of a whip was needed to start the packhorses. Twenty well-armed engagés of the American Fur Company, Skye, Victoria, and No Name, who mysteriously appeared when Skye stepped into his stirrups, Bonfils riding a handsome bay and leading a single packhorse, and Drips, gray and weather-whipped, his every motion economical.

Slowly they toiled up a long grade and then, at the last bend Skye turned, his heart wrenched once again by the sight of that beloved, sorry gathering, and then they rounded a spur of foothill and history fell behind them. Within minutes they had entered fog, and then icy mist, and finally they rode into a cruel drizzle, the kind Skye hated most.

All that long, cloud-shrouded day Skye grieved, while his horse plodded dully ahead. The rain quit but the overcast did not, and by noon they were chilled to the marrow. Drips stopped them in a piney glen and had his engagés boil up some broth over a smoky fire while the pack animals rested.

Two days later they cut around the foothills of the Big Horns and headed northeast. For a while Victoria was on familiar ground and bubbling with cheer, but soon they would cross into the lands of the Sioux, and then there might be trouble.

Drips drove them hard the next days, but the weather was fine and they reached the Yellowstone nine days later, covering as much as forty miles in a stretch. Then the sun besieged them, and man and beast suffered under the glare of sun that burst into the heavens at five in the morning and didn't set until ten.

They saw no Sioux, or Assiniboine either, but they fought an enemy that was even worse: black flies devoured them and stung the horses, and if not flies, then mosquitos, droning viciously at most of their camps. Bonfils, ever brave, made jokes and won the admiration of the engagés with his gallantry, but Skye bore the maddening insects dourly.

They faced two difficult crossings. The first would carry them to the left bank of the Yellowstone, and the second would take them across the mighty Missouri to the portals of Fort Union. The post had flatboats, mackinaws, to help with that enterprise, but they would be on their own crossing the swollen Yellowstone.

Drips chose a broad and gravelly reach of the river, negotiable except for a twenty-foot channel, and they spent a whole day swimming horses across that narrow but treacherous current. But the old master knew what he was up to, and by evening he had assembled his caravan on the far bank.

The next evening they reached the Missouri, and Skye beheld a great post, one he had never seen, squatting on the north bank, and bobbing in the river, the paddle-wheel vessel *Otter*.

five

S kye scarcely knew which sight galvanized him more: the white enameled *Otter*, tied fore and aft to great posts set into the levee, or the imperial American Fur Company headquarters, Fort Union, set on a yellow bench above the Missouri River.

It took some while for a pair of mackinaws, poled and paddled by sweating engagés, to carry the entire packtrain, horses and mules, one dog, and various pilgrims and voyageurs, across the sparkling river.

Here was the seat of an American empire, stretching from St. Louis up the river clear to British possessions and the walled borders of Mexico. He saw a snaky pennant flapping airily over the stockaded fortress, but knew even at that distance it wasn't the Stars and Stripes, and the national flag would probably fly underneath if it flew at all. No doubt the masters of this fur empire considered mere national sovereignty of much less importance than their company banner.

Victoria didn't like the look of that fireboat, even though its boilers were cold.

"Dammit, Skye," she muttered. "I will walk."

He laughed. "Twin chimneys," he said. "Thirty-two horsepower of high pressure steam to spin those paddle wheels."

"Bad spirits, and don't give me no guff."

He studied the vessel with a seaman's eye, noting the flat, bargelike hull, which probably had only five or six feet of cargo space; the freight booms fore, the cabins aft, and the privies ahead of the wheelhouses. The white enameled superstructure rose amidships and looked the worse for wear, with soot staining the woodwork. The riverboat looked hard used.

"We will die," she said. "The water spirits will reach up and smash us against a rock because this offends them."

Skye didn't argue. It would take skills beyond reckoning to steer that monster, the first steam vessel he had ever seen, though he had heard enough about it on the long, hasty trek from rendezvous. Andy Drips had waxed lyrical about this steamboat, and the others in the planning stage or being built for the company. "And we have a whole carpenter and smith shop on board. If anything breaks, we can fix it," Drips had said.

Skye had wondered about that. It would take more than a blacksmith to fix a ruptured boiler, he thought.

When their turn came, they loaded their horses and travois and gear aboard one of the mackinaws, while No Name watched suspiciously. At the very last moment, as the engagés pushed away from the south bank of the Missouri, the old dog howled and leapt, landing aboard and shaking himself. Skye remembered another time, long before, when the strange yellow cur had followed a schooner mile after mile along the Columbia River, determined to go wherever Skye went . . . or die. Skye could not think about that without feeling his throat tighten.

The engagés bantered in French with Alexandre Bonfils, who smiled a great deal and made friends easily. Skye wondered how he could possibly win a post from his French rival, in a company that was almost entirely French. Bonfils exuded the optimism that is natural to well-connected young men in their early twenties who have the inside track to everything good in the world.

The flatboat, or mackinaw, passed close to the huge riverboat, and Skye marveled that this machine had fought its way fifteen hundred river miles, against the current, often against the wind, pausing only to load cordwood. It carried a cargo that would supply not only the rendezvous, but also the entire needs of Fort Union and its satellite posts, including Forts Cass and MacKenzie, as well as Fort Pierre and its satellites. And that within this boat's hull would lie a fortune in peltries: beaver primarily, but also otter, mink, weasel, ermine, elk hide, buffalo robes, buffalo tongues preserved in salt, and more.

They debarked at a crude wharf and were met by a crowd of people, including the Fort's factor, Kenneth MacKenzie, James Kipp, his second in command, and assorted Assiniboine ladies, got up in high fashion. These were mountain wives, the mates of traders, the paramours of engagés, and servants who were casually traded from man to man to make the long winters go by swiftly. Many bore the cruel mark of smallpox on their faces, as did most of the engagés. The disease had obviously scythed through this place and left its calling cards.

The post itself rested on an arid bench in a yellow-rock country, a site far less handsome and inviting than Fort Vancouver, the great Hudson's Bay post on the Columbia. Here were no orchards or cultivated fields or granaries or gardens, but only naked rock and sagebrush. Even so, by all accounts, the masters of Fort Union had found ways to fill their lives with amenities, including fine wines imported upriver, along with splendid furniture, spices, condiments, china, silver, handsome woodstoves, bolts of silk and cotton and flannel, and infinitely more.

Skye studied Victoria to see how she was managing, and found her surveying everything, assessing the dark, boisterous Frenchmen engaged to the company, examining the dusky Assiniboine women, famously dressed like tarts in striped silks and glossy satins, their hair beribboned, their feet in dainty moccasins so heavily quilled or beaded they looked like rainbows on each foot.

"Sonofabitch," she said, echoing the trapper vernacular she had picked up. She loved the trappers' expletives and used them with rich imagination, especially when she was in the company of anyone who disapproved of them.

"Greetings, gents, greetings, Mister Skye," said MacKenzie, the huge chieftain, so formidable it must have taken an extra yard of fabric to cover him. Skye thought the man must be six and a half feet, and would weigh sixteen stone. MacKenzie himself was dressed in somber black and looked like an outsized minister or mortician. He had built the post, got into trouble years earlier for operating a still and was removed, but had returned to his familiar haunt once again, the absolute Lord of the North.

"And you must be Victoria. You are a legend, madam. You are the queen of the mountains!"

"Whatever that is," she said. "You gonna put up our horses or must I do it?"

"Tonight, madam, it would be our honor to care for your nags. Tomorrow they'll be boarded."

"On that fire canoe? The horses?"

"Your two saddle horses and equipage. They'll go as far as Bellevue, where you'll pick them up when you return."

"That dog, he goes with us, goddammit."

"Of course. A dog and his mistress cannot be separated."

It all made sense to Skye. Downriver, at Bellevue, on good prairie benchland near the confluence of the Platte River, the factor, Peter Sarpy, would board the Skye saddle horses until Skye headed back upriver, and provide him with packhorses in exchange for the ones he would leave here.

"Kipp here," said the second in command, a short but powerful gent with an iron grip. "Come along now, and see the post."

James Kipp hurried the Skyes and Bonfils and others up a steep path to the fort, which stood close to the Missouri. The interior yard was about what Skye expected, ample and solid, and the tall picketed walls stilled the blustery wind so that the air was quiet within. The great Kenneth MacKenzie, who had built the post, had built well. Encased by the cottonwood walls were warehouses, barracks, a kitchen, a chief factor's home with eight real glass windows and a shake roof. At opposite corners were bastions sporting small cannon for defense, and something more . . . an air, a feeling, a sense of imperial power that Skye hadn't felt since leaving Fort Vancouver, the Hudson's Bay post.

Below, the sweating engagés were loading the packs and bales of fur directly into the *Otter* under the gaze of a man Skye would soon meet, its master, Captain Marsh.

Kipp showed the Skyes to guest quarters.

"Dinner at eight in the chief factor's dining room," he said to Skye. "Mrs. Skye will eat with the women."

"Mr. Kipp, my wife would enjoy the company of the traders."

Kipp paused, scratched his whiskers. "I'm sorry. It's tradition here. The dinner table is set for gentlemen, and includes those of higher rank. There's a dining hall for the engagés—"

Kipp was plainly discomfited.

"I think perhaps we'll eat with the engagés," Skye said.

"Dammit Skye, you go eat with the men," Victoria said.

Skye knew the arrangements bothered him more than her. Many were the functions and meals within her Crow tribe that divided the sexes. He didn't know why he was so unhappy with this arrangement here, but he was.

"All right," he said, reluctantly.

"I'm sure Mrs. Skye will enjoy the company of our many ladies, most of them Assiniboine, but she'll be meeting my Mandan wife, some Sioux and Cree ladies, and so on . . ."

"Hell yes," she said. "Goddammit, Skye, go eat."

Kipp grinned. Barnaby Skye's wife was a legend in the mountains.

At the appointed hour, which seemed very late to Skye, he approached the chief factor's residence and was immediately invited into a sunny parlor for cordials, which turned out to be a robust port wine. Skye drank greedily, remembering all the joys of rendezvous he had surrendered to come here, but thinking that as the chief trader at Fort Cass he could have his nip each evening. Being a trader, with his own table and own wine casks, enough to last a year, enchanted him.

And so he met the great men of the American Fur Company, assessing them even as they assessed him. He met the bewhiskered red-faced master, Benton Marsh, natty in a blue uniform, and his mate, Trenholm. Marsh looked to be a choleric man, but one who smoothed things over out of long practice. Skye found himself peering into cold gray eyes, and felt a certain wariness.

He remained quiet, as was his wont, but Alexandre Bonfils was circulating gregariously, making friends, offering bon mots, and bragging not a bit modestly about the pelts he had acquired at great risk in the heart of Blackfoot country, pelts now resting in the bowels of the *Otter*.

At the stroke of eight, sounded by a handsome pendulum clock in a cherrywood cabinet, MacKenzie escorted his black-clad clerks and motley guests into his long dining room, where a splendid table awaited them. Here were furnishings Skye had not seen in the West, except at Fort Vancouver. A snowy linen cloth and napkins, elaborate silver, Limoges china, crystal goblets, a table groaning with condiments and awaiting the platters of food being prepared by all those pox-marked Assiniboine women.

MacKenzie seated them all by rank, the junior clerks at the far end of the great table, ascending to the most senior men and senior guests at the head of the table, above the salt. Skye and Captain Marsh were seated at MacKenzie's right and left, and that was how the trouble started.

"Ah, my friend Kenneth," said Bonfils, "how is it that Skye sits above me?"

MacKenzie reddened. "Because I have arranged it."

"But I am senior, monsieur," he said blandly.

"I believe, sir, that Mister Skye has been in the mountains far longer than you, and we are pleased here to honor that."

"Ah, you are mistaken. I have been in service to Pratte, Chouteau quite a bit longer than he has, having begun my engagement seven years since."

The room quieted. Young Bonfils, so well connected to the company's owners, was asserting rank.

MacKenzie, the strongest of men, decided to settle the matter. "My young friend, you are my guest here—"

"I will resolve this," said Skye. "Mister Bonfils, by all means, take this seat. I will join my wife."

Skye smiled gravely at this august assemblage, and walked slowly out the door.

six

Skye brushed off the trouble, but Victoria didn't.

"Why didn't you stay?" she asked in the quiet of their small chamber.

He threw a big hand over her and drew her tight. "Some men want rank," he said. "I don't worry about it."

"But dammit, Skye, you should have let the big chief MacKenzie decide."

"Maybe so," he said. "But I did what I did, and it's over."

"It's not. That man Bonfils, he will put this to good use. He will tell the world that you are not big man enough to be a trader."

Maybe she was right. He had felt something sinister brush him as lightly as a feather; something lurking just beyond his understanding.

After Bonfils's outburst, Skye had nodded at MacKenzie and stalked out while the others stared. MacKenzie had started to protest, but let him go. Bonfils was grinning amiably, and the instant Skye neared the door, the young rival edged toward the vacated place near the head of the table. Captain Marsh and the senior men seated at that table like a row of penguins had said nothing, but their gazes followed Skye.

He had headed for the mess hall where ordinary men ate, and was able to catch a meal just as the cooks were clearing away the trenchers. No one there said anything either. He felt more comfortable among them than he did with those zealous men of rank and all their pretensions. There was something stinking and fraudulent about all that faked opulence, so far from the true seats of power and commerce. Everything had been imported, from the casks of wine to the table linens. The Assiniboine women decorating that post, tricked out in bright taffetas and the latest Paris styles, were there to foster the illusion of civilization, but they were merely concubines and servants, the company's pox-marked whores.

Skye dismissed the episode from mind; it was not important. Obviously, Bonfils regarded rank as something so important that he made a public protest. The man had a point: he had been with the Chouteau interests much longer than Skye had. And his trapping brigades had done brilliantly, bringing in more beaver than anyone else's. Maybe he deserved the honor. Maybe it was a passion of the very young, like Bonfils, to enjoy rank. He wore a medal on his chest, and had his family crest veneered to his equipage, so rank obviously meant everything to him, even a thousand miles from any world where rank meant something.

Had Skye casually thrown away the esteem of those substantial men when he bowed out? Company politics were new to him. He had never entertained ambition. He had been too busy surviving in a mountain wilderness even to consider advancement within the company. But now, suddenly, a trading position meant a great deal to him. With it, he would have a future. Without it . . . he didn't know.

Skye remembered his life in the Royal Navy, where he was the lowliest of the low. Rank had been important to everyone with any ambition, and men zealously guarded their rank, and all the manifestations of rank. A lord admiral wanted every honor and prerogative associated with his high position. Even a lowly jack tar might want the ship's company to know he had been in his majesty's service longer than those young whelps.

Skye breakfasted with the engagés the next dawn, and then watched the rivermen build fires in the boilers and get up steam. He watched intently as the deck hands boarded his saddle horses and penned them in a cage on the foredeck. Even as firemen started to build boiler steam, woodcutters were carrying the last of the cottonwood logs they had stacked bankside. An amazing eight or nine cords of firewood rested on the deck, handy to the firemen, and Skye wondered how long that would last. That riverboat would eat wood.

"Ah, so it's you, Skye," said Bonfils, drawing up beside. "An exciting adventure, *oui*?"

"It's Mister Skye, mate."

Bonfils laughed. "So I've heard. A fine cachet for a mountain man."

That sally from a man who wore a royal medal on his chest. Skye remained quiet. That *Mister* was, after all, the rank he had insisted on ever since escaping the Royal Navy.

"Well, *Mister* Skye, we missed you last night. Talk turned to weighty things, including the future of the fur business, the decline of beaver, the advances in firearms, the sonnets of Shakespeare, the means by which redskins can be persuaded to part with furs and pelts for less and less of value, and the ultimate ownership of Oregon. I ventured the opinion that anything dyed a gaudy color, no matter how trifling its value, would fetch a good price from the savages, and I must say, the gentlemen at table largely applauded my observation. But I suppose those things are not of any consequence. You aren't a citizen, I gather, and have no interest in the republic or its commerce, or in belles lettres either."

"And how would you conduct trade at Fort Cass, Mister Bonfils?"

"*Monsieur* Bonfils, if you can manage it. I am for profit, by whatever means, and so I loudly proclaimed. Why hire trappers and hunters when we can engage the Indians to do these, for the price of a few dyed turkey feathers?"

Skye began to grasp the sharp-edged drift of banter like this, and dismissed the young man. "It's time to fetch my wife, sir."

He headed back to the post, hearing Bonfils's easy chuckle behind him.

MacKenzie stood just inside the post, and hailed him: "Mister Skye—"

"Mister MacKenzie, don't apologize. Young men seek their moment of glory. I had a fine buffalo feast with the engagés."

"No, that doesn't do. I regret the whole business." He hesitated, and then spoke. "If you had stood your ground, I would have made it clear who's the host and who's commanding the post. You would have given me a chance to say a thing or two."

MacKenzie offered a meaty hand, and Skye shook it.

Skye found Victoria in their gloomy room, perched on the soft bed which owed its comfort to its tick, which was stuffed with the thick beards of buffalos. Her cheeks were wet. No Name, their yellow mutt, sat at her feet guarding her against a world neither liked.

"Victoria—"

"Dammit, Skye! Something bad's gonna happen! Maybe we won't see the mountains again!"

He knew enough to keep quiet. Over the years he had come to understand her mysterious, sometimes uncanny sense of the future, something she called her medicine. Her spirit helper, the magpie, often darted before her, telling her what lay ahead. And now she sat on the edge of the bed, her honeyed cheeks wet with tears and foreboding.

"You may be right," he said. "Riverboats get into trouble fast. Boilers blow. They snag. Some catch fire. They're always trouble—"

She pressed his hand and stood. "Dammit, we'll be late."

He lifted two battered parfleches, and she grabbed two others, and thus they transported most of their worldly possessions through the yard of the post, out the narrow gate, and down the steep grade to the levee, where the *Otter* rocked and vibrated like a rabid wolf. A palpable fear swept over Victoria, but she walked determinedly beside her man, and they boarded amidships, on a gangway. The dog sulked, bristled, and followed, sniffing the deck and everything on it, and then wet some firewood.

Bedlam prevailed. Everywhere, engagés and sailors were loading goods; buffalo haunches for the cooks, bales of buffalo robes and deerskins and elk hides which had to be lowered with a boom and spars and tackle into the low hold, where another crew pushed and hauled the cargo to spead its weight evenly. A cabin boy threw a pail of slop overboard. A crew rolled casks of water aboard, not to drink but to replenish the boilers.

Skye and Victoria found their way aft to a cramped cabin and entered it, finding several small compartments around a central hall where meals would be served on folding tables. There was a small woman's compartment aft, farthest from the boilers and thus the safest, but Victoria scorned that and chose to bunk with her man.

The quarters were spartan, trimmed in oak but walled with plank. A small glassed window provided the only light. A simple washstand with an enameled tin basin and pitcher supplied the only bath.

No Name whined, sniffed the corners, and vanished into the cabin, and then out the door onto the deck, where he sat, quivering with dread. Skye followed him, feeling suffocated by that tiny dark compartment, and knowing that Victoria would snarl at him if he stayed longer. She was plainly having a bad time of it, wrestling with a thousand new things as well as a terror beyond describing.

Now he could hear the rumble of the firebox and smell the billowing smoke as it descended over the vessel. The escapement pipe, which released used steam, began to pop and hiss as the boat turned into a living thing, a monster trembling on the great hawsers that pinned it to Fort Union.

A crowd gathered at the bank; the gaudy Assiniboine women in their finery, the engagés, mostly wearing leather and wool, the breed children scooting about, the black-clad monkish clerks, and scores of tribesmen and their squaws solemnly wrapped in blankets to ward off a sharp dawn chill, the low sun gilding their bronze faces.

Skye had put his mealtime with the ship's company to good use, asking innumerable questions. This riverboat ran 120 feet and needed four feet of draft loaded, which was too much, especially with the river lowering almost daily as the spring floods receded. There would be sandbars just a foot below water level, sinister sawyers, the broken limbs of sunken trees, waiting to tear the hull apart, currents whipping the boat into rocks and obstacles, and always the desperate need of wood.

Ten cords each day this monster burned. And many hundreds of miles along the Missouri where there was not a tree in sight. A single trip up the river and back consumed the wood of over fifteen hundred trees: hardwoods down near St. Louis; softer woods, such as the prolific cottonwoods and willows upstream. A full load of wood weighed thirty to forty tons.

Then, suddenly, a shrieking whistle blew, and the mate bellowed in the megaphone. No Name laid back his head and howled. Captain Marsh stood on the upper deck, called the texas, and watched his sailors loosen the hawsers.

Skye marveled that such a complex piece of equipment could pierce so far into utter wilderness. From the jackstaff a triangular American Fur Company pennant fluttered, and a Stars and Stripes hung from its staff at the rear. There were shouts, men winding hawsers on capstans, and then the boat shuddered free and into the swift cold current, its speed sickening.

Victoria caught his hand and squeezed it. The dog bristled. The cannonade of the escapement pipe deafened them now as the wheels rumbled inside their housing and thrashed the river. Fort Union began to shrink into a blurred blue horizon.

Up above, standing next to Captain Marsh like the Angel Gabriel, was Alexandre Bonfils, whose uncles owned this vessel.

seven

lexandre Bonfils lounged beside the helmsman in the pilothouse seething with importance. He had perched himself at this lofty station so that he might view the passing world from the best perspective, yet didn't see the shaggy old buffalo bull lapping water at the bank, or the soaring golden eagle, or the kingfisher diving for minnows, or the stretching green distances of the northern plains, as the river passed through mysteries.

His vision was focused elsewhere, no matter what the world brought to his empty gaze. He wanted that position at Fort Cass, and knew he could not win it unless he took certain measures. Fort Cass wasn't much of a post, merely a satellite of Fort Union, and the Crows didn't do a large trade. But it was the only trading position available because there were so many senior men, all veterans, in the company; the only one likely to open in the next several years, the only one that would advance his ambitions. Some day, he would take over the firm from his mother's cousin, Pierre Chouteau, and be the Emperor of the West, and the Prince of St. Louis.

He had been a brigade leader, but what did it matter? Any seasoned mountaineer, like the barbarous Skye, could reach that position with a few trapping and survival skills, and a way with men.

But being the factor at a trading post, being a licensed trader for the company, that was something else. A trader was advanced up the chain of command if he did well. A trader could swiftly take his share of the profits and retire in St. Louis a wealthy man, high in the ranks of the fur company, an annual annuity comforting him. A trader operated a wilderness enterprise, lived in solid comfort within a building instead of freezing or boiling or starving or thirsting or running from savages. A trader was a weighty man, not some hireling bought and sold by the company. A trader was noticed; an engagé lived in obscurity. And a trader could do whatever he had to do far from prying eyes, the sovereign of his own kingdom.

He knew all about traders, having grown up in the business. The man who put his thumb in the cup while measuring out sugar or flour or whiskey or coffee was the man who tweaked a profit. The man who watered the second or third gill of spirits sold to the savages was the man who got good robes at less cost. The man who sent agents skulking into the night to bribe chiefs away from the opposition was the man who got the furs. The company that sold cheap cast-iron hatchets and axes, instead of steel ones, was the outfit that pocketed the profits, not only from the cheaper tools, but because the savages returned again and again for more soft-metal tools. Poor red devils never grasped the difference.

It all amused him.

Bien. He would be a trader, and it would not matter that Skye was senior in years and experience. Skye would be dealt with, and that is what occupied his every thought, even as he stared, unseeing, at a stationary horsed Indian on a distant bluff, without seeing the man; why he scarcely noted the riverboat slowing and stopping. Why he didn't watch the steersman in the yawl row ahead, make soundings, and then direct the packet toward a newly washed channel where the riverboat would not ground on a bar.

It would have struck a stranger observing Bonfils that this was an odd man, stationed exactly where he could see everything, but gazing on the day's events with a blind eye. Bonfils didn't even hear the quiet exchanges between the pilot, the captain, and the helmsman as they negotiated a dangerous passage where the murky Missouri broadened, the shifting sands built new barriers, and murderous sawyers, dead trees, lurked just out of sight under the placid sun-washed surface of the river.

How much did Skye know, and how much would he tell in St. Louis? It came down to that. A word from Skye would carry weight in the Gateway to the West. Bonfils had no illusions about family connections. The fur trade was exacting, brutal, cruel, risky, and precarious. Pierre Chouteau and General Bernard Pratte wanted the best men in the field; profit depended on it. Men without an excess of honor, which certainly qualified him.

He laughed softly. Being a relative wouldn't count for much, at least not at a certain level of responsibility. The hard-eyed seigneurs who ran the Upper Missouri Outfit would not permit mere blood or lineage to affect their choice—but neither would his connections hurt him. The company was closely held.

Alexandre Bonfils had advanced with breathtaking speed; a brigade leader after only one year in the mountains! And now he would be celebrated as the man who brought the most beaver packs to St. Louis, a fortune snugged in the gut of this riverboat!

But certain matters needed to be concealed, and certain rumors squelched. He had no way of knowing how much Skye knew, or what the gossips at the rendezvous had been whispering, or how much of all that Skye would drone into the ear of old Pierre Chouteau, thus ending Bonfils's career in the mountains, and his hopes of being a dashing dauphin of Creole society in St. Louis, with an unending supply of supple and eager mademoiselles to brighten his life and warm his bed.

Both the Chouteaus and the Prattes knew why he had escaped to the distant fur country in the first place at the tender age of seventeen. He had gotten Marie Therese Lachine with child, and faced with marrying or fleeing St. Louis for the fur country, he had fled, spending time clerking at Fort Clark and Fort Pierre before drifting west to the beaver country.

He was a father, but had never seen the child, for the maiden had swiftly been sent downriver to Baton Rouge, where she was hastily married to a Robidoux cousin. What a relief! He might have been stuck with that whiny and simpering little snip for the rest of his life. All she had to offer was a pubescent sweetness, which no doubt had already vanished under layers of lard. He smiled. He fancied that the little episode had made a man out of him. It would not count against him. What man in the mountains hadn't just that sort of difficulty in his past?

He spotted Skye leaning over the beak of the boat, watching the mysterious river eddy by, the man's black beaver hat glued to his unkempt locks. What a comic figure the barrel-shaped man was, ruffian to the core, ill-kempt, his body webbed with scars, his little pig eyes caught between a glacier of a nose. And yet the man evoked fear in Bonfils. That disreputable slug from the Royal Navy had hamlike fists that could pulverize a foe, a catlike grace that belied his awkward top-heavy carcass, and a withering stare that caused most men to turn away.

But that wasn't what evoked fear in Bonfils. There was something uncompromising about Skye; something simple and solid and unyielding that set the man apart. Skye would do what he had to do, and say what he had to say, without a scintilla of social grace or cunning. Maybe it was some sort of brutal honesty, exactly the sort of transparency that Bonfils detested in a man. He himself was more civilized and saw life's nuances.

He wasn't sure just why he feared Skye. He didn't fear anyone else. And that fear cropped up every time he encountered Skye, turning him into pudding.

Skye probably knew everything there was to know about Bonfils; all the rumors, all the gossip that passed quietly from man to man in the mountains, especially when they were sharing a jug of mountain whiskey. He would know . . . about the dead Blackfeet. He would know . . . about the losses of trappers. He would know . . . about killing the Piegan woman. He would know . . . about that business with the five Cheyenne women. He would know about the sly coup against the Hudson's Bay Company, and how he snatched twenty-three packs of beaver just by taking them when the fools weren't looking. Surely he would know everything, and that was rankling Bonfils now, as he stared down upon his fellow passenger.

Maybe Skye hadn't heard a word.

A shudder ran through the boat, followed by a lurch, and then sudden immobility. The *Otter* had struck something.

From his aerie he watched deckhands peer over the bow, beside Skye. One had a pole, and when he thrust it into the brown water, it hit bottom only eighteen inches or two feet down. They were grounded. Men peered over the side, looking for damage. Others scurried down the hatch, seeing whether they were taking water. Behind him he heard the captain and the pilot shouting directions. He heard a clank and a thunk, and then the snap and hiss of steam rattling out of the escapement pipe, and the rumble of the pistons. The paddle wheels thrashed thunderously, churning up foam. The *Otter* backed away from the bar, and soon floated free.

These crewmen knew what to do. They lowered the yawl from its davits and the steersman and his fellows began taking soundings, looking for passage around that new sandbar, a barrier that hadn't existed only a few weeks before when the boat had thrashed upriver. The riverboat slowly backed upstream, propelled by the reversed paddle wheels, and waited for the crew in the yawl to find a way, if a channel existed.

Bonfils didn't much care. What was all this to him? He studied Skye, who was observing the whole operation with the experienced eye of a seaman.

Bonfils knew suddenly how to proceed. He badly needed to befriend Skye, share confidences, reveal the soul, and maybe find out what Skye knew or suspected; find out what his adversary would do in St. Louis—if he ever reached St. Louis. There might be an accident, man overboard in the night, plainly drunk. And his squaw too, dead from the effort to save her lout of a man. Bonfils had a splendid cache of Kentucky bourbon in his kit; maybe he could put it to use.

He smiled. Who could offer more bonhomie than the young man who had invented the art? He abandoned his post near the helmsman, tipped his straw hat to the mate, and clattered down the companionway to the boiler deck. Bonfils then went forward to the place where Skye leaned over the rail, his moccasined foot on the coaming, his shoulder pressed against the jackstaff, his mutt watching warily.

"Ah, there you are. A close call, eh, Mister Skye?"

Skye nodded, his gaze quietly measuring his fellow passenger.

"They know how to proceed. I imagine they'll find the channel, and we'll be off."

"What brings you down from the pilothouse, mate?"

"We haven't really had a chance to talk, *mon ami*. I want

you to know that whoever is chosen, I will abide amiably with the decision of the company officers. You're a man I've always admired, Mister Skye."

"What do you want?"

Bonfils laughed. The man was so crude. "Want? We have a fortnight of travel before us, time to enjoy the adventure. Perhaps we'll shoot buffalo together, or drop ducks for our supper, or saddle these horses and hunt . . ."

Skye didn't reply. The crew in the yawl had found deep water, and he was watching them jab their sounding pole deep into the river, and measure an opening for the ship.

"Actually," Bonfils said, "I've always regarded you as my mentor, and studied your ways. You're a legend, Mister Skye, and now at last I have a chance to learn more about you, how you think, what you do, how you approach the company throne at St. Louis . . . and what advice you have for a poor, young supplicant."

Skye shrugged, his smile contained. "I'll meet them, we'll palaver, and they'll decide," he said. "And so will I."

In that artless answer, Bonfils found menace.

eight

Through much of that first day on the river, Skye suffered the unwanted company of the young brigade leader. Bonfils made a show of patrolling the vessel, acquainting himself with its operations, but sooner or later he arrived again at Skye's side, there to flatter the older man with small, adroit compliments, admiration that Skye supposed was more feigned than real, and all of that combined with a peculiar humility, in which Bonfils derided his own skills while inflating those of the man next to him.

Skye had had no experience with flatterers; they were unknown in the mountains, and he had never heard a word of flattery aimed in his direction during all the time he spent in the Royal Navy. But here was this honey-tongued Creole admiring Skye's hunting skills, his ability to survive in bad weather, his handling of tough scrapes, his skilled dealing with Indians, his bluntness. The man had plainly inquired about Skye, and seemed to know more about Skye than Skye knew about himself.

What did it mean? Skye imagined that the young man wanted his approval; maybe a kind word given to General Pratte or Pierre Chouteau. Maybe he wanted to find out something to use against Skye.

At one point, Skye pointed at a distant cliff where half a dozen Indian women stood.

"Ah! What fine vision you have, Monsieur. I would not have seen such a sight, myself."

"I think you would have, Mister Bonfils."

"Ah! No. Now I am beginning to understand why you are a legend in the mountains. You see around corners and over the brow of hills, to the war party lurking on the other side."

Skye felt annoyed, but held his peace. Whatever Bonfils was up to would become clear in due course. In the space of half an afternoon, Skye had received more compliments than had come his way over an entire life.

But once in a while, Bonfils probed a bit. "What are your plans, Monsieur? If you become a trader, I would envy you. A good life, settled in a comfortable place, *oui*?"

"Yes, a good life. I would see to it that the company has the loyalty of my wife's people . . . and I would see to it that they receive good value for the skins and furs they bring me. The Crows aren't numerous, and they need weapons and powder

and everything else white traders offer. The Sioux and Blackfeet outnumber them. So, sir, my loyalties would be evenly divided between the company, and the Crows."

Bonfils smiled brightly. *"Quell magnifique!"* he said, but
Skye knew that his own words would be used against him in
the privy chambers of St. Louis, where profit mattered most
and fairness to the Indians was a consideration only so far as
to keep their allegiance. But he would not alter his position.

He was a stubborn man. If he traded with Victoria's people, he would see to it that they were generously treated.
There would be no fingers or thumbs in a measuring cup, and
no extra river water in the spirits, and no weaseling down the
price of good furs placed on the trading counter, in order to
pay less. Not for Victoria's people. Not for any people, anywhere, ever.

The *Otter* rounded a sweeping bend flowing between low
gloomy bluffs, and headed for a notch on the left bank where
the green of a wooded patch bloomed brightly in an ochre
world. The vessel slowed, and the thunder of the wheels
muted into a soft sloshing, and the rattle of steam popping out
of the escapement dwindled to a mutter.

"Wood stop," yelled the mate. "All able men report."

Skye had heard of these episodes. The crew and every male
passenger would soon be debarked at that patch of trees, to
chop, saw, cut and haul seven or eight cords of firewood aboard.

"Ah! A chance to stretch!" Bonfils said.

Skye wondered whether the young man would contribute.
These wood stops would be a good test of a passenger's char-
acter. There would be slackers, and there would be workers,
and he wondered which category Bonfils would fill.

The boat drifted into shore, and bumped gently into the
bottom. Two boatmen, one fore, one aft, slipped into the
muddy river and waded ashore, carrying manila hawsers,
which they tied to tree stumps. Other deckmen lowered a
gangplank. It didn't quite reach shore, so they added a few

loose scantlings to the gangway until a small dry passage ran from the coaming to the grassy riverbank.

A deckhand gave each parting crewman an axe or a saw, and the crew, save for the master and pilot and engineers and firemen, fanned into the cottonwoods and willows and box elders.

Skye received a huge two-man crosscut saw, and headed onto shore.

"Monsieur, that's a two-man saw; we can work together," Bonfils said, catching up.

Skye grunted.

Behind him, the last of the crewmen abandoned the vessel, and he saw Victoria slip down to land, along with No Name, and begin to hike upslope. He knew her thinking: here were all these stupid white men cutting wood, vulnerable, not knowing who or what lay just over the brow of those yellow bluffs. She would look. That was her nature, bred into her by generations of her ancestors, whose life and safety depended on just such caution. He blessed her and loved her. Maybe, on one of these woodcutting stops, her vigilance would spare them disaster.

Four deckmen with axes headed for green trees and began girdling them, chipping through bark and cortical fibre so that these trees would be dead and dry next riverboating season. But the rest headed for the gray skeletons of trees killed the previous year and now ready to fell and burn.

"*Ici, monsieur,*" Bonfils said, pointing at a gray giant that once was a noble cottonwood.

Skye stared up at the noble ruin, a tree so grand he was sure a dozen cords of firewood might be gotten from it. But it was close to other less noble trees, and would be dangerous to fell so close to so many toiling men.

"Maybe we'd better pick something smaller. It'd take an hour just to saw through that trunk," Skye said.

"We shall do it. We shall show them what we're made of."

"That's what I'm hoping to avoid," Skye said gently.

Nonetheless, Bonfils grabbed one end of the long saw and stationed himself beyond the gray trunk. Skye peered about, decided a warning or two would clear the area before the tree fell, and they began to work.

Bonfils didn't shrink or slack. The saw bit fiercely through cottonwood as they scraped it back and forth. They cut a notch in the direction they hoped the tree would fall, and then attacked the other side, the keen-edged saw ripping noisily into the dry wood. Skye began to sweat, even in the coolness of the woods.

In the distance he saw Victoria clamber the last fifty feet to the edge of the bluff and stand there, a tiny statue against an azure sky, with No Name beside her. She was beautiful, he thought; a guardian of her family, and all these other blind white men.

A breeze eddied through the woods, carrying the scent of grass and sun and the day's heat. Bonfils sawed furiously, and Skye wondered whether the man regarded this as some sort of competition; whether the man, in his own soul, would brag to himself that night about how he sawed harder and produced more than old Skye. How odd that was to Skye. How odd that Bonfils had to prove himself, if that was what he was doing.

The cottonwood teetered on its dwindling base, and Skye shouted at the deckmen nearby, pointing the way the giant would fall. For his efforts he received only curses: it meant that the deckmen would have to abandon their own valuable labor, and perhaps deal with the giant tree. Skye privately cursed his luck, and vowed never to let Bonfils draw him into trouble again.

They sawed furiously while the sweating and sullen sailors backed away, and then with a creak and a snap, the giant toppled down, carrying four smaller trees with it. The crash shook the earth, and caused others to pause fearfully, until the mate roared at them to get busy.

Just as Skye expected, the downed giant was so tangled with the lesser trees that the hands had no choice but to cut up the larger one. Skye heard them muttering; the blame came in his direction, and he owned up to it. It had been a stupid and vainglorious act to fell that tree.

But swiftly, the experienced crew hacked and sawed the giant into usable pieces, most of them four-foot lengths that could be stuffed whole into the fireboxes under the twin boilers. A crew toted the heavy logs aboard, while the firemen arranged them into neat stacks adjacent to the maw of the hungry fireboxes.

The trunk of the giant cottonwood was so thick it was useless, so the crew reduced the limbs until there were no more, and then returned to their own felling, their glances sharp and unkind. If Bonfils had attempted to cover himself with glory this afternoon, he had failed.

Within an hour, the teeming crewmen had loaded all the wood aboard that the ship could hold. Skye stood, sweating, as he watched the last of the limbs and trunks go up the wobbly planks. Some short blasts of the whistle alerted those on land, including Victoria, who had returned to the riverbank. She and No Name boarded, the dog sniffing every stanchion and post. Skye reached over and petted the yellow dog, his boon companion along a thousand wild trails, and the dog licked his hand.

Silently, keeping her thoughts to herself, Victoria studied the ruin of that wooded notch in the bluff, the site of a tiny spring-fed creek, and then she wordlessly headed aft to the fantail, the place she had anointed for herself, even as Skye had chosen the prow. It was as if he loved the future, while she clung to the past. He didn't doubt that this trip was a disturbing change in her life; she was witnessing great changes, and knew that these things would soon disrupt the ancient, timeless traditions of her people.

Two short blasts of the whistle. The deckmen loosened the

hawsers and scrambled aboard even as deckhands slid the gangway past the coaming. The ship drifted free, soon was tugged by the current, and then Skye heard the great splash of the paddle wheels rumbling inside the wheelhouses and felt the vessel shudder.

Bonfils had vanished somewhere. Skye headed for the prow, where he hoped to cool off. But a deckman waylaid him.

"The master wishes to speak to you, sir."

Skye clambered up the companionway to the pilothouse and found Marsh.

"Mister Skye," Marsh said without preamble. "We think perhaps you lack experience felling firewood. You dropped a tree with a worthless trunk—much too large for us to use—and disrupted the work of a dozen men. Some judgment is involved in collecting the wood."

Skye nodded.

"From now on, sir, please report to Haines when we fetch wood. He's the one down there at the capstan. He's a veteran riverman, and he will put you to more productive use."

Skye started to salute, and then remembered he was not in the Royal Navy anymore. "As you wish, Captain," he said, and retreated, his thoughts focused on that clever Bonfils and his schemes. Marsh's opinion of Skye would count in St. Louis.

nine

So many were the mysteries of the white man that Victoria thought she could never fathom them all. The greatest of all mysteries was the absence of white women. Before she had boarded the fireboat, she thought maybe she would find white women on it, but that proved to be wrong.

That was puzzling, because Skye had told her that white women were frail and lived in houses. Here was a house on water, with rooms for frail women, but she saw none at all. Only men. Somewhere, there had to be white women, unless these white men sprang from the bosom of the earth, or were borne here by strange beasts who lived in the East. Were there such things as white children? She had never seen those, either. Aiee! What a strange tribe these pale men were!

She was determined to get to the bottom of this, and hoped that in this place of many houses, St. Louis, all might be revealed at last.

The fireboat wasn't a mystery. That first day she had gingerly studied it; had seen how the roaring fire in the metal box had made steam, which was captured in a great iron kettle until it acquired great power, and she saw how this great power drove the paddles and made this fireboat go against the wind, against the current, against nature, wherever the white men made it go. That was no mystery at all.

But Captain Marsh was a mystery. The Big Chief of this fireboat wore a costume of dark blue, plainer than any other costume. He wore a small cap with a little beak on it, but that was dark blue also, and without honors. If he was the Big Chief, why did he wear no honors? Where were the marks that told the world that he was the Big Chief? No feathers or quills or beads or paint. No stripes or chevrons. He did wear a close-cropped brown beard, trimmed almost daily to the contours of his red face, she supposed. But he never painted his face and never carried a lance or shield or staff. He wore nothing around his neck; no bear claws like her man Skye; nor an amulet.

He should be acting like a chief; wearing eagle feathers, painting his face. He should begin each day as father sun climbs over the horizon by seeking his medicine from the sacred medicine-givers, and then exhorting the men under him, pacing back and forth, his oratory inspiring them to make this great steamboat go forth into the world. But he did none of these things.

And instead of inspiring his men to great efforts and feats, he said almost nothing, and with hard eyes, merely watched everyone from his aerie they called the pilothouse. If he was commanding, why didn't he command? And yet, somehow, his will got done and that too was a mystery. How did those sailors know what to do when no one was telling them? Did white men have some secret sign language she didn't know?

She had asked Skye this and he had laughed, and she had gotten angry at him. He explained that the men knew what to do without being told. But that didn't explain the mystery. What made them do it if no one told them to?

She and No Name had padded about, learning everything they could about this strange boat. No one paid her the slightest heed, except Bonfils, who eyed her with frank admiration and invitation, as if he wanted to sample Skye's woman! No, the machinery was no mystery. It was wondrous, but she understood it. She understood the speaking tube by which Marsh directed the engineers to do something. She understood the black metal chimneys that drew the smoke up. She understood the davits that raised or lowered the little yawl. She understood the six-pound brass swivel cannon that was like Skye's rifle but bigger, and made much more noise. It could slay twenty men at once, and she feared it.

Once she understood, she stopped worrying so much. Magpie, her spirit helper, hopped along the riverbanks, or flew over, keeping an eye out. Her fears diminished, and now she began to enjoy the boat, and study the mysterious shores of the river, where unseen eyes studied the boat as it passed.

That evening Captain Marsh stopped at a long wooded island, which afforded fuel and protection from marauders. She knew exactly what to do. No sooner had the gangway been lowered than she took the haltered Skye horses out of their pen on the foredeck, and led them down to the island. They drank thirstily, and she could see the muscles of their necks working the water up their throats and into their bellies. There was plenty of good grass there, and no place for the horses to go, so she would let them graze all night if Captain Marsh permitted it.

These were good Crow ponies, selected with care by Skye and her family. The Crows were the finest horsemen of the northern plains, and these horses could carry Skye's bulky body easily, and heavy packs as well. They weren't the fastest horses in the great Crow herd, but they were chosen for a more valuable trait: endurance. They would continue onward, while fast horses faded. They could run away from trouble, and there were times when she and Skye had been grateful for their strength.

They had hooves of iron, and never grew footsore even on gravel and rock, unlike so many of the horses brought from the land of the white men. And they could make a living on almost anything green, and didn't need all the grain and hay required by white men's ponies. Good horses had saved their lives, and would again, which is why Skye and Victoria treated them well.

In the soft summer twilight, the crew and passengers cut firewood. Here were willows and cottonwoods, and a great heap of driftwood at the upper end of the island, awaiting the axe and saw. They made short work of the task. There would be ample wood to fire up the boilers the next morning.

And they could sleep this night without a guard, because the river protected them. Deep channels isolated the island from the sere and lonely plains beyond. She strolled the island, relishing the feel of soft, warm earth beneath her moccasins, rejoicing that she had survived this day upon the fireboat without mishap. Skye finished his woodcutting and joined her while the cooks prepared a meal.

"Marsh says we can hunt tomorrow, you and I; he'll put us ashore with the horses, hour or two before they launch. Trick is to keep up. That boat's traveling fast, downstream, we have to stay ahead of it. If we shoot a deer or a buffalo, we should try to drag it to the bank. They'll see it and send a yawl for it. He said his hunter, Drouillard, hasn't had luck. He has a crew to feed. Tomorrow he'll put Drouillard on the left bank and we'll take the right."

"Ah, dammit Skye, I like that."

"So will our animals," he said. "No Name will get himself a run; the horses never did like that pen and all that noise."

"We got damn good horses, Skye."

He peered into a lavender twilight, pensively. "When I first came to this country, I didn't know a good horse or a bad one, and didn't care. Now I care more than anything else except for you and that worthless dog. Someday, I'd like to train up a colt my way, make him do what few horses do. Teach him how to make war, and when to run, and how to run. Get your brother and father to help me."

"My brother can teach a horse those things."

"Then we'll give him a gift and have him start a colt for me when we get back."

She loved those moments with Skye. They were bonded so closely that often they knew each other's thoughts without speaking a word.

The next idyllic days, she and Skye hunted the right bank of the river, plunging into giant coulees, topping bluffs, poking into copses of willow or cottonwood, under a cloudless azure dome of heaven. No Name slithered ahead, pretending not to notice or care, but pointing at game, or stopping cold to signal his allies—no one would ever accuse No Name of being part of Skye's family—of the presence of something or other nearby.

But hunting for a river packet proved frustrating. Twice they shot a buck and dragged it to shore, only to see the faint

smoke of the vessel far downstream. Once they shot a prong-
horn only to scare away several elk they hadn't seen.

By nightfall of the first day of hunting they were thoroughly humiliated, and the thought of returning to the vessel
empty handed gnawed on them. Then, No Name stiffened,
and she saw a buffalo cow and calf watering in a slough back
from the mighty river. Skye shot them both, the boom of his
Hawken echoing hollowly in the silent wild. They approached
the dying cow gingerly; buffalo were dangerous. But she was
supine, and leaking blood from a chest wound into the waters
of the slough, lying in a bed of crushed sedges. The calf had
died instantly, and lay on muddy land.

They rode to the riverbank just in time to hail the boat,
which was probing through the waning light as Marsh looked
for a place to anchor and refuel.

The yawl showed up promptly, and a crew of six cook's
helpers and deckmen began butchering the massive buffalo
while Skye and Victoria mounted to the ridge to keep watch.
This was dangerous country, not a place to be caught off
guard. The *Otter* slid as close as the channel allowed, and idled
there at anchor in the purling purple waters, while the cook's
crew butchered, nipping and tugging back the bug-ridden
hide, cutting the huge tongue out, and then sawing the tender
flank meat, and the delicious hump ribs, the most succulent
part of the bison. No Name sat patiently next to the butchering
and was rewarded with offal, which he devoured glutton-
ously to the sound of boatmen's laughter. From the hurricane
deck, the tight-lipped Captain Marsh watched silently, and
Victoria felt ill at ease whenever she glanced at that man.

"Ah, we'll feast tonight!" bellowed a deckhand. "Fat cow!
And it was them Skyes that finally brought in the meat!"

Victoria sat on her restless horse above, a lone mortal on a
mournful sunset ridge, listening to them rejoice below, knowing that one buffalo and one calf wouldn't feed the men on

that boat more than a day. The fireboat slaughtered wood and buffalo. White men lived prodigiously.

"Cap'ain says there's an anchorage mile down," the cook yelled up at them.

Skye nodded.

But the next day, Marsh called off the hunt.

"We'll reach the Minnetaree villages tomorrow," he told them. "They like to trade for corn and vegetables, and they usually have plenty of meat, too."

Victoria seethed with excitement. These people called themselves the Hidatsa, and they were ancient friends of the Absaroka, her people, and spoke a tongue so close they could understand one another. They lived in houses of mounded earth, and raised crops, and hunted buffalo, and were allied with the Mandans, just downstream.

"Is that not the people of Amalie, Bonfils's woman?" she asked, knowing the answer but testing Skye.

"Believe it is," Skye said neutrally.

"I wonder why he didn't bring her here," she said, wanting to gossip.

"We'll know tomorrow," he said. "Alexandre will be among his wife's people. See his wife's family."

Victoria felt a chill creep through her.

ten

s the *Otter* rounded a bend, Alexandre Bonfils beheld the largest of the Hidatsa villages on the right bank of the Missouri. He had been there before; it was Amalie's home. The arrival of the steamboat excited these bronzed agricultural people who

mostly wore white men's cloth, and they flocked to the riverbank. There would be fevered trading and excitement and
dances to celebrate this wondrous event.

The river packet was too distant for him to make out faces;
he would have to wait. Amalie's large and powerful family
and clan would be present, as would the man she had been
married to before Alexandre wandered into the compound of
earth-mound communal houses. That brainless hulking brute,
a village soldier, would not welcome him. The thought evoked
some merriment in him. He had pilfered her from him just for
amusement. She had been a gorgeous young mademoiselle,
sloe-eyed, of sinuous figure, with a bold gaze and a come-
hither smile embedded in her coppery cheeks. He had known
at a glance she was his for the taking.

But that had been the easiest part of it. Fending off the af-
fronted husband, if indeed these savages actually married,
proved to be more entertaining. The Hidatsa cuckold had not
been content to fight alone, but had sent kin and clan after
Alexandre, including Amalie's brothers, one of whom had met
his demise in a small hollow in the prairie, where Alexandre
had ambushed him; the hunted stalking the hunter.

So this visit would be an adventure. He loved adventure
and danger, and never felt fully alive unless he was walking
the edge of some abyss. He provoked danger, sought it out
like a lover, and toyed with it, which is why some of his more
timid confreres in the fur business avoided his brigades, even
though his luck held and always would because the advantage
always fell to the audacious.

Little did Marsh know that there was bad blood between
one of his passengers and these Minnetaree people, bad
enough blood to evoke a pitched fight if it came to that, which
Bonfils hoped would be plain to Marsh. He had plans and
ambitions.

Alexandre was the last of seven children, of whom four
still lived. His mother had cried, Enough! and taken refuge in

a separate bedroom. From then on his father had seemed distant to the child, and was more and more absent from the white porticoed redbrick family manse on Rue Papin, for reasons unfathomable to one so young. His mama, Alexia, had indulged him wantonly, a fact he appreciated only because of the whining and pouting of his older siblings, who had not seen their every whim gratified the way this youngest and last child was cosseted.

So he had grown up unchallenged and thus bored, and swiftly discovered that life in St. Louis, where he was a dauphin of the merchant class, awakened his senses only when he was doing something absolutely scandalous, such as seducing Creole virgins or in one case a plain and swooning convent novitiate, or drinking absinthe in waterfront dens while fondling the lush hard breasts of serving girls, or copulating with languorous and gorgeous black slave women in the carriage houses of his Creole friends.

Now, as the boat slowed and the steersman eased it toward the right bank, he anticipated new amusements, and perhaps a chance to make impressions. He headed for the rail and stood prominently there, a dark, bright, insouciant figure who would galvanize attention on the shore, as soon as one or another of Amalie's clan discovered him.

This early July day had scorched every scrap of moisture out of the close air; the heat bore down like rolling thunder over the dun earth-mound houses and the tawny fields of maize and squash and melons and tobacco. It raised mirages and made images waver drunkenly. The crowd of virtually naked brown males and bare-breasted brown-fleshed women rippled with excitement as the *Otter* hove to, and seamen cast anchor well out. Marsh had said he always traded well away from shore, for safety's sake. There was little forty crewmen and a few passengers could do against four or five hundred visitors, if a showdown ever came. The dugout canoes of the village would ration visitors and impose some sort of control.

A shrill blast of the whistle paralyzed the Indians for a moment, and then they danced and jostled their way to the riverbank, a hideous gallimaufry of savages, many of them carrying woven baskets laden with maize and other grains and fruits. On board, the mate and a few sailors doubling as clerks were organizing a trading store, with blankets, bright bolts of cloth, packets of vermillion, sugar, knives, awls, axes and hatchets, beads strung in loops, and assorted smoothbore muskets and flintlock rifles for hunters, all of it jamming the foredeck near Skye's horses.

A dozen dugouts, each hollowed from a giant cottonwood log, launched simultaneously, chocked with Hidatsi people, the men with pomaded hair rising high above their faces, the women with straight jet hair hanging loosely over golden shoulders.

Bonfils discovered Victoria Skye staring at him, her face guarded. But what did she know? If he couldn't have a Hidatsa girl tonight, after lubricating matters with a little good whiskey from his silver flask, he might try her.

Even as the first wave of dugouts sped across the choppy blue waters of the river, other craft were being prepared, as these river-dwelling people brought baskets of maize, or haunches of buffalo swarming with flies, or dead fowl hanging on a pole by their legs, to the floating store on the foredeck.

Marsh nodded to several sailors who were standing at the gangway, ready to board a few dozen Hidatsi at a time. The traders—experienced men, Bonfils thought—had swiftly set up their shop, even including some bushels and a scales.

"About twenty at a time," Marsh yelled through a megaphone from the pilothouse.

They swarmed in, the dugouts nosing into the low coaming of the riverboat, and clambered aboard, some on the gangway, but most simply over the rail or under it.

Bonfils knew the tongue.

"Ah, we shall buy a knife! Oh, look at that blanket. I will

sleep warm in the winter! Ah, what will they give me for a basket of corn?" The women were gabby; the men taciturn, lithely patrolling the deck of the boat, their quick knowing gazes settling on the heaped firewood, the horses, the master watching these proceedings with caution, the Skyes, who stood aside, with that mutt at their feet; and then at Bonfils, who had gauded himself up for the occasion in fringed buckskins, a bone necklace, a bright red calico shirt, quilled moccasins, and a flat-crowned black hat decorated with a band of rattlesnake skin.

He recognized none of them. These Hidatsi were friendly people, not armed with anything other than a sheathed knife; carrying bows and quivers of arrows would have been considered a hostile act.

It was, actually, an old crone who recognized him. She wore a simple frock of patterned purple calico, which hung from a bony body topped by a seamed brown face and a mouth lacking most teeth. But she walked directly at him, stopped, frowned, and he knew the woman was one of Amalie's many grandmothers, venerated for her medicine and wisdom.

"Ah!" the woman said. "And where is she?"

"She is not here, grandmother."

"You have put her out of your lodge?"

He wasn't really sure. He'd grown tired of Amalie and had lent her to a friend. But the old crone's challenge, which was not at all friendly, decided him.

"I gave her away to a great white chief. She is honored to be the woman of a mighty trapper, grandmother."

"She lives?"

He smiled and shrugged.

She pursed her lips, spat, and turned away. Bonfils was aware that Victoria Skye had listened and probably understood the Hidatsa tongue, so close to her own.

He smiled at her, and wandered toward the trading, which now proceeded furiously a few yards away.

The old woman had not been silent. Now as he approached, others turned and stared at him. He smiled and doffed his splendid chapeau, so they might see him in sunlight and confirm that yes, it was the legendary Bonfils, who had arrived in their village, wooed many a maid, and made off with the wife of Barking Wolf, a clan leader with much medicine and a bad temper, and then dispatched her brother when he came after her with a war party. *Sacre Bleu!*

Allors, it was time to greet them. "See, it is Bonfils," he said in Hidatsa, jabbing a thumb into his chest. "The very same. I am going to the village of many houses now, on the fireboat, to be given a higher position. I will become a trader, you see. Maybe I will trade with you. Ah, I see you now, Barking Wolf! How swiftly your clan brothers have whispered of my presence here! See me now. I am going to return, and all your people will trade with me."

That wasn't quite exact. These people traded at Fort Clark, and sometimes Fort Pierre, and rarely got to the Yellowstone Country, where Fort Cass stood. But he wished to impress them. He wished to laugh merrily.

Barking Wolf was a soldier not much older than Bonfils, stocky and short and smouldering. He had always smouldered. He had smouldered in the company of Amalie, smouldered with his clan-brothers, smouldered while hoeing corn in the fields, smouldered toward his rivals in the buffalo hunts that kept the Minnetaree villages in meat.

"Monsieur Bonfils, what is all this?" asked Marsh from above.

"It is my mountain wife's family and her former mate, *monsieur le capitaine*. They are discovering that I am present, without my Amalie, and they are looking forward to whatever trouble they can cause me."

Marsh didn't like it. "Bonfils, we are trading for food, and you must retreat to your cabin at once. I will not have trouble, and trouble is what I see here."

Indeed, the Minnetaree people had stopped their frantic trading and jostling, and were observing the exchange.

Victoria Skye whispered something to her man, and the pair of them retreated aft. Bonfils watched them sidle away. Skye had always been too prudent for his own success, he thought.

A subchief Bonfils knew, old Standing in Water, snapped an order, and the trading ceased altogether. The clamorous crowd slipped away from the traders, until a no-man's land stretched between the crew and the Hidatsi.

Harshly, the hawknosed elder orated, gesticulating toward Marsh, who stood above, staring at this confrontation on his boiler deck.

"What is he saying, Bonfils?"

"He's saying that they will not let this packet leave if I am on it."

"Why do they want you?"

"I haven't the faintest idea," Bonfils said, amusement playing with the corners of his mouth.

"What is the trouble?"

"Offer them a big damn gift," Victoria Skye said.

"Don't give them a feather," Bonfils said easily, loving the confrontation.

And there it stood.

eleven

Skye smelled trouble, and began easing aft with Victoria. None of the sailors were armed; most of the Hidatsa wore sheathed knives. Marsh must have scented trouble too because he gestured sailors to the capstan to pull anchor if need be. Others gathered casually around the six-pounder at the prow, where an enameled chest contained powder and grape.

But there was Bonfils, a charismatic, mesmerizing figure talking volubly to the Indians, a vast smile wreathing his face, his body arched and confident and somehow larger to the eye than it really was. Skye had never seen anything quite like it: this young Creole was gradually defusing the moment, pawing about like some giant cat, the sheer force of his voice and will subduing every spirit within earshot.

The man radiated something Skye couldn't fathom, some mysterious and commanding force that derived from his sonorous, compelling voice, the easy tenor of his tongue, a smile, warm dark eyes that feasted carnivorously upon whoever was in his sight; a line of clean and regular white teeth, not to mention that costume, the elaborately fringed buckskins, the quilled moccasins, the red shirt, the bone necklace, the splendid beaver hat with its rattlesnake band, and not least, the bronze medal on blue watershot silk decorating his chest. No Indian ever paraded in ceremonial clothing more effectively than Bonfils.

"What's he saying?" Skye asked Victoria.

"I don't get it all. But he's telling them that in himself lies their future. Treat him as chief and they will be chiefs; treat him badly and there will be no more blankets, shot and powder, awls, knives, axes and hatchets, for the window of the trading company will be forever closed, and the people will be ruined."

Whatever it was Bonfils was saying in easy oratory, the tension seeped from the charged moment, and those brown hands that clutched the hafts of knives relaxed.

Marsh, above, obviously knew enough to say nothing, and simply waited for events to play out, his relentless glare on Bonfils. The sailors ready to pull anchor—the farther from the village, the safer the *Otter*—no longer stood at the ready.

Then, at last, with a sweep of his red-shirted arm, Bonfils invited the Hidatsa to trade once again.

Skye watched the angry ones closely. Were these warriors somehow related to Amalie? But even those most likely to spill blood seemed to retreat into themselves. Soon the trading was going again; the sailors and clerks accepting baskets of maize, pelts, squash, buffalo robes, and tanned hides, while the shoppers were examining awls, feeling the edges of hatchets, fingering flannels, and studying the three-point blankets heaped on the boiler deck.

"Sonofabitch," Victoria said. "He did it."

"Did what?"

"He has big medicine, Skye. Those warriors, they were going to kill him. That one there—the one called Barking Wolf, he was Amalie's husband once. And that one there; he is a brother of Amalie, and made medicine to kill Bonfils."

"But they didn't."

"Big goddam medicine."

Even now, Bonfils, slim and confident and springy on the balls of his feet, greeted the Hidatsa like some potentate. The crowd swelled as more dugout-loads of Hidatsa arrived, clambered on board and deposited their pelts and baskets of grain and vegetables before the traders.

Marsh, red-nosed and irritable, appeared on the boiler deck, and corraled Bonfils. "Monsieur Bonfils, what was all this about?" he asked in a dulcet and icy voice.

"A private matter, *mon capitaine*. Some wretches in this friendly village have taken umbrage, and I reminded them forcefully that the entire village would suffer if they acted rashly."

Bonfils smiled, and Skye felt the presence of galvanic energy, almost lightning, shooting and sparking out from him.

Marsh was not placated. "And what was this private matter?"

Bonfils laughed softly. "A woman, of course. What else?"

"Is that all? Is there more? Are you telling me everything?"
Bonfils laughed easily. "All that matters."

Marsh struggled not to say something or other, and finally
subsided. "This is a profitable stop," he said grudgingly, swallowing back whatever was on his mind.

Bonfils smiled that galvanic beam again.

Marsh turned to Skye. "He rescued us; a cool man, wouldn't
you say? I saw you heading aft, out of harm's way."

It hung there, this gentle insinuation of cowardice.

Skye might have argued that he and Victoria were preparing for war by fetching some weapons. Not for nothing had he
been in the Royal Navy. But he saw the captain's mind snap
shut, and let it go. This was the second time he had incurred
Marsh's disfavor. And maybe it would not be the last, given
the length of the trip and the difficulties a steam vessel on the
upper Missouri would surely encounter.

"Yes, sir. Mr. Bonfils has turned the tide in his favor," he
said.

"A remarkable young man," Marsh said, satisfied with
Skye's response.

"Goddamn reckless sonofabitch, get us all killed," Victoria said.

Marsh, taken aback, stared at her, and then smiled wolfishly.
"They will enjoy you in St. Louis," he said to her. It was not a
compliment.

The trading continued for another hour, and by its end
Marsh was well provisioned with meat and grain and had
added scores of pelts and robes to his cargo. Skye and Victoria
watched closely, alert for trouble that never seemed very far
away. The unhappy young men with Barking Wolf hung together in sullen knots, refusing to leave the boat, and glancing
boldly at the unarmed clerks and sailors.

"They haven't quit," Skye said to her. "This isn't over."

Bonfils, either recklessly or with incredible courage, meandered toward the sullen clique and began addressing them in

the Hidatsa tongue, his confidence glossing them all like sunlight. Most tribesmen loved a show of confidence and courage, and Bonfils was oddly welcomed even among those schemers seeking his doom.

The traders were totting up ledgers, stowing unsold goods, hauling pelts and skins to the hold, or carting maize and meat to the kitchen. Most of the Hidatsa had left, and the remaining ones were stepping gingerly into their dugouts.

Firemen began stuffing big willow and cottonwood logs into the firebox, and a cloud of acrid smoke blew downward over them all. Steam began popping from the escapement.

"Mr. Bonfils, would you invite your guests to depart?" Marsh said through his megaphone from above.

The young man nodded, and gestured toward the remaining dugout snugged to the side of the packet. But this last group of six men didn't budge. They ranged in age, the eldest showing gray in his loose-hanging hair. That one bore the marks of war: a puckered wound along a forearm; a rough-healed gash across the left side of his face. His gaze focused unblinkingly on Bonfils. The young man who had once possessed Amalie as wife was declaiming.

Skye didn't like it.

Around him, the crew prepared to sail. Men gathered at the stem to raise a kedge that had steadied the vessel offshore.

Victoria jabbed Skye in the ribs. Startled, he followed the point of her finger. These six Minnetarees had spread slightly, two of them quartering around Bonfils. They all looked poised for action of some sort.

Slowly, the elder one slid a long and rusty skinning knife from a sheath.

Skye and Victoria edged toward the group, with No Name advancing ahead of them. Skye saw that Victoria had her own little knife in hand.

They surprised the warriors, who turned, too late, to discover the company.

Skye never paused. His massive hand clamped over the wrist of the man holding the knife; Victoria pressed her blade hard on the neck of the one on the other side. And No Name, his hair pricking upward snarled, baring a pair of canines that could only win respect

The moment passed. No one in the work crew readying the packet to sail had seen any of it. The older man twisted around, his eyes brimming with rage, and Skye strengthened his grip with one hand, and prepared to knock the man flat with the other.

At last Bonfils grasped that he was in mortal peril, and backed out of the circle of fire.

"Tell them to get in their canoe," Skye said, in a voice that didn't carry.

Bonfils did.

The Minnatarees left reluctantly, in stiff, proud spasms that told the world this was not over; Alexandre Bonfils was a marked man in that clan, and maybe in that tribe. These people might have been farmers and hunters, living sedentary lives beside the great river; but they had not neglected the arts of war.

Skye released the wrist of the older warrior, probably a clan chieftain, ready to block a thrust with the knife. But it didn't come. No Name crouched, ready to go for the man's throat. The warrior, seething now with something so foul and raw it landed palpably on them all, backed off to the coaming and stepped over, and into the dugout.

The mate barked a command. The crew at the capstan twisted up rope until the boat drifted in the current. A shout from the pilothouse down the speaking tube energized the engineers, who engaged the pittman rod to the flywheel, and the giant paddles sliced water.

No one else on board, least of all the powerful master or his mate, had registered the last taut drama at the riverside village.

The vessel soon rounded a bight and left the Minnetaree village in memory.

Bonfils smiled brightly, but that charismatic quality that made him look larger than life had vanished. The smile was veneer; he was a shaken and angry young man.

"Well, you certainly made me look bad," he said.

"What we made you look, Mr. Bonfils, is alive," Skye said.

twelve

ame Deer hoped she would not be too late. For days she had hastened along the Cheyenne River, ever eastward toward the house of the rising sun, the happiest of the four winds. No war parties had molested her and she had seen no fresh pony tracks. The buffalo were elsewhere, and so were the hunters. If she had come across Lakota, she would have been welcomed and protected, for those were ancient friends of her people. If Pawnee or Arapaho, she might have suffered a cruel fate, including captivity.

She rode a gaunt red roman-nosed pony, swaying steadily step by step, her velveteen purple skirts hiked high to seat herself in the high-cantled squaw saddle that was one of her proudest possessions. In her bony lap sat her daughter of two winters, Singing Rain, and behind her rode her boy of four winters, Sound Comes Back After Shouting, on a sore-backed gray packhorse burdened with precious robes and pelts and a parfleche with a little pemmican and jerky in it.

Her man, Simon, had given Singing Rain another name, Molly, and had called Sound Comes Back, Billy. She was going to the place of many lodges to find her man, whom she had not seen for an autumn and winter and spring and now summer; four seasons too long. Simon MacLees was his name; he was a trader. He had a partner in the place of many lodges he called St. Louis, a man named Jonas. He had called himself the Opposition, and she gathered that meant he was a rival of the American Fur Company, like a fox pup among wolves.

He had built a sturdy log trading post on the Belle Fourche River, within sight of the sacred mountain of the Cheyenne People, Bear Butte, and there had done a good trade with the Cheyenne, the Sans Arcs, the Blackfoot Sioux, the Hunkpapa, and sometimes other peoples as well, but that business was fading because so many of her people had moved south to trade at a great fort called Bent's.

For five winters she had been his woman, sharing his life in the post built of big cottonwood logs and chinked with mud against the winter winds. She had always been happy there; never far from her people. But she knew he had fits of loneliness and was sometimes restless, especially when the snows trapped them in their wooden lodge and there was no one else to talk to, and he paced the flagstone floors.

Four springtimes in a row, his partner Jonas had shown up in the moon of the flying geese, sometimes with other white men, bringing new tradegoods—bright-colored blankets, awls, knives, hatchets, rifles, lead and powder, and bolts of red and green and blue flannel. Then Jonas would load the packs of robes and the pelts on the big gray mules he always used, and vanish to the east.

Then last spring, Jonas didn't come and there was little to trade. And then in the autumn, her man Simon left for the place of many lodges, St. Louis, with many promises that he would return. But he hadn't returned. She lived alone, with her little children, waiting for his boots to print the dust.

Her kin among the People told her to forget him. White men were like that. But she could not. She had sold the last few goods in the store and then waited as the summer faded into yellow leaves, frosts and bare limbs, and the winter howled, and then the sun burned away the snow and green grass burst through the drifts. Surely he would come with the warm tide of the sun, but he had not, and she knew that some bad thing had happened, and he was detained.

She had subsisted as long as she could at the post, sometimes given a haunch of venison or elk by the Sioux, because her people rarely stopped by. The Cheyenne had moved south. But he didn't come. She roamed the hills for wild onions and greens and edible things—but never fish, the unclean water creature. And still he had not come.

"Ah, return to us, and some good Cheyenne will take you," her friends said. But she had always shaken her head. She wore the rope, as she had as a maiden, so that she might remain inviolate; no Cheyenne man would touch her for as long as she wore it. She belonged to Simon, for all time, until they were gone from the earth and had become stars in the heavens. And she found in her children the proofs of his presence within her heart, and she bided her time.

Simon had made her proud. She had been the wife of a trader, a man who brought precious and magical things to her people in exchange for something as ordinary as a pelt. By what mysterious power could white men conjure metal pots and knives and awls and hatchets? How did they make blankets? Where did Simon and his partner get these marvels?

But that was only the smallest part of it. Cheyenne men ruled their women, and sent them away if a woman was not obedient, for it was a grave offense to defy him or the elders, and a woman faced unspeakable evils if she did. Simon was different. He was *Hoah*, a friend. What Cheyenne husband consulted his wife as Simon did? A woman kept the lodge and raised the children and answered his every beck and call. But Simon MacLees had been a companion and she liked that.

She did not know of any other woman of the People who had a male friend; they had husbands and sons and fathers, but that was different. Their entire life consisted of visiting with their sisters and mothers and other women. So she considered Simon MacLees a treasure beyond price because he was a friend as well as husband.

He was strange; all white men were strange. He had no medicine and worshiped nothing visible. He never sought the help of the *Ma i yun'*, the Powers who governed the fate of mere mortals. He never talked about where he had come from, or what his people were like back in the place of many houses. It was as if he had been born from a whirlwind, without a family. And now he had gone away as mysteriously as he had arrived one day at the village of Red Robe and opened his packs to show the People what he would offer them for beaver pelts, ermine and fox and deer and elk and buffalo robes.

She had been standing right there, in a whitened doeskin dress with fringed sleeves, and high beaded moccasins. She had many suitors but was not yet taken and her parents had bided their time, wanting the best young warrior for their daughter. Like all Cheyenne girls, she had been a virgin, wore the sacred rope about her loins, and was carefully chaperoned. Nothing was worse for a Cheyenne girl than to be used by several men.

Ah, what a moment that was, when his gray-eyed gaze settled on her, paused to see into her, and swept over her young figure, and then back to her face, where his warm gaze seemed to pierce right to her heart.

Ah, Simon! She would track him to the ends of the earth. She would bring his children to him, and help him escape from the troubles he was in. It didn't matter what the People thought: she would go to the place of many lodges. Even her spirit helper the raven *Okoka* told her not to, and old Four Braids, the elder with great wisdom and an eye upon the mysterious future, the keeper of a medicine bundle, had warned her sharply.

And yet she had come because she had to come, and she would find Simon MacLees and joyously show him how the children had grown, and how much they had learned, and how beautiful they were, partly pale and partly brown like herself, golden children like sunrises in the Moon of First Frost.

She knew all the news, for such things were cried to the entire village of Red Robe. She knew that the fireboat had come to the trading post where the Big River and the Elk River—the white men called them by different names—came together, and soon would go down to the place of many lodges.

She had inquired how she might ride on that boat, though her father had told her not to set foot on it because it offended the evil spirits under the water. But she did learn that she might find the boat and board it if she hurried. She resolved to go at once. Nothing remained within the cottonwood logs of the post. She had nothing to sell, and Simon brought her nothing to eat.

She packed the skins and robes she possessed on one of her two scrawny horses, one sore-backed with a cracked hoof, the other a sullen mare that would not move unless she lashed it. That was all she had, but that would do. She would go to the Big River and wait for the fireboat. She had no idea how she might obtain a ride; but she knew that white men traded almost anything for furs, and of furs she had a few.

She did not think about the chance that the boat might have passed by. If that was true, and it didn't come after many sleeps, she would walk down the big river to this place where white men lived. Simon had said the river would take him there; it would take her there too.

It would be a hard walk. She would walk past the Arikaras, sometimes enemies of her people, but this was the land of the Miniconjou and Yanktonai, and there she would be safe. What power would a woman with two small children have against an enemy? And yet, most would respect her, for a woman of the People, traveling alone, was a wonder, and would be honored except maybe by the Pawnee.

For Simon she would risk all that. She and Simon had talked of many things. He had told her about schools and buildings made of red blocks of fired earth; of wagons, and theaters and books. He had shown her some books, and the mysterious little signs within them had intrigued her. Now she would see where these came from!

It was because Simon was a friend, and few other women of the People had a male friend, that she would go to Simon now. She was very proud to have a man friend; not just a husband who gave orders and expected much labor and then went off to smoke with other men, or pray to the powers together, or perform secret dances, or drum for victory, or ride away to hunt and fight.

Once she had yearned for just such a proud husband; a slim, brown, sharp-eyed man with long braids, a man who would win great honors in war, count many coups, save his people, bring them plenty of meat, ride first in the parades, wear many eagle feathers in his hair, find favor with the elders and the shamans. Oh, how she had yearned for such a man, so she might be proud and looked upon as the most fortunate of the Cheyenne women.

But then she discovered friendship. Simon made her laugh. He rarely forbade her anything. He showered gifts upon her; a new awl, a skein of beads, a blue blanket with black stripes and four bars on it, indicating the heaviest weight.

Ah! What woman among all the bands of the People had such a friend?

Now she hastened her reluctant four-foots eastward, toward the Wind of the Rising Sun. Sound Comes Back was always hungry, and she could not feed him enough. Singing Rain was docile, and sat quietly behind her mother, accepting whatever life visited upon her. Lame Deer made do with cattail roots, which she mashed to pulp and boiled into a white paste that filled the belly and sufficed for food.

The Cheyenne River flowed lazily eastward through lonely steppes and grassy bluffs. At least there were willows and cottonwoods in the bottoms, and plenty of places for a small woman to hide from distant eyes, though no one tracking close or hunting her would fail to find her.

The weather that moon of the ripe strawberries grew hot, slowing the horses, but she would not let them pause except for a while to graze, or lick water, or scratch themselves by rubbing against a willow to rid themselves of fleas and flies.

The Cheyenne widened into a formidable river as its tributaries added their flow, and then she descended long coulees choked with brush, and passed through a dense forest, and beheld the Big River, a vast expanse of shimmering blue water.

There was no sign of anything or anyone, except some hard-used trails along its vast valley. She feared the fireboat had passed. She feared it might came and not see her. Or maybe the white chiefs who steered it would not accept her gifts; several robes for three passengers; some smaller pelts for the ponies.

And so she made a small camp that sunny and quiet afternoon, and waited.

thirteen

Victoria saw the woman first as the packet rounded a bight, and motioned to Skye. His eyes weren't as keen as hers, and he almost missed her. But the woman was making herself known to the crew by waving a red banner on a stick, the sweeping flourishes of crimson brightening the right bank across the dull water of late afternoon.

"She's got horses and some children," Victoria said, and once again Skye squinted into the shadowed spit of land where she stood, until he could make out the small buckskin-clad figure of a boy, and a smaller child grasping the woman's leg.

"She wants something," Victoria said.

"Trade, probably."

"One woman? Trade? Dammit, Skye."

Skye nodded. The distant woman's signaling was urgent, even violent, her flag on a stick describing great arcs, her whole body twisting with the intent of being seen.

Skye touched Victoria's hand, and headed up the companionway to the hurricane deck and the pilothouse.

"We see her," said Marsh. "Can't stop for a lone trader."

"That doesn't look like a woman trying to trade, mate."

"Squaw alone like that. A white man would be different. We can make another six, eight miles before dark. Boilers eat wood, Mister Skye."

"Six miles? Suppose you let Victoria and me off, with our horses. We'll see what she wants, and then hunt along the way to your night anchorage."

Marsh said nothing. The riverboat was passing the woman, who waved her banner ceaselessly, almost furiously. Skye knew the woman was calling, maybe screaming; he could see it in her face, though the rumble of the paddle wheels and the rattle of steam from the escapement kept him from hearing anything resembling a woman's voice.

The pilot and helmsman were following the channel, veering toward the right bank. Below the left bank was a vast shallows dotted with snags and gravel bars, and the helmsman was cautiously edging the vessel closer to the steep bluffs of the right bank.

They passed the woman, who leapt and jumped and cried out, and Skye suddenly felt bad.

"All right," Marsh said. He pointed to a place where the

channel cut close to a sharp grassy bluff. "Get your horses; we'll be six miles down. There's a creek there with a good patch of timber. Bring us meat."

Skye heard the clanging of a bell as he raced down the companionway to the boiler deck. He motioned to Victoria, who had been standing at the rail, her small foot on the coaming, looking unhappy.

"We'll see," he said. "Talk to her, make meat, meet the ship downstream."

That's all it took for her to race to the pen, throw her small pad saddle on her nag, and fetch her bow and quiver. No Name circled restlessly, ready to go wherever his partners went. Skye saddled his ugly, roman-nosed grulla horse and led it to the gangway amidships.

A few minutes later, the ship drifted into the right bank, bumped bottom, and pulled away. The gangway didn't reach, but it wouldn't matter. The crew dropped the far end into the river and Skye and Victoria rode down the incline and urged their ponies toward the steep bank, which the horses took with violent leaps that almost unseated them both.

Marsh wasted not a moment. The boat was already adrift, the gangway drawn up, and the helmsman steering it back into the channel. With a shudder the paddle wheels engaged, splashing water, and the boat raced downstream again.

In an amazingly short time, the world was veiled in silence. Smoke hung in the quiet air. The bluff cast a long lavender shadow over the water. The sinking sun colored the world orange and gold and dun. A streak of green filled the eastern sky.

The woman came running. She was leading a saddled ewe-necked pony and a gaunt packhorse, dragging a child, and carrying a smaller one in the crook of her arm.

"Cheyenne," Victoria said sourly. Enemies of her Absaroka people.

Skye always marveled that Victoria could read the tribe in

a glance. He couldn't, and never got the knack of it. They waited for the Cheyenne woman, and when she did finally stop before them, she was out of breath, and Skye sensed a wildness and despair and defeat in her.

"Fireboat. I want to go," she cried.

This Cheyenne knew a little English.

"Well, maybe so," Skye said. "Who are you?"

"The woman of Simon MacLees," she said, half gasping it out between gulps of air.

Skye knew the name. Opposition. A trading partnership. He sat uneasily on his restless, dripping horse. "You want to trade, is that it?"

"No, go on fireboat. To . . ." she paused, searching for words. "Place of many lodges."

That surprised Skye.

He would get the story en route. "Tell us. Maybe you can go. Fireboat's going to stop a way down for the night. Wooded flat with a creek on it."

The woman gulped air and nodded. She handed the smallest child, a girl, to Victoria, and pointed to herself. "I am named Lame Deer," she said. "That is the People's name, as I am born. Simon MacLees gives me other name. This is Singing Rain, called Molly by him, and Sound Comes Back After Shouting, my boy, he calls Billy."

Skye beheld a solemn child clinging tightly to his mother's hand, half afraid, half truculent.

"I am Mister Skye; this is my wife Victoria, Many Quill Woman, of the Absaroka.

"Aiee, those are names I know," the Cheyenne said, suddenly wary.

She lifted her generous velveteen skirts and clambered aboard the gaunt horse. The boy clambered behind her, sitting on the rump behind the high cantle of the squaw saddle.

"We go to the fireboat?" the woman asked.

Skye nodded. They followed a dusky and difficult riverbank trail, circling marshy flats full of sedges, until Skye found a way up to the tableland above where the going would be easier and straighter. They pierced from indigo shadow into golden light from a horizontal sun that raked the land and painted every bush and tree.

"My heart is big with the dream of my man," the woman said in a voice that sang of music. "He walks across the mountains; he fills the valleys. He comes into our lodge and brings meat and comfort. He has stars in his eyes, and he lights the night like a big moon. He smiles and all my fears fall away like the leaves of autumn. He floats high in the sky like an eagle, walking over clouds, seeing what is to come from afar, and it is so. He says one soft word, and it is stronger than a hundred men shouting. When he sings, the wolves sing too. When he laughs, the coyotes laugh too. He gathers the blossoms, and gives them to me, and my heart grows big. Now I am called to him, and I go."

Skye marveled. She had few English words, and yet she used them so sweetly, and with such lyrical power that he believed she was a born poet.

In the space of a half hour, Skye got her story. She was going to find MacLees, who hadn't returned after a trip east. She had a few robes and pelts to trade for passage.

Skye suspected that if MacLees lived, and indeed, if he had reached St. Louis safely, he would not want to see his squaw. Traders and trappers had routinely formed temporary liaisons with Indian women, often serially, even bigamously. These were called mountain marriages, and many was a trapper or trader who simply abandoned his dusky bride and his breed children when the urge came over him to head back to the States. Many a mountaineer had married a white girl and never spoken a word about the half-breed family he left behind in the impenetrable reaches of the West.

He had heard nothing of MacLees's death, though the names of all trappers and traders who were killed, or died of disease, or had vanished, were bruited through every camp in the mountains. He suspected the man lived. He suspected the partnership had gone broke, trying to buck the powerful attractions of Bent's Fort, which had drawn the Cheyenne southward and had captured most of the trade with that tribe. He suspected that MacLees and . . . yes, Jonas, that was his partner's name, had quit the mountains. And now this beautiful and poetic Cheyenne woman, probably in her early twenties, was determined to find him.

But of all this he said nothing. He gauged Victoria's sharp glances, and concluded that her thoughts largely paralleled his own. This ragged family looked hungry. Skye found some jerky in his kit and handed a fistful to the woman, who took it gratefully and gave each child a piece. Jerky was an unsatisfying food that left one hungrier than before. It took a while to soften in the mouth, to become edible, and then it vanished down the throat with one small gulp. But it could keep a body alive.

They rode steadily into a descending twilight. The sun set, momentarily illumining the bowl of heaven with salmon and pink, and then they pierced through the long summer's twilight, the heavens from north to west a bold blue band. There was light enough to travel; light enough to spot the vessel. Ahead a mile or so he discerned a dip in the hills and a dark patch at its base, next to the river. He could not see the packet, but it would be there.

He felt cool night breezes eddy over him, the colder air rolling down the long slopes to the river bottoms. He heard terns and sandpipers, and watched crows gossip. He spotted the streak of a black and white magpie, and wondered whether Victoria had seen her spirit helper.

Victoria had; her gaze followed the bird, and her face radiated serenity. The Cheyenne woman might be an enemy of the People, but sisterhood formed a stronger impulse.

He saw two does drinking at river's edge, far below, too

far to shoot at; he didn't feel like hunting anyway, and rode past them. If he had veered in their direction, they would have vanished into the wrinkled slopes.

They descended into the creek bottom at dusk, and could hear the whack and thump of axes before they saw the riverboat or the woodcutting crew. Skye led the uneasy Cheyenne woman to the vessel, which rocked gently bank-side, tied stem and stern to trees. They waited while the crew manhandled cordwood up the gangway. The Cheyenne children looked terrified, but their mother solaced them with soft words. She looked ill at ease herself, her black eyes focused on the white superstructure, the busy white men, the smoke eddying from the chimneys from the dying fires under the boiler.

Skye led her and the children on board, while Victoria held the horses, and then up the companionway to the pilothouse.

Marsh stared sharply at the young woman and her brood.

"She's Lame Deer—Cheyenne—and wanting a ride to St. Louis," Skye said. "She'd like to take the two ponies, too. She's looking for her husband. I guess he's there all right."

"I can't take her."

Skye studied the master, finding him in a testy mood, wanting to finish the day's work.

"She brought twelve fine-tanned robes, some beaver plews, and some ermine. Says she'll trade it all for the ride."

"I don't want a squaw and some breed brats."

Skye felt the rumble of anger building in him. "Maybe I'll ride horse down to St. Louis with her. You can tell Chouteau why."

Marsh backed off. "Deck passage."

"No, women's quarters. She needs shelter for the children."

"They're not used to it. Never saw a chamber pot."

"She's a trader's wife."

Marsh sighed. "I'll regret it," he said, but he nodded.

fourteen

Benton Marsh was an irascible man, and now he was even more so. He didn't like vermin-ridden Indians on his packet, a view he kept private because the American Fur Company depended entirely on trade with the savages.

He peered out upon the world from behind a brown beard which he kept neatly trimmed to within an inch of his sallow face. Some might have called him handsome. His composure was so total that few guessed that behind his quiet calm raged a man of harsh and savage judgments, which he kept entirely private, veneered with a faint smile on occasion.

His ability to ferret out the frailties of every mortal had earned him the respect of Pierre Chouteau and the other chiefs of the American Fur Company, who treated him as a sort of privy counselor and consulted him about personnel. He found more pride in that role than in his mastery of the river.

If the trip upstream was perilous, the trip downstream was even more so. The paddle-wheel boat was carried along by the seven- or eight-mile-per-hour current at uncomfortable speeds, at the very time when the water levels were dropping daily as the spring runoff vanished. It was on the downstream trip, when the boats were burdened with a year's prize of peltries, that they most often succumbed to assorted disasters.

He stood in the pilothouse, along with his pilot and helmsman, studying the treacherous river, reading the currents, examining the heavens for rain and wind and storm, all dangerous to navigation. Not to mention Indians, who could amass along the bank at any point where the channel took the boat close to shore.

Simon MacLees's squaw!

Marsh was appalled. Of all the wild strokes of bad fortune! But maybe not so bad: knowledge is power, he thought. He could deal with it; with her.

If he had known who Lame Deer was, he would have flatly rejected passage. But Skye had brought her aboard and settled her before the whole story emerged. Now there was trouble, and Marsh fumed. This was a personal matter, affecting his family, as well as a business matter.

The red slut was going to St. Louis, and she would get there one way or another unless he found a way to prevent it. He wished he had never set eyes on her. She was Simon MacLees's mountain woman, and that spelled trouble right in the bosom of his family. His stepdaughter, Sarah Lansing, was soon to be married to MacLees; in fact, within days of the time he expected to return to St. Louis.

Marsh had known MacLees and his partner, Jonas, for years. St. Louis might be a bustling and brawling city of thousands, but the fur business was a small, closed circle. MacLees and Jonas had been an opposition firm until Pierre Chouteau, with his usual ruthlessness, had crushed them every way possible—by undercutting, by causing them license problems with the Indian superintendent General Clark, by filing complaints about the use of alcohol, by establishing a rival post nearby, where American Fur Company traders bought pelts for more, and sold goods for less, even at a temporary loss, until MacLees had virtually run out of options. The drift of the Cheyennes down to the southern plains and Bent's Fort had been the final blow.

And here came his filthy squaw! When he got to St. Louis he would have the squaw's cabin fumigated and scrubbed down. For that matter, he would have the Skyes' quarters fumigated. Victoria was another squaw he couldn't do anything about until he got his boat back. This was Chouteau's bidding; if Marsh had any say about it, the dirt-crusted redskins would be allowed only on the boiler deck for trading, and that as little as possible. And never, not ever, in the cabins.

Marsh grunted. There were going to be some explosions in St. Louis. He was privy to some things no one else on the boat knew. The American Fur Company was about to offer MacLees a position, which is what it often did with defeated rivals. Unknown to Skye and to Bonfils, MacLees, a veteran trader, was Pierre Chouteau's first choice for the Fort Cass position. The man knew Indians, knew trading, knew how to make a profit, and that was more than Skye or Bonfils knew.

It helped MacLees that he was betrothed to Sarah Lansing, daughter of a Chouteau company attorney, August Lansing, who was once married to Marsh's wife, thus adding to the threads and connections that gave him the inside track for a high position. Sarah Lansing was Marsh's own stepdaughter; his wife's child by the earlier marriage, raised by the Lansings.

And now, along comes MacLees's mountain woman! Just in time for the wedding! How delighted Sarah would be to learn about this red whore and her breed brats! Marsh smiled sardonically. What a fine scandal it would be . . . if the woman actually reached St. Louis. It would break Sarah's heart. But that would not happen.

Marsh hadn't decided what he would do about her, but he knew that he would unload her somewhere and send her back to her people, with a stern warning never to set foot in Missouri. If he took that squaw clear to St. Louis, and raised a scandal, his friend Pierre Chouteau, and his acquaintance August Lansing, not to mention his own wife and stepdaughter, would land on him and he would never hear the end of it.

So MacLees had himself a red woman! And that red woman was riding the *Otter*! Marsh enjoyed the irony.

Mountain wives were an unspoken part of the trade but one didn't hear about them in polite society—unless they showed up on someone's doorstep. MacLees had abandoned his, and never dreamed he would see her again.

MacLees was the obvious choice to trade with the Crows. That Cheyenne squaw wouldn't help matters. Not that Sarah would go west into an utter wilderness. MacLees would do what so many traders did: impregnate her and leave for a year; and then return and repeat the cycle. After a few years, he would have his fortune and his children and would retire in St. Louis, while she would be busy managing a family in St. Louis.

Marsh watched carefully as his pilot and helmsman negotiated a broad shallows, pocked with a thousand stumps and other debris. The channel ran straight through the middle of it, braiding itself around islands and bars. It was one of the most treacherous spots on the upper Missouri, and the doom of half a dozen captains before him, all of them running Opposition boats.

That took the better part of an hour, with only one crisis, when some invisible sawyer scraped along the port side, banged on the wheelhouse, and levered the entire packet sideways. But no damage was done and the boat drifted through another hundred yards of trouble before striking a clear channel again.

"We made it, no thanks to you," he snapped at his pilot.

He rang a bell, signaling the engineers to open the throttle, and was rewarded with a chatter of popping steam from the escape pipe.

The crisis over, he returned to his musings. Somewhere, he would unload the Cheyenne woman. Fort Pierre was next. It was Chouteau's new fort, the headquarters for the whole region, and the supply depot for the satellite posts the company had established in the area. Chouteau himself had picked the site several years earlier on his first excursion up the river.

He wondered what to say to the woman, and decided he would not say anything: he would simply put her off and tell her to go home. He would have liked to put Skye's squaw off too, but thought better of it.

He had little use for Skye. The man might have a reputation as a mountaineer, but he was a cockney oaf, without the brains to make anything of himself. He was doomed to the life of a mountain exile, attached to that barbaric Crow woman, and St. Louis would swiftly mock him and send him back to the wilds.

He had even less use for Bonfils, primping dandy, reckless fool, but Marsh could do nothing about it. Bonfils was connected by blood to the owners. Nonetheless, Marsh intended to catalogue Bonfils's follies during this voyage south, and make mincemeat of the young man in the privacy of Pierre Chouteau's study.

Chouteau was particularly eager to learn the weaknesses of his relatives; and Benton Marsh had been his primary source for years. Just why Chouteau cherished the salacious news about his cousins and uncles and nieces and nephews more than any other gossip, Marsh could only guess at. Amusement, probably. Pierre Chouteau loved to offer witty toasts at family affairs that harpooned one or another of his Creole kin.

Tomorrow, if the wood and water and weather held, they would dock at Fort Pierre, the most splendid edifice on the river save for Fort Union. It stood on the right bank, upon a generous plain well above high water level, a rectangle of pickets encasing a dozen or so commodious buildings. Its factor, Pierre Papin, traded with the Teton, Yankton and Yanktonai Sioux, and sent a great harvest of buffalo hides and robes southward each year, an increasingly profitable trade for the company.

The *Otter* would take on as much of this wealth as it could, and catch the rest on a return trip this far up the river if there would be water enough. The Bad River, which flowed into the Missouri just below Fort Pierre, usually made the difference, supplying the water for late-season navigation.

Marsh turned the vessel over to the pilot. This stretch of the river offered no obstacles and cut serenely across open flats guarded by distant amber bluffs. It was a monotonous land, suited only for the savage spirit. White men required a country with more amenities. The entire area was useless, save for cattle raising, whenever the buffalo were exterminated along with the tribes who fed on them.

Yes, Fort Pierre would be the end of the journey for the squaw, who even now was circling the deck, gazing at wonders beyond her sullen comprehension.

He would tell her at Fort Pierre to debark; she and her brats and those two scrawny ponies. Yes, that was all that was required. A word. If necessary, he would have Skye or his squaw put it into the finger-language of the plains. But that probably would not be necessary. He would send Trenholm to her cabin and have him evict her.

He would like to debark the Skyes, too, but they would be another matter. Skye was no fool. Marsh knew he would need a good reason to debark them; something that would stand up with Chouteau. He would come up with one. Bellevue, downstream, would be the obvious place. That was where the Skyes would leave their horses and pick them up again en route to the Crow country.

That would narrow the field to MacLees and that reckless fop Bonfils. The master of the *Otter* would make sure MacLees was selected—for the good of the company, of course. And for Sarah.

fifteen

Victoria found good company in the Cheyenne woman, Lame Deer. The young mother could understand English well enough. Apparently Simon MacLees had been able to converse with her in Cheyenne, and they had employed both tongues.

The Cheyenne and Absaroka might be hostile, but that did not wither the blossoming friendship between them as they roamed the decks of the riverboat, sometimes leaning over the rails to watch the turbid river flow by; sometimes sitting on the hurricane deck where they could see the majestic stream in all its grandeur flowing between distant slopes.

For Victoria, the chance to coddle the little ones was a moment precious beyond words, for she had borne no child and felt that she would be forever barren. She scarcely knew which one she loved more; the bright girl, Singing Rain, with red bows in her glossy black hair, or the feisty boy whose name she shortened to Echo. To Lame Deer she explained that Echo was the English word for sound coming back, and Lame Deer repeated it with a smile.

It was good to have a woman of the People for company; they could be together all the way to the big place where all the white men's wonders came from.

Victoria wanted to see where metal came out of the earth, and where the powder that exploded came from, and the little brass caps Skye slid over the nipple of his rifle. She wanted to see how cloth was woven and how blankets became so thick, and whether a thousand frail white women were employed making these things, out of sight.

But those things didn't interest Lame Deer at all.

"I will find my man, and he will be gladdened. His heart will grow when he sees the children we have made. He will stand taller than the others. He will look upon me with wisdom. He will walk with the footsteps of a great chief of his people. He will touch me and I will shiver with gladness.

"He will take me to his father and mother, and they will welcome me. I will present our children to them, and they will make blessings and do the sacred things of their people, and sprinkle them with sacred waters, for this is what Simon MacLees told me once, when the night was very black and our robes were very warm.

"They will tell me the story of their people; where they came from, and how they were made, and who this Christ is, just as I have told him about Sweet Medicine and how he teaches the People. And we will all be friends and kin together, in a moment of great feasting. And I, Lame Deer, will be very proud and my heart will sing. And after that we will go back to my people again, and he will be great among them."

Lame Deer spoke these things almost in a dream state, as if she were in the midst of a vision quest. She made the white men's words so beautiful that no white man could ever match her. If she were an Absaroka woman, she would be revered as a story-giver, and given much honor by the People because she could see beyond vision, and hear beyond what the ears knew.

But Victoria listened sadly. She had been around reckless white trappers a long time, and she sensed that the happy young woman's dream might be dashed on the rocks of things the Cheyenne didn't grasp. Such as that the white men got tired of living so far away from their own kind and often abandoned their Indian families and married white women; the very white women that neither Victoria nor any other Crow had ever seen.

"It is a big place, this St. Louis. How will you find him?" she asked the Cheyenne.

Lame Deer only smiled and shrugged. "I will say the name, and the town crier will take me to him," she whispered. "For all the world knows that name.

"I have been to Monterrey, a city far to the west, the place of a people called Californios, so I have seen a place with many houses," she said. "There are more than can be counted. And they have habits we do not know. There was no town crier there, to tell them about those who come. There are some places a woman can't go. And they have a religion that is very strange. To enter a place where they hide their God, I must wear something upon my head.

"I will find MacLees."

"I'll help you," Victoria said. "I know white men better. I'm not afraid to ask. I will see a man in the street and I will ask him if he knows Simon MacLees. And if he doesn't, I will walk into a place they have called a taberna, and ask the men there. That is the Californio word; it is a place to drink whiskey. And maybe they will tell me."

"You will help me, then. You know them better than I do."

They were standing at the blunt prow, watching the river part before the flat-bottomed boat. There was little to see; the far shores revealed no life; the water was blank and told her nothing. The children peered at the murky tide, at the solidly built boat, and accepted it all, though Victoria was not at ease surrounded by water-spirits and white men's mysteries.

"What did your man tell you when he left?"

Lame Deer puzzled that shyly. "He said he was going to St. Louis, the place of many lodges, to do business."

"Did he say when he would be back?"

Lame Deer slowly shook her head, a sadness in her brown eyes that touched Victoria. "He come back sometime."

Victoria didn't want to say what she thought, but she

needed to prepare this girl-woman for rejection. "What if he will not come back?"

"He come back. Simon MacLees, he come back. For he has held me in his arms, and touched my lips, and gazed into my heart. He is like a lion roaming the hills for food for us."

But Victoria caught the doubt in her tone.

"What if he can't?"

Lame Deer stared. "Why do you say such things?"

"This company, American Fur, it is big medicine. Very strong. MacLees, little medicine. Maybe this big outfit, it says no to MacLees; he can't trade no more with your people."

Lame Deer's lovely face crumpled. "Sometimes I think that," she said sadly. "But he come back. He's my man. These be his boy and girl. See how they have the look of us both. No good man leave behind his own child."

Victoria wondered whether to suggest other possibilities, and decided she had a whole trip of many days to do so, and it would be best to prepare Lame Deer for bad news a little bit at a time.

The riverboat was making good time this day, plowing the river under a cloudless blue bowl. She felt a change in the rhythm suddenly, a slowing of the engines, and saw the boat veer toward a patch of willows and alders and cottonwoods ahead. The master would stop for fuel. She had seen so many of these stops that she knew the drill: soon the bell would summon every able-bodied man to the boiler deck, and when the gangway was lowered, these men would fan out and begin sawing and chopping carrying wood. Soon there would be no trees left along the big river, because these men always killed several more for future use, by girdling them.

She saw Skye present himself to the mate, who handed him a crosscut saw. Skye was always one of the first off the boat and last to return. No Name always joined him, his tail wagging slowly, eager for a run and a chance to wet a few trees. Skye worked hard. This was women's work; no Absaroka man would stoop to such a thing, but that didn't bother him. White men were different.

The boat slid close to the bank, bumped something and rocked in place while the deck crews shouted, threw hawsers over the rail, and slid the gangway outward. From where Victoria sat high above, she could see that this woodlot had been much depleted by other visits.

She followed Skye until he vanished behind foliage, and then she studied the brooding slopes for danger, squinting as her gaze swept ridges and gulches, pausing at anything the slightest bit unusual or strange. But she saw no sign of trouble. She glanced forward toward the pilothouse and saw Bonfils there. The young man had ceased to go on the refueling trips, and Marsh said nothing. She wondered about it: was that an honor, not being asked to cut wood? Was Skye being dishonored? She could not know, but resolved to ask Skye about it.

She loved the quiet, when the fireboat idled in the lapping waves and the steam made no thunder and the big paddle wheels did not rumble and slap and splash. This machine of the white men ate trees, and someday that would all come to a stop because there would be no more trees.

It didn't take long. The further they progressed into this trip, the faster were the woodcutting stops, as passengers acquired skills and organized themselves better. She watched the deck crews carry the fresh logs aboard and stack them neatly, within reach of the firebox. A bell summoned those on shore, and soon she saw Skye and No Name walk wearily to the deck. She was always careful about No Name, remembering how that dog had once followed a boat carrying Skye and Victoria for a long distance, never giving up. No Name was a spirit-dog, and he made Victoria feel chills sometimes when she gazed at the mangy creature.

They progressed easily the rest of the afternoon. Skye clambered up to the highest deck and sat with the women, watching the shoreline slide by. They passed a woodlot where white men were sawing planks and others were cutting logs, and the mate, Trenholm, told them they would reach Fort Pierre in a little over an hour.

It seemed a greener land than upriver; verdant grasses shivered in the breezes, and the hills weren't so arid. Then, far ahead, she saw the thinnest veil of smoke, and in a bit, a distant palisade, the famous Fort Pierre, a rectangular stockade like the others she had seen, composed of pickets, a massive gate in front, and various buildings within. But this post was on a broad flat, and around the trading center rose more lodges than she could count; smoke-blackened buffalo-hide cones, one after another, a sea of bright-painted lodges built after the manner of the Lakota, with distant people running now to the riverbank to greet the fireboat.

She saw a small puff from a corner bastion, heard the crack of a cannon, and knew the white men at the post were welcoming the fireboat. Another crack, and then the deck hands fired the little brass six-pounder on the foredeck in response. The penned horses stirred nervously. The fireboat slowed and shuddered as the big paddles stopped revolving and the boat slid quietly toward a muddy levee, where it would soon be tied to posts.

She could not yet see individuals who were gathering and jostling at the riverbank, but she knew who they were: enemies of her people. These were Sioux, mostly the Dakota ones, Yanktons, Yanktonai, but also some Tetons, or Lakota. Many was the Lakota scalp dangling from an Absaroka lance! Lame Deer stared raptly at the gathering crowd of Sioux.

Now a few of the post traders appeared, men in black suits and stiff white shirts, quieter than the frenzied Sioux but no less delighted to see the fireboat.

A shrill blast of steam announced the arrival, and now every living person in the whole area was crowding the shore, cheering the boat as the pilot and the master and helmsman eased it home. Finally the deckmen tossed the hawsers to waiting hands on shore, and the boat slid to a halt.

Aiee, she wondered whether she had the courage to walk down to the boiler deck and onto land, with so many Sioux waiting to separate her from her hair!

Then the mate, Trenholm, appeared on the hurricane deck and addressed Lame Deer.

"End of the ride," he said. "Captain's putting you off."

The woman stared.

"Got your stuff on the deck. Bring the young 'uns. We'll unload the nags in a bit."

The Cheyenne woman looked bewildered. "Is this the place of many houses called St. Louis?"

"Nope, but this is as far as you go."

Victoria intervened. "She paid robes to go to St. Louis."

Trenholm laughed. "Off she goes! Come along now."

Slowly, Lame Deer gathered her little ones in hand and followed the mate to the companionway.

sixteen

Skye stood at the rail watching the hubbub. On shore, a crowd jostled and pushed. The arrival of a riverboat was a great event at Fort Pierre Chouteau. The Sioux added to the press of bodies, studying this amazing machine of the white men, their thoughts private and unfathomable. Skye thought them handsomely formed, and taller than most tribes. Most of the males wore only breechclouts that hot day, but many wore white men's shirts and britches, and stovepipe hats. The calico-clad women stood back, knotted into clusters, holding their children close. Dogs circled crazily; No Name watched them from the deck, his neck hair bristling.

When the deck crew finally slid the gangway to the levee and the boat was snubbed to massive posts set in the earth, a great traffic commenced on the gangway; passengers heading for land, and a few company clerks fighting the tide to reach Marsh, their hands clutching manifests and bills of lading. Skye thought he would wait. There would be time enough to roam the post, meet Laidlaw, its factor, and patrol the Sioux lodges to study the ways of these powerful people.

Fort engagés were hurrying bales of buffalo robes, beaver pelts, and other furs to the bank. The *Otter* would carry a fortune in furs and hides back to St. Louis. On its upstream trip, it had dropped off a year's supply of trade items and household goods for the post; now, en route to St. Louis, it would carry the annual returns, as the fur trade called the accumulated peltries.

Deckmen opened the cargo hatch and several dropped below to begin the mighty business of storing tons of furs in the cramped hold and moving all the furs brought from Fort Union aft to make room for the new load. The boat drew four feet of water loaded; the hold was only five feet high, and a man had to stoop. Other deckmen swung a cargo boom toward shore, where a fort crew waited to load the bales of fur.

Two deckmen were in the horse pen, sliding hackamores over the Cheyenne woman's wild-eyed ponies, and that seemed odd to Skye. Maybe they would exercise all the horses, including those belonging to the Skyes. But they didn't halter any other horses. He spotted Trenholm leading Lame Deer, the Cheyenne woman, and her children down the companionway. He was carrying her things; two parfleches, some blankets, and a canvas sack. Behind, a cabin boy was carrying her packsaddle.

Was she getting off?

He spotted Victoria, looking agitated, and he headed toward the companionway, curious about this turn of events.

Lame Deer passed him, her face granitic and proud, but her eyes betrayed sorrow.

"Say, mate, what is this?" Skye asked.

The mate grinned. "Cap'ain's putting her off. Don't want some lice-bait squaw on board."

Victoria appeared at the foot of the stair. "He's making her go!"

"Why?"

"He says he don't want her."

The mate continued toward the gangway, passing the lounging firemen and stacks of cordwood.

"You sure she isn't just getting off because she wants to?"

"I saw it. The big chief, he just tells the little chief to unload her."

"Is he giving her back her fare? The robes?"

She shook her head angrily.

He pushed into the crowd. Lame Deer was waiting near the gangway.

"You getting off?" he asked.

"He make me go."

"You want to go to St. Louis?"

She nodded. She stood resolutely, tall and straight, her face blank and empty as an August sky.

"Want me to talk to Marsh?"

She stared silently, and now he saw an edge in her. The boy clung to her skirt; she held the girl on her hip.

Skye did not understand any of this. "Don't get off until I see about this," he said.

She looked fearfully at the mate, Trenholm, who was getting her horses readied to lead down the wobbly gangway.

Skye vaulted up the companionway to the pilothouse, which was now jammed with company clerks in black suits.

Marsh looked up, his face showing displeasure at the unauthorized presence of a passenger.

"Why are you putting that woman off?" Skye asked.

"Because I choose to," Marsh snapped and returned to his
examination of a paper the clerks had handed him.

"You returning her fare?"

Marsh, already choleric, exploded. "Get out!"

"I said, you returning her St. Louis fare?"

Marsh wheeled about and faced Skye. The captain was
about the same height and build, and probably was just as
hard as Skye.

"This is my ship, Skye. I will do what I choose, when I
choose, and for whatever reason I choose. Now get out."

Skye didn't budge. "Not until this is settled. And it's *Mister* Skye."

He wondered what it mattered to him. Why did he care
about the Cheyenne woman? Was it because Trenholm had
called her a louse-ridden squaw? Or was it simply his ancient
hatred of injustice, a tidal wave of feeling that went straight
back to the Royal Navy and the endless cruelties he had seen
there. He remembered those naval officers, their arrogance
and contempt, and with the memory came a hardening of his
own. Damn the consequences. The heat rose in him, even as it
filled the face of Marsh, who glared at him furiously.

"You owe her a fare. Get those robes back to her, or let her
stay," Skye said quietly, an unmistakable menace in his voice.
The pilot and helmsman stared. The fort's clerks gaped.

Marsh pointed. "Off," he said. "You and your filthy
squaw. Off my boat!"

"Give the Cheyenne woman her fare back."

Marsh was totally unafraid, and Skye knew the man
would fight, and fight brutally if it came to that. The master
closed in, his fists balled, his hard gaze steady.

The pilot and helmsman circled to either side, ready to
help. A dead silence pervaded the pilothouse, a silence so pro-

found that it seemed to blot the hubbub on the boiler deck and riverbank.

Then all three leapt at Skye simultaneously. Skye didn't fight back; there was no point in it. They escorted Skye to the companionway and pushed. Skye stumbled downward, caught a rail, and tripped down to the boiler deck.

"Aiee!" Victoria cried. She had obviously seen at least some of it.

"We're getting off. Get the horses saddled. I'll get our truck."

The second mate followed, ready to throw them off if they didn't leave on their own. Above, Marsh watched from the pilothouse.

Skye headed for the cabin, filled with regret. What had he done? Had he ruined his future with American Fur? Were his old feelings about injustice, feelings dating back to his slavery in the Royal Navy, still governing his conduct? Had he not grown since those youthful days?

It was too late to have regrets. Marsh had ejected him from the *Otter*, and that was a captain's absolute right. Marsh hated the Indian women. His boat was for whites, not redskins. But that puzzled Skye. There was something else at work here; something he didn't know about; something connected to Lame Deer, or her husband, Simon MacLees. Marsh was a choleric man, but that explained nothing. A minor incident had exploded into something darker. Skye wondered whether he would ever know the answer.

He stuffed their few possessions into Victoria's handsomely dyed parfleches, checked to see if he had left anything in the gloomy little cubicle, and emerged on the boiler deck—right into Bonfils, who was lounging aft, watching the furious business of loading the packet.

"Why, Skye, you leaving us?" the young man asked, delight in his eye.

Skye ignored him.

"Handsome ladies out there. I suppose I'll go see what a few trinkets will purchase," Bonfils said, following Skye past the firemen to the midships area where the gangway stretched to land. "You are abandoning us. Is it that you have given up your little, ah, quest to impress your magnificent virtues and skills upon my uncle Pierre?"

Skye stared at the handsome brigade leader, and then returned to his business.

It took a few minutes for Victoria to prepare the horses, and then they led the nervous, whinnying animals down the wobbling gangway and onto the levee, where scores of Sioux eyed them solemnly. Here they were safe; beyond the fort, Skye and Victoria would be fair game. No Name slunk along with them, his neck hair bristling.

Skye stood at the levee, rein in hand, while Victoria finished loading the horses. He was looking for Lame Deer, who had vanished in the hurlyburly of the crowd.

"You see the Cheyenne?" he asked Victoria.

She squinted. "What for?"

"Take to Saint Louis."

"You still going there?"

He nodded, lifted his battered topper, and settled it on his long locks. "Got unfinished business there. And the least the company can do is get the Cheyenne woman there safely, long as she paid her fare."

"You still with the company?" Victoria's gaze bore into him; she was confused.

"Haven't resigned," he said. "Maybe I will in St. Louis."

"How we going?"

"I've got a little credit. We didn't have time at rendezvous to drink up the last of the salary." He grinned. She grinned back.

"Maybe they got some goddam whiskey here," she said, cheer leaking into her hard glare like sun bursting into an overcast sky. "We got to find that Cheyenne. They treat her bad."

"Marsh doesn't like Indians."

"Well, sonofabitch, I don't like Marsh!"

They found Lame Deer at the fort, her horse tied to a hitch rail, her children clutching her. She might be a trader's wife, but a post of this size was plainly intimidating.

Victoria approached. "Hey, you want to go to St. Louis? Place of many lodges?"

Lame Deer looked uncertain. "My heart is two hearts now. My mind flies away from my spirit. My children weep."

"We'll take you," Victoria said.

"Long walk. Marsh, the big chief, put us off too," Skye said. "But we're going to St. Louis."

Lame Deer studied Skye with knowing eyes, and a determined look in her soft young face. "I will put wings on my feet. I will walk and leave no footprints upon the meadows. I will walk beside the river, and the fish will play beside me. My feet will carry me to the end of the world, for there will I see Simon. He gives me a big heart. I will go with you."

seventeen

Skye wasn't very sure about what to do. Maybe he should just hightail it for the mountains, and see what came of that. But all his instincts told him to finish what he had started: he would submit himself to the directors of Pratte, Chouteau and Company and if they made him a trader to the Crows, that's what he would do.

Marsh's conduct puzzled him, but since he could not fathom it, he dismissed it. Marsh probably favored Bonfils, and this contretemps was as simple as that. The captain would tell Chouteau that he had been forced to put the disobedient

Skye ashore, and that would be the end of the contest. A ship's master was a law unto himself. There was little he could do to change that.

He headed for the store, intending to provision, and glad he had not spent all his hard-won cash at rendezvous. He would have to provision for Lame Deer and her children too. He had no great wish to take her to her wayward husband in St. Louis, and wished the woman would head back to her people. But she was as determined as he was to reach St. Louis, and so they would make common cause. The more he thought of it, the better he liked the idea. If her arrival in St. Louis upset some powerful people, that was all the more reason to take her there.

The trading store at Fort Pierre Chouteau stood just inside the big river gate, and was open for trade but largely empty because the throngs at the fort had clustered around the *Otter* to gape at its white enameled hull and cabins, its elaborate fretwork, its twin black chimneys, and all the wonders of civilization aboard. It seemed so improbable, this traveling city anchored in a wilderness; so defiant of nature and nature's God, that he found his own gaze drawn to it over and over, as the crew walked its plank decks, and gangs lowered bales of fur into its smelly hold.

He steered Victoria into the post and the trading room, which was crammed with every imaginable item that might appeal to the Indian imagination. What he wanted mostly was staples: tea, powder, lead, percussion caps, and some canvas tenting for shelter, since he had left his lodge with Victoria's people.

The sole clerk on duty, a sallow Creole in a black suit, was provisioning two Yank frontiersmen, one skinny, big-toothed and redheaded; the other short, stout, freckled, and jittery. They both wore broad-brimmed, low-crowned gray felt hats that kept the fierce sun out of their faces. They were both

armed with wicked-looking knives and other lethal accouter-
ments, including horse pistols and boot knives.

"All right, Leblanc, bring 'er out to the flatboat," the redhead said. A heap of goods, ranging from flour sacks to tins of
sugar, lay on the rude counter.

"*Oui, monsieur*," the clerk said.

Skye waited to see what sort of payment would be required, but the man offered nothing, and no bill was laid before him by the clerk. Probably Company men, requisitioning
goods, Skye thought.

The redhead turned around, studied Skye a moment, and
unwound himself, his gait so langorous and catlike that he exuded sheer menace. Skye supposed that the Yank frontiersman in the blue chambray shirt had won a few scrapes. The
other, whose step was oddly swift for one with rolls of fat
rolling off his jaw and belly, was no less a menace. The pair
weren't ones to trust.

The clerk summoned a breed boy to tote the mound of
goods out the door, and turned to Skye.

"Sir?" he said.

"I'm provisioning," Skye said. "Now first, how many
leagues is it to St. Louis?"

"By land or water?"

"Land."

"You're not on the riverboat?"

"We just got off it."

The man blinked. "A great oddity, sir. You will need cash
to provision."

"Got it. Company credit, on paper."

"But they put you off the boat?"

"How many miles?" Skye asked, an edge in his voice this
time.

"Ah, four hundred and some—"

"That far?"

"In leagues, monsieur."

"A thousand two hundred miles, then?"

"Ah, oui . . . one thousand and three hundred, more or less."

"Twenty days on a flatboat," said a voice behind him. Skye turned and discovered the redhead, lounging at the door. The man had been listening.

"We're traveling by horse."

"Mighty strange thing to do with a river to float you there in comfort."

Skye nodded. How he traveled was not the stranger's business. He would need provisions for seven or eight weeks for his entire party. He hoped to supply much of his provender with his heavy, octagon-barreled mountain rifle. Buffalo, deer, antelope, maybe some elk. . . .

Skye turned to the clerk. "You have any mules or packhorses for sale?"

"Ah, no, only mustangs. Subdued horses are scarce here and valuable. They are hard to keep; hay, feed, and there is always the, ah, shall we say embezzlements of the Indians. . . ."

That was bad news. Skye needed two more pack animals. St. Louis was a long way.

The redhead was grinning. "You want a ride, easy trip, you got a ride. Me and my partner got us a mackinaw."

Skye turned. "Who are you?"

"I'm Red Gill; him out there, he's Shorty Ballard."

"And what is your business?"

"Independent company out of St. Louis."

"What are you carrying in your mackinaw?"

"Some hides, tallow, buffalo tongues . . ."

"What did you bring upriver?"

Gill grinned, revealing gaps where incisors should have been. "Oh, I reckon a few tradegoods for the Opposition, but not on that there mackinaw. We bought that boat at Fort Clark from the Chouteau interests."

Something didn't sound right. "You running an account here, I see."

Red Gill grinned. "We're teamsters. We brought some stuff by packtrain, and now we're taking some robes back by water. There's just two of us, and that ain't enough to man a flatboat proper, much less fight Injuns. You come along, and we won't charge ye but a little."

It was a temptation. Thirteen hundred miles of horseback would be an ordeal, and without pack horses and supplies, it would be reckless.

"I'm Mister Skye," he said. He motioned them out the door and into the hot July sun. "Maybe you can persuade me," he added.

"Show you," Gill said, motioning Skye. Ahead, a breed boy and Shorty were toting sacks down to the riverbank, where a small mackinaw was anchored well downstream from the riverboat.

Skye had never been on one. He found himself boarding a scow made of thick handsawn planks still oozing sap, with a beveled prow and a squared off stern. A rudder on a long tiller dangled from the rear. Amidships was a cargo box, and behind it a small cabin with plank walls and a doorless entry at the rear. For a roof, a chunk of old, tallowed buffalo-hide lodgecover stretched over curved ribs. The mackinaw was perhaps forty feet long, with a beam of twelve, and it rode lightly in the water, drawing scarcely even a foot though it was loaded.

This was a one-way craft, to be sold for scrap at its destination. There were oar sockets forward, and various poles and oars lying on the planking. There was one oddity: a glorious bouquet of prairie asters, red mallow, and prairie evening primrose poked from a holder in the prow, a rainbow-bright and startling gaud upon a utilitarian scow.

"It beats riding," Gill said. "Have a lookaround."

The craft was sturdy enough; that didn't worry Skye. The nature of the company was what troubled him.

"I think we'll take our horses," he said, watching Shorty and the breed boy stuff a sack of corn, a cask of flour, a keg of tallow, some salt and sugar and pepper and mustard into the rude cargo box.

Skye edged toward the box and discovered it was full of packs of buffalo hides, and some casks.

Red shrugged. "We're just a pair of entrepreneurs out of Saint Louie," he said. "We've had our fun; Yankton women and all. Delivered upriver, and going back now."

"Delivered what, and to whom?"

Gill laughed until he wheezed, and Skye watched the adam's apple bob in his skinny throat. "You sure are choosy," he said. "Them squaws, they'll be safe with us, and the little ones too."

"The Cheyenne woman is returning to her husband," Skye said carefully.

"Oh, who's that?"

"A trader," Skye said.

"Well, we're pulling out in a little bit. You want a ride, we'll charge you ten apiece; the wimmin cook and take care of things; you help pole and row and steer, and if there's a fracas, have that piece ready to help. We got a little protection here," he said, waving at the plank-walled cabin. Several rifle ports had been shopped into its sides.

Skye laughed shortly. "Not much protection for the man on the tiller," he said.

Gill laughed. "It's been thought of."

"It's not Indians I'm worried about."

Gill straightened, fire blazing in his blue eyes. "Well, then, you just go get yourself to hell on a horse," he snarled. "We offered you a cheap ride if'n you share the load, and that's all I'm going to say. If we ain't for you, quit palavering and wast-

ing our time. We got to make St. Louis with these hides or we
don't make a profit."

Skye refused to budge. "You have an account with Pratte
and Chouteau?"

Red Gill turned wary. "No, not as I know."

"How was all this truck paid for?"

"They owed us, and that's the last damned question I'll
answer."

Skye pondered it. "I'll talk to the women and let you
know. We have to provision, too."

"*You* got an account?"

"Brigade leader with the company."

"Mister Skye, is it? I heard of you. Now I got a question for
you. How come you ain't on that riverboat?"

Skye smiled.

Gill waited, cheerfully, until it was plain to him he would
get no answer. Then, "I got me a one gallon jug in there, and
it ain't mountain whiskey either; it's good Kentuck I been
presarving."

Barnaby Skye felt his resolve sliding from under him, and
headed for the women to talk things over. Captain Gill—the
name fit perfectly—had made a proposition he couldn't turn
down.

eighteen

enton Marsh was worried. His
hold was crammed with furs, and
an additional nine packs had been
stuffed into the women's cabin. He had a full complement of

passengers, too, mostly Creole engagés who were returning to St. Louis after fulfilling their contracts with the company.

The *Otter* was drawing a full four feet of water, and that spelled trouble this late in the season. Worse, he would be loading forty cords of wood at Farm Island, just downstream; wood cut for his use by the post because there was so little of it in this area.

Once he left the island, he would be overloaded, though that burden would lessen as fast as the wood was burned. Within an hour after the Fort Pierre returns, as the company called its fur harvest, had been stowed away and the ship properly balanced, he was sailing toward the island for the fuel.

He was an irritable, irascible man, and his worries didn't improve his disposition as he stood in the pilothouse watching his pilot and helmsman ease the ship into the glittering river. Nor was it improved by the presence of the well-connected Alexandre Bonfils, whose professed goal was to become a trader, but whose constant presence in the pilothouse suggested that he might have other motives. Was he Pierre Chouteau's eyes and ears?

Marsh held his temper, but just barely.

The vessel moved sluggishly into the channel, leaving the post behind. There were no visible snags or bars ahead, no sharp bends to whirl the boat toward shore, and Marsh relaxed.

"There," he said, pointing at a rude levee at Farm Island.

The helmsman was already steering in that direction.

"How many new passengers?" Bonfils asked, peering at the motley crowd on the boiler deck.

"Twenty-seven," Marsh said, wondering why he answered; indeed, wondering why he permitted this scion of the owning families to be there. But he knew why.

"Minus a few." Bonfils laughed. "Thank you for the great favor."

Marsh stared coldly.

Bonfils met the gaze. "Skye and his squaw, left behind.

That eliminates the only real problem I face. He's formidable in his way, but of course has his little difficulties."

"What difficulties?"

"He's a deserter from the Royal Navy and makes no bones about it. Ah, *mon ami*, I think that is a black mark upon him."

"It doesn't improve his chances," Marsh replied curtly.

The pilot pulled the bell cord, and soon the rumble of the paddle wheels lessened and the rattle of popping steam from the escapement died. The vessel slowed, drifted toward the woodlot, while Trenholm readied the deck crew and instructed the passengers, who were about to perform their first wood duty.

The fort's engagés had stacked the four-foot cordwood in orderly piles next to the landing, and in short order the crew and passengers were hauling it aboard and noisily stacking it on the foredeck under the direction of the burly firemen who could each lift an entire four-foot log and jam it into the inferno.

As usual, Bonfils had escaped the task by standing there in the pilothouse like some laird. Marsh was tempted to direct the young man to go to work, but bit back the command. He seethed at his own frustration; why couldn't he summon the courage to put this dubious princeling to work like ordinary mortals?

The task was going smoothly but would require two hours, even with so many hands. It took two passengers to lift a single four-foot log aboard. Marsh didn't much care for this softer upriver fuel, mostly cottonwood, willow, box elder, and even driftwood, though the driftwood didn't burn well and had to be mixed with other wood or burned with resin. Occasionally he burned some ponderosa pine, which worked better.

It took twice as much upriver wood to feed his boilers than the better hardwoods downstream, such as the solid, heavy, oak and hickory and walnut and maple. No one had found coal. In three or four years, every tree here on Farm Island would be gone, and then what?

It was during this fuel stop that the pilot spotted the mackinaw bobbing up from behind, and pointed at it. Marsh picked up his spyglass to see who it was; he knew most of the rivermen.

This one was newly made of raw wood; maybe at the Navy Yard north of Fort Pierre; its planks not yet weathered. It had the usual cargo box amidships, and a rude cabin. He focused on the man at the tiller, and knew him: Shorty Ballard. Red Gill and Ballard were teamsters and boatmen licensed by General Clark to transport goods in the Indian country. They supplied the Opposition, and as far as Marsh knew, had no connection to Pratte, Chouteau and Company. But they had never lacked cash, which they spent unwisely in St. Louis, and there had always been question marks surrounding them.

His glass then revealed some unpleasant news: the Cheyenne woman was en route to St. Louis after all, and the Skyes as well, and even their damned dog. The Skyes must have sold their horses for passage, because there were no beasts of burden aboard.

They were continuing downriver!

So his efforts to protect his daughter and wife might well come to naught after all. There might be a scandal. MacLees might find his future clouded and his marriage in distress.

Irritably he glassed the whole flatboat, wondering what was in the cargo box, and wondering whether he ought to overtake the craft downstream, bring it to heel, examine the box, and confiscate the goods if there was the slightest sign of illegality. Maybe he could stop them all in their tracks. Not for nothing did he have a six-pounder and a large crew.

He'd see. Meanwhile, he'd arrive in St. Louis a week or ten days ahead of the flatboat and would have time to warn MacLees, and influence Chouteau. It would be tricky, but it would protect the company. And protect Sarah Lansing.

The flatboat drifted by, riding a relentless current that averaged seven or eight miles an hour, and its passengers waved lazily. They would be a half hour downstream before the *Otter* was ready to go. But there were ways . . .

"There go your passengers," Bonfils said.

Marsh grunted.

When the wooding was done, Marsh set out again, pushing hard through the midday heat until he sighted the flatboat a couple of miles ahead. The *Otter* would overtake the flatboat in an hour, about four in the afternoon. He knew all about flatboats. They could make excellent time going downriver, and could more easily travel at night because they drew so little water they didn't need to stick to the channels. Many a flatboat had been navigated by moonlight on the shoulders of the mighty river. Neither did a flatboat have to make wood stops.

He eyed Bonfils irritably. "Perhaps you wish to retire from the pilothouse for a time?"

"No, this is the place to be," Bonfils said. "Best perch on the boat."

"You may take our leave," Marsh said directly.

Bonfils looked startled, and then cloudy, as if this was something to remember and make use of in the future. Nonetheless, he retreated to the hurricane deck and down the companionway, his brow furrowed.

Marsh turned to his pilot, Lamar DeWayne. "Give that flatboat as much grief as you can."

The pilot stared a moment. The helmsman turned to peer at the master. The command jeopardized DeWayne's federal pilot license.

"We are far from St. Louis. I don't wish for you to swamp the flatboat. Just brush it and make sure it's caught in our wake."

DeWayne reddened. "Why?"

"Because I told you to."

Marsh could see the pilot wondering whether to obey, or whether to face the master's wrath and ability to make his life miserable.

"I don't suppose you would supply me with a reason," the pilot said.

"Smugglers and rivals."

"If they're smugglers let's pull them over and have a look."

"I am considering it."

"Weren't those our passengers on it?"

"Yes, unfortunately."

"Is this connected to them?"

Marsh exploded. "Do it or give me the helm."

DeWayne glowered and ordered the helmsman to ease to the right edge of the channel, where the flatboat was proceeding. Unfortunately the channel was plenty wide there; the episode could not be dismissed as an unfortunate navigational problem.

"Add steam," Marsh said.

DeWayne clanged bells. Moments later the chimneys billowed black smoke and the thunder of the paddle wheels noticeably quickened. The current gave them seven miles an hour; the thrashing wheels doubled that. That speed would be safe enough until they reached the bight a mile ahead where the channel cut to the right bank and then swung hard left.

"Slow as soon as you pass the flatboat," he said.

DeWayne nodded.

They gained on the flatboat, loomed behind it. Shorty Ballard peered behind him and eased toward the right bank. The helmsman followed, closing on the flatboat.

Now the people on the flatboat leapt up in alarm, and Ballard yanked the tiller hard heading for shore. Skye had removed his topper and was waving hard at them, even as his squaw was shepherding the Cheyenne woman and her brats to the right side of the flatboat.

The *Otter* overtook the flatboat and the helmsman spun his wheel until the steamboat was veering back to the channel. The flatboat rocked violently, toppling its passengers and taking water. Ballard was thrown into the river, and Marsh watched him surface, shout, and start swimming. Gill threw him a line, Ballard caught it and crawled back, hand over hand, to the pitching flatboat.

"Make a log entry, DeWayne. 'Collision with flatboat in channel narrowly averted by skillful maneuvering of the *Otter.*' "

"Write it yourself," DeWayne retorted.

nineteen

Skye picked himself up from the slimy floorboards, found his top hat, and stuffed it over his stringy hair. Murky water sloshed about, floating debris with it. His britches were soaked on one side.

He checked Victoria. She was sitting with splayed legs, her skirts in a pool of filthy water, a sober expression on her features. He offered his big rough hand and helped her up. Water dripped from her fringed buckskins. No Name peered at him inquisitively and with some vast resignation.

Gill was helping Shorty over the transom. Water was rivering from the helmsman's blue chambray shirt, and it plastered his dark hair to his skull. With a grunt, Shorty landed in the slop, cursing violently, fulminating great oaths against the pilot, helmsman, captain, company, and all steamboats in general.

Gill was all right, smiling thinly, and taking stock of the flatboat. But Lame Deer was not. She crouched before the crude cabin, her whimpering children clinging to her, worry glazing her warm brown eyes.

"The river devils have reached up from under the water to pull us to them," she whispered. "We ride on top of the dead, over the waters that want to pull us under and hold us down. Ahhh . . ."

Victoria reached the woman and began jabbering in some sort of Indian lingua franca, but Lame Deer only nodded, her face grave, and her gaze trailing the steamboat as it diminished far ahead and finally swept around a bight. The children remained stonily silent, as most Indian children did in a crisis.

Gill unbuttoned his soaked shirt and wrung it, his grin returning as he surveyed the vessel.

"Close one," he said.

"You think the pilot didn't see us?" Skye asked.

"Not a chance of that. You ever been in a pilothouse? You see the whole layout."

"It was deliberate?"

"Couldn't have been other; channel's two hundred yards wide here." Red squinted at him as he pulled the soaked shirt back on. "He got something against you?"

"Not this big a something. Not the sort of something that would overturn a mackinaw."

"Marsh sure had something against someone, brushing us like that. What do you suppose he meant by that?"

"Warning," Shorty Ballard said, getting a grip on his tiller and steering the boat back into the channel where the current would be fastest.

"Who's he warning?" Red asked.

No one could answer that.

Skye thought he saw a wary look pass between Red Gill and Shorty, but he couldn't fathom what was inspiring their caution. It puzzled him. Why would Marsh do that? The man didn't want Indians on his boat, but that hardly explained it.

Lame Deer lifted her soaked children onto the dry and sun-warmed planks of the cargo box, and there the two little ones rested solemnly while the sun pummeled moisture from their clothes.

Gill found a collapsible leather bucket and motioned everyone to his front corner of the flatboat so he could scoop up the filthy water accumulating there. He couldn't get much at a time, and Skye thought the sun would evaporate it faster than Gill could dip it out, but Gill kept working.

Even though the sun shone brightly, a cloud hung over the boat. What had been a cheerful start down the river had deteriorated into silence and caution and fear. The bravado wasn't working; Lame Deer's fear was palpable, a tense terror that contrasted sharply with the quiet certitude and courage that had brought her so far from her home and tribe.

Gill quit dipping and sat down. "If Marsh's got something against you 'uns, me and Shorty want to know about it. This here's dangerous country. Why'd he put you off his boat?"

The question was aimed at Skye.

"He put us off after we tried to help the Cheyenne lady," Skye said. "We arrived at Fort Pierre, and without a by-your-leave had his mate tote the woman's gear from the cabin and put her and her nags off. She'd paid in furs for passage to St. Louis, and Victoria, she got her dander up and we went to talk to him about it. I was thrown out of the pilothouse, and they put us off too."

Red shook his head. "He's an ornery sonofabitch, but that don't make sense."

Skye didn't argue the point. He didn't like being on any boat, helpless, under the control of others. He didn't like being on the riverboat, and didn't much care for the trip on the flatboat either, at the mercy of a pair of men he didn't know and whom he suspected of being less than forthright.

Skye figured maybe it was his turn. "What did you say you do for a living, mate?"

"Rivermen."

"Where'd this flatboat come from?"

"They built it at Fort Pierre, up in their yard north of the post."

"How'd you get it?"

Gill paused, for the first time growing wary. He shrugged. "Deal we did with the company."

"And how did you get up here from St. Louis?"

Gill grinned. "Forget it, Skye."

"Whose furs are these in the box?"

"Them robes and pelts are ours, lock, stock and barrel."

Gill turned away. Shorty was frowning. Skye had the distinct feeling a lot was left unsaid.

Skye tried another tack. "I think you'd better report this to General Clark, if that's the man to talk to. Someone should be pulling that pilot's license. That was a deliberate act, I think."

"Aw, Skye, it wasn't nothing. Just forget it."

"It's Mister Skye, mate. And it's not something to forget. You'd better report it. Or I will."

Red shrugged, and once again Skye sensed there were things unspoken.

"You just mind your business, Skye," Shorty growled from the stern.

Between the warm sun and the labor of crew and passengers, the flatboat dried out. Gill and Skye spent the next hour putting gear in order, coiling hempen ropes, checking the cargo box for leakage, mopping river bilge out of the boat. Shorty steered in the exact center of the channel, swearing profusely, a low monotone of cussing that Skye found inventive and odd. The women vanished into the cabin, and when they emerged Lame Deer was wearing a dry skirt and Victoria's buckskins had been wrung out and smoothed.

Skye wandered to the prow, peered into the water, and tried to put it all together, but he only ran into mysteries. Something more than Marsh's ugly temper and powerful racial antagonisms had caused him to put the Cheyenne family off his boat; and the Skyes too. What was it? And what was this outfit's real business? Why were Red and Shorty so secretive?

He discovered a heavy stubble of beard on his face, dug a straight-edge out of his kit, lathered with a sliver of soap, and scraped carefully. He lacked a looking glass, except the rippling surface of the river, but his fingers served to tell him what surfaces had been missed. Victoria loved his smooth cheeks and she grew testy about his bristly facial hair. The little Cheyenne children, Singing Rain and Echo, as he called the boy, watched solemnly.

"Bet you watched your father shave," Skye said.

The boy stared, and turned away.

The boat creaked with every swell, but Lame Deer never quite accepted the groaning, and he saw her studying the planks, the oakum calking, the crudely joined corners, doweled together for the want of screws or nails. Often they were a hundred yards from a bank; a hard swim in swift cold water, especially when dragged down by doeskin clothing.

They made another twenty miles that day and camped on a gravelly bar stretching out from an ash grove. Skye wished he had a horse to reconnoiter the country; they were vulnerable not only to predatory war and hunting parties, but also to bears, migrating buffalo herds, and wolves. He cradled his mountain rifle in the crook of his arm and hiked in his soaked moccasins across a grassy flat and up a ravine until he topped the bluff guarding the valley, and saw only a silent plain, undulating westward toward the sunset, shrouding its secrets. No Name patrolled before him, acknowledging only that he and Skye were bound by Fate, but not by affection. No Name lived by his inner lights, which Skye had never fathomed or changed.

Skye felt incredibly lonely there, so far from other mortals. Loneliness was nothing new; he had been lonely ever since the moment a press gang had hauled him off the London Dock and stuffed him into a warship. He had been thirteen years old, and never saw his family again.

This vast plain reminded him of the sea; desolate, hollow,

but grand and ever-changing too. He hoped he might hear coyotes this night; he wanted life around him. He knew there would be deer and antelope and all manner of small creatures patrolling the riverbanks this evening, and maybe he would make meat. But in this twilight he felt not life, but a deadness, a forsakenness in this solemn and flat land without landmarks. He preferred the mountains.

He found Victoria and Lame Deer boiling cornmeal. They would have corn mush again, tasteless and dull but filling. It satisfied the belly, but not the tongue.

Shorty and Gill insisted that people sleep on the flatboat at night, rather than on dry land, and maybe there was reason in it, Skye thought. When everyone had eaten from the mess tins, and done their ablutions in the brush, Gill herded them back aboard, and he and Shorty maneuvered the boat twenty or thirty feet offshore, and set anchors. Skye slept on a buffalo robe, wishing for soil which he could sculpt into a decent bed. The planks of the flatboat were unyielding. The bunks in the cabin were occupied by the women and children, luckier than he by virtue of sex and age.

But the starry night passed, and even before dawn Shorty was stirring, and soon Red was too. They pulled anchor as soon as Shorty could see to navigate, and drifted through another humdrum morning, watching the plains march by, the bluffs change from tan to orange to white, the tributary creeks tumble into the Missouri, and the fishing birds wheel through the sky, dive for minnows, shrill their warnings, and flap away from carrion.

Then, midday, they spotted the *Otter*. She lay crosswise of the channel, her deck tilted sharply, her chimneys askance and emitting no smoke.

"Will ya look at that," Red said. "She's run aground."

"Hit a bar," Shorty said, squinting.

"Hit a bar and it twisted her around so that bar runs along

her keel, looks like," Red said. "They're gonna need some lighters to clear that hold and float her over."

That's when the six-pounder cracked, a puff of white smoke ballooning from its barrel even before the sound reached Skye's ears.

twenty

Shorty Ballard ignored the shot and steered the flatboat straight ahead on a trajectory that wouldn't come within a hundred yards of the marooned riverboat. Crewmen stood on the sloping boiler deck, but other people, passengers mostly, had splashed across a gravelly shallows to the left bank and stood on a knoll.

Skye didn't like it. "He means for you to stop and render assistance," he said.

"After what he done?" Shorty's bellicose retort was intended to settle the matter instantly.

"You'll see your license pulled," Skye retorted. Failure to render assistance was a grave matter.

Red Gill grinned, and motioned to Ballard.

"The hell I will!" Ballard spat. Skye sympathized. The wake of the riverboat had pitched Shorty into the Missouri and endangered his life. But Skye could see a deck crew charging the cannon, and this time with more than just powder. He nodded to Victoria, and both of them lay flat on the warm boards, as close to the plank side of the hull as they could. Lame Deer vanished inside the cabin, herding her children with her.

Marsh's voice, amplified by a megaphone, boiled across the water. "Gill and Ballard, bring that flatboat in at once!"

"Go to hell," Ballard yelled.

Time slid by, while the flatboat approached the point where it would pass the grounded steamer.

"Bring her here!" Marsh bellowed. "Or face the music."

Shorty bristled. "Go to hell, Marsh."

The response this time was another crack of the cannon. Skye watched someone with a fusee dip it to the touch hole. Skye ducked and covered his head, knocking off his topper in the process. The ball crossed the bow and hit water near the right bank. Skye slid his head over the gunnel and stared. A crew was frantically recharging the piece.

"Gill, pull over," Marsh bawled. "Next time we won't miss."

Red crawled back to Shorty. "Give me the tiller," he said.

"Hell I will. They won't shoot a hole in a boat they need."

Skye lifted his head. "It will be cannister, and it'll clean you right out of the boat."

"Then I'll lie on the planks and let this sonofabitch drift by; it's in the current anyway."

They were opposite the riverboat now, and Skye heard the snap of small arms, and felt lead pop into the planks. He'd had it with this pair. They were up to no good. He gathered himself, crawled aft under cover, and then sprang at Shorty, catching him unprepared. He heard the pop of rifle fire, and then he landed on Shorty, ripping him loose from the tiller and landing on him in one swift motion.

Red dodged sideways, not wanting a part of this, but Skye spotted a drawn Arkansas Toothpick in his hand. The blow knocked the air out of Shorty, who gulped for breath, gasping on the floorboards. Skye leapt for the tiller and stood up, braving the pistols of crewmen, and swung it hard toward the left bank. The flatboat had already passed the *Otter*. For a terrible moment the bore of the six-pounder followed him as the crew swung it, but then they saw the flatboat veer sharply, its skewing wake showing them the sudden turn.

Shorty recovered but chose not to fight. Red, his furious

gaze darting from Skye to the riverboat, crouched ready for action. And then he did an odd thing: He dug into a tackle box at the prow, and with his back to the riverboat, dropped his jug of Kentuck overboard.

Skye mourned, but at last had an inkling of the business this partnership was in.

He studied the riverboat, watching the six-pounder swivel in his direction; watching Marsh up on the hurricane deck watching him; watching the crew watching him. Everyone on that steamer had seen the whole business.

Red slid his Green River knife into its sheath, and grinned.

Shorty started cussing again, a nonstop, profane damning of everyone's ancestors, parents, animals, connections, children, grandchildren, businesses, profits, and anything else that caught his wrath. Victoria was so fascinated that she crouched beside Shorty, blotting up locutions for future use.

"Goddam," she said, her face wreathed in joy.

"Skye, run that flatboat into the bank there," Marsh bawled.

"It's Mister Skye, mate."

The captain looked even more choleric than usual. Behind him on the hurricane deck stood the helmsman, hefting a rifle.

A party of boatmen had stepped off the riverboat and advanced down a spit of gravel to the point where Skye was steering the flatboat, and in moments they caught the lines that Red pitched to them. Red eyed Skye, his gaze so odd, so twisted, that Skye couldn't fathom what was going through the man's head.

Shorty oozed sheer hate, and Skye knew he had made an enemy, and when this pair got their flatboat back, Skye and Victoria and the Cheyennes would not be aboard.

The flatboat bumped gravel, but the crew pulled it upstream to the looming riverboat. Skye stepped to land, and helped Victoria. The riverboat rode on a sandbar, canted prow and starboard down, stern and port side up, entirely in water.

The gangway provided a bridge to a gravelly driftwood-littered island, one of many separated by shallow flowage of the river, which formed a huge oxbow there. Even when unloaded, it would be a hell of a thing to float that ship and ease it out to the current in an area of braided channels.

The starboard paddle wheel had shattered.

"Skye, why didn't you stop as directed?" Marsh bellowed.

Skye ignored him. Marsh knew perfectly well who had stopped the flatboat to render aid, so there was nothing to say, not one damned word.

"Trenholm, examine that flatboat and bring me a manifest."

The mate and two crewmen boarded, probed the packs of robes in the cargo box, poked around in the cabin, and emerged.

"No manifest," Trenholm said to the man above.

"Then what's in there?"

"Nineteen bales of robes and pelts and some loose furs."

"Whose pelts?" That question was directed at Red Gill.

"Reckon they're ours."

"We'll see. If you don't have papers, they're contraband."

"Contraband hell!" Shorty yelled.

"We'll take this to Gen'ral Clark," Gill said.

Marsh laughed. "You will, eh? Get those packs out of there and tow that flatboat around to midships and tie up. Get busy. We're losing time."

Skye watched, wondering whether Gill and Ballard would end up with their buffalo hides when they got their vessel back. For that matter, he wondered whether he and Victoria would be stranded two or three hundred miles from anywhere.

"You can't do this," Gill said hotly.

"Get busy," Marsh yelled.

Crewmen from the riverboat swarmed over the flatboat, hoisting the hundred-pound packs out of the cargo box and onto gravel. Lame Deer drew her children away, hurried them across wet rock and settled them at a distance on a gravelly spit. Skye knew she didn't understand any of this and was finding safety in distance.

That afternoon sweating boatmen hoisted pack after pack of furs out of the hold of the *Otter* and into the flatboat, and then poled the flatboat to a point just downstream where the cargo could be unloaded on dry ground. There, the furs could be reloaded onto the flatboat and lightered back to the steamer after it had floated over the sandbar.

The riverboat didn't budge. The pressure of the current pressed it to the bar. Evening came, and still the boat didn't float free. Crewmen built bonfires downwind, and continued to lift cargo out of the hold through the twilight and into darkness, while Marsh paced his hurricane deck furiously, emanating rage but saying nothing.

Ballard and Gill, helpless against this armed commandeering of their boat, glared at Skye, who was the author of their misfortune, and Skye figured he and Victoria would be walking to St. Louis when all this was over. Ballard cussed nonstop, softly, profanely, witheringly, his wrath washing over Marsh, Trenholm, every deckman in sight, as well as Skye and Victoria. Skye wasn't worried about him: a man venting his spleen in such fashion was less dangerous than one bottling it up, like Red Gill, whose silent assessing gaze hid calculations and bitterness.

His stomach told him it was time for some good biscuits and corn, but no one started a meal. Marsh paced relentlessly; his mate, Trenholm, oversaw the operation, the steersman stood at the pilothouse, rifle in hand, and the crew worked silently, saying nothing about food or rest under the palpable rage of the master.

Then, when the flatboat was poled away with yet another mound of peltries, the boat ground against gravel once, groaned, creaked, and floated over, gradually righting itself. The crew anchored just below the bar but well away from shore, just downstream from the heaped cargo on the gravel.

At last Marsh halted for a meal. A cool night wind whipped the light of the bonfires. He and Trenholm and young Bonfils descended to the gravel spit to examine the shattered right paddle wheel along with his carpenter and blacksmith. Skye quietly splashed across a flowage and joined them. In the dim light of a distant bonfire, and the ineffectual light of a bird's-eye lantern, Skye thought he saw half a dozen shattered paddles, each of which would need to be unbolted from the wheel and replaced.

Marsh fumed. "Get busy. I want this repaired by daylight," he snapped at his carpenter.

The man started to protest, and then held his peace.

Marsh noticed Skye. "What are you doing here?"

"Looking."

"Go back with the others. I'll deal with you later."

Skye lifted his battered top hat. "Deal with us?"

"I'm busy. Don't get in my way."

"We'd like to get some of our food out of the cabin of the flatboat. We have hungry children to feed."

"Skye, get the hell out of here."

Bonfils laughed. "You're out of luck. It's the company you keep. Those gents are smugglers. Maybe you are too."

So that was it. Skye wasn't in a mood to argue with the master or his ham-fisted mate or the scion of the company.

He splashed across the shallows again, headed straight to the flatboat which was riding the water loaded with the last of the ship's cargo.

He walked up a plank, boarded, headed aft to the cabin, all without protest from the deckmen. No one stopped him. Inside, he opened a food box, pulled out a sack of cornmeal, found a kettle, a firesteel, and other items, and returned to shore. An hour later Victoria and Lame Deer fed cornmeal mush to the children, and then the rest.

Lame Deer sang, this time in her own reedy tongue, smoothing the hair of her children, her voice soft and melodic, the cursing of the nearby rivermen contrapuntal. The children nestled, and she held them close, blanketing them with her courage as the darkness enveloped them all.

Skye sat in the dark, his belly full of fried corn mush, wondering whether to make his fate or wait for it.

twenty-one

low growl from No Name awakened Skye. He peered about, disoriented, a thick ground fog obscuring everything in the gray predawn light. He could not remember where he was; then the hard gravel he was sleeping on reminded him. He was on a spit of land on the left bank of an oxbow of the Missouri River, an island of sorts but only for the moment. When the river dropped another few inches, it would be shoreline.

He had learned to respect No Name's warnings. The dog was an ally rather than a pet, an independent, cantankerous, wily peer who made common cause with Skye and Victoria, but whose tail rarely wagged, and whose affection was fleeting and reserved. But the very qualities that had made No Name a master of survival had been offered to Skye; and now the dog was softly warning his human companion of trouble.

Skye glanced about. He and Victoria had spread their robes beside some red willow brush, next to a stack of driftwood. She did not stir. And yet he felt a moving presence in that camp. He remembered that the Cheyenne woman and her two children were closer to the shore, nestled in the roots of a cottonwood. He didn't know where Gill and Ballard were and didn't care. The flatboat bobbed nearby, a gray blur, with some of Marsh's crew aboard. Just downstream, on the other side of the gravel bar, floated the *Otter* in shallow water. The ship was obscured by fog. The noise of repair had ceased in the middle of the night, either because Marsh called a halt or the carpenter and his mates had finished installing new paddles.

Skye lay quietly on his back, listening closely, seeing nothing but sensing trouble. He pulled back his robe, collected his mountain rifle, pulled his powderhorn over his neck, and then lifted his hightop moccasins over his feet and laced them. He nudged Victoria, who sat up in one lithe motion, glanced about, and silently collected her bow and quiver.

The dog was pointing toward the mountain of fur bales stored on the gravelly spit, and Skye thought perhaps the rank smell of the furs and uncured hides had drawn a predator, maybe even a bear. He sensed but didn't hear motion around the pile.

Then he saw the shapes of moving men, walking single file, filtering through the foggy dawn, so close he thought surely he and Victoria would be discovered. *Indians.* That much he knew. Now there were more, scores of them peering and poking, examining the flatboat without boarding it, and vanishing in the fog downstream, where the riverboat rode the night on tethers tied to trees.

Many Indians. Victoria was cussing softly. "Lakota," she whispered. "Goddam war party. Painted up."

He couldn't fathom how she knew, but Indians could recognize one another far better than whites.

Painted for war. But probably not against whites. The Teton or Lakota Sioux as well as the Dakota Sioux had been at peace with the traders for years.

He couldn't put numbers to this crowd, but there were plenty of Sioux around, poking, probing, reconnoitering, maybe looking for easy plunder. They would find it. Marsh had posted no pickets and had assumed he would be safe enough in this friendly country. Not that Marsh was equipped to fight a war. He knew there were but five or six rifles aboard, and maybe a few pistols, and even those weapons were largely owned by passengers, mostly engagés returning to St. Louis. There was the six-pounder mounted on the foredeck, maybe still loaded—and probably useless. Anyone trying to aim or arm it would be mowed down in a hail of arrows.

Skye sighed, wanting to act. For much of this trip he had been under the command of others, his own will counting for nothing. His fate was not in his own hands. He was at the mercy of the company, and its factors in the posts, and then its riverboat captain and his crew, and was finally in the hands of the operators of a flatboat; men apparently engaged in some sort of illegal traffic.

He had, moreover, taken upon himself the protection of a Cheyenne woman and her children. So there he was, unable to give a command and see it followed, as he had when he was leading a trapping brigade. Quite the reverse: here he was expected to obey instantly. Even Gill and Ballard expected it. Ever since he had landed in North America, he had controlled his destiny; and now he was not in command, either of himself or others.

He had no friends among Marsh or his officers; and no friends on the flatboat either, not after tackling Shorty Ballard and seizing the tiller and steering the flatboat toward the *Otter*.

He watched more shadowy figures patrol the site as the light quickened noticeably. At any moment, these Sioux would be discovered and all hell would break loose. And yet the Sioux had not engaged in bloodletting. Their tomahawks and knives rested in their sheaths. They probably had not yet figured out what this camp was about, and what they might do without resistance if they chose.

Skye supposed the best bet for his people would be the flatboat, which could be unloosed quickly and supply them with the safety of water as well as the drift of a current. He nodded toward it, and Victoria nodded back.

Barely forty feet away, obscured by the fog, a knot of warriors huddled, whispering furiously, plainly at odds, confused, and wary. There was traffic now, warriors walking back and forth, splashing across the gravelly shallows between this meandering spit of gravel and the one lower down, where the riverboat bobbed on the quiet river.

Victoria slipped back into the brush and disappeared, and Skye knew she was awakening the Cheyenne woman and maybe reconnoitering.

Skye had a decision to make and only moments to make it. He knew somehow it was portentous, and the wrong move could cost him his life, and maybe Victoria's too. He could shepherd Victoria and the Cheyennes out of the area before the daylight pierced the veil of fog, using the braided gravelly islands as their escape route. Or he could try to save the furs and boat and ultimately, Pierre Chouteau's company. Almost half of the annual returns were stacked there on the gravel. A fortune by any measure. He could try to keep hotheads, including Bonfils, from starting a fight they would only lose. These warriors, after all, had yet to lift a war axe, fire an arrow, or lance a sleeping boatman.

He knew what he had to do, and finished dressing, clamping his black beaver topper to his head. Then he whistled, and then he called.

"Gents, come visit me; I'm right here, plain sight if you move a little closer. Welcome, Lakota!"

His voice seemed muted in the choking fog; had anyone heard?

"Hey, Lakota! Dakota! Here I am!"

Now at last shadowy shapes materialized, and in moments he found himself surrounded by warriors, eight, ten, fifteen, armed and dangerous. They were Sioux all right; tall, sinewy, light-skinned, wearing war garb, which is to say, very little but paint. Some wore eagle feathers in their hair; war honors. Others wore medicine bundles or amulets suspended from their necks. Most wore summer moccasins. They were vermillioned and ochered, in chevrons, stripes, handprints, and mystical designs.

Skye felt the prickle he always felt when he considered how easily an arrow could pierce him. But he lifted his hands and made the peace sign, the brother sign, the friend sign. They stared.

He identified himself with the sky sign, and some recognition filled their faces. His name had come to mean something among the western tribes. He had fought for Victoria's people, the Crow.

Finally a headman of some sort emerged from the thick fog, and stared at Skye. This one was a long-nosed giant, a foot taller than Skye, built like a bear.

"Who you?"

That was English. The chief had been around a trading post.

"I am Mister Skye. My wife and I and others are assisting the captain of that fireboat. He is making repairs."

The words didn't register. This one knew all too few.

So Skye told him again, simple words, many signs.

"What will you give us?"

Ah, there it was.

"Gather your warriors here and I will give you food and a gift."

He wasn't sure what sort of gift. The headman weighed all that, eating up time.

"Be quick about it," Skye said. "They will shoot you if they see you." If those aboard the riverboat weren't all dead.

He heard some of the crew that had spent the night on the flatboat talking. The daylight was intensifying. He heard a scuffle, some grunts, and then the boatmen, along with Gill and Ballard, appeared, prisoners of still more Sioux. They looked frightened but knew enough to shut up, their gaze fixed on Skye, who stood in the center of a mob of fifty warriors.

"Who are you?" Skye asked the headman.

"Bull Calf, a war leader of the Sans Arcs, as we are called by the white men. We are going to kill the lying Pawnee, and bring back slaves and many horses."

Bull Calf was a noted war leader, a force to be reckoned with. "How many are you?" Skye asked.

"We are many. Ten times the fingers of my hands."

Skye gambled. "You will need to cross the Big River to go to the Pawnee."

"Yes. That is why we are here; this is a good place. But we found you and the fireboat."

Skye calculated swiftly. "We will give you a gift. We will take you and your ponies on the fireboat across the Big River. Then you will be strong and fresh. If the fireboat is not fixed, we will take you across the Big River in that flatboat." He pointed. "A few at a time. Then you can kill the Pawnee."

Bull Calf translated for his warriors, who listened solemnly, craning their necks to see Marsh's boat slowly emerge from the fog in the morning sun. He saw curiosity, fear, anger, and awe on their faces. Most had never even seen such a boat, much less ridden on one. And here was a chance to cross the Big River without getting wet or losing horses or endangering themselves.

Bull Calf nodded.

But even as he nodded, he saw Bonfils and Marsh's boatmen on the fog-shrouded riverboat swing their six-pounder around until its muzzle was a black hole facing this throng.

twenty-two

Skye yelled. The Sans Arcs fled, stumbling over one another to escape the bore of that six-pounder on the hurricane deck thirty yards distant.

Dawn light glinted on the brass barrel. Bonfils, wielding a punk, jammed it into the touchhole. Smoke erupted. Skye felt grape blow the top hat off his head, sear his ribs, smash into his thigh. Felt himself punched backward, flying through air.

A sharp boom reached his ears as he fell. He heard screams; saw warriors bloom red; saw Ballard fly backward and tumble to earth; heard a child's sob and then his pain deafened him and he heard nothing but the roaring of his pulse.

He heard, from some vast distance, the roar of the sixpounder again; horses splashing across the gravelly flowages; the ululating howls of the Indians; the crack of rifles and carbines, and again, the bark of the cannon. He writhed on the ground.

Victoria raced up to him, weeping and cursing.

"Where, where, dammit?"

Skye ran his hand along his ribs, and found blood there and seared flesh, and hurt that lanced him and stopped his breathing. He tried to suck air but raw pain stopped his lungs. His shoulder hurt viciously and shot pain along his arm, numbing his hand. His right thigh stung—pounding, throbbing, relentless pain shot up his leg and into his belly. Nausea engulfed him; he wanted to puke, but couldn't move his lungs. Dizziness engulfed him.

He gasped for air; wheezed and sucked, but the pain paralyzed his diaphragm. Something had shattered ribs and torn him up. He felt his bones click and scrape when he moved. He felt himself whirl out of consciousness, and fought his way back. Stay awake. Blackness hovered. Sticky blood soaked his shirt, hot, red blood. His bad arm stopped working. He needed sweet air, and his lungs were quitting.

"Goddam, goddamn," she sobbed.

"Can't breathe."

Skye drifted in and out of the world. Once, when vomit rose in his throat, he tried to puke, but he couldn't. It settled down his gullet, sour and obscene.

Sobbing and fierce, Victoria poulticed the wounds, all the while giving Skye a running account of the battle. The Sans

Arcs fled to the left bluff, carrying three or four wounded and maybe some dead. A few of them formed a rear guard, shooting their carbines at the riverboat crew on the hurricane deck.

He heard shouts, howls, sobs, and anger. He tried to sit up, and fell back, with Victoria snapping at him to lie still. He wanted to orient himself. His pain had melded into rage at Bonfils, who had destroyed a peaceful parley, wounded him and others, and made enemies of the Sans Arcs and other Sioux.

He lay defeated, sick, nauseous, wondering if he was dying, feeling the pain stab in and out of his body with each breath. Then he turned his head and saw Ballard, lying still, with a blue hole in his forehead. Gill was sitting beside his partner, dazed, silent, and bitter.

Painfully, Skye rolled his gaze toward the sobbing he heard behind him, in the cottonwoods. There, Lame Deer sat, weeping, the still form of her son, Sound Comes Back After Shouting, in her lap, while Singing Rain clung to her mother.

Victoria was weeping.

The grapeshot, fired at that distance, had spread into a broad pattern, scything down every living thing in a twenty-yard swath, including a Cheyenne child.

"He dead?" Skye gasped.

"Through the neck."

Skye sagged into the earth, desolated, hot tears collecting in his weathered face. Two dead. Others injured. He felt too nauseous and weak to do anything but lie quietly and listen to the ebbing sounds of flight. Soon, all he heard was flowing water, and all he felt was pain and the warmth of the sun.

Victoria was working on him, shooting pain through him as she dabbed at the rib wound.

"Stop it," Skye muttered, but she didn't. "Can't breathe . . ."

A shadow crossed his face, and he looked up to find Marsh and Trenholm and Bonfils staring down at him.

"You alive, Skye?" Marsh asked.

Stupid question. Skye glared.

"This is a mess," Marsh said. "I don't know what happened. You're welcome to ship's stores. We've some morphia."

"Go away," Victoria snarled.

Gill rose, faced Bonfils. "You killed Shorty," he said in a low and deadly voice.

Marsh stared at Bonfils.

"Didn't know you were in that mob of thieving redskins," Bonfils said.

Skye struggled to focus on Bonfils. "They weren't thieving."

"They were painted up. I saw them from my cabin; painted up, carrying bows and tomahawks, creeping through the fog, getting ready to jump the *Otter*, steal every pack of fur sitting there on that spit."

Skye listened quietly, too sick to talk, but Red Gill wasn't silent.

"Goddammit, Mister Skye had them quieted down. They were going after Pawnee, and planned to cross the river here and ran into us. He offered them a ride across, and their chief, Bull Calf, agreed. It was all settled, peaceful."

"A ride on my boat?" That was Marsh's voice, waxing indignant.

"It or the flatboat," Skye mumbled.

"What gave you the right to tell them that? I wouldn't have a bunch of filthy warriors and their crowbait horses on my boat. It was a trick. Once aboard, they'd loot it and kill us all."

Skye didn't argue. Blackness crept through him.

"Marsh, they was just looking for a ride and maybe a meal and maybe even a trade or two," Gill said. "Now, I'm going to St. Louis, and I'm gonna visit Gen'ral Clark, and he's going to hear the whole story, and I'm going to blame Bonfils here, you can damn well count on it."

Marsh snarled something.

Bonfils began to snap, like a crackling fire. "I drove off marauders. I spotted them in the fog, sneaking up. I saved the company's furs. And that's how Clark and the company will see it. . . ." Bonfils sounded excited, his voice harsh and pitched. Skye felt his wounds throbbing.

"You killed that little boy. Simon MacLees's boy," Skye said. "And MacLees is going to hear about it, I promise you that."

Marsh and Trenholm and Bonfils stared at the distant Cheyenne woman, registering her grief, and the dead child in her lap for the first time.

"Accident of war, couldn't be helped," Marsh said. "Just an incident. I'm sorry about it. Sorry about Ballard, there."

"An incident?" Skye struggled to sit up, wrath driving him, struggled to stand. It was foolishness. Pain and nausea engulfed him. Dizzily, he tumbled back to the gravelly ground, gasping for air, willing his lungs to pump.

Boatmen from the *Otter* had gathered around, though a few patrolled the area, rifles in hand.

"Start loading those bales," Marsh snapped. "We'll sail as soon as we have our cargo stored." He turned to several of them. "Gather driftwood. There's plenty here."

"Give me my flatboat back," Gill said.

Marsh laughed shortly. "You're a smuggler and you'd just better get used to what we'll do to you."

Gill cussed helplessly.

"At least, bury Ballard," Skye said.

"You can manage. We don't have time," Marsh said.

Skye struggled against the blackness engulfing him, and when he opened his eyes again he peered up at the confident-looking Bonfils, Marsh's hero of the day. "Look for me," Skye said, swallowing back his vomit.

Bonfils smiled broadly and tipped his hat.

The rest of that morning passed in a haze of pain and confusion, but he knew the boatmen were ferrying bales of furs back to the steamboat and loading them, using Gill's flatboat.

He knew they were confiscating Gill's bales because Gill was raging at them, and they were holding him at gunpoint.

He knew that poor Ballard lay in the sun, unburied and unmourned, and that the bereaved Cheyenne woman had retreated into the willow brush with her dead boy, to be alone with her grief and out of sight of the authors of her sorrows. He heard her singing; a low, monotonous, strident wail unlike the sweetness he had heard earlier.

He knew that Victoria hovered over him, slid water into him, put compresses and plasters on him to cool the mounting fevers. He felt her tears fall wetly on his cheeks, and felt the gentle touch of her fingers, sending love, willing him to heal, comforting him. He felt himself being rolled onto a softer robe so the gravel would not stab his back.

He smelled woodsmoke, and knew the firemen were building up steam. That meant that the paddles had been repaired and the steamboat was being readied to travel. He knew that Bonfils was parading about, the company-certified hero of the hour, the man who had saved the *Otter* and all its precious cargo, not to mention the entire crew.

He knew that three of those balls in the cannister shot by Bonfils hit him; others had butchered a child, murdered a St. Louis frontiersman, and wounded or killed several Sans Arcs.

Marsh pulled out mid-morning. Skye heard the snap of steam exiting the escapement, and heard the rumble of the wheels and the splash of the paddles as they thrashed the river. Then they were gone.

He saw a blue heaven above him, and magpies flicking over him, and crows sailing the breezes. He heard the soft lap of the river. He moved and felt his ribs scrape against cartilage, and felt Victoria's tight bandage. He coughed, shooting wild pain through his torso, and then sucked air desperately. The poultice comforted him.

It was very quiet, save for the angry muttering of Red Gill. Skye turned, and could see Gill poking around in the flatboat.

At least Marsh had returned it, raped and empty, to its owner. It rested just off the gravel spit, moored fore and after by hempen hawsers to the willows.

Gill approached him after a while, squatting down.

"How you doing?" he asked.

"I'll live."

"I can't hardly navigate without another man. You up to it?"

"Victoria can help you."

Gill looked about to say something, but held his peace. "You ain't up to it."

"Soon," Skye said.

"I got to bury Shorty."

"You might offer to help Lame Deer first."

"Bury a redskin?"

"She will wrap the child in a robe, put it in a tree, and offer it to the sun."

Gill pondered that. "Maybe I should do that with Shorty. I don't hardly know how to bury him around here, on gravel, a foot above the river."

Skye nodded, feeling delirium wash through him. He hoped it would be a long time before he was carried to the flatboat. He hoped the gentle rocking of the flatboat wouldn't make him any more nauseous than he was.

Victoria had vanished and he knew she was consoling the Cheyenne woman, the pair of them just as far from white men as they could get on that gravelly island.

He wondered what MacLees would think upon hearing the news that Bonfils had killed his boy. Maybe MacLees wouldn't care. Maybe Marsh and Bonfils wouldn't say anything. Maybe the log of the *Otter* would show nothing, nothing at all . . . Maybe Marsh and minions would spread their own carefully wrought version among the powerful. At any rate, the steamer would reach St. Louis weeks before the flatboat did—if Gill managed to reach St. Louis at all.

Skye pondered that, and amended it: if he and Victoria

and Gill and Lame Deer and Singing Rain ever reached St. Louis at all, and were allowed to see the general, or were welcomed into the offices of Pierre Chouteau. There were too many ifs and ors.

twenty-three

The river glistened; nothing stirred. The sun beat mercilessly upon that place where so recently the horrors of war had carmined the gravel with blood.

Victoria's heart lay heavily within her, but she pushed aside her desolation to help those in need; her man, Skye, gasping and nauseous; and Lame Deer, the stoic mother, staring helplessly at the body of her son, killed by a thoughtless act of fear by that Creole sonofabitch.

She brought cold water to Skye, who sipped it gratefully. He didn't want much; only to be left alone. But he was lying in full sun.

"We got to get you into the cabin," she said.

"Leave me."

She ignored him, and found Red angrily putting the flatboat in order, his own cursing a match for Shorty's. He had dragged Shorty aboard and wrapped him in an old blanket.

"Thieves! Killers! Wait 'til I tell Chouteau!"

"Ah, Mister Gill, I need your help."

He stared at her and then nodded.

"I got to get Skye into the cabin. Out of the sun or he maybe die."

"He's too shot to move."

"We carry him together in a robe."

"You?" He eyed her slim frame doubtfully.

She didn't reply but dug around in the cabin for a blanket, and waited for him.

Together they rolled Skye into it and half-dragged, half-carried him up the wobbling plank and into the flatboat. Skye groaned. She settled him on the bunk, checked his bloody bandages to see whether this passage had reopened the wounds, and then went back for his rifle and top hat. Tenderly, she settled his possessions beside him, his rifle within easy reach, just as it always was.

He reached up and clasped her hand in his. She saw tears in his eyes. His cold hand, weak as his grip was, spoke to her of profound love. She fought back the roar of anguish in her, and smiled. She would not let him see her own tears.

The shade of the cabin would protect him from Father Sun. She pressed her palm to his brow and found it fevered. Soon she would give him herb tea if she could find what she needed.

She found Red Gill slumped on the deck. "Now you got to help me with Lame Deer."

Red nodded morosely. She plucked up the small robe the boy had slept in and brought it, along with some thong.

Lame Deer sat silently in a private bower she had found, screened by red willow brush, a place to be alone with her grief. She stroked Singing Rain absently, calming the fretful child, but her spirit was far away, and Victoria thought her mind's eye was gazing upon her homeland, her Cheyenne people, the lodges of her kin.

"We send Sound Comes Back After Shouting to the place of the spirits now," she said gruffly.

Lame Deer stared, saying nothing.

Victoria motioned to Red. The child lay on the gravel, flies collecting around the fatal wound, a thin layer of browning blood covering the boy's neck.

She spread the small robe on the gravel, lifted the child

onto it, and pulled the robe over the boy. She lashed the bundle with thong, driving away the swarming flies, and nodded to Red.

She found some box elders flourishing on a slight rise, and a place where one might anchor some crosspieces to a low fork in one of the trees. It took her and Red Gill a while to complete the little scaffold, but at last she was satisfied. Here the Cheyenne boy would lie, under the rustling leaves, while his soul climbed the long trail.

She returned to Lame Deer's bower and tugged at the woman's hand while Red gathered the bundled body of the boy. That was the funeral procession: Red, carrying the bundle, Lame Deer and her daughter, and Victoria, her sharp quick gaze checking distant ridges for trouble even as she grieved.

Red lifted the bundle onto the scaffold, as if the boy weighed no more than a feather.

Lame Deer stood before the scaffold, her countenance solemn but composed.

She was plainly seeking English words, and then did speak.

"This was good child. MacLees, him and me, we make him one winter night, very cold, and then I see the owl float by, and so this is the owl prophesy. This I know long ago, that this good boy would not be alive for long. But I put that in my heart and kept it until now. It make me sad now.

"MacLees, he love this boy, want to make him a trader like himself. Now MacLees will be sad. This boy, he was going to be in white man's religion; big medicine, bigger than maybe Cheyenne medicine. This child, the one whose name is known, he walked with big steps, a little man so soon. He comes into the earth lodge and now he goes, and leaves an empty place inside of me. Where he goes, he will be a great one, with many honors."

She wept then, tears leaking from her warm brown eyes.

"MacLees, now he must be told. I go to Many Houses to tell him. He will do what he will do when he learns this."

What was Lame Deer saying?

Red was listening impatiently, some innate courtesy keeping him from returning to the flatboat. Victoria watched him, read him well. Hard man, good man, wild and reckless, not a man to live in Many Houses place but out where no elders and chiefs curbed him.

Lame Deer reached upward and placed something on the bundle.

"Turtle stone," she said to Victoria. "It says who he is to the spirits."

An amulet.

She led the way out of the grove, and into the blinding sunlight, with the subdued girl, Singing Rain, beside her, hobbling across the rough gravel.

Red and Victoria followed.

"Got to wait until Skye's up," Red said. "I can't handle a flatboat alone. Need a strong man up front with a pole, among other things."

"I will steer," Victoria said.

He considered it and shook his head.

"You steer, the Cheyenne and me, we pole or row or whatever you want, dammit," she said.

"You're too small."

"All right, sit here and starve!"

She had touched the sore point. The cornmeal wouldn't last long.

He grinned suddenly. "Can't get into a worse jackpot than I'm in now," he said. "But we got to hold a little service for Shorty first."

He headed for shore and began collecting the larger stones from the gravel banks, and these he carried aboard and placed next to Shorty's wrapped body. She fathomed his intent, and collected stones herself, but Lame Deer retreated to the front of the bobbing boat and settled on the planks.

When Red had collected enough stones, he opened the blanket and placed them alongside Shorty, who lay there open-mouthed and sightless, and then tied the blanket tight, using up all the thong.

Then, grunting under the heavy load, he lifted Shorty and slid his partner into the river, and stood, panting. The soft splash radiated outward and vanished in the flow. Somewhere, not far below, a mortal lay, perhaps tumbling slowly downstream. Victoria didn't like it; giving the body to the water demons, which were the worst spirits of all, as any Absaroka knew. But maybe white men were demonized by other things, from the sky.

Red stood at the side, panting, somber, upset.

"Don't know what to say, Shorty, so I'll say good-bye, and good luck wherever you are. I'm proud to know you, proud to ride the river with you, Shorty Ballard. I guess, well, I'm not good at prayers, so I'll just say, like the Spanish, *vaya con Dios.*"

Skye's muffled voice rose from the cabin. "I can lead you," he said.

"I'd be obliged."

"The Lord is my shepherd, I shall not want . . ."

Victoria listened to these familiar words, so different from the medicine of her people, but a great comfort to white men. Even to a smuggler like Red Gill, if that's what he was. She wasn't quite sure what Red Gill did and why it was considered so bad, or what else was wrong with him that the big chief of the riverboat would treat him with such contempt, and without even a moment's regret.

Skye finished reciting, his voice soft and gentle and barely audible in the afternoon quiet, and then Red thanked him and untied the front hawser from the bankside brush. He loosened the rear rope and scurried aboard as the current caught the flatboat and nudged it away. He yanked the plank into the boat and headed for the tiller. The flatboat, unburdened by cargo, floated high and skimmed into the river.

She watched the place of death and darkness fall behind.

"Where's No Name?" asked Skye from within the cabin.

Fear lanced her. She hastened around the flatboat.

"Stop. The dog is not here," she said to Red.

Red immediately pulled the tiller and the flatboat drifted toward shore. Even before it bumped the riverbank, she leapt out and began trotting back toward the place of death, swallowing back her fears.

She reached the flat and saw nothing.

"No Name," she cried. "Spirit Dog, where are you?"

She discovered only silence.

Maybe it wasn't so bad. No Name lived his own life. If he felt like it, he would keep up with the flatboat while hunting along the shore. But the more she tried to persuade herself of all this, the worse she felt.

She began a thorough examination of that brushy flat, visiting the places where Skye had fallen, Shorty had died, the little Cheyenne boy had breathed his last, and several Sans Arcs had either died or been gravely wounded. She saw nothing but blood on gravel.

Then, some distance back from the river, she spotted the familiar yellow, and pushed through thick canebrake to reach the dog.

No Name lay under brush, in a small hollow. He was very still.

"Aiee!" she whispered.

She crawled under the brush to the dog. It lay unmoving. A bloodless hole pierced its chest. She reached, frightened, to touch the dog, find breath, find life. But there was no life.

Bonfils's cannister had snuffed out yet another life.

She gathered the dog in her arms, and staggered to her feet, carrying a heavier load than she had ever known.

twenty-four

lexandre Bonfils stood in the prow of the *Otter*, congratulating himself. Had he not rescued this ship and all its crew? Had he not saved the entire cargo, half the company's annual returns, from the theft of savages? Had he not acted with speed and decisiveness? As a result of all this, had the company not halted smugglers and confiscated nineteen bales of pelts? And while it was unfortunate that some ruffians and savages got shot, he could scarcely have hoped for a better result.

The riverboat gathered its muscles and plowed downstream, leaving the savage squaws, Skye, and the smuggler to mend themselves, and maybe mend their ways if they had any sense. Bonfils doubted that Skye or any of the others would reach St. Louis now; in any case, if they did show up in a few weeks, Pierre Chouteau and General Pratte would have long since awarded the trading post position to him; how could they not? And once he showed some skill there, dealing with the Crows, some sharp improvements in the profits, he would swiftly advance to greater things.

Trenholm appeared at his side.

"Marsh wants you," the mate said.

Bonfils smiled and nodded. The commendation from the captain would be music to his ears. A kind word from the powerful captain in St. Louis would assure success.

He hastened up the companionway to the hurricane deck, and forward to the pilothouse, where he found Marsh dourly writing at a small desk. The captain peered up, and the look in his red face was not pleasant.

"Let's get something straight, Bonfils. You will never again touch that cannon or fire any sort of shot from this vessel without my permission."

Bonfils was taken aback. "But there was no time . . . we were on the brink of disaster."

"Disaster!"

"*Mais oui*, the savages were about to overrun us."

Marsh sprang to his feet, his face reddening.

"You endangered my ship. You acted without permission. You started a war! You ruined the company's trading with the whole Sioux nation! And all because you didn't wake me, ask me!"

Bonfils resented the outburst. "*Monsieur le capitaine*, I beg to remind you the savages were gathering on the riverbank, only ten yards away; scores of them, ready to plunge into the water and overwhelm us and strangle us in our sleep! I beg to remind you that on that gravel beach, just a few yards distant, lay half the wealth of Pratte, Chouteau and Company! And that is where the savages collected, right there, ready to commandeer that flatboat, ready to pitch the bales into the river if the spirit moved them! I saved the day; I drove them off! I collected two of your crew and we defeated them. We are safe here, we have more pelts than when we started! We—"

Marsh waved a hand so forcefully that Bonfils abruptly stopped.

When the master spoke, the tone was low and deadly.

"If I had irons I'd put you in them. As it is, you'll be confined to your cabin the rest of this trip."

"Confined!"

"You will learn, Bonfils, that dangerous passengers are confined."

"Dangerous!"

"From now on, every trip I make up this river will be

frought with danger from the Sans Arcs and maybe other Sioux. And from now on, every robe and pelt from that band will go to the Opposition."

"But I saved your life!"

Marsh barely whispered. "This is not the mountains; you are not leading a trapping brigade and fending off Blackfeet. Those you shot are our trading partners. They were not about to pillage this ship; far from it. I have confirmed that indeed, they were looking to cross the river, as Skye said. One of the Fort Pierre engagés who knows the tongue listened to several of the Sans Arcs who were collecting their wounded, and got the story. Skye had no business offering them this vessel, but at least he didn't mow them down with grapeshot. Nor did he murder a white man in the process."

"It was an accident of war!"

Marsh peered into the sunlit waters ahead. "There are things you don't know," he said.

The helmsman and pilot cast furtive glances at Bonfils, and Trenholm stared away from them.

"Maybe this should be dropped. It is a mere incident."

"Dropped? It is already in my logbook. An unauthorized discharge of my cannon, twice, into trading partners standing peacefully yards from this boat. And I have named you. This will scarcely go unnoticed. I plan to discuss it with Pierre Chouteau. I'm sure that when that flatboat reaches St. Louis, Skye and Gill are going to say a few words, not only to Chouteau, but General Clark. And there may be a warrant issued against you."

Bonfils's mind raced. This could hurt him with his family, with his petition, his life, his career.

"I see it differently," Bonfils said. "I will not sit in confinement the rest of this journey, a punishment I don't deserve. Put me ashore."

Marsh laughed meanly, and nodded to Trenholm. The

burly mate laid a hand on Bonfils, who violently threw it off. Then Marsh himself grabbed a fistful of shirt.

"Bonfils, you may be connected, you may be your family's choice, but here on my ship you're a piece of manure. Get your revenge in St. Louis. Whine all you want."

He nodded to Trenholm, who led Bonfils out of the pilot-house and down the companionway.

"Do I post a guard, or do you give me your parole you'll stay in?" Trenholm asked when they reached the cabin.

Bonfils hated the moment, hated the indignity. How had his life come to this? He wouldn't let some river rat tell him what to do.

"Say it."

Bonfils stood rigidly.

"All right, if you won't give me your word, you're confined. I'll post a deckman outside your door," Trenholm said.

Bonfils slammed the door behind him. He peered through a small porthole at the passing shore, and suddenly realized he had lost not only his freedom but also his reputation. And for what? Rescuing the ship from those idiots.

The *Otter* was two weeks from St. Louis. Two weeks confined to this miserable cubicle! Told when to eat, when to relieve himself! He paced; he flopped onto his bunk. He peered out the porthole at a free and serene world. He raged at the master, the mate, and everyone else aboard. He plucked up his Hawken Brothers .53-caliber rifle, a finely wrought octagon-barreled weapon that could drill a ball through a buffalo.

This was madness! He would draft a report and deliver it to his uncles and cousins. He would take this matter straight to the powerful families who ran St. Louis. He would have Marsh's scalp. He would ruin the man. He would see to it that neither he nor Trenholm ever served on another American Fur Company ship.

His rage, his fevered visions of revenge, lasted twenty minutes. Then he stood wearily, paced his compartment. Three paces door to wall. Two paces across. He peered out the window again. The scenery was exactly the same as before: nameless bluffs, empty skies, every blade of grass free to live as it could.

He flopped onto his bunk again, and tried closing his eyes. *Mon Dieu!* How could any mortal submit to such confinement? And all because he rescued the ship and cargo and crew from a pack of savages!

He tried thinking of women, ah, Emilie, ah, Marguerite, ah, Bridget, ah, sweet Cherise, ah . . .

And what of the future? Was he disgraced? No, never, not after he had had a chance to explain himself, tell people what had happened. But would he lose his chance? Would Skye now have the inside track? Ah, there was a new pain on top of all the rest.

In an abstract sort of way, he was sorry Skye got shot, though in fact it amused him. His rival, the London lout, just happened to be in the path of the cannister! Still, it was another thing to explain to his uncles. The fog! Yes, of course, the fog! How could any man tell what lay in the fog?

And if he could not tell what he was shooting at, then why did he fire that six-pounder?

Ah, *mon pere*, it was necessary to save the ship, save lives, save the cargo by which we all grow rich!

He endured an hour more, then opened the door a crack. A deck man stared at him.

"I am going to the closet," he said. The man didn't stop him. He walked forward, entered the cabinet that hung over the river, just ahead of the wheelhouses. There was a bench within, with three holes in it. The river skirled below. The blades of the wheel slashed into the river, spraying water about.

He lingered there, just because he hated to return to his

cabin, but finally he stepped out into sunlight, relishing it, relishing liberty. But the burly deckman was waiting, lounging against the rail, his bare foot on the coaming.

Bonfils returned to his room, his eyes hungrily raking the boiler deck, the firemen, the sunny prow, the broad river glinting in the bright sun. He entered his cabin and shut the door behind him, knowing what he had to do: escape. No innocent mortal could endure two weeks cooped up like an animal!

A cabin boy brought him some slop in a bowl. Marsh wouldn't even give him proper food! He caught the boy.

"Marcel, bring me food, eh? Much food, wrapped up in a bag. I will slip you a few pieces of eight."

The boy looked frightened, but finally nodded.

The chance came at dusk, when Marsh stopped for wood. All hands reported to Trenholm, who handed the crew and passengers axes and saws. Bonfils discovered that his guard had vanished to shore with the rest. Even Trenholm had gone ashore.

Bonfils gathered his rifle, his powderhorn, his kit. He pushed his straw hat over his long locks and stepped out. No one stopped him as he walked down the gangway and into a grove of willows, past the work party and up a game trail leading to the top of the bluff.

He turned at last to look down at the *Otter*, only to discover the master's spyglass upon him. Marsh waved casually, an exaggerated flap of his arm. So the master had foreseen it all, and let Bonfils walk.

twenty-five

The fever and nausea departed abruptly, and Skye grew aware of the world once again. His shoulder and thigh ached numbly, but the wound that still tormented him was the one that shattered his ribs. That one hurt so much his body refused to breathe, and he gulped air in pain.

He heard the lap of water against the plank hull, and the gurgle of the river. Somewhere forward, the Cheyenne woman crooned softly. She had been crooning all day, a low, melancholic song that tugged at the roots of his heart. He wondered what it would be like to lose a son, and was overcome with a sadness that he and Victoria had never conceived one.

The woman sang her sadness, and her melancholia suited him. She had lost a boy; he had lost a dog. He had loved that dog like a son. He had tried to put the dog out of mind; what was No Name but a miserable cur that had attached himself to the Skyes and kept its distance? And yet he could not. No Name was a magnificent dog, fierce and loyal, great-hearted, mysterious, independent, and sometimes tender. Now he was gone.

When Victoria had stepped aboard carrying that limp yellow bundle of fur, her lips pressed tight and her face etched with sorrow, Skye's own spirits had plummeted to that netherworld where the Dark Prince guarded the gates of hell. No Name dead. For that little while, Skye didn't care whether he lived or died. He had loved the dog. Even now, days later, the numbing loneliness he felt when he thought of his faithful animal was more than he could endure. They had wept, buried the dog in the river with songs and prayers, and set out upon their journey. For days afterward, Skye had the eerie sensation that the dog was running along the riverbank, beside the flatboat.

From his bunk he could see Gill at the tiller, looking dark and vacant-eyed, his thoughts upon his partner and not the currents that shouldered them ever southward. The boat carried no load, drew only a few inches of water, and scarcely needed steering. Skye grew aware of Victoria beside him, and reached out to her. His hand caught hers and squeezed it.

"You better," she said.

He nodded.

She began to change his poultices, which hurt. But when she had pulled loose her dressings, he could see that the hard red inflammation had subsided. Somewhere along the way, she had gathered her own medicinals from alongside the river, and had packed the wounds with them. He did not know what herbs and leaves she had used, but the presence of green moss over the wounds surprised him.

Gill shadowed the door, and then he entered.

"Heard you talking. You some better?" he asked.

"Who's at the tiller?" Skye asked.

"It'll take care of itself a while."

"Better," Skye said.

"Anyway, you made it; Shorty didn't."

Skye didn't respond to that. He knew what was on Red Gill's mind: if Skye hadn't wrestled Shorty down and steered the flatboat over to the beached steamboat, none of it would have happened. Maybe he was right. But maybe the next cannister shot from that six-pounder would have cut Shorty to pieces; maybe the next shots after that, fired from the looming riverboat, would have raked them all. In any case, the iron law of the seas and rivers was to stop and render assistance. Red was bitter. He'd lost his partner and his cargo, which was to be his profit, and had unwanted passengers as well, and nothing but debt back in St. Louis.

"I'm sorry about Shorty, mate."

Red glared, watched Victoria work on the wounds, and then retreated to his post at the tiller.

The dolorous song continued. Lame Deer was singing away her sorrows.

They drifted through a quiet and partly cloudy day, sun bright one moment, and obscured the next. He saw Red turn over the tiller to Victoria and heard him pacing the boat. The singing stopped.

By afternoon he felt well enough to sit up a few minutes, and he pulled himself upright in the bunk, resting his head on the forward wall of the cabin, which was the rear wall of the cargo box. The Missouri had grown into a majestic flowage, drawing waters to it from a vast basin. He felt he was traversing a lake rather than a river.

A rifle crack shattered the peace, and as his body jerked in response, his wounds stung him.

Gill yelled, and Skye saw him peering over the water, trying to locate the source of the distant shot.

Victoria stood beside Gill at the back of the flatboat, and finally she pointed to the left bank.

"Some sonofabitch standing there," she said.

Skye strained forward until he could see out of the small porthole sawn into the side of the cabin. Indeed, a man stood on a high prominence forty or fifty feet above the river. He was waving his hat and beckoning the craft to him.

Skye watched Gill pull the tiller, and watched the shadows and sunlight move across the floor of the cabin, and knew that Gill was heading for shore. Even as the flatboat veered toward the riverbank, the man scurried downslope to the water's edge and waited, rifle cradled in his arms, with a sack in his hand. He looked vaguely familiar.

Skye sank back on his bunk, unable to stand the pain of sitting, and waited restlessly for news.

Then Gill began cursing, a low monotone cussing that his partner Shorty had employed to voice all manner of opinion from hatred to joy.

"Who?" asked Skye.

"Bonfils."

"Bonfils!" The author of his wounds. The man who killed No Name. The author of the death of Shorty. The author of the death of Lame Deer's boy. "You going to stop?"

Red grunted.

Skye lifted himself from the bunk for a look, and discovered Bonfils thirty yards across water, his rifle at the ready across his chest.

Skye fell back weakly. Victoria swept into the grimy cabin and worked feverishly, loading Skye's rifle from the powderhorn that hung over the corner of Skye's bunk.

"Bonfils got that rifle pointing at Gill, almost. I'll kill that sonofabitch," she muttered.

Skye held up a hand and she subsided.

He waited patiently, listening to the water lap and gurgle. Then he felt a jar, and the flatboat bumped shore.

"How about a ride?" yelled Bonfils.

"What are you doing here?" Gill asked.

"I left the riverboat."

"Why?"

"Felt like it."

"I said, Why?"

"Had a little trouble with Marsh."

"About shooting us with the goddamned cannon."

"I want a ride to St. Louis."

"You killed Shorty."

"How was I to know he was in there with all those redskins?"

"I think you can walk," Gill said.

"Is Skye in there?"

"You're going to walk, Bonfils."

"I think you are going to take me and be glad of it. In fact, my friend, this rifle says so."

"The hell with you."

Skye heard Gill pick up a pole to push the flatboat farther away from the riverbank.

"Gill, you don't listen. This rifle is pointing at you. Your fate is in your hands. What a pity. The two smugglers go up-river and never return! Now listen: Would you like to get your cargo back?"

Gill paused.

"Monsieur, I know things. All day, many days, I talked with Marsh in the pilothouse, and from his lips come many things. I will tell you something I know. The one who employs you is not the Opposition, but Pierre Chouteau, is that not so?"

Skye heard only dead silence. He wished he could take a good look at Gill. The assertion was so astonishing that Skye could barely fathom it. Chouteau? Why would the company employ Gill and Ballard?

"What else?" Gill asked neutrally.

Bonfils laughed. "There is much. I can help you. A word in the right ears in St. Louis will return your cargo, yes? I will tell you as soon as I step on board; as soon as we are heading for St. Louis. This I promise you."

Gill must have changed his mind, because Skye felt the boat bump bottom, heard the brigade leader step aboard, and felt a faint rocking of the flatboat. Moments later the boat was riding the current again.

Bonfils slipped into the cabin, laid his rifle on the other bunk, and smiled. "Ah! So you are alive and in good flesh!"

Skye was too worn to resist the man, so he kept quiet.

"I will tell you something, Skye—"

"It's Mister Skye, mate."

Bonfils laughed. "The *homme* with the best chance for the trading post, he is in St. Louis now preparing to marry a niece of General Pratte, the stepdaughter of Capitaine Marsh. Her name is Sarah Lansing, and her beau is Simon MacLees, and he is a great favorite of the capitaine."

"MacLees?"

Skye lay on his back, contemplating that. "If he's the choice, why did they want us to come to St. Louis?"

Bonfils shrugged. "I do not read minds, Skye. But when we arrive with MacLees's mountain wife, and there is a fine fat scandal, the unexpected may happen, *oui*?"

Bonfils abandoned the cabin and headed aft to talk to Gill. They palavered in such low tones that Skye could not catch it all, but he knew Victoria was hovering about. She had a way of being invisible to white men. He needed only patience and he would know.

A while later she slipped into the cabin.

"They going to St. Louis day and night. No stop. They gonna pass the riverboat. It ties up at night. It can't see nothing in the dark, so this boat pass them up some night soon, and get there first."

"Why, Victoria?"

"Get to Chouteau ahead of Marsh."

"But why?"

"So Chouteau gives the robes back to Gill. I got that much, anyway. Gill and the one who is dead"—she avoided naming the name of the dead, as always—"they take whiskey upriver by pack train, many mules, make big circle around Fort Leavenworth where the bluecoats watch the river.

"They get pay in robes, bales of robes and a flatboat to bring them down the river. No record is ever made. Gill and the other, they talk about working for the Opposition, but that is not so. Bonfils says he get the bales back for Gill."

Skye pondered that and thought it might be true. But he didn't doubt that Bonfils had private designs that would affect him and Victoria, and Lame Deer too. But he could only wait and see.

twenty–six

lexandre Bonfils held the aces. He knew things. And the few things he wasn't sure of, he could guess at with all the shrewdness of a wealthy young Creole reared in St. Louis society. Odd, how the affairs of St. Louis threaded westward into an utter wilderness. He had discovered secrets! And now this flatboat was drifting toward St. Louis, brimming with them! Oh, ho, the ways he knew to embarrass Pierre Chouteau!

The *capitaine*, Benton Marsh, had not said a word to him about the Cheyenne squaw, or why Marsh had abruptly ejected the woman and her children from his steamboat. But Bonfils knew! Ah! It was delicious to think about it. Scandal! The Beaujolais and brie of St. Louis society!

The Cheyenne woman was a threat to Marsh's future son-in-law, and an embarrassment. Children, too! Ah, proof of dalliance far away from prying eyes. Her arrival in St. Louis would trigger a splendid scandal that would embarrass Marsh's stepdaughter, Sarah Lansing, and wreck Simon MacLees's chances in Pratte, Chouteau and Company, and probably wreck the nuptials. Ah! What fun it would be to arrive in St. Louis ahead of the steamboat, and make sure that the Cheyenne woman and her brat were properly introduced! Especially the little breed girl, whose papa everyone in St. Louis knew!

And of course, MacLees's downfall would clear the way for the appointment of Bonfils to the trading post. MacLees was the rival to worry about: a shrewd trader, experienced in the art of running a trading post, a man of great talents—and a little squaw no one in St. Louis knew about!

Bonfils chuckled. The woman was his ace. She sat there in the front of the flatboat, her back to the cargo box, fussing with her daughter, oblivious to the white men behind her. Little did she know she was a future debutante, and Bonfils would arrange for her coming out, right down to her ball gown.

Skye could be easily dealt with. A simple visit with General Clark would do the job. Clark was the man who issued permits and licenses. Anyone trading with Indians in United States Indian Territory had to have a license, and had to be an American citizen to get that license. Skye was an Englishman. That detail had been overlooked by Pierre Chouteau. Bonfils laughed. It was all so simple, so easy. General Clark might even eject Skye from the United States. A pity. Poor devil might have to rejoin the Royal Navy.

Still, it would take some doing. A flatboat was scarcely the speediest mode of travel. But if it progressed continually, night and day, it would indeed reach St. Louis ahead of the river packet, which could not navigate at night unless the moon shown bright. It was crucial to get to Pierre Chouteau first, tell him that Marsh stole the packs from Gill. That would put Marsh on the defensive. Uncle Pierre had gone to great lengths to transport spirits to the posts far from the prying eyes of the government, and now Marsh had ruined the fragile and private arrangement. Ah, what fun to know how things worked. If Uncle Pierre dreaded anything, it was the exposure of his whiskey-running.

The other matter would be more entertaining, like watching a Molière comedy. Introducing the lice-ridden Cheyenne squaw around town, as MacLees's mountain lady, and her breed child with the blue-green eyes and light brown hair, would start things in motion. That would be the *coup de grace*.

He meandered back to Gill.

"We must never stop. Night and day, we must never stop."

"Got to eat, rest, sleep—" Gill said.

"Non, non, we must catch up. Marsh is leagues ahead of us!"

"Don't know that he is. He's got to take on wood once, twice a day, and we just keep on a-going."

"You sleep; I will steer at night. I am not afraid of night. And this bateau, it draws only four, five inches. We go over bars, over snags, over the top. We get to St. Louis ahead of Marsh, and I will get your furs back from Uncle Pierre."

Gill shrugged.

Bonfils paced restlessly, back and forth, from stem to stern, aware of the gazes following him. The river had broadened into a noble stream, carrying a vast burden of water from the distant mountains and the everlasting prairies ever south and east. The country had become monotonous. Who was there to talk with? The only interesting person was Skye, who lay abed.

He would talk with Skye anyway. The man had been sitting up; his fever had vanished. He was taking some broth. Bonfils ducked through the low door and into the dark and grimy cabin where Skye lay. His squaw sat across from him, silently watching the river.

"*Bonjour, mon ami*, how are you this day?"

Skye nodded curtly but said nothing.

Bonfils tried again. "Soon we will be in St. Louis, eh? Now what will you be saying to Uncle Pierre? I will tell him that we had a little bad luck."

Skye looked better; less flushed, quieter. But he didn't respond.

Bonfils felt faintly defensive and annoyed. "Ah, it is that you do not wish to talk with the one who put some grape into you. This I understand. But of course it was purely an accident. No harm intended. And it did stop a war party from pillaging the company furs, or capturing the riverboat."

Skye would tell Pierre Chouteau a different story, and it was necessary to find out what the Englishman would say, so it could be dismissed. But Skye wasn't cooperating; he just lay there, eyes closed, as if he wanted Bonfils to leave.

"Madam, your man recovers nicely because of your care," he said to Victoria.

She made no sign of having heard.

"Truly, he will be almost fit by the time we reach St. Louis. Well enough to hobble around, don't you think? Pierre Chouteau will admire him for his courage, coming clear down the river with a body in such need of repair and rest. Do you suppose he will need to winter in St. Louis, where he can get good care, before he ventures back to the mountains?"

She didn't respond; didn't smile, didn't nod, didn't speak. He felt as if he were being examined, not by some savage woman but by a surgeon, or maybe by a confessor listening through the grille.

"The Cheyenne squaw, she sings well, *oui*? I am listening to her send her boy along the spirit trail, and am filled with utmost admiration. She sits quietly at the front of the boat, like a goddess, watching the river and singing. Truly, she will be the queen of St. Louis! I myself will present her to society, letting all the world know she is Simon MacLees's wife, and that the pretty little creature is his daughter!"

Neither of the Skyes responded, which annoyed him. So that's how it would be! Here he was looking after them, making sure they got to St. Louis ahead of Marsh and his vitriolic accusations, but they showed no appreciation. Very well, then.

"Bonfils," Gill yelled.

"Ah, pardon, *mes amis*, the man wants me," he said, rising to leave. He ducked through the low door, into sunlight, and headed for Gill, who was steering for shore.

"Why is it that you stop? Are we not trying to keep on going no matter what? Go on, go on!"

But Gill just shook his head and pointed.

Ahead was a great turmoil. Bonfils strained to see what Gill had spotted. On the left bank was a swarming brown mass, slowly undulating toward the broad, sparkling river. And clear across the river, forming a barrier, was a brown band, quietly and powerfully moving from shore to shore, a thousand snouts and horns and heads; buffalo. And on the right bank were thousands more, clambering upslope, rivering the water out of their brown hair, and following the rest of the gigantic herd up and up and over the crest of the bluff, as if they were all marching into the heavens.

"Buffalo crossing," Gill said.

"It's amazing. There must be tens of thousands."

"All of that."

"How long will it last?"

"Who knows? Hour, day, several days."

"*Mon Dieu!* I have heard of such a thing, but never have I seen it!"

He clambered up on the roof of the cargo box to see better. Countless bison were moving sinuously down the far slope, driving into the river at a good launching place that had turned into muck, and were slowly paddling a third of a mile across the water, their heads and horns and snouts making vee-shaped waves. They were six, ten, twenty, fifty in a rank, and the ranks spread like a brown carpet clear across the Missouri.

Gill was heading for the right bank, and he clearly intended to hole up until the herd had crossed. But that was foolish.

"Just go ahead, go ahead. The beasts will let you through."

Gill shook his head. "Them buff'lo, they can hook a horn right through the planks. Don't matter if they're in water. Get into the middle of them, and the buff would cut this poor flatboat to splinters."

"How do you know that?"

"Just do."

"We're losing time!"

"Nothing anyone can do about it."

Bonfils could see no end of the herd, no stragglers topping the left bluff; only a vast brown column of animals appearing on the ridge and working downslope to the river. He had never seen such a sight; more buffalo in this one herd than he thought existed in all herds everywhere. None of the beasts bawled; yet a faint rumble, the impact of thousands of hooves, the struggles of tens of thousands of animals to swim, the shuddering and labored climb up the mucky right bank and the walk up the slope, made a faint hum, but what struck him most was the odd silence in the midst of so much motion.

Gill reached a point a hundred yards upstream from the crossing and close to the right bank, and there he turned the flatboat into the shore until it ground to a halt. He eased off the gunnel with a rope in hand, and splashed to shore in a foot or two of water, to tie the rope to a sapling.

Bonfils endured it for a while, growing more and more restless. The great flow of animals never ceased, never slowed, and with each passing minute, his patience eroded and his temper mounted.

twenty-seven

Barnaby Skye struggled to sit up so he could see the herd swimming the Missouri. He fell back weakly, the shattered ribs shooting pain through him. He gasped for breath, and tried again, this time struggling upright. Ahead, he saw the procession slowly wending down the left slope, swimming across the river like some brown tide, and emerging slick and wet on the right bank, just a hundred yards below where the flatboat was tied to river brush.

The sight awed him. He was seeing a majestic wave of buffalo that vibrated the boat even as it lay quietly beside the shore. He scarcely heard the noise of passage, and yet the air was not still, and some obscure thunder filled it, and some suffocating force seemed to draw the oxygen out of it. The herd possessed within it so much energy that it was unfathomable; all the energy of thousands of square miles of grasslands; more muscle and breath than the whole human race. He thought that never in the rest of his days would he see such a spectacle, and he counted himself privileged to witness it.

He had never felt so helpless. His body was not obeying him. He could not will his pain away. He could not exist now without the help of others. Victoria spooned broth into him and changed the poultices on his three wounds. Red Gill steered the flatboat and looked to its safety. Even the Cheyenne woman, Lame Deer, took her turn looking after him.

This weakness was new to him. He had been helpless in the Royal Navy, too; imprisoned and dependent on others. But not ill, not so drained of vitality that he could barely manage to sit up. That was different. He had never before been gravely injured, and now he realized how fragile was his flesh, and how much his very life depended on others.

The only person who no longer visited him was Bonfils. Maybe it was just as well that the aristocratic Creole stayed away; whenever Skye contemplated his wounds, and the unending ache in his shoulder and thigh, and the sharp pain that rose and ebbed every time he breathed, and his dead dog, he knew he could not endure Bonfils; not for an instant.

How strange it was to be weak; to be cared for, to be so helpless.

As soon as Gill tied up, he collected his Pennsylvania long-rifle from the cabin, along with his powderhorn.

"Gonna have some good cow for supper," he said.

Skye nodded. He might manage some broth, and a few bits of meat, but he would not be able to eat even the most succulent of the parts of the cow, the humpmeat, one of his favorite foods.

He watched Red Gill progress down a plank he had run from the flatboat to the sedge-lined shore, and then walk downriver toward the awesome herd. A while later he heard a crack, oddly obscured by the gutteral noise of the passage.

Gill had gotten his cow.

Skye watched the vast herd, wondering when it would end. He had heard somewhere that sometimes they tied up a riverboat for two or three days.

Gill shouted toward the boat.

"Bonfils, ladies, help me butcher," he said. "The cow strayed out from the herd; we're safe enough."

Skye heard movement forward, and low voices. Then he watched Victoria and the Cheyenne woman, with her little girl, edge down the shaky plank to shore, and start toward the carcass somewhere ahead, beyond Skye's vision.

Where was Bonfils?

Skye heard footsteps toward the front of the flatboat, but plainly the young brigade leader was not leaving the boat, even to cut up the buffalo or start a fire to cook it. Skye was on the wrong side of the cabin to see much of what was happening on shore. But he knew the women would be gutting the cow, cutting out the tongue, and sawing away at the shoulder hump, which made the best of all roasts. It would take a long while to butcher the huge animal and cook a haunch or boil the tongue.

He drifted in and out of awareness, as he often did in his sickbed. Some moments, he smelled the sharp, rank odor of the herd, or listened to the muted rumble of its passage, or followed the soft patter of footsteps on the planks of the flatboat. Other moments he was far away, in the past or future, his mind roaming far from his wounded body.

Sometime soon he would be in St. Louis, facing a powerful and ruthless man he had never met, seeking a position that would ensure him a life of relative comfort and ease, as well as the prospect of a good future. Or maybe not. He had heard enough to know that he might not be appointed; Bonfils or MacLees might well receive Chouteau's favor. Maybe this trip would all be for nothing. Maybe these wounds, which had bled the strength out of him and rendered him little more than a bedridden wreck, might defeat his purposes.

He heard footsteps, and knew his rival was heading aft. A moment later Bonfils darkened the door and stepped in.

"Ah, Monsieur Skye, we are alone at last. How do you fare?"

Skye stared.

"Truly it was regrettable that you were trapped in the middle of those thieving Sioux."

Skye was tempted to argue that Bonfils had been a damned fool, but he held his peace. The man was obviously here for a purpose.

The young Creole found a seat on the opposing bunk, which was nothing but a stretch of planking, like that which supported Skye. "You are progressing?" he asked politely.

"No fever. No infection."

"A blessing. You have a gifted woman."

"She packs the wounds with a blue moss she scrapes off the north side of trees."

"The Indians, they are crafty healers, *oui*?"

Skye nodded. These pleasantries were not why Bonfils had settled his lean and dark self in the cabin. Skye wondered what would come next.

"I myself am mad with eagerness to go again. These buffalo are an unexpected frustration," he said.

"Most amazing thing I've ever seen," Skye said. "I'll remember it the rest of my days. More buff than I've ever seen in all of my life; brown river of them."

"Ah, you are a sentimentalist! I see only hides and meat."

Skye settled deeper into his robes. Speaking taxed him and made his ribs ache. "I think you're here for some reason," he said. "I am very tired."

Bonfils smiled brightly. "You are discerning, *mon ami*."

"Now I'm your friend, am I? Would I be more of a friend if you had put four holes in me instead of three?"

Bonfils laughed easily. "You have wit, monsieur. No, what I wish to discuss with you is simply your future."

Skye waited. Breath came harshly because his lungs rebelled when his ribs ached.

"I shall tell you exactly what my plan is. First, I must overtake the riverboat and reach my mother's cousin, Pierre Chouteau, before Marsh does, to settle certain accusations he will make against me, things that might damage my chances. And of course, introduce him to the Cheyenne woman, MacLees's squaw. That will be a very pleasurable moment, taking her and the little breed child in hand and into that handsome house, where the women will stare at the squaw and see whether there really are lice in her hair." He laughed softly.

Skye was hurting from his attempt to sit up, so he lay very still, listening.

"I think that once Lame Deer is known, MacLees will no longer be a contender for the post on the Big Horn River."

"I didn't know he was a contender."

Bonfils laughed. "There is much you don't know. MacLees abandoned his squaw and is soon to marry a lovely white girl, Sarah Lansing, stepdaughter of Captain Marsh, and related to General Pratte. But when Lame Deer reaches St. Louis, I suspect the outcome might change."

"And?"

"That brings us to you. You are an Englishman, *oui*?"

Skye nodded.

"A deserter from the Royal Navy, is it not so?"

Skye waited for whatever was coming, staring at Bonfils, who was enjoying himself.

"You know, if you become a trader for the company, you must become an American citizen. General Clark does not license foreigners for the fur trade, or people of bad character such as deserters. Nor does he permit them access to Indian lands held by the United States. You are here illegally."

That was a revelation to Skye.

"My design, Skye, is to tell the general that you are not an American. . . . should you arrive in St. Louis."

Skye absorbed that. Chouteau must have known, must have counted on him becoming an American citizen. Still, the subject had never been mentioned, and it irritated him.

"We are rivals, *mon ami*. And I will do what I must to acquire the post. It is the boulevard to success. A little while out there, earning the company a good profit and befriending the Crows, and I will have the credentials I need. Chouteau insists on practical experience. The senior men are very rich, monsieur, and so shall I be."

"And what's your design for me?"

"Bellevue, Skye. Get off the flatboat at Bellevue and head west with your woman. You will be safe. No official will know of your whereabouts or try to remove you from Indian Territory. You see? What I propose is in your interests!"

Bellevue was the site of an American Fur Company post near the confluence of the Platte River and the Missouri, a trading center run by Peter Sarpy for the Omahas and other plains tribes, a depot for the furs coming down the Platte River, and a supply point for much of the mountain trade. It would be only a few days away once they were traveling again.

"Sorry," Skye said. "We're going to St. Louis to try our luck with Chouteau. We'll not turn back now. And there's no way Clark can keep me from returning to my wife's people if I choose to go there."

"Regrettable," Bonfils said. "You force my hand."

twenty-eight

Victoria ripped hard through the brisket until the guts burst out into a steaming heap. The cow was scarcely dead. Red Gill waited a few yards distant, wary of the stream of buffalo that were shaking, snorting, dripping water, shivering the very earth. Victoria didn't like it either, and wondered whether some minor excitement would send the vast herd trampling over her. She and Lame Deer worked only yards from the riverbank, and only yards from the undulating edge of the herd.

A calf bleated nearby and refused to meld itself into the herd. Victoria felt a moment's sadness, for this dead four-foot was its mother. But the calf would live; it was three months old, and nibbling grass.

Lame Deer had sliced open the flesh behind the jaw of the cow, and was carefully sawing off the massive tongue, a great delicacy, while Victoria was scooping out the brisket, aiming for the huge liver, another delicacy. A cloud of black flies whirled and whined over them all; with the herd came every vicious biting fly on Mother Earth, and all types of them were swarming over this dead animal. Victoria knew that by nightfall other predators would congregate, and by dawn this cow would be bone and hide. She shivered.

Red Gill retreated irritably, leaving the filthy work to the women, but he hovered not far off, and began gathering drift-wood and brush to build a fire. The flatboat bobbed and bumped land just a few rods distant. Victoria paused to examine the skylines; all sorts of predators followed the herds, including the two-footed kind, and it paid to be wary. But she saw nothing.

She reached into the warm, pungent, slippery carcass and clamped her hand over the liver and tugged, while gently nipping away tissue with the other hand until she released the dark and slippery organ.

Her hands dripped blood, and the black flies swarmed in thick clouds, and she wished this ugly task were done and she was feeding the mighty strength of Sister Buffalo into her wounded man.

She sliced thin strips of raw liver and popped one in her mouth, feeling its succulence between her teeth. She sliced another and handed it to Lame Deer, who gave it to her daughter, and then bit into a second piece. What finer meat was there than buffalo liver? It carried the strength of the buffalo in it, and made one strong.

She set the liver aside in the grass and began sawing along the backbone, working toward the hump. She would not try to save this hide; she could scarcely harvest a day or two of meat before night fell.

She parted the hide along the ridge of the back, releasing swarms of worms and beetles buried in its thick brown matting. This cow must have been tormented, and no doubt the long swim across the river had helped cleanse some of the nesting parasites.

Lame Deer sliced with sharp, deft strokes, working from the incision under the jaw, until at last she had freed the tongue and it could be pulled out of the mouth. Oh, there would be a feast this night! Boiled tongue would put power into them all. Sister Buffalo would give her strength to the two-legged ones.

When Victoria had exposed the humpmeat which lay over the dorsal ribs, she motioned to Lame Deer and they grabbed the legs of the animal to flip it over so Victoria could work on the other side of the hump. This took a mighty effort, but the two women succeeded, and soon Victoria was skillfully slicing out the hump, which lay at the base of the neck, and which contained the most tender and edible of all the flesh of a buffalo. It was no easy thing to cut the humpmeat free.

She peered up and found Bonfils staring at her, but he didn't venture into the cloud of vicious black flies, and she wished she didn't have to feed him.

Gill set up an iron tripod, hung a black kettle from it, and then collected the tongue, brushing off the black flies. He dropped the tongue into the kettle and fed more wood to the fire.

But Victoria and Lame Deer slipped liver into their mouths, licking up the salty blood, nurturing themselves and little Singing Rain, even as they worked. Let the men have the tongue. The women had the liver. And tomorrow there would be a hump roast.

The herd made her uneasy. Every little while it undulated close, and the dripping buffalo trotted by, churning up a muddied slope, so many that the earth quivered under their countless hooves, and the air was filled with soft noise, breathing, pent-up energy, and their sharp odor.

Then she noticed other animals nearby. Half a dozen wet wolves sat on their haunches on the riverbank, their coats glistening after the long swim across the broad river. A chill shot through her.

She picked up a rock and threw it at them. She liked wolves; they looked after her people, and some of the Absaroka warriors had wolf medicine. But she didn't want them there, twenty yards distant, contemplating her and the other women, smelling meat and death. The rock bounced between two of them and they lazily parted a few feet, undeterred.

She returned to her work, wishing she had her bow and quiver. She would drive an arrow into the big one who watched her with a feral and patient gaze. She turned to Gill.

"Wolves," she yelled.

Gill nodded, looking around for his weapon, when a rifle cracked. She saw smoke erupting from Bonfils's weapon. A wolf catapulted backward, yapping, shivering, and then dying. The others retreated sullenly. She and the Cheyenne woman held this ground for a little while, but the instant they abandoned the buffalo cow, the wolves would be upon it.

She stared at Bonfils, who stood grinning, proud of himself. He set down his rifle, poured a fresh charge of powder down its barrel, patched a ball and drove it home with the hardwood rod that clipped under the barrel. Then he cleaned the nipple with his pick. The rifle was armed, except for a new cap.

It took another stint of hard, filthy work to saw through bone and gristle and meat, but she and Lame Deer freed the hump and laid it in the grass. Victoria severed enough of the filthy hide to cover the hump and liver and the rest of what they had cut loose, and together they dragged it away from the carcass.

Even before the women reached the cookfire, gray wolves swarmed over the carcass; not just the six she had seen, but a dozen more, snarling and tearing, their feasting drowned out by the mutter of the passing herd, which still stretched from the distant bluffs across the river to the bluffs on this side of it.

She and Lame Deer dragged the bloody meat aboard and laid it near the front of the boat. Lame Deer began crooning in her own tongue, and Victoria knew she was giving thanks again to the animal that had been sacrificed to feed her and her daughter; and to rejoice in the goodness of the bountiful world, and the kindness of Sweet Medicine, the sacred brother and lawgiver who looked over the Cheyenne people.

Victoria washed herself at the riverbank, floating away the

slime and blood, cleansing her brown face, slapping the black flies that still swarmed around her. The fragrance of the boiling tongue reached her nostrils, and she was ready to feast again. But first, she would feed her man.

She sawed off some half-boiled tongue and dropped it into one of the wooden trenchers Gill kept on board, and then headed for the cabin. She found Skye gazing up at her, drawn and ill.

"This is tongue," she said. "Good for you. It will put the strength of the buffalo into you. Eat!"

He struggled upward, breathing hard, wincing with every movement, but eventually sat up. He looked haggard.

"Eat buffalo, goddammit! It make you feel good."

But she had to cut each piece because he was too weak to saw at the dimpled tongue meat. He ate slowly, a few tiny slivers, and then waved the food away.

"Eat!" she cried.

He tried another piece and then stopped.

Outside, Bonfils and Gill were devouring the tongue and contesting something in low tones. They were on the riverbank. She could not make out what they were saying, but their words were cross even though they were filling their bellies.

Dusk was settling over the flatboat, plunging the cabin into darkness. Skye drank some broth, and then pushed aside the tin cup she had given him. He hadn't eaten enough.

"You got to eat and get strong!" she said, irritably.

The muted hum of the herd, the vibrations reaching her even in the flatboat, the mutter and snort of the animals, was wearing on her, rubbing her raw. The snarl of the wolves was irritating her too. Was there no end to this?

"Learned a few things from Bonfils," he said. "He says I'd have to become an American citizen to get a trading license."

She didn't understand any of it. "What is this license?"

Skye translated the idea to her in jargon she would understand, as he often did. "It's like a yes. I have to have a yes. Big chief in St. Louis says I got to join them or they won't let me trade with your people."

"How come?"

"They say the fur trade's for Americans. Not for others. Especially not for English. Makes sense, I guess. Maybe I won't be a trader if I can't get a license from this General Clark."

"We come all this way and you don't be a trader?"

He sighed. "Lame Deer's man, MacLees, he's likely the one going to be made a trader to your people . . . if Bonfils knows what he's talking about."

"MacLees?" she marveled. "He's the Opposition."

"He's been driven out. Now it looks like maybe they'll give him a job, put him to work. He's a veteran trader. That's how they do it. Drive out the opposition and then hire the best of them. They're even employing Gabe Bridger now."

She understood only part of it, but fumed at the very idea.

"Him I don't trust," she said, gesturing toward the dark shore where the two men sat at the fire.

"Bonfils, he's got his own schemes going. He says we should get off at Bellevue. That's a big post down the river some. He says I should stay out of St. Louis for my own good. That's what he talked about a while ago. You want to quit?"

"Hell no," she snapped.

He grinned in the obscure light. "Thought so," he said. It was the first time in days he had smiled.

twenty-nine

C ame Deer awakened to deep silence. Not even crickets were chirping. Her hand found Singing Rain beside her, sleeping peacefully in the bunk across from Mister Skye.

She understood the silence. The buffalo brothers had crossed the Big River at last, and had vanished to the west. And the wolves had vanished with them. The night was no longer restless, and the very earth did not tremble under the impact of so many dark hooves.

She could see nothing. No moon lit the landscape or glinted off dark waters. She stirred, wanting to step outside into fresh air. Skye's sour breath filled this dank cabin, and she wanted to escape it and suck sweet fresh air into her lungs. Her friend the Crow woman slept across the floor of the cabin, rolled into a robe. The men slept outside.

She heard stirring in the fore part of the flatboat, and knew Bonfils was awakening. She hated and dreaded Bonfils, and marveled that such a one could be here in this flatboat with those he had hurt. She thought again of Sounds Come Back After Shouting, and grieved, the pain so sharp and so bitter that she wanted to scream in sorrow and cut her hair and deface herself as an act of mourning.

She had not known at first that this man, Bonfils, was the killer of her only son. That awful moment when the Sans Arcs had gathered around Skye, in the fog of dawn, she had seen two men aboard the fireboat dancing about, sometimes obscured by the whisps of fog, dark obscure figures she paid little attention to because Skye was conferring with the Sans Arcs, and she was listening to all of that.

Then the shocking blast came, and she heard screams, and beheld her boy tumbling to the cold earth. He fell onto his back, and she saw a dark, wet hole in his neck and another in his head, and his lips moved once or twice and then his spirit departed for the long trail. His eyes did not see her. Sound Comes Back After Shouting was gone, after four winters of life, and she heard another blast of the cannon and more screams, and white men's cursing, and then the Sans Arcs shouted, raced about, gathered their fallen, and vanished . . . and she began to weep.

It was not until the Crow woman told her about Bonfils that she learned who had killed her son. And now this very killer was aboard. She could not fathom it. That man had also killed Shorty Ballard, partner of the owner of this boat, and put three wounds upon Mister Skye, gravely injuring him, and yet that man walked the planks of the flatboat, lorded over them all, and acted as if nothing had happened. He had even been saying he had done a good thing and had rescued the company's furs.

She had thought often of killing Bonfils. But she knew she wouldn't. It was not in her to do such a thing, though sometimes she longed to stick her knife deep into his ribs and let him see what a woman of the People could do to the killer of her beloved son.

But she had chosen another course. She would tell MacLees about it; tell him everything, let him grieve for Billy, as he called the boy he doted on, and then Simon would be filled with wrath and seek justice against this man Bonfils, after the manner of the white men. And then this Bonfils would be driven from the midst of the white men.

But here he was, walking among the aggrieved, and she could not fathom it. Why had the boat chief, Red Gill, permitted this man to board? But she knew the answer to that: Bonfils had held a rifle on the boat chief.

She heard Bonfils walking rearward, heard him awaken Gill, who yawned and cursed after the manner of white men. She heard subdued voices, and Gill's snarl, but then the owner of this big canoe arose, and she could hear him making water over the side of the flatboat, and talking with Bonfils.

She threw off her robe, caring tenderly not to awaken her child, and stepped out upon the deck. A chill night wind caught her hair and an overcast hid the stars and Brother Moon so she could not fathom the time. But some intuition told her that Father Sun would soon appear upon the horizon.

It was much too dark to navigate, but she realized they were untying the boat from the bankside brush that tethered it, and a moment later she felt the craft bob and move slowly into the bleak darkness. She knew only that Gill had turned it outward from shore. He had great medicine, that man, and maybe he would steer the flatboat just by keeping it in the swiftest current. The boat rode high, carrying so little, and he feared nothing.

How impatient these men were, and how little they saw. All the trip, she had seen a world unfold that they never perceived; the black bear, the ravens, the Arikara women digging roots, the black snake swimming, the minnows, the turtle that paused to watch them, and the eagle climbing the stair to the sky.

But Gill saw things she could not; the way the water ran, the place where currents drove ahead, the meaning of the lines of foam, the snag that made a vee-shaped pattern in the water, the changing color of the river as it took on more mud and silt. She respected Red Gill, not only for his river medicine, but because he was strong and shrewd and watchful.

So they were once again moving. She exulted. Soon she would come to this place called St. Louis, and she would find Simon and his heart would be gladdened. The sharp breeze reminded her that it was not long before dawn, and she was hungry. Roasted hump meat hung from a mast forward; to fill herself she needed only saw at it with her skinning knife. She worked forward, through an inky darkness.

"The buffalo, they let us go," said Bonfils, materializing beside her.

She did not speak to this man; neither did she look at him or let him peer into her spirit. There was something possessive about him. She could not quite fathom his interest in her. It was not like a man's desire for a woman, but something else, as if she were something to use; something that would help him. She wished she knew what was in his mind.

"Don't want to talk, madame? Very well. It is not necessary. We will watch over you all the way to St. Louis, and then we will present you to the world." He laughed softly.

She found the meat hung well above where a creature could nip at it, and she reached upward, standing on the tips of her moccasins, to cut off the cool and succulent flesh of the blessed buffalo. She gave thanks again to this mother who gave herself to feed the two-foots, and then sliced a piece and popped it into her mouth, and then several more. And then she sliced a few small pieces and carried them back to the cabin. They would suffice for Singing Rain, and keep her strong.

She felt her way back, entered the cabin, and discovered that Victoria Skye was awake, and crooning softly to Singing Rain.

"We're on the river," she said.

"Buff gone?" Skye asked from the darkness of his bunk.

"Yes, the brothers have passed by and the wolves too."

She handed a slice of meat to her child, who began to mouth it. The girl would gum the juices out of it but eat little.

"Can Gill steer?"

"No, he is letting the boat go where it will go. He can see nothing."

"Sort of like my life," Skye said. "No one at the tiller. But the river's taking me somewhere."

She heard Bonfils and Gill far forward, trying to see what they could see. She liked the dark, and the soft gurgle of the water on the hull, and the closeness of the cabin.

"You any better?" Victoria asked Skye.

"Some."

"Want to sit up?"

He grunted. Victoria wrestled her man upward until he was resting against the cabin wall. She gave him a tin cup of water, which he drank slowly.

"Maybe I'll walk today," he said. "Need strength, if they put us off at Bellevue."

"What is this?" Victoria asked sharply.

"I think Bonfils is going to try to put you and me off at the next post. I'm guessing if I don't go voluntarily, he and Gill will put us off by force. He figures the fastest way to get rid of a rival is to keep me out of St. Louis."

"Sonofabitch," said Victoria.

"Why would he do this thing?" Lame Deer asked.

"Get me out of the way. That leaves only Simon MacLees," Skye said.

"My man?"

"Your man." Skye looked uncomfortable.

Lame Deer could make no sense of it. White men were mysterious to her, and there were undercurrents that she knew she would never understand.

She did not want to ride in the flatboat with only Red Gill and Alexandre Bonfils. The Skyes were a comfort to her. Victoria had become a friend and also a mentor, explaining the strange ways of white men. And Skye himself was a great chief among them, well known to her people and all the Peoples.

"My man no work for American Fur."

Skye stared into the gloom. She could barely make out his face. "I hear that Chouteau—he's the big chief—is going to hire your man. He's got trading experience with your people."

A faint light began to pervade their universe, a light so false that she dismissed it. Yet she knew dawn was not far off.

Simon had said nothing to her about any of it. Maybe he didn't know. But he could have sent word up the river with the men who brought messages.

"If you get off the boat, then we will too, and we will walk to the place of the many lodges."

Skye peered at her. "I don't think Bonfils would let you," he said.

"Let me go? Him?"

Skye shook his head. The light had thickened, and she could see him clearly now, staring at her from those intent blue eyes. He coughed and turned his head away, clearly letting her know he didn't wish to discuss what he knew. He was hiding things.

She felt an unnameable fear crawl through her. Something strange and unknowable and evil was crushing her. She thought of this place Bellevue, and thought that she might escape there—if she could. And then walk to St. Louis.

thirty

Red Gill was in a sour mood. His annual trip upriver had been ruined and his partner killed. He would arrive in St. Louis penniless after a summer of hard and dangerous work—unless he could get his furs back. He scarcely knew who to blame, but Skye was one, Marsh was another, and now Bonfils.

If Skye hadn't knocked Shorty down and steered the flatboat toward the stricken *Otter*, the trouble wouldn't have happened. Shorty was going to take his chances with that six-pounder, and he was right. All of Gill's troubles were launched when Skye steered the flatboat toward the steamer.

If Skye hadn't intervened, Shorty would be alive . . . probably, anyway. Marsh wouldn't have confiscated the bales of furs as smuggler's contraband. Skye wouldn't be lying in the cabin recovering from three wounds, Bonfils wouldn't be on board, goading Gill onward like some madman.

It was that goddam Skye's fault. Probably, anyway. Gill didn't want to think about what might have happened if Shorty had continued to plow past the stranded steamer under the mouth of that cannon. Well, he'd never know whether Marsh would have fired or not, after putting a ball across the bow. Just one ball from that cannon would have blown the flatboat to bits; one cannister of grape could have killed everyone aboard.

But Red Gill refused to think about it. He would have taken his chances, just like Shorty. He'd been taking chances all his life, and this was just one more chance—until Skye wrecked everything.

But a small voice in him kept whispering that Skye had done the only thing, and he had saved lives doing it. Gill hated to admit it, and pushed the thought out of mind.

Damned Skye.

Gill manned the tiller, not wanting Bonfils or the squaws to do it. And Skye was too weak, even though he was wandering around the deck now. They hadn't overtaken the *Otter*, and Gill didn't expect to, even though Bonfils insisted on floating day and night in pursuit, like some madman.

And that brought up another matter that was irritating Gill: what the hell difference did it make if the flatboat arrived in St. Louis after Marsh did? Bonfils had been saying he had to reach Pierre Chouteau ahead of Marsh or Gill would never get his furs back, but the more Gill thought about it, the less sense it made.

Gill intended to have it out with Chouteau: return them furs or get into big trouble with the government. Chouteau would understand. Gill was not above going to General Clark and telling the Indian superintendent the whole story, how Pratte, Chouteau and Company had employed Gill and Ballard to sneak ardent spirits to the trading posts, and were being paid off in buffalo robes and other furs, all off the books.

Chouteau would make sure the furs were returned, and probably chew out that damned Marsh for seizing them. So why the hell was Bonfils in such a rush? Why was the Creole pacing the boat, urging Gill to find the fastest current, talking like a wildman of overtaking the steamer, looking for the *Otter* at every wood stop, lamenting every minute the flatboat stopped to cook a meal or hunt for game to put in the pot? What was the matter with the man?

They had been drifting downriver for days, through a hot summer, enduring flies and mosquitos, seeing no one except for the occasional Opposition post, shabby little affairs, along the way.

But now they were approaching Bellevue, or Sarpy's Post as the company was calling it. It wasn't much of a trading center, but it served as an entrepôt, storing furs coming in from the Platte River, and tradegoods destined for the upper Platte and upper Missouri.

The closer they got, the wilder Bonfils became.

"How soon?" he demanded.

"Soon as the river takes us."

"Can't you hurry? Put up a sail?"

"What's at Sarpy's Post?"

"*Otter*. We'll pass them there."

"*Otter*'s down in Missoura now, near to Independence."

"No, it can't! Ah, my friend Gill, when we arrive at Bellevue, there are some small matters to take care of; very important for you and for me, *oui*?"

Gill glared. He was tired of all this.

Bonfils drew himself up, and whispered intensely. "Under no circumstances must the Cheyenne squaw be allowed off this boat."

"And who's to stop her? I sure won't."

"But you don't understand."

"Damn right I don't understand."

Bonfils smiled. "Monsieur Gill, there are things beyond your knowledge that affect you. Just trust me."

"Bonfils, that woman goes where she wants to go, because I ain't stopping her."

Bonfils smiled, nodded, and retreated. "Very well, but there is another matter. I want you to eject Skye and his squaw. Put them off."

That flabbergasted Gill. "Why?"

"As a favor to me, one that will benefit you, as you will see."

Gill didn't mind that idea so much. He had no use for Skye or that sharp-tongued little Crow woman he called his wife. Still, Bonfils was obviously a man full of schemes, and Gill wanted some answers.

"I want to know why, because if I don't like it, I ain't going to do it."

Bonfils sighed. "Ah, friend, when Skye arrives in St. Louis and meets Pierre Chouteau, I fear he will say things unflattering to me, and reduce my influence. It is because of my influence with my relatives that I can make sure you'll get your furs back, and your name will be cleared, and Capitaine Marsh, he will suffer for his rash conduct in seizing your cargo, *oui*? Trust me, my friend."

Gill didn't believe a word of it. "And what am I supposed to do?" he asked.

"Very simple. Tell him he must get off your boat."

"Let me get this straight. You want me to keep MacLees's woman aboard at all costs, but dump Skye."

"Ah, you have a discerning mind, monsieur."

"And for this I get my cargo back."

Bonfils smiled broadly, something velvety and soft in his brown eyes.

"I'll think on it. But I'll tell you one thing, Bonfils. That steamboat's a week ahead of us by now, and you won't see it again unless you've got wings. That buffalo crossing wrecked your little plan."

Gill fumed. He didn't trust the sonofabitch. He didn't need Bonfils. He needed one quiet word with Chouteau. And he didn't doubt that Pierre Chouteau would give him whatever he wanted. If the company lost its trading license for smuggling spirits into Indian Country, that would be the end of an empire. Gill had his own lever. So Bonfils could go to hell.

No sooner had Bonfils headed forward than Skye appeared at the cabin door. He looked weak and pale, but he was standing now, and the pain was gone from his eyes.

"I heard that, mate," he said.

Gill didn't reply.

"You want the story?"

Gill nodded, ready to discount everything the mountaineer said. He'd be just as bad as Bonfils.

"Well, there's a position open . . ." Skye said, his voice so low it scarcely carried to Gill's ears. Skye laid it out in simple terms: he and Bonfils were being considered for the trading position at Fort Cass, and maybe Simon MacLees too, though Skye said he had no direct knowledge of it.

As for MacLees, Bonfils believed that the arrival of his mountain wife in St. Louis would embarrass the former Opposition trader and ensure that Bonfils got the position, which was why he was obsessed with getting her there.

Gill cussed softly, a long, gentle stream of epithets that substituted for rage or amazement or sometimes wild humor. But he wasn't laughing now.

"How come you know this?"

"I've told you what I know. And what Bonfils said. I don't know the truth of it."

Gill believed the English sonofabitch, leaned over the transom, and spat. It was clear now. Alexandre Bonfils wasn't interested in doing Gill a favor; all he wanted was to get to St. Louis fast, with the Cheyenne woman he could use like some chess piece to embarrass a rival.

Gill spat again. He had Bonfils pegged now; should have seen it long ago. The Creole was a smooth, flattering bastard who made everything he did sound like a favor, even while he was using everyone in sight. Next thing Bonfils would do is tell Gill that shooting Shorty was a favor, too, because Gill would end up with all the furs, instead of half.

Gill had a redhead's temper, but now he held it in check. He wanted to think. If it came to trouble, he could knock that Creole right over the gunnels and let him swim. Gill wondered why he believed Skye, and realized there was something in the man that commanded respect, and that was the difference between Skye and Bonfils.

The country was changing now; more trees, some hardwoods, lower hills. The river had accumulated the waters of a dozen more streams and had grown majestic. Above the confluence of the Platte, they passed various Opposition posts and the ruins of several others. Fur outfits had fought over this country from the beginning. He even saw some stacked cordwood, offered by local woodhawks to steamboats for a price. The river was changing.

He knew he would make Sarpy's Post at Bellevue by sundown or soon after, and there he intended to stop. He was no longer in a rush. What difference did it make if Marsh got there first? Pierre Chouteau was no fool. He hadn't built the most powerful fur empire in the world by being gullible or reckless. The hell with Bonfils.

As if in response to the thought, Bonfils appeared aft.

"Is this it? Is this Bellevue?"

"Couple hours, maybe three."

"Are you ready?"

Gill spat, making a white dimple in the muddy brown river. "Guess we'll take our time," he said. "I want to visit with old Peter Sarpy, eh?"

"But we must hurry!"

"Not we; you. I'm going to stop for a good visit."

Bonfils smiled, even laughed, but Gill didn't miss the fleeting calculation in those liquid brown eyes.

thirty-one

Benton Marsh was so pleased with himself that he neglected his daily tongue-lashing. Normally, he selected one or another boatman who had shirked his duties, and rebuked the man in sardonic, withering language intended for as many ears as possible. The boat ran better because the crewmen never knew who would be next.

He had driven the *Otter* up a treacherous, shifting river to the farthest reaches of the unknown continent and returned bearing a fortune in furs and hides, along with the usual riffraff out of the mountains, plus precious information, worth plenty to the right parties.

Now he was negotiating the lower Missouri, still cautious even though the volume of water was greater, because of the many snags lurking just below the innocent surface, ready to tear out the hull of his boat and shatter men's dreams. Soon he would be in St. Louis, and then he would ride a hack triumphantly up the slope to Pierre Chouteau's ornate home, and whisper things into Chouteau's funneling ear, strictly in private. Benton Marsh knew himself to be an invaluable asset to the entrepreneur.

There, in a private warren of Chouteau's home, he would whisper the news. Such as that he had saved the company a great embarrassment. And that he had confiscated nineteen bales of buffalo hides from smugglers and scoundrels. And that he had concluded on good evidence that Skye was an ignoramus, an East End London hooligan, unsuited for so demanding and diplomatic a profession as trading; and alas, the company's favorite nephew, Bonfils, was impetuous and reckless.

With relish, he would tell Chouteau about Bonfils's rash and unauthorized use of the cannon, its fatal results, and its deleterious effect on trade with the Sioux. So much for that wretch! He would add that in his estimation, MacLees was the only man fit for the trading position. He wasn't sure whether he would say anything to Chouteau about the Cheyenne squaw, or that Marsh had rescued the young man from a scandal. He would decide about that when the time came.

Marsh could well envision Chouteau's response; always subdued but appreciative, the gravity of the man evident in his intent gaze, and his odd humor blooming in the small, almost smirky smile that would soon build in his dark face. There would be a bonus, of course. Maybe even a partnership share in the firm, at last. Chouteau knew whom to count on.

Soon Marsh would be seeing his lovely stepdaughter, Sarah, and would relish her happiness as the nuptial day approached. He had bought her a new pianoforte, and she was mastering it and singing, too. Her voice was a little less than sublime, but no matter. She could hold a tune as long as she didn't get into the upper ranges.

He watched the riverbanks roll by. They were tree-lined now, and the forests closed down upon the great stream, with rarely a patch of grass in sight. For two days he had been traveling through settled country. Now fueling was easy. He had only to pull up at one or another woodhawk's lot and load the heavy hardwood logs aboard, pay the man or leave a chit that was as good as cash anywhere. Sometimes the woodhawk's wife had fresh potatoes or carrots or greens, and these he bought too for the mess. His passengers had grown weary of buffalo and elk and antelope.

The *Otter* churned past rude hamlets, which always erupted whenever the boat passed by; dogs, children, adults, all of them waving, shouting, barking. Sometimes horses shied, and once in a while his passage sent a herd of cattle thundering away from the frightful apparition on the river. The passage of a steamboat was no small thing.

Now, fifty miles out of St. Louis, Missouri seemed totally civilized. Farms dotted the slopes. Towns of red brick and whitewashed cottages clustered along the banks. River traffic increased: ferries, sailboats, rowboats, fishing ketches, flatboats, and keelboats, all hauling goods and people up and down or across the broad river. Civilization at last.

He marveled that only a few weeks earlier he had reached a point near British possessions far to the north, after passing through an impenetrable wilderness that would remain that way for a century. Only a few days before, red-skinned savages had congregated about the boat, dumbstruck by its power, superstitious and frightened when he rang a bell, shot steam up the escapement, blew a whistle, or ordered the great paddle wheels to thrash water. White men understood such things; red men never would.

He would arrive in St. Louis at dusk, maybe at twilight, but with just enough daylight to reach a safe anchorage. Word of the *Otter*'s arrival would have reached the pier ahead of him, carried by horsemen, and by the time the packet eased to shore, a hundred lamps would light the way, dimpling the black waters with pricks of light. And a crowd would be gaping at the boat that traveled clear to the unmapped land of savages, some unimaginable distance away, and safely back.

Maybe even Chouteau.

Yes, he hoped Pierre would show up to celebrate Marsh's triumphant journey. It would be fitting.

Just as he hoped, he raised St. Louis just as blackness was lowering, and his pilot edged the riverboat through the inky waters until it gently bumped pilings in the levee. The rumble of the paddles suddenly ceased. At that moment, his pilot blew the whistle, and the engineers shot a great bang of steam through the escapement, and he could see the throng recoil, and then shout and cheer. Hats sailed, bull's-eye lanterns swung crazily, ladies in black lace sitting in ebony carriages watched demurely from behind their accordion-folded fans, well apart from the hoi polloi. Maybe one of those shining vehicles contained his wife or even Sarah Lansing. He would welcome the hugs, the exclamations, the sweet perfumes, the promise of bliss, the domestic hearth, the sweetness of one's own home.

He watched his crew run the grimy gangway to the levee, watched others tether the boat fore and aft with great looped hawsers, making it secure. He was in no rush. In fact, he was observing the crew: this was a test. The better men worked faithfully until dismissed. The worse ones were looking for ways to bolt for the nearest dive, or head for their wives, or paint the town. He had the answer to that, though. The pay envelopes would not be distributed until he was good and ready.

He saw a carriage drawn by a pair of dappled drays clop down the cobbled grade to the levee, and sensed that this time the chief officer of Pratte, Chouteau and Company would soon appear in his cabin instead of waiting for his arrival up the hill. The coachman drove straight to the gangway as the crowd parted, and indeed the man who emerged, stocky, dark, square-set, and splendidly if a bit casually dressed, set foot on the glistening cobbles, and then upon the gangway. He looked up at the master, and waved languidly.

Marsh beckoned him up and set out a bottle of cognac and some glasses on the small walnut table within. He lit the hanging oil lamp with his striker, and awaited the emperor, who swept in grandly.

"Ah, Benton, so good, so good, *mon ami*. You are back safely, and we see the vessel is heavy-laden and rides low. How do you fare? How is your health? Did we lose anyone?"

"No one I didn't intend to lose. And your health?"

"We are well, though madame struggles with gout, and there has been dysentery again. The whole city smells of excrement."

"Well, Pierre, we're in St. Louis with good news aplenty. You are rich, once again. Very, very rich."

"Ah! We shall see. In New York they speak dolorously of dropping prices. They have us by the throat." Chouteau plucked up the cognac and poured a generous dollop into the captain's cut-glass snifter.

"Tell us everything! But first, what do you carry?"

For an answer, Marsh pulled out his papers and ledgers and lay the cargo manifest before Chouteau. The entrepreneur donned his wire-rimmed spectacles, and began reading the watery black script, lifting the ledger pages up close to the soft light.

"*Manifique, c'est marveloux*. So much. Is there insect damage or soaking?"

"No, no trouble this time."

Chouteau read and reread the manifest. "There is more here than we were led by the expresses to believe we possess."

"Ah! Some nineteen bales of buffalo hide, and odds and ends I picked up along the way from savages."

"We are sure there is a story in it."

There was indeed.

Trenholm knocked politely. "We're secure. Crew wants to go," he said.

"No, not until every bale is safe in the warehouse."

"They're grumbling."

"Let them. Every bale accounted for, and a receipt for it.

They'll be freed in a few hours. Except for you, of course, and a half dozen men you select. They stay."

"Aye, sir."

Trenholm left, and they heard him clatter down the companionway.

Oddly, Chouteau's smile had vanished.

"Monsieur Marsh, is there anything urgent we should know?"

"Oh, a few small matters, an incident or two, and some action on my part that will save the company from embarrassment."

"Really, we shall relish the story."

"Yes, it'll take a bit, but we have time."

"Ah, my captain, was that not your wife and the lovely Miss Lansing we saw on the levee, awaiting your presence?"

"Yes, it was. They can wait a little. That's the fate of the wives of sailing men, I'm afraid. The lamp in the window."

Chouteau smiled gently. "We see things differently. A man who returns to his wife after a long absence should fall into her arms—assuming, of course, she is of a certain age and not infirm."

They laughed.

Chouteau stood. "You have mail from the posts, we presume?"

"Yes, as always. Quite a packet of it."

He handed Chouteau all the letters he had collected en route, reports and complaints that would give the fur magnate a fine idea of the situation at each fur post, and the preoccupations of each trader.

"We will read these, my friend. Come to our house at ten, and we will have a cigar in our study, and you can tell your anecdotes, eh?"

"Very well, sir."

"*Bien*! And tell your passengers, Bonfils and Skye, to come to our offices midmorning."

"They are not aboard, sir."

Chouteau stood stock still. "You have much to tell us, then. We will read this correspondence while you put this bateau in order and embrace your enchanting wife and family. Then, *mon ami*, we will see."

thirty-two

S arpy's Post, on the right bank of the Missouri at the confluence of the Platte, looked different from any other post that Skye had seen. This one was simply a hilltop farm, with a farmhouse and a few buildings scattered about. It was not fortified.

Were they that close to civilization? Or were the tribes in the vicinity, such as the Omahas, that pacific? Gill had steered the flatboat past several posts, mostly Opposition outfits, in the Council Bluffs area, but now he pulled the tiller and steered the boat toward the bank, where a few people stood watching.

"There's more to it than it looks," Gill said, reading Skye's mind. "This place—Bellevue—been in the middle of the fur trade from the get-go."

"Will we see white women?" Victoria asked.

Gill grinned. "Not as I ever heard. Some comely Omaha ladies, maybe."

"Where the hell are your women?"

"There ain't any. We get borned a different way. We cut off a toenail, put her in whiskey, and it grows."

Victoria laughed.

Skye saw that the people on shore were Indians after all, but dressed entirely in white men's duds, duck cloth pantaloons and chambray shirts, mostly. And the sole woman was in printed calico. Tame Indians, the mountaineers called them. Not the furred and feathered variety in the far West.

Gill steered the flatboat toward the crude landing, and tossed a hawser to one of the men, who wrapped it around a post poking up from the mud. Bonfils threw the plank gangway to the bank, stepped ashore ahead of the rest, grinning broadly. For once he didn't seem to be in a rush.

Lame Deer followed, her walk wary and cautious. She carried her girl in her arms, and then set Singing Rain on the damp earth. She was dressed in a fringed buckskin skirt and moccasins, and a blue cambray shirt, all quilled in the Cheyenne tradition, and sharply different from clothing of the tame Indians.

Skye followed, still weak on his pins and wobbly, but Victoria helped him alight. He wondered how he could manage the hundred yards upslope to the store, but taking a few steps at a time he worked his way forward, glad to be walking. Gill secured the boat, wrapping another hawser forward, and then joined them in the trek to the store.

"There's a mess of Sarpys in the fur business," he said. "Pete here, he's the son of old John, and coming along smartly in the company. His pa's a partner in the company, got a thirty-second of it, I think. Tom, an uncle, got himself blown up a few years ago, messing around a powder barrel."

By the time Skye reached the store, he was exhausted, and settled on a plank bench to catch his breath. He wasn't healing as fast as he had hoped, and was still just about useless. At first it had been the rib wound that tormented him; now it was the thigh wound, which ached mercilessly and drew the strength right out of him. Still, the wounds had scabbed over and weren't infected, and with some time he might recover his health. Victoria had taken good care of him, but he was still just about worthless.

The view was handsome from up there, and he studied the sparkling blue river while his heart thudded and slowed, and a dry breeze toyed with him. Victoria headed into the store, along with Bonfils and Lame Deer.

"I got some private business with Sarpy," Gill said, heading for the farmhouse.

Skye guessed it had to do with smuggled alcohol. Red Gill struck him as a bold, likeable, daring frontiersman who would make his coin any way he could, no matter what the rules were. He might well have supplied Sarpy's Post with ardent spirits, if indeed that was Gill's real business.

After Skye recovered his breath, he wobbled to his feet and entered the post, which looked more like an ordinary store for white people than most trading posts. But he spotted the usual blankets, awls, trade muskets, shot and powder, knives, pots, skeins of beads, along with sacks of cornmeal, sugar, coffee, and all the rest. He loved these stores, with all their small sweet luxuries, and meant to buy Victoria something. A black-suited clerk hovered behind a plank counter, keeping a wary eye on customers, but his eye betrayed a lively curiosity as he looked over these latest specimens from the far West.

"Out of the mountains?" the clerk asked.

"From the Stony Mountains," Skye said.

"You've come a piece." The man was itching to find out Skye's business, but Skye wasn't in a talking mood.

"We got good prices, better than mountain prices," the clerk said as Skye studied the stock.

What struck Skye at once was Bonfils, who was holding up a gaudy red and blue blanket for Lame Deer. Her eyes shone with pleasure.

"Madame, it is for you!" he said with a gallic flourish. "And now I shall buy one for the *petite fille!*"

He dug through the two-point blankets and plucked up a green one for the child.

"Ah! I see smiles! Now, how about a little paint, eh?"

He led the Cheyenne woman toward a shelf filled with small, papered cubes of vermillion, and handed one to her.

"There's this, but perhaps you'd like some ocher too! And of course some lamp black, and some cobalt!"

"Ah!" she cried.

"And let us not forget some big beads, and thread and needle, and a string of jingle bells! Now, how about some to-bacco? Ah, a few plugs, and a clay pipe! You shall have a good puff or two, all the way to St. Louis!"

Lame Deer was laughing and shaking her head. Skye had not seen her laugh for weeks.

"Now, madame, what about a hatchet, and some vel-veteen for a skirt? You'll have time to work it up, and when you find Simon MacLees, you'll look like a Cheyenne queen!"

"What is queen?"

"Very beautiful and important lady. MacLees will go mad with happiness!"

"Ah! Ah!" she cried, fondling the purple velveteen.

Bonfils raised two fingers to the clerk, who cut two yards of it and folded it neatly.

"You got a little lard?" Bonfils asked.

The clerk nodded, and pulled a tin off a shelf.

"Good. We'll mix us some paints!"

Swiftly, Bonfils heaped the goods on the counter, and then added cornmeal, coffee beans, parched corn, sugar, molasses, and chocolates.

Even as the clerk was totting up the cost of all that, Bonfils was mixing vermillion with the lard until he had a shiny red paste, and then he began painting Lame Deer, a thick red streak down her forehead, chevrons of red on her brown arms, while she laughed and squealed. When Bonfils was done, he stepped back to study his handiwork.

"Yes, yes," he said, "you'll be the belle of St. Louis. Ah, the perfect savage!"

"Goddam," said Victoria, approving. "Skye, why don't you get me that stuff?"

"With what?"

"You gonna take me to the city with all the lodges dressed like this?"

Skye grinned. "When I get that job, I'll dress you in satins and silks, like all those Assiniboine ladies up at Fort Union."

Victoria grunted, not certain she liked that.

Skye found a barrel to sit on. He could scarcely stand up for five minutes.

Bonfils pulled real gold out of some inner pocket, and paid the clerk with yellow coins so bright that they stole sunlight from the room.

"Where's Sarpy?" Bonfils asked.

"At the house, talking with your friend."

"Well, say hello to him, *mon ami*, and help me load this stuff."

The clerk lugged sacks of food and the heap of Lame Deer's goods down the steep slope, and left them in the flatboat cabin, while Bonfils added a few yards of gaudy ribbon to his purchases, and then handed the ribbon to Lame Deer.

"You come along, *ma cheri*, and we'll tie some ribbons to your hair, *oui*? Then we'll have a big smoke!"

Lame Deer's eyes lit up again. She had turned into a wild beauty, with the vermillion striping her face and arms, and the gaudy blanket drawn around her, and the clay pipe in her hands.

Soon, Lame Deer, her little girl, and Bonfils retreated to the flatboat, and the clerk finished his hauling and returned, winded, to the store.

"Haven't seen gold out here ever," he said, fingering Bonfils's ducats. "I had to do some calculatin' as to the value."

Victoria was sulking. "How come he bought all that stuff for her, eh? Maybe he could buy some for me! You gonna fix me up for when we get to this place of the lodges? You gonna make me happy, or am I gonna look like some damn Injun around all those white women in all their silk stuff, eh?"

Something about all this puzzled Skye, but he had no

answers, and figured he would find out soon enough. Was Bonfils courting the Cheyenne woman? Did he plan to steal her from MacLees?

Skye had some residual credit with the company, but he wasn't inclined to spend it on foofaraw. When he returned to the mountains, it would be with a new percussion rifle, made by the Hawken Brothers of St. Louis, some good DuPont powder and shot and caps, some real cow-leather boots, and a load of necessaries. And a jug or two if he could manage it. Not just trade whiskey, either, but some real, potent, smooth Kentucky.

He was out of sorts, had been ever since he was wounded, and his spirits were darkened by uncertainty. He wanted that trading job badly. It would provide him with a living, and put him in daily contact with Victoria's people. But as much as he wanted that, he felt doubts gnawing at him, things just beyond the pale, things unfathomed, a thundercloud just over the horizon.

There was the question of his health. Would he ever recover? And if he were offered this job, and took it, he would become a company man, and that meant obeying instructions and doing things he would not otherwise do. . . . Would he be required to cheat? Put a thumb in the sugar cup, the way he had seen traders do? Water the whiskey, adulterate the flour with clay, all for a profit? Would he be at the beck and call of Chouteau? He had been a free man of the mountains for many years, but would he still be free? Would he still be honorable?

While he was fretting over that, and Victoria was poking her way through the tradegoods and muttering happily, he heard Red Gill yelling. The boatman stepped into the trading room, peered wildly at the people within, spotted Skye, and beckoned.

"He's gone!" Gill roared at the puzzled Skye. "Bonfils!"

Skye hastened to the door and peered down the steep path to the riverbank. The flatboat had vanished. It was so far gone that Skye could not even spot it down the long sweep of the river.

thirty-three

Benton Marsh was feeling testy as he stepped from his cabriolet and faced the front door of the brick Chouteau residence, which he privately regarded as a grotesque melange of porticos, gargoyles, dormers, cornices, motley architectural styles, and gallic gaud.

For some reason, Pierre Chouteau put him on the defensive and he didn't like it. For that matter, he didn't like that frog, Chouteau. After months on the steamboat, where he was absolute master of his universe and his word was law, he suddenly found himself back on the ground, and in a world where there were masters of men, chief among them the man he was about to visit.

A handsomely liveried house slave appeared out of the darkness and led the cabriolet off. The trotter's hooves clopped hollowly on the glistening cobbles as Marsh headed for the enameled door of the famous house where all the spiderwebs of ambition in St. Louis were spun. It was an ostentatious house, though actually a large, homey and comfortable one.

The door swung open even before he reached it, and a graying slave in black brocaded silk with white ruffles at the collar and sleeves let him in and took his top hat and umbrella.

"He's off there in the parlah, suh," she said.

Marsh trod over an Aubusson carpet with bold golds and blues in it through the parlor to the lamplit study, Chouteau's private and secluded den, where much of what happened west of the Missouri River was decided over snifters of brandy or glasses of amontillado. The captain saw no signs of other life in the house, and supposed that Madame had retired to her chambers.

Chouteau was standing, a certain smile on his face. That smile, which always resembled a smirk, had always annoyed Marsh. No one but a dark-fleshed Creole frog would smile like that, as if in amusement or disdain. But Marsh had endless experience smoothing over his own choleric temper, and smiled warmly as he and the master of an American empire shook hands and proceeded through the wine-pouring and cigar rituals.

Marsh was no good at small talk, and wished that this St. Louis Midas, this bilingual Western Caesar, would get on with it.

"Anything in the mail?" Marsh asked, impatiently.

"Ah, *mon ami*, why is it that our traders complain that they have too much of this and not enough of that one year, and the opposite the next year? We have a time supplying them with whatever feathers and beads and trinkets their tribes demand at the moment. Fashion, it is ephemeral, *n'est pas?*"

Chouteau swirled a stiff drought of ruby port in his glass and swallowed it in a gulp.

"Ah! We have discovered the cure for aches of the body," he said. "But my dear *capitaine*, we believe you have some stories you wish to divulge, in strictest privacy?"

At last, the cue, Marsh thought impatiently. He scarcely knew where to begin. But the Cheyenne squaw was a good enough place. Later, when Chouteau had imbibed more wine, Marsh would talk about such disasters as firing a cannon into the Sans Arcs, killing a boatman and wounding Skye, jettisoning Chouteau's own relative Bonfils, booting Skye off the boat, and a few small items like that.

"Well, yes, in chronological order. We were proceeding homeward when we were flagged by a squaw on the riverbank. I was reluctant to stop, but did so because Skye pressed me to. A *squaw*, after all. The squaw, a Cheyenne woman, spoke a little English. She wanted a ride to St. Louis for herself and her little brats, and had some robes and a few fox and otter pelts to trade. . . . So I offered deck passage; nothing to lose, of course. . . ."

Marsh described what he learned from Skye. "The squaw was the mountain wife of Simon MacLees! Imagine it! Going to St. Louis to find out what happened to her man!" Marsh laughed darkly. "When I found that out, I put her off at Fort Pierre, along with her brats, fumigated the cabin, too. Camphor works well. And so . . ." he spoke softly, "I saved you and also my family embarrassment. Poor Sarah! How agitated we all would have been! Imagine that squaw and her little breed brats showing up at his doorstep on the eve of the wedding! And of course," there was a question in his voice, "I saved embarrassment to the company too. You were considering MacLees for the Fort Cass position. Am I not correct?"

Chouteau nodded softly, and said nothing. That was one of the maddening things about the man. He funneled vast amounts of information through those hairy ears poking from his wavy black hair, yet offered none; not even his reaction to events. Marsh swallowed back his choler but nursed a grievance. Chouteau had not yet said one word to him about his successful trip up that dangerous river. Not one word thanking him for all his devotion and skills.

Chouteau whirled the red ambrosia around his wineglass and waited, quizzically.

"I must tell you candidly, the Skyes took the squaw's part, and so vehemently I was forced to eject them as well," Marsh said. "I will not have mutiny or rebellion on my ship."

This time the whirling of the glass ceased altogether. "Tell us more," Chouteau said softly.

Marsh did, stressing the insolence of the man, the sheer stubborn arrogance of this common slug off the docks of London. But Chouteau simply stared blandly, his odd smirk gone, and Marsh had the feeling he had displeased Chouteau.

"I will not have anyone interfering with my command of the ship!" he said firmly, "Any more than you would tolerate someone meddling with your operations."

"Did Skye ask anything of you?"

Marsh shook his head, not wanting Chouteau to know that he had kept the squaw's fare to St. Louis, the robes and pelts.

"We will get his story," Chouteau said. "Is he coming?"

"I suppose so. Don't put much credence in anything he says; the man is utterly unreliable."

Chouteau arched an eyebrow, and that smirky smile emerged on his face once again. "And?" he said.

"I'm afraid I had some difficulties with Alexandre Bonfils as well," Marsh said reluctantly. This interview was not proceeding as he had hoped.

"Ah! Tell us!" Suddenly Chouteau was all ears.

Marsh sighed. "It's a complex story, my friend. And I must backtrack a bit. You see, Skye and the squaws arranged passage with two flatboat operators, a pair of scoundrels named Red Gill and Shorty Ballard. Do you know them?"

Chouteau's gaze turned opaque, and Marsh could not fathom what was passing through the skull of that man.

"Well, one day we hit a gravel bar that hadn't been there before, and far from help, too. The usual procedures didn't lift us over, and along came that flatboat with Ballard at the tiller . . ."

He went on to describe how it had taken a shot across the bow to bring in the boat, saying nothing about Skye's role in the process; the unloading of the cargo to a gravelly island just the other side of the bar, and the refloating of the boat.

"We were about to reload, having passed over the bar and repaired the paddle wheels and anchored in safe water, when at dawn, in fog, we were beset by a Sans Arc war party, which was filtering around the shore opposite the boat, obviously dangerous.

"Bonfils discovered them. They had collected around the

camp of the flatboat people, and it turned out that Skye was negotiating with them. What they really wanted was a ride across the river; they were in hot pursuit of the Pawnees. Skye, without authority, offered them the use of the riverboat. But Bonfils was unaware of that. He rounded up a crewman or two and charged the cannon with grape and fired, scattering and wounding the Sans Arcs, killing Shorty Ballard, injuring Skye, and killing one of MacLees's brats."

Chouteau pursed his lips.

A silence stretched out, and Marsh listened to the ticktock of the grandfather clock.

"Of course the shots awakened me. When I found out about it, that Bonfils had done this without authorization, risking the company's trade with the Sioux and killing a white man, I of course put him ashore at once."

Chouteau's liquid eyes seemed to flare and then the light in them faded. "Skye is alive?"

"I suppose."

"Ballard is dead? And of the Sans Arcs what is known?"

"Nothing."

"Ah, *c'est mal*. And where is our young relative?"

The words were meant to remind Marsh there were blood connections between the brigade leader and Chouteau, and Marsh didn't like to be reminded of that.

"Coming down the river, obviously," Marsh retorted crisply.

"Is that all, then?"

"No. It was obvious to me that Ballard and Gill were hauling cargo gotten in illegal trade, no doubt supplying spirits to the Opposition, so following many precedents done by this company and encouraged by the army, I seized their cargo, which is why we have more bales of pelts than were on the manifests supplied by the posts. A fine coup, if I may say so. You are more than a thousand dollars richer."

Chouteau's soft white hand went still again, and the wine

stopped its mad whirl around the glass and settled into a placid red pool. "And you are going to report this smuggling and seizure to General Clark, we suppose?" he said at last.

"Of course! That pair were up to no good; and we have an extra thousand dollars of profit from it. And we have, to borrow your phrase, erased the Opposition."

"My capitaine, please go to the levee at once and arrange that those bales, the confiscated ones, be separated from the rest and put in another part of the warehouse and guarded carefully."

Marsh nodded curtly. The command was a rebuke.

"We think it would perhaps be best for us to discuss matters with Red Gill when he arrives. Say nothing to General Clark."

"My navigator's license requires me to report such matters promptly."

Chouteau's smirky smile appeared once again, and he nodded.

"Very well, monsieur. Go report to General Clark in the morning. We would not want you to lose so important a thing as your livelihood."

Marsh started to stand, but Chouteau stayed him with a wave of his soft hand. "How far behind you are they?"

"I don't know or care. I have done everything in my power to preserve the good name, profit, and influence of this company, and what a boatload of smugglers and malcontents do is not my business."

Chouteau merely smiled, a response Marsh did not like. There still had not been the slightest commendation of his considerable efforts, or his good judgment, or his formidable skills.

"Is your report now complete, my *capitaine*?"

Marsh nodded.

"*Alors*, Hannah will show you out."

Marsh retreated, seething.

thirty-four

Bonfils gone. The flatboat gone. The Cheyenne woman and her daughter on that renegade boat.

Skye squinted, hoping to see the distant vessel, but he saw nothing but a broad blue stream wending its way to the sea. It was very quiet at Sarpy's Post.

Red Gill cursed softly, a string of oaths that seemed to vent his anger the way a valve hissed steam from a boiler. He wheeled around and headed for Sarpy's house again.

"I'll fix this," he said.

Skye felt weary; he was far from healed, and an hour's sojourn here had exhausted him. He wanted only to find refuge in his bunk. He had nothing but the clothes on his back. His mountain rifle, powderhorn, beartooth necklace, top hat, blankets and robes and spare clothing lay in that flatboat, along with all of Victoria's spare gear and duds. He wore only a blue calico shirt, duckcloth trousers, and summer moccasins.

He hadn't the faintest clue about the future. By rights, he should stay here and heal up, and then try to arrange some credit with the company. He still hoped to get to St. Louis but that prospect was looking bleak now, and the chance of winning that trading position was leaking away with every mile that Bonfils put between himself and his rival.

He turned to Victoria, who was standing beside him.

"Don't know what to do," he said.

She wasn't even cussing. Instead, she was studying the river.

"Maybe Sarpy would hire me long enough to get well and earn an outfit."

The thought discouraged him. An outfit would require a year of hard labor.

"You any ideas?"

"Horses."

"Don't know how we'll pay, but I'll go talk to Sarpy after Gill's done with him. They owe us a couple of pack animals, at least."

She squinted at him. "You going back?"

"No. We've started something. Let's finish it."

"You think Bonfils, he gets to be the trader?"

"I think Bonfils thinks we're going to quit and go west. He's counting on it. And I'm not going to satisfy him."

"You got some wounds ain't healed up, but you ain't quitting."

"No, not quitting. Never quit. Just keep going. People who quit, they just betray themselves."

She reached over to touch him, and he felt her hand press against his forearm.

They would go on, never quit, never surrender. Even in failure, it is a good thing to know you've tried with all your strength.

Which reminded him that he didn't have the strength of a baby, and he needed to sit down before he toppled over. He eased to the earth, and she joined him, watching the river to St. Louis flow by.

In a while, Gill appeared, and with him a short, thin young man.

"Mister Skye, this is Pete Sarpy, the trader here. I told him what happened. In fact, I told the whole story. I told him about Bonfils, and Lame Deer, and the riverboat, and all the rest of it."

Sarpy extended a smooth hand, which Skye shook. "I've

heard of you," he said. Upriver, Skye's a name to be reckoned with."

"And so are your family," Skye replied.

"You going to talk to old Pierre, eh? He keeps to himself pretty much. Gill here, he knows Pierre better than I do."

Something passed between Gill and Sarpy that Skye couldn't fathom.

Sarpy looked at Skye and Victoria. "Your outfit went down the river, eh?"

Skye nodded.

"Go in there and pick up a new one."

"With what?"

"On my say-so. I will forward the bill to Pierre Chouteau. Gill's getting an outfit too. Then you'll take that sailboat down there."

Skye saw a small craft tied to the levee. A sail was wrapped around the boom. He doubted the homemade boat reached twenty feet stem to stern.

"We use it to get across the river, pick people up," Sarpy said.

"You won't need it?"

"Sure we'll need it, but we'll get it back."

Skye felt a stir. He knew sails and he knew wind, and he saw that the little craft below could maneuver easily in the broad river.

"I can sail it," Skye said, even though he had never set foot in so small a sailing craft.

"Royal Navy," Sarpy said.

Gill was grinning. Skye knew intuitively that all this was Gill's doing, and he wondered what hold the boatman had over Sarpy. There were mysteries about Gill. Maybe someday Skye would get the story.

Skye and Victoria hiked down the slope to the little boat, discovering a hand-crafted vessel made of hand-sawn planks caulked with oakum. The flat bottom would be unstable in a wind, but he could see nothing else wrong with it except that it had no cabin, no shelter against the elements. There was nothing within; no oars, no anchor or rope. Just some flat benches. A tiller operated the rudder at the rear.

"Does it have a keel?" he asked Sarpy.

"Small one, about a foot."

"It'll do," Skye said.

Wearily he hiked up the steep slope, wondering whether his leg would give out, but he made the hill and paused to catch his breath at the store. Victoria was already within, piling blankets and gear on the counter.

Gill came in, grinning. "Guess I got some pull, eh?" he said.

"I don't know how you arranged it. This is the only boat they have here."

"Like I say, old Red Gill's got a way to get around in the world. You'd better remember it. You ever sailed a small boat?"

"No, but I know I can."

"They flip over easy, just a freshet will do it. This has a squared bottom, and it don't lay over like a round-bottomed hull."

"We'll manage."

Skye headed for the rack of rifles, and plucked up each one, hefting it, finding them unbearably heavy. He knew when he was stronger they would feel lighter. But for the moment, his still and sore arm was crying out whenever he lifted a weapon.

He tried several, some of them old longrifles from the eastern states, knowing they would be clumsy in the mountains. They were all flintlocks, and he wanted a percussion lock. But the only percussion weapons were brand new.

He found a Hawken .53-caliber mountain rifle, heavy, half-stocked short-barreled, built to endure the abuse of the wilderness. He knew that he had a quality weapon in his hands. The rifled barrel looked clean to the eye, and the oversized lock looked like it would survive all manner of battering. He checked the nipple within the wire mesh protective basket, looked at the hickory ramrod, cocked and lowered the hammer gently, testing the trigger mechanism.

It would do.

His arm hurt like the devil.

He found a used powderhorn, a pick with which to clean out the nipple, and a box of fulminate of mercury caps, good quality ones of brass rather than copper. He picked up a bullet mold, and some small pigs of lead, but also a pound of pre-cast balls. A one-pound can of DuPont would do for the time being, and he added some patches.

Victoria's heap on the counter grew at an amazing pace. She had added flint and firesteel, a butchering knife, a tin cookpot, a skillet, some tin messware, a ball of soap, an awl, thread, a hank of hemp rope, thong leather, and a dozen other items.

"Victoria, we can't pay all that back. Not with this too." He hefted the rifle.

"That's a damn pretty gun," she said.

"We'll see if it shoots true."

She eyed him. "You can hardly lift it."

That was true. All of this hefting of heavy metal objects had started his arm howling and his rib wound aching so badly he was having trouble breathing again.

"You get down to the boat, dammit," she said.

He didn't. He stubbornly helped gather the outfit, even as Gill got his together, along with plenty of parched corn, sugar, coffee, tea, cornmeal, and other foodstuffs.

"They're not going to let us walk out of here with this," he said to Gill.

The boatman grinned. "I got ways," he said.

"You got powers beyond mortal knowledge," Skye retorted.

It proved to be true.

When the clerk tallied up the goods, Skye's outfit came to

over two hundred dollars, and Gill's came to a hundred fifty, including food for the three of them. But the clerk offered no quarrel. Gill began grinning.

"See what powers I have, Skye?"

"It's Mister Skye, mate."

"Then it's Mister Gill, if that's how it is."

They laughed. Skye's ribs howled.

The clerk helped them tote the heavy loads down to the levee and even helped stow the goods in the little sailboat, under the neutral stare of a few Omaha women.

When the stuff had been settled in the hull, the clerk stepped to shore, and stood by.

Gill undid the ties, while Skye unrolled the sail and ran it up the mast and tied it off. A summery beeze ballooned the linseed-oiled linen, and it tugged the little boat outward.

From above, Sarpy waved.

Gill replied with a casual dip of the arm.

And Skye marveled at the hold Red Gill had over Pratte, Chouteau and Company.

thirty-five

lexandre Bonfils had exactly the cargo he wanted, and had put his rival behind him. For as long as he could peer backward, toward Sarpy's Post, he had seen no one on the levee. The Skyes were within, dickering for some goods, and Gill was off visiting with Sarpy.

To be sure, the Cheyenne squaw glared at him darkly, and he knew she was angry about all this. She paced the flatboat, knowing she was a prisoner. But he would deal with her after he put a few river miles between him and the fur post. Just then, he wanted to keep the flatboat in the fastest current and make his escape so successful that Skye would never catch up.

Poor old Skye! Bonfils laughed. He had Skye's outfit aboard, effectively stopping hot pursuit by horseback or canoe or any other means. He also had Gill's possessions, a kitchen outfit and some sacks of meal and old clothing. Gill could not move until he replenished everything needed for river travel.

But best of all, Bonfils had the squaw and the brat, and once he arrived in St. Louis, he would play that card for all it was worth. And that was going to be pure fun. He could hardly wait to see the shock and embarrassment on the faces of the bride's family; the astonishment with which MacLees would discover his mountain squaw and brat.

Oh, the secrets would tumble out, and St. Louis would chuckle up its sleeve and gossip about it for months. And old Uncle Pierre would come to laugh secretly at MacLees, and en-joy the whole spectacle. The Creoles would make much merri-ment out of it, but the miserable Protestant English-speaking population would cluck, cluck, cluck and whisper the scandal from ear to ear.

It was usually easy to find the channel and he had no trou-ble steering the flatboat to that fast-flowing heart of the Mis-souri. It was only on the long sweeping bends that he found he had to steer the flatboat into the swift current and keep it from being swept toward shore.

The squaw's relentless gaze disconcerted him. She never looked elsewhere; always at him, as if assessing his very soul. Not that she would know what a soul was. Savages wouldn't fathom such a thing. And yet that unblinking examination of him was a little unnerving. She had drawn her brat to her, and was absently comforting the child with her hand as she stud-ied Bonfils. Would the woman never even blink?

At last the squaw studied the shore, and Bonfils wished to know what thoughts passed through her head. He would have to be careful not to let her escape. She was the prize. St. Louis was a vast distance away, and she would have her chances every time they cooked a meal or otherwise approached a riverbank. Islands! He would make sure they anchored only at islands so she couldn't just pick up the brat and hurry away in the night. Ah, there was always a way!

She probably entertained only one thought in her head, and that was to find Simon MacLees and present her little girl to him, and begin nesting with him again. Well, Bonfils would help her do it! And that was why she would stay with him. She could not get to St. Louis unaided.

A few hours elapsed, with the woman alternately staring at him from a blank face, and viewing the shore. When the time to stop and rest and eat had passed and twilight lowered, she grew agitated but said nothing. Bonfils found the travel easy: the river took them along without effort or even steering. The empty flatboat cleared all snags and bars, and seemed unstoppable.

Then, at twilight, the woman arose, negotiated the passage alongside the cargo box and cabin, and confronted Bonfils.

"You left them behind," she said.

"We will go to St. Louis faster this way. You will see your man sooner."

"Why did you leave them?"

"Because Skye and I want the same job as trader. If I get there ahead of him, I will get it."

He wasn't very sure of that but it sounded good. He still had to deal with whatever Marsh told Chouteau about the Sans Arcs.

"Why am I here with you? Why did you not leave me back there with the others?"

"So that I can take you to your husband."

She stared at him again, her warm brown eyes unblinking.

"It is not so," she said.

"Of course it is so, *madame*."

She sighed. "We are hungry. My girl need food." She pointed. "There is a place. See, many trees. We will have a fire and eat."

"No, we have to get to St. Louis."

She stood silently a minute. "I will walk to this place, St. Louis," she said. "Let me go."

"Too far to walk."

"I will walk for many suns. I am not afraid."

"No one can walk that far."

She seemed puzzled. "I can walk as far as I want."

"Well, you just wait. Maybe after dark I will find a place."

He could use some food himself but there had been no islands.

He took another tack. "If you walk, you won't be able to carry all the things I got for you."

"Why did you get those things?"

"So you can look pretty. When we get to St. Louis, you must wear your paint, and put feathers in your hair, and wear the jingle bells on your feet, yes? Then you will look like a queen of the Cheyenne, and all the white men will look upon you with wonder."

She did not reply for a moment. Then, "Is that what the white women wear?"

"Oh, yes, feathers and beads and warpaint. They are all savages at heart."

He felt her stare raking him again, and didn't like it.

"Marriage is sacred among the People," she said softly, carefully choosing words. "We mate for life. My man MacLees is mine forever, and I am his. I will go to him and give him all that I can. All that I am. He will be sad because we have lost a son. But he will be glad to see our daughter again, and see how she has grown. She walks in beauty. She is a wise child. He will rejoice to see me. See? I know how to say these things in English."

They sailed into dusk, and then Bonfils did discover a

wooded island. A swift survey revealed a thin strand of wooded land, dividing two sweeping branches of the river.

He pulled the tiller and the flatboat headed for a clear area of the shore, where there seemed to be no tangle of submerged limbs.

She watched him, studied the island, studied the shoreline, looking like a caged eagle wanting to fly away. He would have to be careful. Keep his rifle in hand, keep her away from it, keep her away from the boat, compel her to gather wood, build a fire, and start a kettle of cornmeal boiling while he watched over her and the girl. The girl, that was it. The girl was his hostage. He wondered whether she would resist when it came time to travel again. The girl would solve that, but he didn't want to be so obvious. In the morning he would step aboard with the girl. Lame Deer would come because she had to.

They bumped the shore, and she leapt gracefully to land, carrying her baby in one arm. He followed, tied the flatboat to the thick brush, and unloaded some kitchen goods. She and the child had vanished into a thicket. He swiftly cased the island; it covered perhaps two hectares and neatly divided the river. The banks seemed a vast distance away, low black walls across moon-silvered water.

She took an interminable time, but finally she did emerge from darkness carrying an armload of dry kindling. She carried flint and steel in a small beaded pouch at her waist, and after much effort—a moist breeze discouraged fire-making—she nursed a small flame. An hour later they were eating yet another meal of cornmeal mush; if it were not for some salt he acquired at Sarpy's store, it would have been almost unbearable.

She ate with her fingers, dipping them into a bowl, and fed MacLees's brat the same way.

"It was an accident," he said. "I didn't see the boy—"
She stared at him.
"I didn't know your son was there. There were the Sans

Arcs, and the fog, and we were being attacked, and I drove them off."

"The one who died," she said, "he was my man's son. I will tell my man about it. Yes, I will tell him that you put powder in the big gun and aimed it, and killed the one who we are talking about, and also the boatman, and wounded Mister Skye very badly. This I will tell my man with a tongue filled with fire. I will speak words of smoke and flame, like the crackling of wood. He will know what to do."

Bonfils heard the threat in her voice. "You haven't grieved. You should grieve. Don't women who lose a son or husband cut half their hair off? Isn't that the sign of grief among the Cheyenne? A woman's hair cut on one side?"

She nodded. "It is the way of my People. But not MacLees's people."

"You should do that. Ah, yes, it would truly tell MacLees that you grieve." And make her even wilder looking and more barbaric to St. Louis sensibilities, he thought.

Lame Deer suddenly looked desolate.

She scooped the last of the mush and slid her laden fingers into Singing Rain's mouth. Then she walked to the river and washed her hands and Bonfils could barely see her in the blackness. She stayed there a long time, while the moon climbed and then vanished behind clouds. He scanned the night sky and decided it would not rain; not for a while. He was uneasy about sharing the flatboat cabin with her. In fact, he thought he might disarm her; especially that knife she wore and used so deftly.

He heard loons calling on the water and a disturbance on shore. Unseen creatures swept through the air about him, and he wondered what they were, and what they were hunting. And still she did not return.

He kicked the fire to pieces and poured water over the ashes, not wanting to be the cynosure of any eyes.

The moon emerged from a silver-lined cloud, and he

beheld her again, a dim figure in the pale light. He intended to travel at once, and motioned her toward the flatboat, which rocked quietly in the river, shedding sickly moonlight from its dull hull, thunking softly against a submerged log.

She followed him, stepping into the boat, helping the little girl, offering no resistance.

It was then that he noticed: she had sawed away the left half of her jet hair. On the right, it hung loosely braided over her breast; on the left, it dangled in crude strands to ear-level. The barbaric sign of mourning. She turned to him, letting him see her disfigurement, her head thrown back in faint disdain, something proud and savage in her ravaged face. Perfect! He exulted. It would add to the sensation she made in St. Louis.

thirty–six

*V*iolent gusts threatened to tip the crude sailboat and swamp it. Skye had to drop the sails during windy moments for fear of capsizing. A south wind at times checked their progress.

They drove downriver for two days without spotting the flatboat. The plan was to sail night and day, taking turns at the tiller. But the second night a massive cloud cover obscured the shores and plunged them into inky blackness, and they could only drift across the currents until they struck land, and wait for better visibility.

The next day they started downstream under cast-iron skies that soon began to drizzle, chilling them all. Victoria kept glancing at Skye, worried that the cold rain would further weaken him.

"You all right?" she asked.

Skye nodded from his pallet.

"You ain't," she said.

Skye agreed. He was maddeningly weak and the numbing rain was bringing on a fever. She nodded to Gill, and they headed for shore again. Gill dropped the sail and wrapped it around the boom, while Victoria pulled a tarpaulin over the boom and anchored its corners to the gunnels, supplying a shelter of sorts, open at both ends but at least a haven of dryness.

The rain pelted down, spattering the river about them, dripping through a hole in the canvas, gusting inward from the aft end of their tentlike shelter. It chilled all of them. It drizzled into the belly of the sailboat and Skye knew they were going to have to bail soon, or slosh around with inches of water on the planks.

He remembered the crude comfort of the flatboat with its enclosed cabin, and he knew that Bonfils and Lame Deer and her daughter were enjoying some measure of comfort.

Gill, cussing softly, scooped water out of the boat using a cooking kettle and a skillet. Skye wished he could help, and at one point sat up to take over the bailing. But then he fell back upon the stacked supplies.

"Don't do that," Victoria said.

"Got to help Red."

"You get sick."

Skye was feeling plenty sick. The rain had halted his healing and left him weak and shaky. "I have no fire in me," he said.

"You'll get better."

"I wonder."

"It take long time; you got three wounds, two very bad."

Skye sighed. Would he ever get well? What if he sank into sickliness, and became dependent on Victoria to keep him going? Was his life going to change because of his wounds? He'd seen plenty of shot-up men fumbling through hopeless days.

"You stay in there, Skye. I'll pitch this damned water out," Gill said.

"You'll get sick yourself."

"Been sick before. I don't have no holes in me."

Gill scooped another thin load of water with his sheet metal skillet.

They could not manage a fire that day. Skye felt a ravenous thirst for tea. If he could have a few cups of steaming tea his soul and body would be repaired. But there wasn't a dry stick of wood in sight. So they all starved.

"I'm ready to eat a catfish," Gill said. "You got to understand that's the sickliest flesh ever I ate, but I'd eat one now and lick my chops too."

Skye lost his hunger and lay quietly, a blanket over him that only partly subdued his shivering. Wet gusts bulged the tarpaulin, spraying water within. He wondered if he would ever be warm again. This was worse than trying to get through an arctic night in the mountains rolled in a pair of buffalo robes.

Red sat inside the shelter, only to bolt outside every few minutes, never happy. He dripped water. His coppery hair was plastered to his freckled face. He looked like a trapped animal. Finally he began untying the boat.

"I'm steering out and letting it drift," he said. "I'll watch the bends and keep a hand on the tiller sometimes."

Skye nodded. He would have done the same thing.

The boat slowly drifted into the channel while the shores fell away, veiled by the rain and mist, and they were nowhere, sailing through a private world, going wherever the current took them.

Skye felt a chill settle in his bones. Victoria discovered it; she was always checking on her man. She piled her blankets over his but this did not stop the shivering.

"You ain't well yet," she said crossly.

"I'm too cold."

He shook until he could shake no more and slumped into stupor as the heap of blankets gradually warmed him. He did not know how long he lay like that, but when he returned to this world the rain had stopped; the distant riverbanks were clearly visible, and the cast-iron overcast had given way to light cloud cover.

"Some way to get a job," he said to her. He was sick of travel, sick of weakness and pain.

"You get better."

He didn't feel better. Gill was at the tiller again but not employing sail because the tent shelter still stretched over the boom.

He heard Skye and came forward, ducking under the canvas. "You mind if I raise the sail?"

Skye shrugged.

Gill undid the canvas at the gunnels, pulled away the tarp, untied the sail and raised it. The unstable craft heeled and then settled. They were plowing downstream again, driven by a steady northwest wind.

Skye watched the world roll by. His life seemed to be out of his hands.

"I'd like to see the mountains again," he said.

"I don't like this country neither," Victoria said.

"Hope to get shut of it soon."

"We'll dry out," Gill said. "Clouds getting lighter all the time."

Skye felt a little better, and not so fevered. But he was not fooled. Injuries left their mark.

He felt Victoria's small hand on his forehead, and then felt it run through the stubble of his beard.

"You gonna be strong soon," she said.

She knew what he had been thinking even though he had spoken not a word of it.

The trading position meant everything to him. He would have a living and a future. She would be comfortable. He would be able to help her people. The Crows would have a friend in the trading room. With the beaver trade fading, the position was his bright, sweet tomorrow.

That is, if he ever recovered his strength. He had been so gravely wounded that he might not recover the strength of his youth; this might be the great divide, separating the strong young man from the weakened older one. This terrible assault on his body might force him into a different and sedentary life, or one filled with chills and sickness, such as he had experienced here in this rainy prairie land, where the vegetation grew thicker, and moist breezes dampened everything.

He rose shakily. "I'll take the tiller," he said.

Red grinned. "Long enough for me to stretch," he said.

Skye liked Red Gill. The man was simultaneously secretive about his livelihood and open, brash, straightforward about everything else, including his passion for flowers. Let there be a bloom along any shoreline and Gill was steering toward it to have a closer look. Sometimes the man collected asters or daisies and decorated the prow of the little boat, with all the pride of a Venetian gondolier.

"You regret going to St. Louis, given as how you got shot and robbed and all?" Gill asked.

"Nothing is without risks," Skye said. "And the more something is worth, the worse the risks."

"You gonna get that job?"

"I hope I do."

"Me, I'm going to put in a word for you, and a word against Bonfils."

They sailed through the rest of the day under a cloud cover, and then headed for an island.

"Maybe we can get a fire going," Gill said, eyeing the long, thin strand of woods.

When they bumped into the shore, Victoria made the boat fast, and they strolled along the narrow place, scaring up ducks. There were plenty of campsites visible, some of them recent, and even some gathered wood. But only with great difficulty was Victoria able to nurse a glowing ember bedded in the underside of some bark she peeled from a cottonwood into a tiny flame.

They ate hot food that night, and Skye drank what he thought was a gallon of tea. They set off as the light was fading, and a half hour later Victoria spotted a small orange glow on another island.

"Bonfils," Gill said.

"You want to stop and take him?" asked Victoria.

Gill said, "It's a temptation. Get our stuff back from that sonofabitch."

"You sure that's him?" Skye asked.

"I can make out the flatboat."

Skye pondered it. "What I'd like most, mates, is to pull over, wait for dark, take down our sail so we're less visible, and slide by. We'll get to St. Louis days ahead of him. I think there's advantage in it. We've got the sail and we've got three people to navigate all day and night. We'll get our outfits back when he gets there."

"You think he's expecting us to follow?"

"You, maybe. You live in St. Louis. Not me. He probably thinks we quit and headed back to the mountains," Skye said.

"I'd like to take the bastard."

"Then what?"

"Get my stuff back. And the boat."

"Are you ready to keep him prisoner? I can't help much. You'd have to steer, ward off Bonfils."

"Me, I'd just put him off, like he put us off, go on without him."

"You figure you can take him?"

The boatman reflected. Bonfils was larger, harder, and had just spent several years in the mountains. "I don't know," he said.

Gill was plainly tempted to surprise Bonfils, but in the

end, acquiesced. They all wanted to talk with Pierre Chouteau before Bonfils did. They swiftly dropped the light-colored sail and headed for the shadowed right bank where they waited until the night was inky, and then steered out into the current. In an hour they had passed the wavering orange flame and left it far behind.

thirty—seven

*O*ne day they passed a settler's cabin. Smoke issued from a rock chimney. Tilled fields planted to corn and wheat surrounded it. A pole fence held some cows in a paddock.

"Is this a white man's village?" Victoria asked.

"Nope," said Gill, "just a farmer."

"What is a farmer?"

"One who grows food for a living."

"But there is food everywhere—"

"Farmers, they plow and plant, and work a heap for nothing much except feeding the grasshoppers. You ain't ever catching me behind a plow, looking at the south end of some mules."

Victoria absorbed that, without grasping much of it. "Is there a woman in that house?"

"Most likely."

"But she never comes out? All white women live inside the logs and never come out?"

Gill, who was at the tiller, smiled. "Where'd you get that notion?"

His attitude annoyed her. "I know about white women.

They are weak creatures who have to stay in their lodges and are afraid of the sun. That is why they don't come with their men."

"They're busy cooking and caring for the little ones, I guess."

"No, they are weak. They faint away, make the little death, in the sunlight. So it is said among my people."

"Reckon we'll see one soon, and outside, too."

"What is 'outside?' "

Gill looked startled. "Why, there's the outdoors, like we're in, and there's indoors, like inside a lodge."

"But no white woman ever came to my land or visited my people. It is because they are frail and die."

Red Gill grinned. "Now, I reckon you have a case."

That day they sailed past several more cabins and on each occasion, Victoria studied the homestead, trying to see a white woman.

"There ain't any," she said after passing a large log house on the left bank. She eyed him skeptically. "You don't have one. Where's yours?"

"I don't want one. I run away from a dozen, and I'll keep right on running."

Skye had been listening idly to all this from his resting place near the bow. "Is this Missouri?" he asked Gill.

"Left bank, I suppose," Gill said. "Right bank's Indian territory."

"Who says this thing?" Victoria asked.

"Gover'mint drew a line; this here is civilization to the east, and that there's unsettled country to the west. We're fixing to pass Fort Leavenworth. That's where the soldiers control the river, look for smuggling and all that."

"We're stopping there?" Skye asked.

"Don't have to. Not going downriver. But they'll be looking at us in their glass."

"Are there women there?" Victoria asked.

"Yep. Mostly officers' wives."

"Then we will stop. I want to see them."

Gill looked uneasy. "I reckon you'll see white women aplenty down the river a piece. No need to stop at Leavenworth."

The way he said it alerted Victoria to his discomfort. "You do something the soldiers don't like?"

Gill clammed up and glared at her. They were sailing a vast expanse of river, wider than most lakes she had seen, with thick forests on either bank. Clouds had settled over the whole country, turning it all flat and gray. She didn't like this moist Missouri land.

"You need a woman," she said to Gill.

Gill grinned again.

"I'll get you a good woman. Maybe Lame Deer. She makes a good woman for you."

He stared at her. "She's MacLees's woman."

Victoria laughed triumphantly. "She was. But white men don't keep their mountain wives. Gabe Bridger told me all about mountain wives and how they ain't the same as real wives."

Gill eyed the shore uneasily.

"Some do," said Skye, from his forward perch.

She turned to look at her man. He seemed earnest and yet she was worrying about this trip. Maybe Skye would abandon her and find a white woman, frail and sickly so he could take care of her. That dark possibility had bloomed in her mind and the closer they got to this place of many lodges, St. Louis, the more the fear gripped her.

"Maybe you gonna take some damned weak woman with pale skin, and send me back," she said, an edge in her voice.

Skye didn't reply. He beckoned to her, and she slipped forward, around the boom and the chattering sail, watching out for her head if the boom swung in a breeze, and stood before Skye.

He still looked sick and most of the time he simply lay there, letting Gill operate the boat.

"When we leave St. Louis," he said quietly, "you'll be with me."

She wasn't so sure of it.

There, in the prow of the boat, was a leather device that Gill had rigged up to hold flowers. He picked a fresh bouquet of them each day, and they brightened the whole boat with their various colors. Yesterday he had picked a number of tall stalks with pastel-colored blooms on them, flowers she had never seen before, and now the pink and blue and purple blossoms decorated the boat. Whenever Gill spotted a patch of color on shore he steered the sailboat to that place and anchored long enough to replenish his bouquet.

Ah, Red Gill. She liked him. He was a strange and secretive man, but she adored his flowers. He called these hollyhocks, and said they were white men's garden flowers, not wild ones. She didn't know what wild flowers were. Garden flowers and wild flowers were as confusing as indoors and outdoors. She had asked him why he gathered the flowers and put them in his boats, and he had said he was an artist at heart, and he liked flowers, and they reminded him of women.

"Them flowers are pretty. That's reason enough."

"Are they just to look at? The People make medicines and spices and food from them, too."

"We have flowers for that," Gill said. "Women have herb gardens. Women especially got a whole list of flowers that cure things. Like foxglove and skunk cabbage and red pepper and mandrake and goldenrod."

"Damn, white women, they good for something anyway," she said, evilly.

At midafternoon, they approached a settled area with white frame buildings that looked very strange to Victoria, all snugged on a bench just above the river, in front of wooded bluffs.

"Leavenworth," Gill said. "Just a little of it's visible from the water. Most of it's up, top of that bluff. Parade ground, officers quarters, barracks, all that. This here, the levee and the warehouses, that's where they do business."

Skye lifted himself from the prow and examined the oncoming post. "Inspections?" he asked.

"From stem to stern, everything going upstream, from canoes to steamboats."

Something in Gill's voice registered worry.

"I want to stop," she said.

"Ain't a good idea."

"Why, mate?" Skye asked.

"You ain't even a citizen, Mister Skye. They'll be wondering how come you're around here, coming out of Indian Territory, without being no citizen."

"Mister Gill, are you saying my presence here is illegal?"

"I don't rightly know. Everyone in Injun country's supposed to be licensed. Me, I'm licensed for the river."

Skye glowered at the distant post, which slumbered in a pale sunlight. "All right, let's get past it then," he said.

Victoria heard strength in his voice. Her man was beginning to come alive again. She had sung many songs over him and driven out many devils.

She spotted men in blue coats standing along the levee, and one was glassing them with a brass instrument. She had seen a few of these in the mountains and marveled that they could make everything come close.

Then she spotted a white woman. She stared, uncertain for a moment, but yes, it was a woman, in brown skirts. Victoria could even make out the pale face, and the straw hat the woman wore, and the woman's hair, which was the color of cornmeal. She had rarely seen hair like that. It seemed to glow yellow, even though the sun was obscured by light clouds.

This woman was staring at the sailboat and talking with

the three men in blue coats. At last she had seen a white woman. For years she had wondered why the trappers came to them without women. She itched to talk to this one. She had a list of questions to ask. What did they wear? What powers did they have? How did they raise their children? Did they care about their men? Were they proud of their men, the way the People were?

She watched the blue-coat men move about on the levee, suddenly in a hurry. Two of them approached a small brass cannon and fiddled with it. Then a ring of white smoke erupted from it, followed by a sharp crack.

Gill sighed. "Dammit all to hell. They want us to report," he said, pulling on the tiller until the boat hove around and headed toward the right bank.

"What for?" Skye asked.

"Who the hell knows?"

Skye pulled himself up, lifted his top hat and settled it over his unshorn locks, and waited for the little boat to dock under the mouths of cannon.

thirty-eight

half a dozen blue-coats stood at the levee. To Victoria, they looked all alike in their uniforms and visored hats. But one wore a sword and had more marks of honor sewn to his clothes. A chief, she thought.

Cussing softly, Red Gill steered the little sailboat toward the bank, while Skye dropped the sail. Gill tossed a line to one of the soldiers, who wrapped it around some pilings set in the muddy earth.

"Mawning," said the man who'd caught the line. "Going downriver are ye?"

"St. Louis," said Gill.

The soldiers were eyeing the cargo, what little there was of it.

"No hides, I see. Is this all personal gear?" the man asked.

"Yessir, corporal," Gill said.

Victoria wondered what a corporal was. The man's honors were sewn on his coat, but she didn't know one from another.

"Any pox you know of upriver?"

"Pox?"

"Smallpox. There's a fright about it."

"Nothing we heard of."

"Who are you gentlemen?"

"Red Gill. I got papers, only they're not with me."

"Gill, yes. And this man?"

"Barnaby Skye, sir."

"Nationality?"

"Formerly a subject of the crown—"

Victoria heard a tightness in Skye's voice, and knew he was tense.

"Canadian, then."

"No, not Canadian."

"Your squaw?"

"My wife."

Several soldiers chuckled.

"What are you stopping us for?" Gill asked.

"Pox. We're vaccinating everyone up or down; there's a scourge in St. Louis, and some of the tribes upstream have succumbed. It's a vicious and highly contagious disease."

Victoria had heard of it, this dread sickness brought by white men to the Peoples, with deadly results. Fear clamped her.

"Kindly step out and we'll innoculate you with Jenner's vaccine."

"You mean scratch us, like I heard is done?"

"That's the idea," the corporal said.

Skye helped her step out. The sailboat bobbed lightly behind them. White men's buildings and equipment crowded the space. She saw only the small brass cannon here, but above, away from the river and higher, she saw the mouths of several big cannon, and felt the power of this place.

Whitewashed buildings with glass windows. She ached to see what lay within, and how all that wood had been so cunningly joined together. A livestock pen with a pile of hay. Wagons and carts, buggies and carriages, such as she had never before seen.

But what riveted her was the woman. Were all white women so beautiful? This one was young, and frankly curious, eyeing Victoria with as much fascination as she was eyeing the woman.

What Victoria had thought was milky hair proved to be the lightest yellow, silky and soft, drawn back into a bun under her straw hat. And her face; what a face, her flesh creamy and rosy, her soft eyes the color of the heavens, and her nose thin and white. She had lips that formed naturally into a smile; she was a happy woman, with her daughter clinging to her soft white hand.

They both wore brown. The white woman was adorned in deep brown muslin trimmed with white. Her generous skirt was gathered tight at her slim waist. Something like a men's jacket completed the ensemble. Her daughter, who might have been five or six, wore a miniature soldier's costume, with brass buttons.

Victoria stared enviously. No wonder white men hid their women from the world. They didn't want anyone else to see them! This one didn't look weak or sickly. Her eyes shown and her countenance was lively. A dread crept through Victoria. If white women were like this, she would lose Skye. So riveting was the sight of this woman that she scarcely paid attention to whatever business these soldiers were conducting.

"Captain Rosecranz, army surgeon," the corporal was saying.

The older one had brown muttonchops and small spectacles perched on his bulbous nose, and his gaze darted from one man to the next, finally settling on Victoria.

"This will only take a moment, gents," the surgeon said, opening a black pigskin bag. "You won't regret it."

"Have we any choice?" asked Skye.

"No, sir. We're vaccinating everyone going up and down the river. For their sake. My good man, until we learned to vaccinate, England alone lost forty-five thousand a year. And Boston was practically depopulated for years on end. It's a vile disease, high fever, followed by lesions on the face and then all over the body, which suppurate and disfigure for life—"

"Is there danger to my wife?"

Rosecranz paused. "Some savage women are more vulnerable. But I assure you, most do just fine."

"How does it work?"

"You'll be infected with cowpox, a mild version of smallpox. Jenner discovered that people who had the cowpox didn't get the smallpox. I have a phial of lymph from cowpox sores and we can perform this procedure easily enough."

Fear burrowed through Victoria. "Sonofabitch!" she snapped.

The doctor stared at her, startled.

"I ain't going to do this!"

"You have no choice."

"I'm going to my people."

Rosecranz addressed Skye. "Hold her. I'll scratch her and it'll be over."

"No, sir. If she's going to take the pox vaccine, it will be her choice."

"We can't let you pass if she doesn't. She could carry the plague—"

"It is her body and her decision, doctor. If she declines, I'll head upriver with her."

Skye seemed formidable, except that he was surrounded by soldiers and helpless.

"Well, let's get on with it," Rosecranz said. He turned to Gill. "You ready? Best to remove your shirt."

While Gill tugged his shirt off, Rosecranz opened a velvet-lined black box with shining medical tools in it. One was a needle on a little stick.

He unstoppered a phial that contained a thick liquid, and then took hold of Gill's arm.

"I don't like this," Gill said. The fearless boatman suddenly looked liverish and upset.

But the doctor had the arm firmly in hand, and squeezed one drop of the terrible liquid onto Gill's arm midway above the elbow and shoulder. Then, with the needle at a low slant, he mauled the flesh, abrading it but not piercing it, drawing no blood.

"Hey, are you sure . . ."

"You'll thank me," the surgeon said, releasing the arm. "All done."

"All done? That's it? Am I gonna die or get sick now?"

"Some feel sick a few days. A mild fever. Most don't. A sore will develop at the site of the inoculation, but it'll go away."

Gill exhaled, as if to release a mountain of tension, and rolled down his sleeve.

The physician turned to Skye. "Next?"

Victoria saw the trapped look in Skye's face.

"Don't do it!" she hissed.

But Skye was unbuttoning his chambray shirt. He pulled it off, and stood hairy and bare-chested. The white woman stared, and then turned away.

The doctor spotted the barely healed wound in his shoulder, and then the deep flame-colored furrow across his ribs. "Those are recent," he said.

The soldiers gazed intently.

"Few weeks," Skye said.

"Where did you say you came from?"

"I didn't."

"How did you suffer these?"

Skye shrugged.

The corporal bristled. "You would be well advised, sir, to answer the doctor. Unless you wish to be detained."

"Shot from the cannon of the *Otter*."

"From Marsh's cannon! And how did that happen?"

Red Gill boiled. "Because some reckless fool named Bonfils thought we were being raided by some Sans Arcs one foggy morning and didn't look at who he was shooting at, that's why, dammit all to hell, and killed my partner and a little Injun boy too, along with some Sioux."

"And what were you doing with the *Otter?*"

"Helping them get off a sandbar."

"In that little boat?"

Skye and Gill explained, as best they could, that they were on a flatboat at the time, but the army contingent looked skeptical.

"We'll report this to Gin'ral Clark," said the corporal, since there wasn't much anyone could do about it. "I'd like to hold you, but there ain't grounds. But believe me, don't think this is settled."

"I don't suppose it is," Skye said, mildly, settling his top hat. "It would be kind of you to care about the injured more than caring about your report. You must have all the details from Captain Marsh, isn't that correct?"

The corporal bristled, itching for a fight, and Victoria thought they would all end up captives.

But the surgeon clamped Skye's uninjured arm to him, released a drop of that evil fluid, and again pressed the needle into the fluid and flesh ten or twelve times. Skye watched, grimaced, and then dressed methodically.

The surgeon turned to her.

Victoria knew she would perish. She had not seen her spirit helper the magpie for many suns. She fought back terror and tears.

Skye gazed kindly, but left everything to her. She knew he would go upriver with her at once if she refused. But she hated the very thought of it, sacrificing himself for her, even as she dreaded sacrificing herself for him. But then she found her resolve.

She pulled up the buckskin sleeve as high as she could, baring her thin brown arm. The white doctor held her brown arm, released a single drop of the fluid, and pressed the needle hard a dozen times, never breaking the flesh. She winced and studied the place where Death had entered her.

It was done. The evil liquid had been pressured into her.

The doctor was putting away his instruments.

She felt a great despair as she rolled down her sleeve. She had to say good-bye to her man. In the boat she would sing her death song.

thirty-nine

The closer they came to St. Louis, the lonelier Skye felt. That was odd, and he couldn't fathom his own feelings. Here at last, in North America, he was seeing familiar things: brick buildings, handsome frame houses, neatly tended farms, bright gardens, cobbled streets, men and women in ordinary attire, and not the exotic buckskin garb of the mountains.

People like himself, speaking the English tongue as he did, engaged in occupations he understood. A branch of England, really, even though this robust young nation had fought free of the mother one, and was absorbing thousands of immigrants from other parts of Europe.

How could he possibly be lonely, just when he was coming into contact with people like himself, after so many years? Maybe it was the dog. He grieved for No Name. Maybe it was Victoria, who was acting strangely, perched in the rear of the little sailboat singing softly, dark dirges that sometimes attracted his concern. She had a stricken look upon her; a bleak, desolate gaze he could not fathom, and sometimes tears in her eyes.

Maybe he was lonely because she had pulled into her own world.

Red Gill had turned quiet too. The memory of his partner Shorty was haunting him. This time, instead of floating down the river with his partner and a fortune in furs, he was coming back to St. Louis without any returns for his effort, and the other half of the partnership had been committed to the riverbed, a long way away.

For days, Skye and Gill had traded stories to while away the boring hours on the river. They had both turned brown and blistered under the relentless sunlight bouncing off the murky river, and pummeling them from above. There was no shade, save for the sail itself occasionally, on that majestic waterway that sluiced through the wooded green shores of Missouri.

A place called Westport Landing, near Independence, had interested him because for all the years of the rendezvous, it had been the jumping off place of the packtrains heading west. It was more of a town than he had realized; handsome red-brick buildings around a square, the simple, plain American architecture yielding its own practical beauty.

It was there that Victoria had finally seen white women going about their daily business, some with baskets in hand on the way to the butcher or baker; others strolling with their children, or hanging their wash on lines, an occupation that intrigued Victoria.

At last, Victoria had come to understand that white women were neither fragile or weak or sickly; they didn't come west with the trappers because this was a different culture, not a bit like hers, and women simply played a different part.

Here, too, she saw her first black men and women, except for swart Jim Beckwourth, the mulatto mountain man who had lived with the Crows for years. But Beckwourth hadn't been very black, and these in Missouri were as dark as ink. She studied them, exclaimed at them, and marveled that so handsome a people could be white men's slaves.

Skye himself bloomed and he was beginning at last to put his wounded body out of mind. He could breathe without feeling sharp pain. His shattered ribs and cartilage no longer grated at his side whenever he moved. He had not yet recovered the full use of his wounded arm, and sometimes it prickled clear down to his fingers, but each day he managed to increase the range of movement. Someday soon he could hold up a rifle again, and even aim it. He walked with a small limp when the torn muscles in his thigh balked at their task, but he worked at healing that, too, by walking round and round the boat, and as much as he could on land whenever they docked.

But what worried him most was Victoria. The farther they plunged into settled America, the darker was her visage. And she had never stopped her private singing.

Once he had observed her studying birds that swooped over the water, or patrolled the shores.

"Magpie is not here," she said.

Gill had confirmed it. The western magpie did not exist in this central part of North America. That news had brought a sharp intake of breath from Victoria. Her spirit helper, the chosen guide she had met during a spirit-dreaming session as an Absaroka girl, was no longer present, no longer flying before her. Maybe that was why she was singing. She was alone, bereft, like a white man so far away he was beyond the visibility of God.

They had no cash, but sometimes stopped at a riverfront town anyway, bartering a few items from their outfits for fresh vegetables, berries, or beef. Oddly, Victoria refused to leave the sailboat, desolately sitting there at the levee, or on a dock, when Skye and Gill tried to trade something for fresh food.

Numerous islands provided safe campgrounds. Missouri was thinly settled, and often they traveled for miles without seeing any sign of habitation or human existence on those brooding wooded shores. Skye sensed that the vast rural areas, still devoid of homesteads, harbored twisted and vicious border men who would stop at nothing. He had seen a few in the mountain camps, and knew that the young republic seemed to breed malcontents and murderers along with the many yeomen who were building a nation.

They were meeting river traffic now; fishing boats, scows, keelboats, and once a proud white steamer, the *Antelope,* along with innumerable rowboats, used by Missourians to cross the river. All these local people used the islands as havens, including runaway slaves.

Still, he wasn't at home in this place. The weather had turned sultry and his clothes stuck to him, glued on by the sweat of his body. The moist air suffocated him and left him yearning for the sweet, dry comfort of the mountains. It stormed frequently, and not even the hastily rigged shelter of a tarpaulin spared them a miserable drenching and sodden moccasins and boots. He had taken to rubbing grease into his Hawken to keep it from rusting, and polishing the steel of his knives each day to fend off corruption of the metal.

He could not fathom why any sane mortal would abide in wet, dank, gloomy Missouri, as hellish a place as he had ever seen. He would have preferred the jungles of Burma to this sweaty, overcast, choking place.

It amazed him that he was willfully traveling all this way just to seek a position. Why was he doing it? He no longer could answer that piercing question. For the sake of a trading position he had endured two thousand miles of travel, three nearly fatal wounds, seen the brutal murder of his beloved dog, watched Victoria slide into fear and isolation, and discovered insult and rivalry and contempt in unexpected places, among unexpected fellow travelers. He could not even explain to himself what the trading position meant to him, or why he was willing to come so far, at such cost, to apply for it. All the reasons fell away.

But oddly, one remained. He wanted to see the United States and fathom its robust people. Was it truly the hope of the world? What a curious reason to travel so far, and yet that wish to see the new nation had grown stronger than any other. He would see the land of the Yankees, and meet the people, not the wild ones who came to the mountains but the ordinary yeomen and burghers and their wives and children. Then he would know. And then he could weigh the grave matter, which was oddly affecting him with such passion, of whether to become a citizen.

They camped one night on a narrow island that showed signs of other visitation; ashes, chopped wood, garbage and bones. Red Gill wandered off, down the long strand, leaving Skye and Victoria alone. Skye was plenty worried about her. His Absaroka wife was shrinking into a shadow of herself in this dank place.

He took her hand. "Let's walk some," he said.

She pulled her hand away.

"You've got something hanging around your neck," he said.

She eyed him sharply and tried to distance herself.

"Let me see your arm."

She stopped struggling, and rolled up her sleeve. The last

crust over a small sore clung to the flesh where she had been inoculated.

"This looks just about healed," he said. "Just like the doctor said. Mine's healed up. You'll be fine, and now you won't ever die of that disease, which gladdens me right down to my bones." He tugged at a sleeve, having trouble rolling it up his massive arm, but finally he was able to show her a small, white dimpled area that was the sole remaining sign of the smallpox vaccination.

He began to fathom her torment. She had been singing a death dirge all these days.

"Victoria, Victoria . . ." he said, clasping her to him. She resisted at first, but then her arms clamped his body and she hugged desperately. He ran his hand over her jet hair, his gesture awkward, and she buried her face in his chest and sobbed.

"Soon we'll go back to our country. I don't much care for this place."

She lifted her head. "No, you will stay here."

He lifted his top hat and settled it, perplexed at her mood, and aching to lift her out of it. "The land of the Absarokas is my land now," he said. "Those mountains with the tops white with snow; the pine forests, the good horses and endless prairies . . ."

She shook her head.

"We'll be heading up the river in a few days."

"I have seen the white women."

He could not make sense of that. "They're not so different from women of the People," he said.

"They are like you, and you will go to them sooner or later. I know this. I have looked at them. They are beautiful, not like some old savage. They dress in skirts, many fine stitches, that no damn savage ever sewed. They got all these things, manners, you got and I don't. You and me, what do I really know about you? You are stranger to me. But they know you, all your thoughts, because they were born like you."

She buried her face in his chest, and then whispered more.

"We get to St. Louis, and they'll all come to you and entice you and show you their white skin, and this old savage woman, she gets put aside. Even black women are better than savages."

At last he had some inkling of what was desolating her. It hurt him that she didn't believe in his love and esteem for her anymore.

"Have you seen me flirting with the white women?"

She didn't answer.

"You think that because MacLees abandoned his red woman, and Bonfils probably will, that I'll do the same?"

"The white men all go back to their kind," she said, her voice smothered in his shirt.

"Have I told you that I love you, Victoria?"

"Sonofabitch," she replied. "In a few suns, you won't say it no more."

forty

Red Gill steered the little craft toward St. Louis in almost steady rain, a relentless drizzle that chafed at Skye, soaked his clothes, bred mold on his leathers, rusted every steel surface on his Hawken even when it was sheathed, and made the air hard to breathe. Victoria had taken to bailing out the sailboat with a tin cup, while saying nothing at all.

The windless wet air made the sail useless. It flapped and dripped rain, and rarely collected a breeze. Skye finally lowered it, and they depended on the steady river current to take them to the great city. Victoria's nose began running, and Skye pitied her. In all the time they had shared together in the dry West, he had never seen her nose run, and had rarely seen her sniffle. But now something in the very air was disagreeable to her, and making her sick. She said not a word, but he knew she was increasingly ill and maybe fevered. It worried him.

The closer they came to St. Louis, the more animated Gill became, and he often jabbered about one landmark or another. The Missouri ran slate gray, its water murky and barely potable, the gloomy banks crowded with osage, locust, sycamore, shagbark hickory, oaks and elms, all of them cheerfully identified by the boatman. He, at least, was glad to return to his home. Skye wondered what sort of home Red Gill had. A room, probably, or maybe no quarters at all. The frontier was filled with vagrants.

"This here's the grand prairie back of St. Louis," he said, waving a hand toward the right bank. "Mostly wooded, but plenty of parks too. Farm land now. There's a limestone bluff near the river, and below that's a bench where the city sits, most of it. The city's bursting up the cliff now, and spreading out."

They drifted past two large islands and then into a vast and confusing confluence with the Mississippi, so enormous that Skye was glad he wasn't navigating because he couldn't tell one shore from another, and often there seemed to be no shore at all.

"The Father of Waters," Gill said, with a grand sweep of his rainsoaked arm. All Skye saw was gray mist stretching into obscurity. But Gill seemed to know where he was going, and hewed closely to the right bank, where a swift current propelled the little boat southward.

At last Victoria stopped her bailing long enough to stare at this strange place where the Big River joined the Father River. She wiped rain away from her face, trying to fathom landmarks in this gray and featureless seascape. Her rain-drenched chambray blouse was plastered to her small body, and once Skye caught Gill staring at her with half-masked hunger.

"We're pretty near there," Gill said. "If the fog lifted, you could see it now; biggest city in the West; biggest north of New Orleans, and still pretty much French, but that's changing. Yanks like me setting it right."

The fog at the confluence gave way to a low gray cloud cover and lighter rain, and in time the ghostly city did emerge from the dark mist, a gloomy prospect of warehouses and other buildings crowded along the levee. But what astonished Skye was the number of steamboats, one after another, as far as he could see, tethered to pilings along the levee.

"Pretty busy place, eh?" Gill said, some pride welling up in him. "Those there boats, they're from the Alleghenies, come down the Ohio to here; or up from New Orleans, or down from the north, Illinois and Iowa and up there, or like us, down from the west. This is where it all comes; the goods, the commerce, the people. A New Englander can ship a cargo down the coast, around Florida, to New Orleans, and up here."

The magnitude of the city stunned him. It seemed almost a London, and this seemed more than a Thames.

"There now, you can see the new cathedral of St. Louis, that spire yonder where the Frenchies worship. That's on the south edge. We won't go that far. I'm going to head for La-Clede's Landing, the old dock where it all started, because near there's where I've got my room. That street the church is on, that's called Church Street, *La Rue de l'Eglise*, and this street on the riverfront, along the levee, it's Main, *La Rue Principal*."

"The streets have two names?"

"Yep, you can't expect Yanks to twist their tongues like that speaking French. Next in is Barn Street, *La Rue des Granges*, and that cross street, heading up the slope, that's Tower, *La Rue de la Tour*. See, it ain't so hard."

Skye wiped rain off his face, and glanced at Victoria, who was staring in rapt bewilderment at something unfathomed in her mind, and beyond imagination.

The slap of water on the hull reminded Skye that Gill was

steering the craft across the current now, toward a small, stinking dock area where keelboats and flatboats crowded so tightly that they were tied to one another instead of to land. Gloomy warehouses and mercantile buildings lined the levee like black teeth, disgorging and swallowing the contents of the riverboats. And amid them, he saw grog shops, low, sullen buildings with rough characters lounging around their doors. Not a woman was in sight.

"Rough quarter," he said.

"Roughest in the world," Gill said, heading for a small opening between two flatboats. "They'd as soon slit your throat as let you pass. Unescorted woman has about as much chance as a shoat on a butcher block."

He eased the boat into an awkward corner, where projecting boulders threatened to hammer the hull, and the boat jammed suddenly against the levee. Victoria grabbed a line and jumped out. There was nothing to tie to, so she tugged the prow up a muddy incline.

"Goddam," she said, squinting at a scene so alien to her that she might as well be on another planet.

The whole area stank of sewage, dead fish, effluent, rotting food, and decay. Skye stepped onto the black mud of the levee and stretched. For this had he come two thousand miles. This was the United States. He had never been in the United States before, at least its settled region. And even this was barely settled, though French and Spanish had been on this river for nearly a century.

The rain mercifully ceased. A breeze immediately rose, the air chilling him as it cooled his soaked shirt and buckskins.

St. Louis! From here had come his succor for many years, and here would his future be decided.

Everywhere, drays, freight wagons, buggies, carriages, carts, and even a few elegant victorias and landaus crowded the waterfront, with the cacophony of neighing, whinnying horses adding to the din. Black stevedores hefted enormous bales of cotton, or massive crates, or heavy casks, in and out of shadowy interiors. Great noxious puddles silvered the cobbled street. Rain had blackened the backs of horses, and still dripped noisily from eaves.

Victoria gaped at the hubbub, the wagons, the Negro men, the white men in handsome suits, the roustabouts in duck cloth britches and loose blouses, and blue uniformed officers on the river packets. Skye thought she looked frightened but determined; a native woman trying to absorb the fantastic and show no shameful fear.

He stepped toward her and slipped an arm about her waist, his hand clasping her and sending assurances toward her. She turned away from him, not toward him, and he sensed she did not want him to see her face, or the fear and awe and fascination in it; things a Crow woman would marvel at for the rest of her life; things too fantastic to repeat to her sisters around the lodgefires of her people; things that would make the Absarokas call her a liar if she tried to describe them.

She said nothing, but found his rough hand and squeezed it.

Behind them, Gill was shuffling goods forward in the sailboat and raising the dripping sail just enough to let it dry. It would rot if he wrapped and tied it wet.

Skye watched, absorbed, and stayed on guard, knowing waterfronts well. He eyed his outfit lying in the prow, wondering how to store it and where. He was penniless.

"Red, are we saying good-bye?" he asked.

Red grinned. "You going to see old Chouteau, like I am?"

"Yes, but we need to find a place to camp."

"Nearest camp, I suppose, is four or five miles up that cliff and out on the grand prairie. All privately owned, but you could get permission. And it's gonna be wet."

"We'll find a spot," Skye said. He was worried. They had too much gear in their kit to tote on their backs for more than a few hundred yards. Those vultures lounging across the mucky street would pounce on anything lying loose in that open sailboat the moment the boat was not guarded.

"Come with me," Gill said.

Skye divided the load, giving Victoria the lighter things, including the blankets, while he loaded the sacks of staples and tools on his shoulders. The weight strained his wounds, and he felt flashes of the old pain course through him, making him want to drop every burden. But eventually he and Victoria and Gill shouldered their gear and wobbled northward, past the frenzy of the levee and up a slope to a dirt street hemmed by tawdry tenements. Gill grinned, led them around a mucky path to the rear of a grimy building, and dug an iron key out of a flowerpot. Moments later he ushered them into a dank room, with one small window admitting light. A narrow iron bed occupied one wall; a commode and dresser the other. That was it.

"Home sweet home," Gill said. "Leave your duffel here. It's safe enough, long as I lock up. I ain't got anything to eat, but we can boil up some cornmeal. There's a little kitchen down below."

A sorry home for a man who risked life and limb to smuggle whiskey for the Chouteaus, Skye thought.

Skye wasn't hungry. His fate was about to play out, and he didn't want an ounce of food or drink to deaden his senses. This was it. His fate would become clear right here in this grubby city.

Victoria shook her head. He watched her touch the rough plaster walls, examine the iron bedstead and try the cotton-filled tick, study the commode, with its vitreous porcelain pitcher and basin atop it, and then swing the cabinet door back and forth, admiring the brass hinges that held it up.

She stared at everything, probably repelled by this dreary little hovel, but she had slipped into deep silence and he knew enough not to disturb her. They heaped their outfit in a corner, apart from Gill's, and Skye headed outside to a washstand and outhouse he saw in the tiny rear yard, there to freshen himself as best he could before heading toward the mansion of the man who would decide his fate. But he put that thought at a distance, not wanting to deal with it. Not yet.

"You ready to meet the man?" Gill asked, combing his matted hair with his fingers, and shaking the grime from his pants.

"I don't suppose I'll ever be ready," Skye said. "But we have business to do."

forty-one

The vaccinations went better than Alexandre Bonfils thought possible. When he learned at the Fort Leavenworth levee why he had been compelled to stop, he envisioned nothing but trouble with Lame Deer. But instead, she had assented at once, and submitted herself and her daughter to the surgeon.

"My man had this thing done," she explained. "He showed me the little place on his arm, and told me he was safe from this pox disease. We will have it done too."

And so they continued down the Missouri in the flatboat with minimal delay; the whole business had taken scarcely half an hour. The assorted enlisted men and officers had scarcely bothered to examine the empty flatboat.

He exulted. For days he had sought out islands as night camps, fearing that his doe would flee if he chose to camp on one bank or another. The only bad thing about steering a flatboat alone was that there was no relief when rain or night fell, and he had to be at the tiller most of the time. Lame Deer and Singing Rain wandered the vessel, or settled in the cabin during the heat of the day. The Cheyenne voiced not the slightest protest at any of Bonfils's conduct and didn't even seem aware that she was a virtual prisoner. And yet . . . her conduct made him uneasy.

Skye and his squaw were stranded back at Sarpy's Post and out of contention, while the squaw would guarantee that Simon MacLees would not be selected. So it would be that the toast of St. Louis, Alexandre Bonfils, would win the trader position, and he would soon head west with the comfort of Fort Cass ahead of him.

He would abandon Amalie, of course. He had grown weary of her. The Crow women were said by the mountain fraternity to be the most wanton of all, and he thought one or two, or even three, such savage ladies would make his winters fly fast. What did they want but a bit of ribbon or a few beads for their devotion? Ah, he could see himself as the dauphin of the Yellowstone, living in wild luxury for a few years, until he wearied of it and uncle called him back to St. Louis and a full partnership in the firm.

The land had changed. Walls of majestic trees hemmed the Missouri: sycamore, locust, shagbark hickory, elm, oak, osage, and many more. The air had turned soft and velvety with moisture, and in his estimation more pleasant than the harsh dryness of the West. It showered almost daily; by afternoon, clouds built up into towers, their bottoms blackened, and a lightning-charged storm crashed through. In those moments, he tied up and waited out the deluge in the cabin with the savage woman.

There was about her a certain dignity that sometimes annoyed him. She spent those rainy moments asking him questions: how do white men raise their children? Do white men have more than one wife? Who is chief among the white men? What do women wear in this place of many lodges?

He responded sullenly. He was aware that she was preparing herself for her sojourn among a strange people, and he didn't want that. He wanted to present her as a wild savage—and MacLees's squaw—and make her a laughing stock and MacLees the cynosure of a thousand tongues.

They arrived one day in Independence, and Lame Deer insisted upon examining the village.

"Why? What is there to see?" he asked.

"I will see the people."

Reluctantly, he stepped aside and let her clamber onto the levee. She helped her child step to land. He intended to shadow her, ever fearful that his hen would escape the coop. She walked slowly among the citizens, drawing some stares even from a frontier population used to wild Indians. It was her ghastly sawed-off hair that drew attention. Lame Deer noticed, and gazed reproachfully at Bonfils, who had taunted her into a display of grief more familiar to her people than to these white people.

"Hurry up; we must be off now," he said. But she chose to take her time, quietly examining the brick buildings, the lovely town square, the glass-fronted mercantiles with all their goods displayed. But above all the people. She paused frequently, absorbing every aspect of men's and women's dress; the fullness of the skirts, the whiteness of the men's shirts, their boots and slippers, their hairdos, the wicker baskets the women carried while shopping, the clothing worn by children.

"We must be off!" he announced, but she simply turned to him and smiled.

"I like this place," she said. "I am seeing things that my man told me of; things I could not imagine. The people are like cranes and herons whose feet never touch the earth. They are all chiefs; this is many-chiefs land. Even the little ones and the women are chiefs. Strong and good are the chiefs. Even like MacLees, these chiefs know all things, and their wisdom is before my eyes, and now I am joyous because I have seen the mystery of MacLees."

They paused at a church, red brick like so much of Independence of the 1830s, with a white spire.

"Is this a store?"

"No, this is a church."

"And what is that?"

"A place where people come to the Creator."

He was getting testy. The last thing he wanted was to discuss white men's religion with her, or dwell on the differences of the churches.

"I wish to see."

"We should be off to St. Louis. There are better churches in St. Louis."

She ignored him, climbed some steps, and opened the door and found herself in a sanctuary, dark and empty.

"I have seen this sign before," she said, pointing to a wooden cross above the altar. "Sometimes there is a man upon it."

"He is a man like Sweet Medicine," he said, invoking the Christ-figure of the Cheyennes.

"Ah! So this is a teacher. Sweet Medicine taught us all the virtues, and how to live in beauty. This is the One that Simon MacLees told me of?"

"I will tell you when we start down the river," he said.

"It is something for me to learn of, so my man can be happy with me and share his life with me."

Bonfils smirked.

It took three hours before Lame Deer was ready to set foot in the flatboat, and when she did, she rummaged about in her parfleches in the cabin, showing sudden signs of industry.

Alexandre Bonfils cast loose the lines, clambered aboard, joked with several rivermen on the levee, and poled the heavy boat away from the bank and into the gentle current.

Lame Deer stayed largely within the cabin, even though the day turned out to be a glorious one. Once she headed forward, and strangely enough, dipped her head into the river, lathered it, and washed her hair. Then she vanished into the cabin again. Later that afternoon he discovered that she was sewing.

They passed other vessels; mostly rowboats, but once a

keelboat with a large crew poling their way upriver close to the far bank. All that while, she remained within the little cabin, and this cloistering of herself piqued his curiosity. From his position at the tiller, he could see in, and knew she was sewing, but he knew nothing else of her busy day.

At dusk he found a fine island and steered the flatboat toward it. The boat scraped over a snag, and then another, and he thanked his luck that it was not loaded. He anchored at the island, which showed no signs of habitation, apparently because river men had feared the snags.

He tied up to some sycamores growing at the bank, and stepped ashore, grateful for a respite from the navigation of the great river.

Then she stepped out of the flatboat cabin, tugging her child with her. The sight astonished him. She had trimmed her hair until it lay almost evenly around her neck. One side was still short, but even that had been carefully cut and shaped, and now her glossy black hair framed her strong features with balance and regularity. And her dress! She had modified one of her crudely sewn squaw dresses into something closely resembling a white woman's afternoon gown of teal cotton, with much tighter sleeves and an even hemline.

"Will Simon MacLees like this?" she asked.

"Madam, it is a great mistake. You must wear just what your people wear, and on the occasion of your meeting, you must be gotten up with paint."

She looked puzzled. "I do not think so. I have seen white women, and that is how I will be. I will be his wife in this place of many lodges, and I want to make him very happy with me, and our girl."

"Madam, he did not marry you because you were like the girls back home, but for your fine savage beauty."

"What is this word, savage?"

"Ah, different from us."

"Yes, we are different. But he is my man, and over many

winters we have come to be more alike. I am happy. I have seen how the women dress, and I will make my clothes like that. And when the sun comes in the east, I will make clothing for Singing Rain too, so that he will be pleased with her when he sees her in this place of the white people."

He felt himself growing petulant, and masked it with a smile. "Ah, madam, just this one time, wear your finest cere-monial clothing. Heap big medicine! Wear the elk's tooth blouse! Wear the quilled doeskin! Wear the elk moccasins! Wear your paint! Wear feathers! Vermillion! Ochre! Let him and all of St. Louis know you are a woman of the Cheyenne!"

"Why do you want this?"

"Because . . . because it will be a great moment."

She smiled. "I think you have other reasons."

He made camp sullenly, realizing that his cheerful fantasy of scandalizing and shocking St. Louis had quietly filtered away with the breeze. All that paint; the vermillion he had purchased, the jingle bells he had expected her to wear, the earbobs, the silver rings, the foxtails, the blue garters, the red and green cock feathers, the blue and white barleycorn beads, the pigeon egg beads, the white and purple wampum, the hawk bell, the hairpipe beads, along with the fine brutal mess of her hair, the unfashionable squaw dress, the clay pipe and plug tobacco, all gone a-glimmering.

He discovered within himself an odd and unexpected emotion. Envy. This squaw cared so much about her man that she was transforming herself into a white woman, believing that her runaway lover would welcome her all the more. Amalie would never have done that; nor any other woman of the tribes he had encountered. Not for Alexandre Bonfils.

His thoughts amused him. In St. Louis he would seduce one or another Creole beauty, maybe several, and none of them would ever hear a word about Amalie.

Lame Deer was gazing on him, and the serene and accept-ing look in her face was unsettling.

forty-two

Red Gill led the way, and Skye was grateful because he hadn't the faintest idea where in St. Louis he would find Pierre Chouteau, Jr. The man had an office, of course, in his warehouse down near the river, but no lamplight shone in the arched window at that hour.

"We'll hike up to his house," Gill said. "It's a piece. Will you be up to it?"

"I don't know," Skye said. "Leg still hurts and I can't pump my bellows much."

Gill nodded. He led Skye and Victoria through dusky streets with brick buildings crowded cheek by jowl, with only pools of light from windows to guide them.

"I guess you figured out Shorty and me by now," Gill said.

"No."

"We pack wet goods for Pierre Chouteau. Not the company. Just him."

Skye sensed he was about to hear secrets. Gill was a smuggler; that much he knew.

"It's the inspection at Leavenworth causes the trouble," Gill said. "The company can't get a drop of whiskey to the posts. Congress even tightened the law. Used to be there'd be a boatman's ration, one gill a day allowed, but no longer. Them puritans in Congress, they don't want nary a drop going up to the posts, or down the gullet of a redskin."

They walked a while more, through narrow streets, and Skye got the impression their direction was southerly, where the land was flatter.

"I shouldn't be saying a word. Get myself into trouble,

only I'm gonna quit. I'm done for good. Shorty getting killed, that did it for me. I don't want no part of this anymore."

Skye nodded, saying nothing. But he was certainly listening closely.

"It takes a mess of spirits to fuel the fur trade," he said.

"Damn right," said Victoria.

"We had to get it to the posts. Every factor at every post knew us and waited for us to show up."

"How'd you do it?"

"Different way each time. This last time, we got us a good pack string, good Missoura mules, and had big tin casks soldered up, and we took it out to the posts that way, never even getting near the Missouri until way up near Council Bluffs. Until then, we just headed north, bunch of mules, through barely settled country. Well, we dole it out as we go, cask here, cask there, and then a flatboat's waiting for us at Fort Union, and it's got our payment in hides in it; just hides, all off the ledgers, and Shorty and me come on down to this here town, sell the hides to wholesalers and cash it out for our profit. It's a trade. They get some good mules up at the posts; we got a flatboat to sell too, so old Pierre, he likes it, we liked it, and them traders liked it. And the flatboat, it brings us extry cash. Someone always buys it to haul stuff down to New Orleans."

"I thought it was something like that, mate."

"Pretty risky. We never done it twice the same way. Some times we headed out like we were going to Santy Fe, and then swung north. The patrols out of Fort Leavenworth cover a heap of country, so that was a bit troublesome. If we get caught, we lose everything. But we always done it."

"Never got caught?"

"Never. People knew we was smugglers, so we let it be known we was hauling for the Opposition." He glanced sharply at Skye. "I'm getting out, so it won't do you no good to go spill it all to Gen'ral Clark."

"Not even on my mind," Skye said.

"The company got into trouble once, you know. When Kenneth MacKenzie had himself a little old still shipped up-river and brewed his own likker, buying maize from the Mandans. Nat Wyeth tattled on him, and they durned near pulled the company trading license, and it was all old Chouteau could do, yanking strings in Congress, to stay in business. But he's got to have spirits. All them others got spirits, and with spirits you just walk off with the business."

Victoria laughed.

Skye didn't laugh. He really hadn't known much about the politics of the fur trade, never having been in the States before or getting some notion of its laws. He thought of all those times when he and Victoria enjoyed a good jug, scarcely aware that every drop of it had been brought illegally into Indian Country.

"That going to continue?" Skye asked, thinking that as a trader at Fort Cass he might himself be doling out illegal spirits, and hiding his stock of it from an occasional traveler or Indian Bureau agent.

"You ask old Pierre that. He shore don't say nothing to no one. Me and Shorty, we smuggled his spirits out there for six years, and no one ever caught on. Only ones that knew for sure was Chouteau and the traders at the posts. Everything was hidden. Buying spirits was off the ledgers. Getting the mules and the tin casks was off the ledgers. Paying us, that was off the ledgers, and in hides, not cash."

"What are you going to say to Mister Chouteau?"

"Well, we'll just see. I got a few levers, including a big mouth, specially since I'm getting out, Shorty dead and gone, my old friend wiped out by that sonofabitch Bonfils. Makes a man plumb bitter, and I ain't walking in there feeling any too kindly toward that Creole and his six thousand relatives that run the whole damned fur business in the country, save for a few independents."

Skye wanted to ask a lot more questions, but Red Gill had

clammed up, and the grim set of his mouth warned against any more talk about a matter so incendiary.

Skye found himself wondering about Pierre Chouteau and his methods. For all his time in the mountains, he had heard tales about the ruthless Mr. Chouteau, and his effort to erase the Opposition, especially the Rocky Mountain Fur Company, Jackson, Sublette, Bridger, Fraeb, and the rest of the old coons. Chouteau had succeeded, too. Nothing remained in the northern and central plains but the American Fur Company, technically the Upper Missouri Outfit, now called Pratte, Chouteau and Company. And the Bents were almost the sole survivors in the southern plains.

It had grown very dark, and houses no longer rose cheek by jowl, or even with their doors on the street.

"Getting close," Gill said. "It's that there."

A brick-walled enclave rose before them.

"You think he'll see us now? Not at his chambers in the morning?"

"Mister Skye, old Pierre, he'd be mad at me if we waited one spare minute. I've come all hours, sometimes right in the middle of dinner, or he's been in bed half a night, or when he's having some Frenchy priest saying the mass to the family, and he just excuses himself and glides out and we go to his study and he lights the wick and we palaver until he's squeezed everything I know out of me."

Skye noticed that Victoria was uncommonly quiet, but she was cruising not only through utterly new turf, but also through a world she didn't understand.

Gill reached an iron-grilled portico, and rattled the closed gate. An old black man in black livery emerged at once from the darkness.

"Got to see old Pierre," Gill said.

The man squinted, surveyed Skye and Victoria from liquid brown eyes, and opened the gate.

"Massah's in," he said.

A slave. Skye hadn't much thought about slavery until he was suddenly confronted with it here in what the Yanks called a Border state. Skye had been a slave; the Royal Navy had made him one, pressing him off the streets of London and locking him into ships of war for seven years. He hated slavery in all shapes and forms, whether open and blatant, like this oppression of Africans in America, or just slightly less blatant, like pressing seamen into the navy and paying them a bare pittance and keeping them for as long as it pleased the lord admirals.

But of course Chouteau would have slaves. A man like him would think nothing of it.

They walked through a flower-decked yard, past magnolias and chestnut trees, toward a gleaming, black lacquered door with a brass knocker. Within, laughter erupted. Light spilled from casement windows, some of them open to the evening breezes. The tongue was French, fluid and soft and amused. Skye saw men in brocades and silk, black pantaloons, waistcoats, high collars, and women in summery white cottons and Brussels lace and pleated muslin.

Gill knocked.

A black woman opened to them. She was ancient, white-haired, sharp-eyed, sorrowful. She wore a black cotton gown rimmed with white, and a large porcelain crucifix on her heavy bosom.

"Mr. Chouteau," Gill said.

"Cadet?"

"Yes, junior. I'm Red Gill."

Skye wondered what that was about.

The black woman nodded and ushered them into a white foyer gilded with gold leaf and lit by six oil lamps in a crystal chandelier. The woman limped heavily, with a world-weariness that could not be concealed.

Another slave. Skye watched her lumber toward the salon where all the festivities were brightening the world, and saw intuitively a will not commanded by her own self; a dream lost and hope squashed by a terrible institution. And what for? Because the Chouteaus chose to keep her as chattel rather than pay her a wage for a lifetime of servitude? Suddenly he hated the abominable institution of the Americans, and thought ill of any human being who enslaved another, including the man who had employed him.

The venerable slave reappeared, this time with stocky, jet-haired, square-faced Pierre Chouteau, Jr., in a handsome blue waistcoat with brass buttons.

"Ah, ah!" he said, a small smirk lighting on his lips. "Ah, at last, messeurs and madame."

He motioned them toward another part of the manse, this area black and shadowed, and steered them into a chamber lit only by a faint light from outside.

"One petite moment," he said, scratching a lucifer. He lifted a lamp chimney and lit the wick and blew out the match with a small, whimsical puff.

"Here we can meet in private," he said, his soft assessing gaze raking in everything visible about Skye, Victoria, and Red Gill.

forty-three

*P*ermit us," Chouteau said in a soft, gallic voice, shaking hands. "We are Chouteau. And you, *mon ami*, are Mister Skye. And madame?"

"This is my wife, Victoria," Skye said.

"Ah! Enchanted, madame. And Mr. Gill we know."

He shook hands with Gill, neutrally, revealing nothing.

"We trust you had a pleasant and uneventful trip?"

Skye found himself wary of this man who was setting snares. It was not an uneventful trip, and Marsh would have told him so, long since.

"I fear we've interrupted a party. We can return in the morning," Skye said.

"*Non, non*, you must tell us everything. Leave out nothing. We have private business with Mr. Gill here, for some other time—"

"No, it ain't private, Mr. Chouteau. I'm getting out of my business and want to settle up."

Chouteau stared at the riverman, not entirely blandly. "Ah, some other time, our friend Gill. Now we must celebrate the arrival of our colleague and his beauteous wife, yes?"

Gill turned surly. Skye was certain that there would be some harsh exchanges, with Gill demanding his peltries back and maybe threatening Chouteau with exposure if he didn't get them. But if trouble was looming, Chouteau was too much of a master to reveal it.

He smiled graciously.

"My friend Skye, we have heard much of you for years; the reports of our bourgeois in the field, the brigade tallies that reach my desk, the impressions of our men, all add up to the best of recommendations. When it came to choices, your name was at once placed high on our list, and over the names of so many others who have neither your experience nor your judgment. You see? We meet for the first time, but *mon ami*, we have been keeping watch over you and know more than you might expect. That is the privilege of the senior partner, *oui*? But tell us about the long trip? And where, *mes amis*, is Alexandre Bonfils? Did he not start out with you?"

"He's coming along on a flatboat belonging to Gill," Skye said, wondering if he could ever sort out for Chouteau just what happened.

"Extraordinary! Your flatboat, Gill?"

"Yes, with a Cheyenne squaw and her girl," Gill said. "We were all together until Sarpy's Post."

"We are astonished. You must explain this," Chouteau said, directing himself to Skye.

"The Cheyenne woman's the wife of an Opposition trader named Simon MacLees," Skye said. "She hadn't heard from him for some while, and found the courage to come out of the mountains to look after him. She brought her children . . . her child now. I understand he's my rival for the trading position."

Chouteau pursed his lips, stared into the flame, and sighed. "Your information is very old, and you must have heard it filtered many times over many tongues, beginning perhaps with our Captain Marsh, and maybe others?" He paused, seeing Skye nod. "We did consider Monsieur MacLees for the position. He's a veteran trader and a gifted man, and gave us a very difficult time in Opposition.

"But you see, when we first approached him, he told us he was soon to marry the lovely Sarah Lansing, one of the great beauties of this city, and had no wish to go out into the West again. He tells us he will live in St. Louis. He has secured work elsewhere, we understand with Robert Campbell, brokering hides and pelts."

"Goddam," said Victoria.

Chouteau's gaze flicked in her direction, and then away, some faint amusement in his face. "Fort Cass will go either to you or Alexandre Bonfils. You are both eminently qualified to trade with the Crows. It is not a large post, but an important one to us, because the Crows are good buffalo hunters, and the future of the fur trade lies in hides, not beaver. And how is your health, Mister Skye?"

"I am doing better."

"You received injuries, did you not?"

"Captain Marsh has been here ahead of us, and you must have the story, sir."

"Ah, indeed, one story. But we like to hear the story from each person."

"Maybe that should wait until morning, sir. We've come a long way."

"Non, non! We have all the time in the world. Who is here tonight? My Gratiot relatives, whom we see all the time. They are partners in the company, you know. We don't see our men from the field but once in a long while, and so, our friend, we want you to divulge the whole story of the trip down the river, beginning at the time you and Bonfils boarded the *Otter* at Fort Union. But first, may we pour you some brandy? And by all means, sit yourself."

Skye nodded. A snifter would drive away some of the aches and cares of travel. And that yellow silken settee looked inviting.

And so the story came out. Skye didn't know what to say, or how much to say, and decided on a bare recitation of the facts, without the slightest shading. He would be especially careful describing Bonfils, and the reckless discharge of grape shot into the Sans Arcs—and others.

Chouteau settled himself in a wingchair with crewelwork covering it, and sipped his brandy, listening intently, and no doubt forming sharp impressions. Skye knew he was being assessed, measured, weighed, and examined. He described the moment when he and Victoria spotted the Cheyenne woman and persuaded Marsh to pick her up; the moment when Marsh ejected her from the vessel without repaying her, over Skye's protests. The moment when Skye and Victoria found themselves afoot at Fort Pierre, and their meeting with Red Gill and Shorty Ballard, and their switch to the flatboat to continue their journey.

"Ah! My *capitaine*, he told us he was beside himself when he discovered that the Cheyenne woman was MacLees's mountain wife! MacLees was about to become his son-in-law! He did what he had to do to prevent the woman from ever reaching St. Louis—scarcely realizing you would take the woman's part!"

Pierre Chouteau seemed much amused, though none of it had been very funny.

Skye saw the moment looming when he would have to describe his rival's reckless conduct at the place where the *Otter* had grounded and the Sans Arcs had appeared one foggy dawn, and decided to let Red tell that part of it.

"Red," he said, "please tell Mr. Chouteau what happened during the time we were helping the steamboat."

"I damn well will," Red snapped, in a voice that wiped Chouteau's perpetual smirk off his face.

Red's bitter story flooded out, beginning with the shot across the bow of the flatboat; Shorty's determination not to stop; Skye's intervention; the rescue operation, in which the *Otter*'s cargo was removed until the boat floated; the arrival of the Sans Arcs before dawn on a foggy morning; Skye's negotiation with them to ferry them across the wide Missouri; Bonfils's reckless cannoning of the group with cannister; the dead and wounded; the harsh treatment of the wounded and dead by Marsh, while the steamboat was reloaded, and then the grief-laden trip downriver.

Pierre Chouteau sipped brandy, twirled the amber liquid in his snifter, stared into the lamp, and grunted.

The rest of the narrative came easily to Skye. He described his own struggle with grave wounds and nausea and pain; Bonfils's astonishing appearance and presence among them; the man's scheming at Sarpy's Post, the theft of the flatboat, and the acquisition of the small sailboat from Sarpy, with which they passed Bonfils in the night and beat him to St. Louis.

The more Skye talked, the more agitated he became. And when he finished his narrative, that shadowed study was plunged into a portentous silence.

"My dog is dead. I came close to the brink. We buried Shorty Ballard in a canvas shroud, weighted with rock, and said good-bye to a good man. We buried my dog. We buried that Cheyenne boy, Sound Comes Back After Shouting, innocent child, eager to see his father. The Sans Arcs took their own with them, but I'm sure they'd buried a few."

"Four," said Chouteau. "Seven more gravely injured. Eight more less injured. We've received an express. They are agitating the Teton Sioux against the company." He cocked his head. "Marsh said you were negotiating ferry passage for that war party on the *Otter* without authority to do so."

"Yes, sir."

"You might have asked him."

"I did what I had to do."

Chouteau waved a hand. "It was the right thing to do. We just wanted your answer to Marsh's accusation. Exactly the right thing to do. Most admirable, and it shows what a veteran of the fur trade you are, Mister Skye. Now, if you will excuse us, we will closet ourselves with Monsieur Gill for a few minutes. We will have Bertha show you to the foyer, where you may wait. We wish to talk further. Meet us at the offices, tomorrow at ten, yes?"

"Ten, at your firm," Skye said.

Chouteau rang a bell, and the ancient, stooped servant slave appeared.

"Take them to the foyer, and Mister Gill will join them shortly," Chouteau said.

The woman silently led them back to the foyer, and they could hear the festivities in a nearby room, where light spilled from a dozen lamps.

Gill joined them in a few minutes, and they plunged into a dank night.

"Old Pierre, he didn't even wait for me to speak my piece. He says my pelts are in the warehouse and I can pick 'em up anytime. He had Marsh put them in a separate place. I guess Shorty's family gets half of the price, when I get them sold. I told him that sonofabitch Bonfils was a disgrace to the company, blood relative of his or not, and that if he had any goddam brains, he'd better put his chips on you."

Skye listened to all that, but he felt detached, as if this was all about someone else. They plunged into the night, and Skye wondered where he and Victoria would spend it. Chouteau's hospitality had not extended to accommodations. Even his slaves had a bed.

forty–four

Skye reported to the brick headquarters of Pratte, Chouteau and Company the following morning, feeling tired. He and Victoria had ended up in Gill's airless cubicle, making a bed by stretching out their blankets on the hard grimy floor.

Victoria intuitively chose not to accompany him this morning, and he resolved to tell her everything that transpired. He had no secrets from her, and the company would not impose any if he had his say about it.

He felt an odd trepidation about the position, not at all what he expected so long ago at rendezvous. But he refused to let those worries rot his resolve or spoil the moment he had struggled toward for so long. If all went well, he would soon be heading for the mountains with a paid position, bonuses for meeting or exceeding goals, the chance to bless Victoria's people, and the prospect of success in the company. Not bad for a poorly schooled refugee trapped in a world not of his making.

He found the warehouse and factor's rooms hard by the riverfront, an austere brick building that radiated none of the opulence of the Chouteau residence. A small plaque, gilded letters on black, announced the company. The cathedral bell struck ten as Skye opened the creaking door and pierced into an unfathomable gloom. The acrid odor of furs and hides permeated the dark corridor. A varnished oak door beckoned, and it opened upon an austere office that shouted business. Chouteau was not present. A porcine clerk hunched over a rolltop desk, putting figures into a gray-backed ledger book, by the gloomy light of a wall of tall windows of wavery glass that faced west, away from the majestic Mississippi.

Skye hesitantly lifted his top hat, which was as well brushed as he could manage, and waited. Eventually the clerk deigned to study him.

"Tradesmen use the other door," he said.

"Mr. Chouteau is expecting me. I am Mister Skye."

"I can't imagine why," the man said, surveying Skye as if he were a side of hanging beef.

But the man sidled off his stool and vanished through a door with pebbled glass in it, and soon emerged from it and beckoned Skye.

"Monsieur Chouteau has arrived and will see you," he said.

The fur magnate's inner sanctum was as spartan as the warehouse, save for large windows admitting generous light.

"Ah, Skye, close the door please," he said.

Skye did, gently. What secrets had spun out here, behind that closed mahogany door?

"We should like to know exactly how you would proceed with business at Fort Cass," Chouteau said, after the barest of preliminaries.

"I would proceed, sir, with an intent to earn a profit. This requires loyalty, I to the Absarokas, and they to the company. I intend to give them good measure, exactly what the company has agreed to give for each sort of pelt and grade. As is usual, I will give the chiefs and headmen gifts of some value, to assure that they do not take the tribal trade elsewhere . . ."

Skye noted that Chouteau was dimpled up again, that amused, impatient look he had seen the previous evening. He looked bored, as if he had heard all this many times.

"Yes, yes, yes, Skye. But we are in the business to make a profit. To spend as little as possible to get as much as possible. That requires a certain, ah, delicacy."

Skye waited silently for more, and Chouteau did not disappoint.

"My friend Skye, there is only one goal: profit. Get us every pelt you can, drive off the Opposition by whatever means, and give as little as you can for what you get. It is clear, is it not? Crystal clear. If an Opposition trader arrives, you must drive him off: temporarily, offer more for pelts than he does; and don't hesitate to use other measures. Your post will be supplied, as always, with the means to attract Indians and affect their judgment. Entertain, my friend, entertain lavishly and buy every pelt in sight even as the savages dance and sing."

Spirits.

Only Chouteau wasn't saying it. In fact, Chouteau was speaking in Aesopean language, charging his instructions with much more than the words would, on the surface, suggest.

"Is that good for the tribe, sir?"

Chouteau was nonplused. "The tribe? The savages? What does that have to do with it?"

"They are my wife's people."

"Ah, but what does a mountain liaison matter? They come and go. Yes, look after the savages, of course. They will come to your door in times of war, wanting arms and powder, and you will be their savior. Eventually, Skye, you'll come to St. Louis and live in splendor. We reward our best traders very well, we assure you."

"I understand I must be a citizen to get a trading license from General Clark."

"A trifle. Don't go to General Clark. They've no reason to assume you aren't a citizen. We shall list you on our rosters as a citizen."

"I think I should go to the general—"

"No, don't do that. It would take too long. You would have to swear allegiance before a federal judge, and even then you would not yet be a citizen. No, let it lie. We have a great advantage. There is no record of you, yes? They cannot prove you are not a citizen."

He smiled, obviously enjoying the thought of putting one over on the authorities.

"Ah, Skye, you are well known to us here. We have watched you from afar, but not without interest. No man comes to us better recommended. You are resourceful. You avoid fights with the Indians, so that your brigades have lived and trapped. But you are a mad dog when you're cornered and then, beware, for Skye will perform the miraculous." He paused, dimpling up again. "It shows in our records. More beaver pelts, better cared for, less loss of matériel, more men coming into rendezvous, and in better condition. Ah, yes, we know of these things, and we are pleased to behold the author of such profit and value in our company!"

Skye scarcely knew how to respond, so he just ran a weathered hand through his unwashed knots of hair. There had been no place to lave himself for this interview, and he wore just what he had worn for a thousand miles of river travel.

"You will go far," Chouteau said, and paused pregnantly. "But of course there is always a condition—absolute loyalty. Your heart may not be divided, Skye. Not in little pieces, one for your wife, one for her tribe, one for England if you still care, one for your dear friends who organized the Rocky Mountain Fur Company, one for Hudson's Bay or another company. Ah, no, your loyalty will be toward us. In the field, you will think only of us, and the profits we require to stay in business. The fur trade is the riskiest of all enterprises, my friend. The profits seem high, but that is how we cover the inevitable disasters.

"So you will wring every cent out of a yard of ribbon or an awl, and every dime or bit out of a blanket or packet of vermillion. We have clerks here assiduously buying these things from all over the world—vermillion from Asia, beads from Venice, fine blankets from England, knives from Vermont.

"We gather these, and ship them out to you at enormous cost, and expect you to turn them into hides, beaver pelts, bearskins, elk, ermine, and now especially buffalo, which makes greatcoats, carriage robes, and a host of other things, including belts for pulleys.

"And all our labor is focused on you, at the trading window, taking in furs, examining and grading them carefully, and then offering no more than their real value. Ah, you see, it is the most important of all vocations! You can make or break us!"

Skye listened to the lecture, not doubting most of it, but there were things here that he ached to understand, undercurrents, ideas unspoken, commands and instructions never made explicit but certainly present. Pierre Chouteau was talking about the underside of the fur trade, yet not really saying anything about it. The finger in the cup, the thumb on the scales, the cheap cast-iron tools that shattered, and especially the whiskey, watered and rewatered and offered for every robe in a lodge, even in the middle of winter.

Skye liked and yet didn't like him. Chouteau was good-natured and filled with humor. But he was also the man who had destroyed everyone in his path. He wished Chouteau would put it on the table, get it out in the open: Would Skye be required to chisel, or could he deal honorably in all matters?

That was the crux of it. Suddenly, in Skye's mind, the tables were turned. He stood there, weighing the man, gathering together the understanding he would need to come to a decision: Would he work for this man or not?

Chouteau talked a while more, but the words were veils, and the purpose was to probe and plumb the bulky, big-nosed Englishman who stood before him, on one foot and then the other. It was odd, finally, how few questions Chouteau asked. Nothing about Skye's background or family; nothing about his service in the Royal Navy; nothing about his philosophy or religion or experience or connections.

It came down to an examination of a man thoroughly known to Chouteau by reputation, if not in person. And the real purpose of this endless interview was instruction, by subtle and indirect comment, about what the next trader at Fort Cass would do and not do.

Then suddenly it was over, and the dimpled, amused master of the fur empire rose, clapped Skye on the back, and told him to report daily. There would be no decision until Chouteau had a chance to review the merits of other candidates.

"And where shall we find you, Monsieur Skye?"

At last, some recognition that Skye was far from home.

"With Red Gill."

"That is not desirable. Can you not find some other billet?"

Skye stood silently, awaiting what would come.

"Ah! Gill works for the Opposition, so naturally we are concerned. Don't believe anything he tells you."

That was not true. Skye made note of it.

Skye wandered through gloomy halls and out the door, into a rainy day, splashing through silver puddles and dodging dripping eaves, intending to find Victoria. He would have to barter something that he had gotten from Peter Sarpy to feed them.

He wandered along the waterfront, heading toward Gill's quarters, when he saw the familiar flatboat nosing to the levee, steered by Alexandre Bonfils.

forty-five

Bonfils maneuvered the big flatboat toward a berth on the levee, a delicate task for a man alone at the tiller. But his luck held; a generous slot had opened because of the departure of a steam packet.

From within the cabin, the Cheyenne squaw watched, bemused, as the city emerged from the mist like some ghostly presence. He would have given his last sou to know what was on her mind as she discovered the legendary place of many lodges before her very eyes, and saw the stained brick structures and grimy frame buildings rising rank upon rank before her.

He was soaked and chilled, even though this August shower had scarcely cooled the summer heat this gloomy day. He did not know quite how to proceed; whether to take the squaw to see Simon MacLees, or bring her with him to Pierre Chouteau's chambers. He was leaning toward the latter. Uncle Pierre would be amused, smile that smirky little smile of his, and elect Bonfils for the job before the whole scandal blew up.

Bonfils laughed with anticipation.

He swung the tiller hard, needing to angle across the steady current of the mighty Mississippi to harbor his awkward boat, but he succeeded, driving it straight toward the mucky stone-paved levee. The moment he bumped shore, he would leap from the flatboat with a hawser in hand and wrap it around any of the numerous pilings sunk deep into the levee, and make fast the vessel.

It was just then that he saw the apparition.

It could not be Skye. He had left the man far back at Sarpy's Post, below Council Bluffs. The sight rendered him witless for an instant. Someone else! He could not fathom it. How did that mountaineer arrive here ahead of him? Impossible! *Sacre Bleu*! But it was Skye, in his top hat, thick-nosed and ugly as sin, limping along in the rain. And then Skye saw him.

With a roar, Skye raced toward the waterfront, the limp slowing him scarcely at all, and suddenly Bonfils knew he was in trouble because Skye was not going to stop on land; he was going to leap straight into that boat.

Bonfils let go of the tiller, confident that he could whip the older man if it came to that; a man barely out of the sickbed, with all-but-mortal wounds weakening him.

Then in one bound, Skye was over the transom.

"Got you," he growled. "Want my outfit back."

"Get off the boat," Bonfils retorted.

Bonfils swung a haymaker that hammered only the air, and Skye landed on the younger man, knocking him to the floorboards. He glimpsed Lame Deer peering out of the cabin at them, her hand to mouth, starting to keen.

Bonfils sprang upward, tossing Skye aside, and confidently began pummeling the older man, but Skye bore in, unafraid, though breathing hard while Bonfils had scarcely started to suck air.

But Bonfils had not met such a man as this, and sensed that all those years as a tar, in shipboard brawls and war, had taught the Englishman a thing or two, because he felt blows rain on him, catch him in the liver, the groin, the jaw, the ears, almost as if Skye were playing with him.

Skye quit pounding, grabbed Bonfils by the shirt, and tossed him to the planks again. The Creole leaped up, but Skye was looming over him. The flatboat had caught the current and was drifting into the side of a steam packet.

Skye stepped back, pulled the tiller to twist the boat away from collision just as Bonfils flew at him. Skye tripped him;

Bonfils landed in a heap, bloodying his lips when his teeth cut them as he landed. He wiped the blood away.

"We're going to see Chouteau," Skye rasped.

Bonfils didn't want to. Not just then. Not until he could concoct something to explain things.

Skye was breathing hard. The brawl had drained him. Maybe there would be some advantage in that, Bonfils thought.

The boat had drifted into the channel, and Skye steered it past the packet, where fifty faces stared into the flatboat, and several men with pikes stood at the rail, prepared to push the flatboat away.

Skye chose a spot several hundred yards downstream, well below the warehouses on the levee, and docked the flatboat. Bonfils tied the hawsers to a tree stump left there for the purpose.

"Come with me," Skye said, retrieving his top hat from the slimy floorboards.

"What if I don't?"

"Then you'll take what I give you. You can walk or I can drag you."

Bonfils knew he could sprint faster than the barrel-shaped, wounded man, and nodded.

"Lame Deer, come with me," Skye said roughly.

The Cheyenne woman edged from the cabin, looking fearful of what might occur. She tugged her daughter with her, and they stepped to shore. She had dressed herself as closely as possible to what white women wore, and had succeeded.

"We're going to see Red Gill first," Skye explained to her. "To get this boat and his gear back to him. Then Victoria and I will find the house of Simon MacLees and we will take you there so that you and he can see one another. We will help you."

Lame Deer nodded.

Skye turned to Bonfils, puzzlement on his face, as if he didn't quite know what to do. "It doesn't matter what I do with you," Skye said. "You're done for. I was going to drag you to your uncle and toss you in his lap. But now I don't know why. Chouteau knows the whole story. All I want is my outfit and Gill's." Skye lifted his top hat and settled it. "I'm going to unload our gear, and Red's, and Lame Deer's, and you can do what you please. Go visit your uncle if you wish. Or head for Tahiti. I'm not holding you."

Skye was dismissing him. How peculiar! Bonfils exulted uneasily.

The Londoner simply turned on his heel and stepped into the flatboat. Little by little, he emptied the cabin of its burdens: Gill's clothing and rifle and trunk; Skye's and Victoria's robes and Skye's mountain rifle, Lame Deer's beautiful summer robe, and the parfleches containing her few things.

Bonfils thought feverishly. He hadn't expected the Skyes ever to come to St. Louis, and he wondered how they did, and how they passed him. And what he should do.

"I have connections," he said to Skye.

Skye stopped his unloading. "Yes, you do," he said. "And you'll rely on them instead of on yourself. If you want anything of yours from the cabin, get it."

The suggestion had an eerie quality to it, and suddenly Bonfils wanted nothing but to get away from there.

"I leave the squaw to you," Bonfils said. "Seeing as how that's where you set your sights, squaw man."

Somehow it sounded hollow.

Skye barely nodded, as if further concourse with Bonfils was no longer necessary. He was straightening the gear on the levee, and at the same time looking for a cart or a hack.

Bonfils nursed his sore lip, wondering what to do. He had come this far, confident that he had eliminated Skye as a rival, and could embarrass MacLees out of contention. He stood there on one foot and the other, unable to decide, and then cockily started toward Pratte, Chouteau and Company, two hundred yards upriver. With each step, his confidence returned.

He was family. What were families for, but to nurture and protect their own?

He brushed himself off, laughed, knew he could silver-tongue his way out of trouble, and hiked jauntily toward his distant uncle's lair. He had been there many times, watching his mother's cousin fling his resources into a wild and unknown land, and many months later, watch the furs float down the mighty rivers and into his warehouse.

The blood on his lip tasted salty, but the minor bleeding would cease by the time he was sitting in Pierre Chouteau's office. He glanced behind him. Skye had summoned a hack, and was dickering with the hack driver. Lame Deer stood aside, her daughter clutched to her.

Bonfils gathered courage, strode toward the dreary brick edifice that formed the heart of an empire, turned into its gloomy corridors, and then presented himself to Pierre Chouteau.

"Alexandre, we've been expecting you," Chouteau said, after studying the young man standing in his doorway. "Is your lip still bleeding?"

"Bleeding?"

"When you landed in a heap after Skye hit you in front of our warehouse."

Bonfils laughed nervously. He should have known that everything of consequence that happened on the St. Louis levee would reach his uncle's ears in moments.

"I am back from the mountains, and ready to assume whatever position you have in mind for me," he said, and then remembered his manners. "I trust you are well, and the family is in good health?"

That dimpled little smirk built on Chouteau's face, and Bonfils knew all would be well.

"New Orleans," Chouteau said.

"I don't follow you."

"New Orleans is where you should go. But of course, we

leave all that to you." Chouteau shrugged, a gesture imbued with gallic charm.

"I would like a trading position. Wasn't that why you summoned me?"

"It was. A most regrettable decision, it turned out."

Bonfils didn't like the gist of all this. "I wish to inform you, sir, that no matter what the captain said of me, my swift action that morning saved an entire cargo of furs, and ensured a profit for you."

Chouteau looked amused, but behind that humor was a dangerous glint.

"We would suggest, young man, that you remove yourself from this city before we do it for you. You could take that flat-boat if you wish. It belongs to Gill, but we'll make it up to him. We trust you have returned his outfit to him, and returned Skye's?"

"*Mais oncle—*" Bonfils was aghast. "You have not even let me tell my story."

"If you should see Skye on the levee, tell him we wish to see him. We will offer him the position. A great step upward for the man. *Au revoir, mon neveu.*"

"I never really wanted that lonely job in that lonely post anyway," Bonfils said. "It was all a game."

forty–six

Skye found Victoria on the waterfront, quietly blotting up the ways of white men. She took one look at the hack, loaded with so many possessions as well as Skye, Lame Deer, and Singing Rain, and ran to it, clambered aboard and hugged Lame Deer. It was the first carriage ride for either woman, and they sat spellbound as the hack driver steered the dray horse over the wet cobbles.

"So?" Victoria asked, waving at the mound of goods.

"Saw his flatboat come in. I talked him out of our possessions."

Victoria glanced at him sharply, noting the torn clothing.

"Where is he now?"

"Seeing the uncle."

"What did you say to him?"

"I didn't. I ran at him."

She smiled at him. "Where are we going?"

"Find Red. He's in the warehouse grading his buffalo hides, I think."

"Driver, the Pratte, Chouteau warehouse first," Skye said.

The man nodded, stared sharply at Victoria, just as he had stared sullenly at the Cheyenne woman, tugged the lines and steered the blindered dray leftward to veer across the wet expanse of the cobbles to the brick warehouse. Skye hadn't a cent to his name, but the man accepted a blanket for an hour's time.

The hack pulled to a halt, and the old, wet-backed dray sagged in its harness.

"We'll be out directly," Skye said to the weary man.

He led the women into a cavernous and ill-lit place, redolent of fur and hide and the acrid odor of ancient dried flesh.

They found Gill immediately, off in a separate bay, examining his hides one by one.

Gill looked up, spotted Lame Deer, and started.

"What the hell?" he asked.

"Ship came in," Skye said. "Got your stuff and ours in a hack."

"Where's that sonofabitch?"

"He's gone to talk to his uncle."

Gill eyed them, dropped the robe without examining it, and sighed. "You want to store the stuff in my place?"

"Just long enough so that it doesn't walk away."

Gill nodded. "We'll get it over there. You got everything of mine?"

"Your stuff, Shorty's stuff, and whatever was lying around that flatboat."

"You got the boat, too? How the hell did you persuade him to give it up?"

Skye smiled, flexing his fists. Gill looked alarmed.

"You get hurt?"

"Some."

He nodded at Lame Deer. "She all right?"

"Ask her."

"Yes," she said. "It was a long trip."

"He hurt you or . . . do anything?"

"No, because I showed him my skinning knife and told him he would not sleep well if he touched me."

Red Gill hoorawed.

They clambered aboard the groaning hack, and the driver took them to Gill's room, and even helped unload the gear. When they were done, there was no space left in that small place. Lame Deer studied the gloomy chamber closely, her lips compressed.

"I like a lodge more," she said softly.

"So do I," Skye said.

The bewhiskered hackman wasted no time whipping his bony dray away from the tenement and back toward the levee, clutching Skye's good blanket as his pay.

"Tell me the story," Gill said, settling on a corner of his narrow cot and pulling out a pipe that Skye had never before seen. "And if I forgot it, thank you. This is a big bundle of stuff, me and Shorty's gear, and worth something. Them rifles alone cost a month's pay."

"A lucky break," Skye said. "Red, you know this town?"

Gill nodded.

"MacLees's place?"

"Think so; if not, I'll find out."

"Think you could take us there? Lame Deer has some business to attend, and I don't aim to leave her alone here in St. Louis."

Gill tamped yellow leaf tobacco into his pipe and struck a lucifer. After he had a fire blooming in the bowl, he nodded. "I think we owe it to her, she being alone and under our care." He gazed at her. "You want to pretty up?"

"I'll help, dammit," Victoria said. "She don't know nothing about big places."

"Skye, let's you and me leave these ladies alone. I'll fetch them some water and good lye soap."

Lame Deer trembled, and Skye realized that this ordeal was coming to its conclusion, and that she was a lonely, frightened, desperate woman of the plains caught at last in the strange and mysterious world of white men. She had borne her troubles well, but he saw in her face a whiteness and exhaustion that bespoke her true condition.

"Go, dammit," Victoria said, pushing them both out the door.

"First time I got booted out of my own room, and by a damned squaw," Gill said, and then apologized to Skye with a grin.

They lounged about under a small portico, awaiting the women. The rain had almost stopped, but water dripped steadily from eaves.

"Tell me where MacLees lives," Skye said.

"He lives with his pa. I'll take you there but I ain't going in," Gill said.

"With his father?"

"Yeah, since he come back from the mountains. I knew him some. Pretty fancy house. They ain't poor."

"What does the father do?"

"Brian MacLees is a banker and what they call an arbitrageur, buying and selling money mostly. St. Louis, it's got no one money, so it's dollars, pence, shillings, state bank notes, pieces of eight, ducats, reals, francs, guilders—you name it, after being part of Spain, France, and the United States. And there's English coin out of Canada to deal with too. Old MacLees, he's made him a pile just straightening the mess out."

"Brian MacLees put his son in business?"

Gill shrugged. "Simon got the money somewheres, but went through it. Chouteau don't let no Opposition company last for long, let me tell you. Now Simon's getting married, I hear. Benton Marsh's stepdaughter, Sarah Lansing."

"Getting married?" Skye was thunderstruck.

"So I heard at the warehouse. Next Saturday, too. Big wedding, pretty fancy goings on. The Lansings, they're rich, and they ain't sparing the horses, I heard. Sarah lives with her real father, not her mother. Nasty divorce a few years ago, rocked St. Louis. Benton Marsh has had his share of women, and then some."

"And Simon MacLees abandoned Lame Deer without a word, never let her know."

Gill shrugged, uneasily. "Mountain weddings, them don't count for much."

Some things about the trip were dawning on Skye. "You think that's why Bonfils was so eager to bring Lame Deer here? Embarrass MacLees? A scandal that could cost MacLees a position?"

Red grinned. "That's how it slices up," he said. "Say, you don't think maybe we should get the women to hustling, do you? They're taking forever."

"I reckon when a woman wants to pretty up, it doesn't matter whether she's a white or an Indian. They're going to pretty up at their own speed." Skye astonished himself with that bit of wisdom, since he had never waited upon a white woman in his life.

Getting fancied up for nothing, he thought. Nothing but a lot of hurt. He wished Lame Deer had never come here; he wished he could whisk her away before this cruel meeting afflicted her. She had already lost a son on this long trip; and now she would find a man who had abandoned her. He felt helpless to stop this terrible reunion, but he didn't have the faintest idea what to do, except to let it play out.

They fidgeted another while, and finally the door to Gill's room creaked open. Skye beheld a beautiful and solemn Cheyenne woman, dressed largely as a white woman might dress, with Victoria trailing behind.

Lame Deer had made herself lovely. Her jet hair looked odd, but it glowed, and there was a red ribbon tied in a bow on one side of it. She wore a green calico dress, with a bone necklace. On her feet were the traditional high moccasins of the Cheyenne, these exquisitely embellished with quillwork. Her soft eyes were alive with joy.

Suddenly Skye felt very bad. He must have shown it, because he caught Victoria staring at him.

"What?" she said sharply.

Skye shook his head.

"No sense in standing in the rain," Gill said. "I'll take you, but I ain't hanging around, no how."

The child had been cleaned and groomed too, and wore a green dress that matched her mother's. Skye stared at the pair of them, and thought of their doomed journey and the mortification they would soon endure, and felt bad as they splashed through mucky lanes that soon soaked their moccasins.

The slow drizzle fit his mood.

Gill led them upslope to the neighborhood where the Chouteaus and so many of their relatives lived, where the air was better, the shade trees majestic, the views generous, and the city they owned lay supine before them.

They reached a two-story Georgian home of red brick, with a shining white veranda across the front.

"MacLees's house," Gill said. "And I am gonna vamoose."

"Red—"

But Gill was hurrying away, just as fast as he could walk.

forty–seven

black manservant opened, and stared at the motley people on the veranda. The man was a slave, but Skye got the distinct impression that the haughty servant was sitting in judgment, and the visitors were found wanting.

"Simon MacLees, please," Skye said.

"Ah will fetch him directly. And who are you?"

"Mister Skye. He will know the name."

"From?"

"From the West."

The man vanished into the dark recesses of the house, made even gloomier by the slate sky and slow drizzle. Victoria as usual was studying, gauging, marveling at what white men had wrought. But Lame Deer's face was a mask, unfathomable to any observer. If she was curious about all these comforts, she showed no sign of it.

Skye had the sense that more than the heavens would be weeping in a few minutes. After a considerable time, a lean, hawkish, raptor-eyed man in a fine silver-embroidered waistcoat and black pantaloons appeared, jaunty until he discovered who was standing at his doorstep. He stared, visibly startled, and then his good humor faded behind a hard mask.

"Mister MacLees, I'm Barnaby Skye, and this is my wife Victoria. And this woman you know."

MacLees stood stock still, not even drawing breath, some wild alarm in his bright brown eyes. "I—don't know you," he said at last, his gaze darting madly from face to face.

"Simon," said Lame Deer. "I come."

"Who? Who?"

"Me. I come. See the child we made, Singing Rain." She herded the girl forward. The little one looked upward at her father, her face solemn, and clutched her mother's hand.

"Who . . . ah, who are you?"

Lame Deer was puzzled. "A long way we have come, Simon. A long way from the People, with many suns on the big river, always toward the East Wind, Simon, my own." Her composure crumbled. "I have bad news. The one who was our firstborn . . ." she was carefully avoiding the name, as was her tradition about those who were dead, ". . . he is gone up the pathway of the spirits."

Lame Deer stood there, yearning, open, vulnerable, and brimming with tenderness.

"Ah, ah," MacLees looked utterly disoriented. And no wonder, Skye mused. The young man had thought he was a safe fifteen hundred miles and an entire civilization away from his Indian wife.

"See, see how your girl has get big," she said, urging the child forward again.

The girl clung to her mother.

"It was a hard trip," Skye said, "but she bore it bravely, her thoughts always on you. She has been worried for many months, because you did not return. She never heard a word."

"I don't have the faintest idea who this squaw is," MacLees said, his voice wavering. "Or why you are here."

Skye was disappointed in the young man, who was hiding behind a feeble and transparent lie.

"You might welcome her," Skye said, relentlessly.

MacLees seemed to harden. "Nor have I met you, sir. I don't quite know what you want or why you're here, but if you have no business with me, then I shall excuse myself."

Skye straightened himself and waited, unbudging. He would not help this spoiled young scion of a wealthy family out of his little dilemma.

A graying man emerged from the gloom of the house. "What's this, Simon?" he asked.

"Some people who think I know them," MacLees said.

"Mr. MacLees? I am Mister Skye; my wife, Victoria, and this is Simon's Cheyenne wife, Lame Deer, and Simon's daughter. They have come a long way."

The world seemed to stop in its tracks. Beyond, in the bleak interior, he spotted a stout woman hovering about, and the manservant standing erect and disdainful to one side.

The senior MacLees turned red. His glare settled on one, then another, and finally on Lame Deer.

"Blackmail," he said. "You are a blackmailer. You want money or you intend to embarrass us upon the eve of Simon's wedding."

"Wedding?" Victoria snapped.

"Wedding. And I won't stand for it. Leave at once, and if I see you in St. Louis again, you'll all be turned over to the authorities."

"Simon, I come long way," Lame Deer said, her hands lifting toward him. "How good to see you. I will be like a white woman to you, and learn all these strange things, and make you happy. It will be like it was, when we had our own lodge, and we were together. This I will gladly do—"

"Out!" The senior MacLees shook his fist.

The great oaken door swung hard, and snapped shut in their faces. But through the leaded glass windows at either side of the door, white faces peered at them.

"He gonna marry some white girl," Victoria said to Lame Deer.

The Cheyenne woman stood erect, summoning her courage, and wheeled off the veranda. Then she began singing, a lamentation that rose and fell in minor chords as she sang the music of grief and loss and stayed the ache of her heart. She turned, stared at the half-timbered house and the velvet lawn about it, and the manicured grounds, and closed her eyes for a moment. When she opened them, she was somehow different.

Skye reached her, clasped his big, scarred hand into hers, and led her into the rain. One bad moment had wiped out her dreams and hopes, and fifteen hundred miles of travel toward her lover. But when at last she reached the lane, and could no longer see the house, or those ghostly faces peering through the windows, she slumped, and he could not tell whether the wetness on her cheeks was raindrops or tears. Victoria caught Lame Deer's other hand, and held the child's hand too, as they retreated not only from a cold home, but also from warm hopes, dreams, and visions of a joyous tomorrow.

They slogged silently down a narrow lane toward the riverfront, scarcely knowing where to go. Between them they hadn't a cent for food, shelter, or transportation.

Skye didn't like St. Louis anymore, and wasn't sure he ever did. The place oozed with its grimy little secrets. The climate was foul, the soul of the city corrupt. When they reached the levee, he discovered that Gill's flatboat was gone. The little sailboat had vanished too. He steered the women toward the Pratte, Chouteau warehouse again, needing to find Gill.

Like it or not, he had several people depending on him for food and shelter, and no doubt, a means to go back to the mountains, and Gill was the only person he could count on.

He turned to Lame Deer. "You want to stay here?"

She shook her head sternly.

"You want to go back to your people?"

She faltered then, unsure of herself. "I do not know," she

said. "My medicine . . . I have no medicine. No vision rises in me to light the way like a torch."

"You have good medicine," he said, but she looked desolate.

He steered them through open double doors into the pungent vaults where the company stored its peltries, and found Gill back at work, pulling each hide open and examining it.

"Told you so," Gill said, surveying the gloomy party.

"We need—"

"Yeah, I know."

"The flatboat's gone."

Gill stopped his grading. "Already? Bonfils didn't waste no time. Old uncle must have told him to vamoose. Chouteau come around here a few minutes ago and told me the same. Long as I was doing his dirty work for him, getting spirits out to his posts, he knew I'd keep my mouth shut. But now that I quit, now he's worrying maybe I'll talk too much, spill his secrets, cost him his license, like the last time the company got into a jam.

"So he wanders through here and asks if I'm satisfied, and I says yes, except Bonfils took my flatboat, and he says he'll pay for that, two hundred dollars, and he says he thinks maybe it's time for me to get away from St. Louis, and the ears of old General Clark, who is sitting there, not a hundred yards from here, governing the whole Indian country, and handing out licenses. So I says I'll think about it, and he says if I think fast, he'll sweeten the offer."

"Like what?"

Gill grinned. "Ain't decided yet. The longer I hang around here, the more he itches for me to vamoose and raises the ante. I could maybe go into the Santy Fe trade. Lots of teamsters making plenty hauling stuff out there. Them Messicans pay silver or tallow or hide for just about anything gets hauled out there, half starved the way they are by all them tariffs and duties and rules their government puts on 'em. I could clear two thousand dollars a trip, maybe more. I'm more teamster than waterman anyway." He nodded toward Lame Deer. "How'd she take it?"

"She is a courageous woman."

"You get in to talk with MacLees?"

"Only as far as the door. He pretended not to recognize us. There he was, facing his wife, the woman who had borne his children, and he said he didn't know her."

Gill spat. "Guess that says all that needs saying about him. Then what?"

"MacLees senior called us blackmailers. Told us to get out of St. Louis or face the constables."

Gill grinned. "More dirty linen no one wants aired."

Victoria said, "What are we gonna do?"

Skye was reminded that he was penniless in a strange city, and had two women and a child to care for.

"Red, would you look after these ladies for a while? I want to talk with Chouteau."

Red grinned. "Have a seat. Or help me grade these robes," he said. "All you got to do is open up the robes and let me have a look-see. When I sell, I want to get my money's worth, and that means looking at every robe."

The women nodded. Lame Deer settled upon a bale of robes and drew her girl to her.

Skye left them, and headed through the dreary warrens of that warehouse until he found his way into the company headquarters, and Chouteau's chambers.

"Ah, Mister Skye, we weren't prepared to see you, but it is just as well," Chouteau said, rounding his desk.

Skye nodded. "I am hoping you have news."

Chouteau's compressed smile emerged on those pouty lips again. "We have rid the city of my nephew. He's en route to visit relatives far away. We saw him only briefly, long enough to reject him for any position in the company—ever." Chouteau was not smiling now. "We have received an express from Fort Pierre. The Teton Sioux are, shall we say, angry. They lost four young men, and others lie in torment. They want revenge on Bonfils, and reparations—blankets, guns, powder, lead, and much more. That grapeshot into their midst not only injured you, sir, but the company.

"We have chosen you, Mister Skye. You will be our trader at Fort Cass."

forty-eight

ow sweet it was. The unknown rival, MacLees, had declined the position, and sullied himself. The known rival, young, skilled, and connected in all the right places, had shown appalling judgment, damaged the company and many innocent people, and now was banished. And the position had settled upon Barnaby Skye.

He could, if he took it, greatly benefit Victoria's people, making sure they were well armed against their clamorous enemies such as the Sioux and Blackfeet, supplying them with good blankets to warm themselves on an icy winter's night, offering them all the tools and equipment they needed.

He could delight Victoria with a solid log home and garden and safety; vest her mother and father and brothers with great status among the Crow people; give Victoria a richer life as various visitors came by; and maybe even provide a place for children, if she could only conceive. All of that and security, and maybe down the line, a better position, more responsibility, more salary, and someday even a share in the company. That was how Chouteau did it. His best traders received a share in the profits, something that inspired them to diligence and enterprise.

He had come a vast distance, over hundreds of miles of land, and over a thousand miles of river, for this. He had endured insult, and then life-threatening wounds, for this. He had endangered himself and Victoria for this. And after this, he would still need to take her safely home, up the Platte and North Platte in autumnal weather, past her tribal enemies, two vulnerable people in a harsh world . . . for this.

Chouteau was waiting, some small amusement building in his face, as usual.

Skye shook his head. "Sorry, mate. I'm not your man," he said, a slight roughness in his tone.

An eyebrow arched. "Not our man?"

Skye shook his head. He didn't know just where or how he had come to that decision, but he had, and now he was sacrificing every advantage being offered him, the one and only time in his hard life, because of . . . something.

He knew, painfully, what it was. Honor.

"Not right for me."

An eyebrow arched. "We never ask twice, Skye."

"It's Mister Skye, mate."

"May we inquire?"

"It needn't be spoken," Skye said. "I owe you my thanks for considering me. And bearing the expense of bringing me here. I trust horses will be waiting for me at Sarpy's Post, as agreed upon, in trade for those I left at Fort Union."

"*Certainment*. We will write a draft, just in case the matter is in question when you arrive."

"And I trust you'll provide river passage that far? The *Otter*'s going that far, water levels permitting?"

Chouteau nodded, and seemed to resign himself. "It would have been awkward," he said. "Your citizenship, General Clark . . ." A gallic wave of the hand dismissed that line of thought.

Skye let it go at that. There was honor and dishonor in the fur trade, and all parties had sullied themselves at times, especially with illegal spirits. Skye did not consider himself any loftier or better than the rest. He had drunk illegal spirits at the rendezvous. He had given spirits to his Indian wife—also illegally. And yet, there were others he knew, among the mountain men, who hewed to honor. Jedediah Smith was one, killed by Comanches in '31, but a man to remember. Skye knew he could never be a man of Smith's caliber, but in a smaller way, he could try. He could do what was right.

He stood reflectively in Chouteau's chambers, upbraiding himself for playing the fool, throwing away all that had been offered. Chouteau sat, reached for his quill, dipped it, and began drafting a requisition for four horses, the quill scratching noisily on the soft paper. The brass pendulum of a cherry-wood grandfather clock swung metronomically, reminding Skye of the passage of his life, time gone irretrievably, and the passage of once-in-a-life opportunity from the one powerful personage who cared enough about him to offer him a chance.

"Please make it passage for me and my party. I want to take MacLees's wife and baby back to her people," he said. "And please direct Marsh to accept us."

Chouteau nodded.

Skye hadn't the faintest idea what he would do or how he would support himself. He might be able to keep himself in galena and DuPont by shooting buffalo and skinning off the hides. Beyond that, his life was a blank. Had he been the ultimate fool? He knew most of his mountain friends would think so; most of the world would think so.

It seemed amazingly quiet for a midday encounter in the busiest quarter of St. Louis, and yet he could not even hear the clop and rattle of a dray outside those tall windows.

Chouteau finished with two drafts, and handed them to Skye. The first granted him and his party passage upriver. The second gave him his choice of four of Peter Sarpy's saddle or packhorses, and tack.

"There, Monsieur, there. A petite surprise, all this. We are mystified. And curious. What will you make—ah, what will you do?"

"Turn into a savage, I imagine," Skye said, a faint amusement building in his face.

"*Sacre Bleu! A sauvage!*"

Then Pierre Chouteau was laughing, this time with big, boisterous gusts. "We make plans, and Fate makes other plans! We will give you some counsel. Don't go into Opposition."

"Don't plan to."

"Ah, they all say that to me, and then they secretly put together a small outfit and head west, thinking that we will never know. But we know. The company has a thousand ears, and ten thousand special ways of triumphing . . ."

Skye lifted his battered top hat, settled it, and grinned.

Chouteau nodded, a sudden dismissal, and Skye found himself alone, unemployed, unprotected by powerful interests, caught in a strange and gloomy city, and with several Indian women to shelter in a cruel and sordid town.

He stepped outside, and discovered that the storm clouds had at last slid by, and a golden sun painted the world, glinted off the puddles, and warmed the breezes. The world was a good place. Even St. Louis was a good place. He sucked fresh air into his lungs, surveyed the awesome river that drained much of North America, which ran most of a mile wide there, and felt at peace.

He decided to make one small call before breaking the news to Victoria. The plain, utilitarian one-story redbrick United States government house stood just a few yards distant, and he had in mind a visit to a man revered by all the world for his exploration of this continent early in the century; a man who held the fate of so many in his hand.

He crossed the stone-paved street, passed a staff with a

red, white and blue flag dangling from it, and entered. General William Clark's chambers were located at the end of a short hall. He was actually not a general in the United States Army, but of the Missouri Militia, but the title, as so often was the case in this republican country, seemed interchangeable. He and Meriwether Lewis had both been called captains at the time they led the Corps of Discovery. Skye opened a plain, varnished door, entered, and found two clerks slouching at battered desks situated by the tall windows to catch the sun.

"General Clark, please," Skye said, removing his topper.

"And who is calling?"

"Mister Skye, sir. Barnaby Skye."

The clerk made Skye's presence known. Clark himself opened his inner office door. The old, weary, redheaded man with a military bearing beckoned. The legendary American wore an ordinary suit of clothes, not a uniform, and wore them carelessly as well. He looked unwell.

"Ah, you are Barnaby Skye. Your reputation precedes you, sir," Clark said, offering a big, solid, meaty hand, which Skye took in his own. A tremor spasmed Clark's hand.

"I can't imagine it," Skye said. "A man like you paying attention to a man like me—"

"Come in and visit with me."

Skye was heartened by this unsteady old American with a hospitable instinct, and settled uneasily in a chair opposite the general.

"I am surprised to see you in St. Louis, sir. You are one of the legends of the mountains."

"How would you know that, sir?"

"Through these chambers, my British friend, come the masters of the fur trade. Both Sublettes, Campbell, Drips, Mitchell, most of the upper echelon of the Chouteau company . . . shall I name a dozen more?

"No, sir. You probably know more about me than I know about myself."

Clark laughed easily. "It is quite possible."

"I came here at Mr. Chouteau's request. He thought to offer me a trading position."

"I see." Clark's affability had suddenly vanished.

"I turned it down."

Clark took some while registering that. "You turned it down? I knew you were coming, and I expected you to inquire about United States law governing the Indian country. Citizenship, especially. You are not an American, I take it."

"No, sir."

"Then I am puzzled."

Skye sought the words he needed. "I am married to a Crow woman, and have been many years. I want to know two or three things. One is whether I am legally entitled to be in your territory. The other is what nature of business I might engage in, if I am lawfully present."

"Simple. A squaw man's entitled to live with his spouse, as part of a tribe, no matter what his nationality. And you can engage in any business you wish, but only within that tribe and to others in the tribe. Save, of course, the purveying of ardent spirits, which are totally prohibited in the Indian territory now."

"I could actually do some limited trading?"

"Within the Crow tribe, yes. It would be no different than if a Crow himself were engaged in business with his tribesmen."

Skye brightened. "That's what I need to know."

"Ah, Mister Skye, I take it that you will not become an American citizen?"

"I am thinking on it."

"I regret that you find it necessary to weigh it, but I understand the case."

Skye nodded, not wanting to pursue that any further. He was still, in some lingering way, an Englishman at heart, and maybe he would end up somewhere in the Empire, such as Canada. And besides, he wasn't so sure about these Americans.

"How else may I serve you?"

"Those are the things I wanted to know, sir."

Clark stood at once, and Skye realized that this official was not one to lounge about. "If you are in St. Louis for a while, come visit me. We will share stories of the mountains, and grizzlies, and Indians over some brandy. And do bring your native wife."

"Victoria, sir. Many Quill Woman to her people."

"Ah! Bring her, then."

"I will consider it an honor."

Skye left, feeling heartened by this old man, but also wary of him. He headed back to the Chouteau warehouse, knowing Victoria would be waiting, and would want his portentous news.

He felt sublimely happy, but he wasn't sure she would.

forty-nine

Victoria listened intently. "You said no?"

"Yes. I just couldn't accept it, and I may regret it, but I had to."

She nodded. "That which guides you inside of yourself, it is always true to you, and that is all there is to say. I am content."

"I would have hurt your people."

"Some other trader will come, and he will hurt them."

"Let it be someone else, then."

"We have come a long way."

"Not for nothing. All this had to happen."

"Aiee, it is so. I have seen this land and this many-lodges, and now I am wiser than I was before."

"We'll get a ride part way back on the steamboat."

She processed that a moment. "With the captain, Benton Marsh?"

"Yes."

"He is a bad man. Maybe I walk."

"Chouteau gave me passage for me and my party. We can put up with him for a week or ten days."

She laughed. "He will put up with us! I will make it hard for that sonofabitch."

Skye laughed too. "We got a long trip ahead. You up to it?"

"My People call me. My country, the mountains, in the foothills, with the prairies rolling away, call me."

"I arranged passage for Lame Deer and her girl. Take 'em with us."

"If she wants to go. Maybe she stays here."

"I suppose we should ask," he said.

The rejected Cheyenne woman was sitting quietly in the cool gloom of the warehouse, watching Red Gill grade his hides and prepare to sell them.

Gill looked up as they approached. "You got the Fort Cass trader position?"

"It was offered. I turned it down, Red."

"Turned it down you say? Ain't that the craziest thing I ever heard. What'd you do that for?"

Skye just shook his head.

"Well, I wouldn't work for the company, neither. That's a rough outfit, and a man can't call his soul his own."

"Something like that," Skye said.

"What're you going to do?" Gill asked.

"Start a little trading store. Long as I'm married to a Crow woman, it's all right," Skye said. "That's straight from the general himself. After I got loose of Chouteau, I hiked over there and talked to him."

"How you going to stock it?"

"I've got two outfits now. I'll sell one for horses and a few trade items."

"You figure that's a living?"

"No," said Skye.

Gill dropped the robe he was examining. "You want to partner?"

"Doing what?"

"Santa Fe trading."

Skye shook his head. There were twenty other outfits in the business, and more coming in each year, and all of them better financed. But it would not suit Victoria, and that was reason enough. And he wasn't sure about lining up with a smuggler.

"I guess not, Red, but thanks for the offer."

Red grinned. "I figured it'd be that. You're a man of honor; me, I'm an opportunist. Tell you what. I'll lend you some start-up if you want."

It was tempting. A few hundred dollars of trade goods would go far. But after a moment's reflection, he declined. He was a man without a country; also, a man who had to go it alone. He couldn't say why.

"I think I'll just weather the bad times," he said.

"Luck," said Red.

Skye and Victoria braced Lame Deer, who was sitting contemplatively, cradling her girl.

"We're going back west. We'd like you to join us," Skye said. "Take you to your people."

"We will walk?"

"Riverboat up to Sarpy's Post, and then horses and pack mules out the Platte River. Long trip, and the weather will turn."

"The same fireboat?"

Skye nodded.

She seemed to harden before his eyes. "I will go. This is a place like a cloudy night. I see no stars. The stars are like friends, and I see no friends. I come to give myself to my man; give my child to him. He sees me and then I am a stranger to him, and they close the door and I am standing with his little girl, and the door is closed."

She shuddered, and then focused on some distant place beyond all horizons.

"He will walk in darkness. He will pass meadows blooming with flowers and not see them. He will stumble when there is no rock to stumble on. He will look behind him to see who is following, even when no one follows. He will smile, but his spirit is sad. He will have friends, but will not be a friend of himself. He will be with many, but he will be alone. I cannot help him. This path he choose for himself; me, I am not welcome in his lodge. His medicine is bad and mine is good and I will walk along soft trails covered with pine needles and my feet will not hurt."

Skye marveled again at this woman's images. Where did they come from? What artesian well, of what sweet water, rose within her? Was this a curse or a prophecy?

"We'll be your traveling companions, and you can call on us," Skye said.

She seemed to come out of some trance, and stood. "We go now?"

"I'll find out," Skye said. "I hope we have some time. I've got some trading to do."

Two days later they boarded the *Otter* under Marsh's baleful eye, and settled in their staterooms.

First Mate Trenholm appeared. "Captain wants you," he said.

Skye followed the mate up the companionway, wondering what more trouble the captain could inflict on his party.

Marsh stood in the pilothouse, massive and choleric as ever.

"You lost, Skye," the captain said, enjoying himself.

"I was offered the position and turned it down."

Marsh wheezed. "You make a poor excuse for a liar," he said.

"It's Mister Skye, sir."

Marsh laughed. "I knew you'd lose. I told Chouteau you

weren't fit. You were better than Bonfils, but that's not saying much."

Marsh had called him a liar. Skye wondered whether to make an issue of it. He knew it was bait. Marsh was looking for an excuse to toss Skye and his women off the steamboat, and a brawl would do nicely.

"That it?" Skye asked.

"Behave yourself. The moment this boat casts off lines, I'm God. I'm the master of this boat and all upon it. You can leave now if you don't like it, or I'll put you ashore at the first wood-lot on any excuse I can find, or no excuse at all if I feel like it. And don't go whining to Pierre Chouteau. He'll laugh."

Skye didn't move a muscle.

"I hear you tried to blackmail MacLees," Marsh said. "I got the whole story firsthand, over some good brandy. It's the source of much humor in that household. You and your slut and that squaw on their doorstep. The wedding, by the way, was splendid."

Skye grinned.

Marsh waited, poised like a cat, his huge red fists ready to hammer Skye. The helmsman was ready too, with a club. Trenholm hovered just outside the door, on the hurricane deck, a thick club in his hand. They were ready to kill him, hoping for it, and were looking for the slightest excuse.

Skye kept his mouth shut and his hands at his sides.

"I'm calling you a liar and a blackmailer, Skye," Marsh said. "I hear no objection. I guess you must agree."

Skye smiled.

"Very well, I get no argument from you about your char-acter. You'll be deck passengers. I'll have a cabin boy get your gear out, and unload it on the deck. Then I'll have him delouse the rooms."

Now at last Skye spoke, softly and resonantly. "Tell the helmsman and Trenholm to back off and put down their clubs.

Then I'll answer you, man to man," Skye said. "You want a reply? I'll give you one."

Marsh eyed the helmsman and the mate, and Skye could see him calculating. He waited calmly, on the balls of his feet. His gaze bore into Marsh. Then he edged forward until the length of a pencil separated him from the master.

"Well?" Skye asked. "What's your reply?"

Marsh didn't blink and the moment stretched long, but then there was a subtle change; nothing palpable, but a change even so, and Skye knew he had won. The master needed his armed thugs and they all knew it. The insults and taunts were dust.

"We're leaving as soon as steam's up," Marsh said.

Skye wheeled away, down the companionway, and back to the rear staterooms. He found the women all together.

"We're getting off the boat."

"Sonofabitch!"

Lame Deer was staring at him. "It is good. I love to walk upon the breast of the earth and feel the grass beneath my moccasins. I love the earth. It is honest and clean. My legs do not grow weary, and I can walk from sun to sun."

Skye nodded.

A preliminary whistle squalled from the standpipe. The chimneys belched black smoke. Steam was up. The fireboxes roared.

A cabin boy appeared, and Skye directed him toward the mound of gear. Skye and the women each collected all they could carry, and hauled it out upon the main deck, next to the gangway.

"All ashore that's going ashore," a second mate bawled at the crowd on the deck.

"Help us get this off," Skye said to the cabin boy. The lad looked doubtful. "There's time, and Marsh will wait if he must."

The lad nodded, and helped them move their truck to the

levee, where a crowd watched silently, curious about Skye and his Indian women.

Up in the pilothouse, Marsh was smiling. The moment the boy was done, Marsh pulled a cord. Deckmen pulled up the gangway. Rivermen loosened the hawsers. The *Otter* slid away from the levee, and began to buck the current of the Mississippi. The wheels thrashed, and the boat shuddered forward, and the captain laughed. He had gotten rid of Skye's party after all.

But Skye, staring up at the man, didn't mind.

In a grove outside of Independence, the last caravan of the season creaked to life one early August morning, and headed out the well-worn trail toward Santa Fe. This one, thirty-two wagons strong, consisted of independent entrepreneurs, except that Ceran St. Vrain was among them with a dozen wagons destined for Bent's Fort and Taos. The Bent brothers and St. Vrain were partners in the other great fur empire, this one stretching across the southern plains, and reaping a harvest of buffalo robes that rivaled Chouteau's.

Skye and Victoria knew several of those travelers, including Uncle Dick Wooton, Kit Carson, and Lucien Maxwell, all of them veterans of the mountains. Some of them had been in St. Louis for one reason or another that spring and summer. It would be grand to see Kit.

Skye had traded his spare outfit for passage on a steamer, *Arapaho*, as far as Independence, and there was enough left over for horses as well, which they took with them on the steamer because there was an acute shortage of mules and horses in In-dependence, where the Santa Fe trade devoured livestock.

With Skye was Lame Deer and her daughter, sharing a small mare Skye had acquired for her. She was smiling, know-ing that at Bent's Fort she would find her Cheyenne people, and maybe even her own kin. The Cheyenne, who had lived for years around the Black Hills and along the Cheyenne River, where MacLees had traded with them, had drifted south in recent years. And now she was going home.

Red Gill was taking a wagon west, loaded with hardware and satins and velvets for Santa Fe, and had put together his outfit just in time to join up with the others before the cold weather roared down on the plains. Even so, the last part of his trip would be tough, with snow on the peaks of the Sangre de Cristos in Nuevo Mexico.

But it was to St. Vrain that Skye was attached now.

"My friend, come work for us," William Bent's partner had said expansively in Independence.

"Maybe for the winter," Skye had replied.

And so Skye had hired on, and now, this fine hot day, the motley assemblage of foul-mouthed teamsters, adventurers, merchants, buckskin-clad mountaineers, trappers' children, and a few Indians, like Lame Deer, rode out. Skye and Victoria preferred their saddle horses, but Lame Deer was content to sit in the van of one of St. Vrain's lumbering, rocking freight wag-ons, and tie her mustang mare to the tailgate.

Skye drew up beside her wagon.

"You happy?" he asked.

"I go to my people," she said. "They are strong and good. They listen to Sweet Medicine, and obey his wisdom. My clan will care for me, and for Singing Rain. They will honor me, and soon I will find a new man with a true heart and I will be given to him, and I will make his lodge a good place. And we will follow the four-foots and the buffalo, and make our lodge warm in the winter, with many robes and much meat."

"You glad you went to St. Louis?"

Her face clouded a moment. "I have been where no Cheyenne woman has ever gone, and I see many things. But my heart is big now that I see the grass and the sky, as far as my eye can see. And I will bring this knowledge of what I saw in St. Louis to my people, and help them know about white men. I am big in my heart, but in St. Louis I was small in my heart. Now you make me happy, and you are my friend, and I will sing about you to my people."

"Thank Victoria, not me."

"Ah, the Absaroka woman, she is a true friend too. She loves Singing Rain, and my girl-child loves her too."

Skye nodded, and spurred his lean, rough-gaited, nondescript nag forward to walk beside St. Vrain.

"You want to winter with me, up at my post?" St. Vrain said. "I could always use a man. You'd be closer to Victoria's people."

"Might. But only if you offer the jug. I have the biggest thirst I've ever had."

St. Vrain laughed. "It is possible," he said.

"I didn't get a sip all summer. First I got yanked out of rendezvous when they were just unpacking, and in St. Louis I didn't have even two bits to buy a refreshment. So I'll let you and William make offers. How many jugs do you bid?"

"I think William Bent could outbid me," St. Vrain confessed. "We don't have to smuggle spirits, you know. We've got Taos Lightning, brewed in old Mexico. Aguardiente, it's called. A fiery brandy, fermented from the agave leaf. Oh, Skye, it bites. It kicks. It makes a man howl."

Skye rumbled, the anticipation of paradise welling up in him.

And so the procession creaked west, the big wooden wheels hammering along rutted trails, winding through mixed groves and prairies, splashing through muddy creeks, and eventually out upon vast grasslands that spread to the mysterious horizons where the future lay, like the seas upon which Skye had sailed for so many years. It would be a good trip if the grass held up. Many Santa Fe caravans had already lumbered down the trail, and the grass had been well chewed down.

Maybe this was the future, he thought. The beaver were gone, and beaver felt wasn't in demand anyway. If there were any more rendezvous, they'd be melancholy affairs at best, a mournful echo of those grand frolics of yore. But a man could still survive out here, far from the cities, far from all the civilizing influences that he would just as soon avoid. There was a living to be had from buffalo, and he reckoned he could make some money someday just taking people where they wanted to go and looking after their safety.

That year of 1838, the Bents and the Chouteaus had divided up the West; the Bents controlling everything south of the South Platte, while the Chouteaus dominated the robe trade to the north. Only a handful of independent traders were surviving against the two giants. Skye had tried the Chouteaus; now he would see about these others.

He found Victoria, who was back toward the rear with Red Gill, enjoying the mild day.

"You happy?" he asked.

"This damned horse! It don't do nothing right. But I got him figured out. He was not gonna walk one more step, so I leaned forward and took an ear, and I whispered into his ear, 'You sonofabitch, you get moving or I'll eat you.' "

"And what did the horse do?"

"Well look at him! He's a prancing fool!"

Skye was content. Victoria wished she could be heading toward her people, but had settled into cheerful acceptance of the turn in their fortunes. She had brightened from the moment they left St. Louis. Skye planned to winter at the great adobe fort built by the Bents, enjoying the mild climate and the good company.

He was glad he had gone to St. Louis, even though the

whole thing had come to nothing. The cost to his body had been terrible, but the trip had opened vistas to him. At last, he had seen the Yanks in their homeland. He no longer wished to work for Pierre Chouteau. Skye knew himself to be a man of honor, and if he paid a heavy price because of his beliefs, so be it. He could always live with himself; other men with more flexible ethics might not like what they saw in the looking glass.

He was no longer tempted to become an American citizen. Not now. Maybe not ever. How could a people with such noble ideals harbor so many cutthroats and ruffians? Skye grasped anew that he was a man without a country, and probably would live out his life that way, apart from the cabals and crowds and schemes of empire.

That was all right. Even if he belonged to no people, he belonged to a land, and that land stretched across the great prairies to the mountains, from British Canada on the north to Mexico on the south. Alone, yet not alone, for no man with stalwart friends is ever alone, and no man with a woman like Victoria is ever alone, and no man who harbors a bright vision of the way things should be is ever without comfort.

St. Vrain had promised him any position he wanted, and he thought he might take some trips out to the Apache and Comanche Indian villages on the Mexican side of the Arkansas River, where he need not worry about having a trading license from General Clark. There could be some danger in it, but Skye was born to danger, and thought he would be all right. Bent regularly sent small trading outfits to the surrounding villages to bid for buffalo robes, and Skye thought he might do that. He wouldn't earn much, but there were some things in life that were better than money. And if he hung around Bent's Fort, he and Victoria would be employed, fed and sheltered for as long as he wanted to stay on the Arkansas River.

That was good enough for Skye. He and Victoria would settle in, and maybe some twilit evening, up in that famous second-floor billiard room Bent had built for his men, he and Victoria would pull the cork on a jug of Taos Lightning, settle down on a thick buffalo robe against the adobe wall, gather his friends for some quiet good times, and rejoice that they had escaped secretive, scheming St. Louis. They were out beyond the rim of civilization, where life was sweet as mead and a man was always free.